P9-DMC-713

INSPECTOR MAIGRET'S CASE FILES

INSPECTOR MAIGRET'S Case Files:

Murder a la Carte

MAIGRET AND THE PICKPOCKET
MAIGRET AND THE TOY VILLAGE
MAIGRET'S RIVAL
MAIGRET IN VICHY

Georges Simenon

Galahad Books • New York

MAIGRET AND THE PICKPOCKET Copyright © 1967 by Georges Simenon
English translation copyright © 1968 by Hamish Hamilton Ltd.

MAIGRET AND THE TOY VILLAGE Copyright © 1944 by Editions Gallimard
English translation copyright © 1978 by Georges Simenon

MAIGRET'S RIVAL Copyright © 1944 by Editions Gallimard
English translation copyright © 1979 by Georges Simenon

MAIGRET IN VICHY Copyright © 1968 by Georges Simenon
English translation copyright © 1969 by Hamish Hamilton Ltd. and Harcourt,
Brace & World, Inc.

All rights reserved. No part of this work may be reproduced or transmitted in
any form or by any means, electronic or mechanical, including photocopying,
recording, or any information storage and retrieval system, without permission
in writing from the publisher. All requests for permission to reproduce material
from this Work should be directed to Harcourt Brace Jovanovich, Inc., 6277 Sea
Harbor Dr., Orlando, FL 32887.

Published in 1992 by
Galahad Books
A division of LDAP, Inc.
386 Park Avenue South
New York, New York 10016

Galahad Books is a registered trademark of LDAP, Inc.

Published by arrangement with Harcourt Brace Jovanovich, Inc.
Library of Congress Catalog Card Number: 92-72505
ISBN: 0-88365-810-0
Designed by Hannah Lerner

Printed in the United States of America.

CONTENTS

MAIGRET
AND THE
PICKPOCKET

1

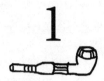

"Sorry. . . ."

"Don't mention it . . ."

It was at least the third time, since the corner of Boulevard Richard-Lenoir, that in lurching she had thrust her bony shoulder into him and pressed her string shopping bag against his thigh.

She mumbled her excuses, neither embarrassed nor apologetic, after which she resumed staring straight ahead, with a settled and resolute air.

Maigret did not bear her any ill will. Anyone might have thought he found it entertaining to be jostled. He was in a mood to take everything lightly that morning.

He had chanced to see a bus with an open platform coming, which was already a source of satisfaction. This kind of transportation was becoming more and more rare, as such buses were being withdrawn from circulation; soon he would be obliged to empty out his pipe before being swallowed up inside one of these enormous modern conveyances in which the passenger feels like a prisoner.

There were the same open-platform buses when he had arrived in Paris nearly forty years before, and in those early days he never tired of riding up and down the main boulevards on the Madeleine-Bastille line. It had been one of his first discoveries.

And the café terraces. He never grew tired of the café terraces either, from which he could survey the ever changing street scene over a glass of beer.

3

Yet another marvel, that first year: you could go out of doors, from the end of February, without an overcoat. Not always, but occasionally. And the blossom was starting to come out along some of the avenues, in particular Boulevard Saint-Germain.

These memories were coming back to him, bit by bit, because this year once again spring had come early, and that morning he had left home without a coat.

He felt a lightness about himself, like the sparkle in the air. The colors of the shops, the groceries, the women's dresses, were gay and lively.

He was not really thinking. Only scraps of thoughts which didn't add up to a coherent whole. His wife would be taking her third driving lesson at ten o'clock that morning.

It was funny, unexpected. He couldn't have said exactly how it had been decided. When Maigret had been a young clerk, there was no question of affording a car. At the time it was unthinkable. And later on, he had never seen the need for one. It was too late for him to learn to drive. Too many other thoughts were always passing through his head. He wouldn't see the red lights, or else he would mistake the brake for the accelerator.

But it would be pleasant to drive to their cottage, at Meung-sur-Loire, on Sundays. . . .

They had just made up their minds, all of a sudden. His wife had protested, laughing.

"Just imagine . . . Learning to drive, at my age . . ."

"I'm sure you'll do very well. . . ."

She was having her third lesson and was every bit as nervous as a young girl studying for her exams.

"How did it go?"

"The instructor is very patient."

His fellow passenger in the bus couldn't have been a car driver. Why had she come to do her shopping in the Boulevard Voltaire neighborhood, when she lived in another part of town? It was one of those little mysteries that tend to fasten themselves in one's mind. She was wearing a hat, an increasingly rare spectacle, especially in the morning. There was a chicken in her shopping bag, butter, eggs, leeks and celery. . . .

The harder object, at the bottom, which pressed into his thigh at every jolt, must be the potatoes. . . .

Why take the bus to buy perfectly ordinary provisions miles away from home, when they were readily available anywhere? Perhaps she had once lived on Boulevard Voltaire, grown used to her local tradesmen, and remained faithful to them?

The young man with the slight build, to his right, was smoking a pipe that was too short in the stem and too large in the bowl, badly balanced, thus forcing him to clamp his teeth. Young people nearly always choose a pipe both too short and too heavy.

The passengers standing on the platform were packed tightly together. The woman ought to have sat inside. In a fishmonger's in Rue du Temple, he spotted some whiting. He hadn't eaten whiting for ages. Why did whiting, too, all of a sudden take on a springlike quality?

Everything was springlike, like his own mood, and it was just too bad if the woman with the chicken was sullenly staring ahead of her, a prey to problems beyond the ken of the common mortal.

"Sorry. . . ."

"Don't mention it. . . ."

He hadn't the courage to say:

"Instead of making everybody out here miserable, why don't you take that wretched string bag of yours and go and sit inside?"

He read the same thoughts in the blue eyes of a large man wedged between him and the conductor. They understood one another. So did the conductor, who imperceptibly shrugged his shoulders. A sort of freemasonry, between men. It was amusing.

The stalls, especially those with vegetables and fruit, were overflowing onto the sidewalks. The green and white bus carved its way through the crowd of cleaning women, secretaries, and clerks hurrying to work. Life was good.

Another jolt. That bag again, with its hard lump at the bottom, potatoes or something of the sort. As he stepped back, he in turn jostled somebody behind him.

"Sorry. . . ."

He also mumbled the word, tried to turn around, and saw the face of a youngish man on which he read an emotion he did not understand.

He must have been less than twenty-five years old; he was bareheaded, with disheveled brown hair, and unshaven. He looked like someone who had not slept all night and who had just been through a trying or painful experience.

Threading his way to the platform step, he jumped from the bus as it was moving. It was at the corner of Rue Rambuteau, not far from the Central Market, the powerful smell of which hung in the air. The man walked fast, turned around as if he were apprehensive about something, then was swallowed up in Rue des Blancs-Manteaux.

For no precise reason, Maigret suddenly put his hand to his hip pocket where he kept his wallet.

He just stopped himself from starting off in his turn and leaping from the bus, for the wallet had vanished.

He had reddened, but he managed to keep his head. Only the big man with blue eyes appeared to have noticed anything amiss.

Maigret smiled ironically, not so much because he had been the victim of a pickpocket as because it was quite impossible to catch him, and all because of the spring, and the champagne sparkle in the air, which he had begun breathing the day before.

Another habit, a mania, which dated back to his infancy: shoes. Every year, with the first day of fine weather, he bought himself a new pair of shoes, as light as possible. This had occurred the day before.

And this morning he was wearing them for the first time. They pinched. It was torture just to walk the length of Boulevard Richard-Lenoir, and it had been a relief to reach the bus stop on Boulevard Voltaire.

He would have been quite unable to pursue his thief. And anyway the latter had had time to lose himself in the narrow streets of the Marais.

"Sorry. . . ."

Her again! That woman with her shopping! He just managed to stop himself from snapping at her:

"Will you kindly take yourself off with your potatoes and leave us in peace."

But all he did was nod and smile.

In his office, too, there was the same light as he remembered from those first days with a haze hanging over the Seine, less dense than mist, made up of thousands of tiny brilliant, living particles, peculiar to Paris.

"How are things, Chief? Anything doing?"

Janvier was wearing a light suit which Maigret had never seen before. He, too, was celebrating spring early, for it was only the fifteenth of March.

"Nothing. Or rather, yes, there is something. I've just been robbed."

"Your watch?"

"My wallet."

"In the street?"

"In the back of a bus."

"Did it have much money in it?"

"About fifty francs. I seldom carry more."

"And your papers?"

"Not only my papers, but my badge too."

That famous badge of the Police Department, the nightmare of all Inspectors. In theory they should have it always with them, to identify them as Crime Squad officers.

It was a handsome silver badge, or to be more precise plated copper, for with age the thin silver coating wears through to a reddish metal underneath.

On one side the badge showed the Republic's Marianne with her Phrygian cap, the letters "R.F." and the word "Police" outlined in red enamel.

On the reverse were the arms of Paris, a serial number, and, engraved in small lettering, the holder's name.

Maigret's badge had the number 0004, number 1 being reserved for the Prefect, number 2 for the Director-General of the Police Department, and number 3, for some obscure reason, for the Head of the Special Branch.

Some officers hesitated to carry their badges in their pockets, because the same regulation also provided for suspension of one month's salary in case of loss.

"Did you see the thief?"

"Very clearly. A young fellow, thin, tired-looking, with the eyes and complexion of a person who hasn't slept."

"Did you recognize him?"

When he had worked on the beat, Maigret knew all the pickpockets by sight, not only the ones from Paris, but those who came from Spain or London for the big fairs or open-air festivals.

It is a fairly closed profession, with its own hierarchy. The top operators bestir themselves only when it is worth their while, and they do not think twice about crossing the Atlantic for a world exhibition or, for example, the Olympic Games.

Maigret had lost sight of them somewhat. He was ransacking his memory. He was not making a tragedy out of the incident. The lightness of the morning was still affecting his mood and, paradoxically, he laid all the blame on the woman with the shopping bag.

"If she hadn't been constantly jostling me . . . Women ought to be banned from bus platforms. . . . Especially when she didn't even have the excuse of wanting to smoke. . . ."

He was more annoyed than angry.

"Are you going to look for him in the files?"

"That's what I have in mind."

He spent nearly an hour examining photographs, front view and profile, most of them pickpockets. There were some he had arrested twenty years before, and who after that passed through his office again ten or fifteen times, almost becoming old friends.

"You again?"

"One has to live. And you, you're still there, Chief. It's quite a while since we last met, isn't it?"

Some were well dressed and others, the shabby ones, dossed down in junkyards, the steps of Saint-Ouen, and the Métro corridors. None of them remotely resembled the young man on the bus, and Maigret knew in advance that his search would be a waste of time.

A professional doesn't have that tired, anxious look. He works only when he knows his hands won't start to tremble. And anyway they all knew Maigret's face and profile, if only from seeing it in the newspapers.

He went down to his office again, and when he ran into Janvier he gave a shrug.

"You didn't find him?"

"I'd swear he's an amateur. I even wonder if he knew, a minute earlier, what he was going to do. He must have seen my wallet sticking out. My wife never stops telling me I oughtn't to carry it in that pocket. He must have thought of it when there was a jolt and those confounded potatoes almost knocked me over. . . ."

His tone changed.

"What's new this morning?"

"Lucas has got flu. The Senegalese was killed in a *bistrot* on Porte d'Italie. . . ."

"Knife?"

"Of course. Nobody's able to give us a description of the assailant. He came in around one o'clock in the morning, just as the boss was going to close down. He took a few steps in the direction of the Senegalese, who was having a last drink, and he struck so fast that . . ."

Routine. Someone would finally turn him in, maybe in a month, maybe in two years. Maigret went to the Director's office for the daily conference, and he was careful not to mention his little adventure.

The day promised to be a quiet one. Some red tape. Some papers to sign. Routine matters.

He went home for lunch and scrutinized his wife, who didn't talk to him about her driving lesson. For her it was a little as if, at her present age, she had gone back to school. She felt some pleasure, a certain pride even, but also some embarrassment.

"Well then, you didn't drive up onto the sidewalk?"

"Why do you ask me that? You'll give me an inferiority complex. . . ."

"On the contrary. You'll make an excellent driver and I can hardly wait for you to drive me along the banks of the Loire. . . ."

"That won't be for at least another month."

"Is that what the instructor says?"

"The examiners are getting more and more strict and it's best not to be failed the first time. Today we went on the outer boulevards. I would never have believed there was so much traffic on them, or that people drove so fast. Anybody would think . . ."

Imagine, they were eating chicken, as, no doubt, they would be doing in the house of the woman on the bus.

"What are you thinking about?"

"My pickpocket."

"Did you arrest a pickpocket?"

"I didn't arrest him, but he relieved me of my wallet."

"With your badge?"

She, too, thought of it at once. A serious hole in the budget. True, he would get a new badge without the copper showing through.

"Did you see him?"

"As plainly as I see you."

"An old man?"

"A young one. An amateur. He looked as if . . ."

Maigret was thinking about it more and more, without really wanting to. The face, instead of becoming blurred in his memory, was becoming clearer. He was recapturing details which he was unaware he had recorded in the first place, such as the fact that the unidentified man had thick eyebrows forming an absolute hedge above his eyes.

"Would you recognize him?"

He thought about it more than a dozen times during the course of the afternoon, lifting his head and staring at the window as though some problem were puzzling him. There was something about the episode, the face, the getaway, that wasn't quite natural; he didn't know just what.

Each time it seemed that a new detail, which would convey something to him, was on the point of coming back, then he would turn again to his work.

"Good night, boys. . . ."

He left at five minutes to six, when there were still half a dozen Inspectors left in the next office.

"Good night, Chief. . . ."

They went to the movies. In a drawer he had found his old brown wallet, too large for his hip pocket, so he put it in his coat.

"If you'd kept it in that pocket . . ."

They went home arm in arm, as usual, and the air was still warm. Even the smell of gasoline was not disagreeable that evening. It, too, was part of the spring in the air, in the same way as the smell of melting tar is part and parcel of summer.

In the morning he found the sun still there and had the window open for his breakfast.

"It's funny," he said. "There are women who go halfway across Paris in a bus to do their shopping. . . ."

"Perhaps because of the T.V. sales guide. . . ."

He looked at his wife with a puzzled frown.

"Every night they tell you on television where you can get the best values. . . ."

It had never occurred to him. It was as simple as that. He had wasted hours on a little problem which his wife had solved in an instant.

"Thank you."

"Does that help you?"

"It saves me having to go on thinking about it."

He added, philosophically, grabbing his hat:

"One doesn't think about the things one wants to. . . ."

The mail was waiting for him at the office; on top of the pile there was a large brown envelope on which his name, his rank, and the Quai des Orfèvres address were written in block capitals.

He knew before he opened it. It was his wallet, being returned. And a moment later he discovered that there was nothing missing, neither the badge, nor the papers, nor the fifty francs.

Nothing else. No message. No explanation.

It irked him.

It was just after eleven when the telephone rang.

"There's someone who insists on speaking to you personally but refuses to give his name, Chief Inspector. It seems you are expecting the call and would be angry if I didn't put it through. What do I do?"

"All right, put it through. . . ."

Using one hand to strike a match to relight his pipe, he said:

"Hello!"

There was a longish pause, and Maigret might have thought he had been cut off if he hadn't heard breathing at the other end of the line.

"Hello!" he said again.

Another silence, then:

"It's me. . . ."

A man's voice, quite deep, but judging by the tone it might have been a child hesitating before confessing to an act of disobedience.

"My wallet?"

"Yes."

"Didn't you know who I was?"

"Of course. Otherwise . . ."

"Why are you telephoning?"

"Because I've got to see you. . . ."

"Come to my office."

"No. I can't go to Quai des Orfèvres."

"Are you known here?"

"I've never set foot inside the door."

"What are you afraid of?"

Because the anonymous voice betrayed a note of fear.

"It's a private matter."

"What's private?"

"What I wanted to see you about. This solution occurred to me when I saw your name on the badge."

"Why did you steal my wallet?"

"Because I needed money at once."

"And now?"

"I've changed my mind. I'm still not quite sure about it. The best thing would be for you to come as quickly as possible, before I change my mind. . . ."

There was something unreal about this conversation, in the voice, and yet Maigret was taking it quite seriously.

"Where are you?"

"Are you coming?"

"Yes."

"Alone?"

"Do you insist that I come alone?"

"Our conversation must remain private. Do I have your word?"

"It depends."

"On what?"

"On what you have to tell me."

Another silence, heavier now than the one at the start.

"I want you to give me a chance. After all it was I who called you. You don't know me. You have no way of tracing me. If you don't come, you'll never know who I am. So it's worth, to you . . ."

He could not find the word.

"A promise?" Maigret prompted him.

"Wait. Once I've spoken to you, you must give me five minutes to disappear if I ask for it. . . ."

"I can't make any promises without knowing more about it. I am a police officer and . . ."

"If you'll only believe me, it'll be all right. If you don't believe me, or if you have any doubts, you could manage to look the other way, to give me time to leave, and afterwards you can call up your men. . . ."

"Where are you?"

"Do you agree?"

"I'm prepared to come and join you."

"Under my conditions?"

"I shall be alone."

"But you promise nothing?"

"No."

It was impossible for him to act otherwise, and he awaited the reaction of the other man with some anxiety. The latter was in a public telephone booth, or in a café, because he could hear the noise in the background.

"Have you made up your mind?" said Maigret, growing impatient.

"Now that I've come this far . . . What the newspapers say about you gives me hope. Are they true, those stories?"

"What stories?"

"That you are capable of understanding things which normally policemen and judges don't understand and that, in certain cases, you've even . . ."

"Even what?"

"Perhaps it's a mistake for me to talk so much. I don't know any longer. Have you ever been known to turn a blind eye?"

Maigret preferred not to answer.

"Where are you?"

"A long way from Police Headquarters. If I tell you now you'll have time to have me arrested by the local police. You've got my description, one quick call . . ."

"How do you know I saw you?"

"I turned around. Our eyes met, as you know. I was very scared."

"Because of the wallet?"

"Not just that. Listen. Drive to the bar called the Métro, on the corner of Boulevard de Grenelle and Avenue de La-Motte-Picquet. That'll take you about half an hour. I will call you there. I won't be far off and I will be with you almost immediately."

Maigret opened his mouth, but the other man had hung up. He was as curious as he was angry, for it was the first time a complete stranger had treated him with such lack of deference, not to say high-handedness.

And yet he could not bring himself to feel any hostility. Throughout their jerky conversation he had sensed an anguish, a desire to find a satisfactory way out, a need to come face to face with the Chief Inspector who, in the unknown man's eyes, figured as his only hope of salvation. All because he had stolen his wallet, without realizing who he was!

"Janvier! Have you got a car downstairs? I want you to drive me to Boulevard de Grenelle."

Janvier was surprised, there being no case at present in that area.

"A private meeting with the character who lifted my wallet."

"Have you got it back?"

"The wallet, yes, in this morning's mail."

"And your badge? That would surprise me, because it's the sort of thing anybody would like to keep as a souvenir."

"My badge was there, my papers, the money. . . ."

"Was it a joke?"

"No, on the contrary, I have the impression that it's something very serious. My pickpocket has just called up to say he's waiting for me."

"Shall I come too?"

"As far as Boulevard de Grenelle. Then you must stay behind, because he wants to see me alone."

They followed the riverbank as far as the Bir-Hakeim bridge. Maigret was silently contemplating the Seine as it flowed by. There were street repairs going on everywhere, with barriers and detours, just as there had been in the first year he came to Paris. In fact, it used to happen in ten-year cycles, each time that Paris started once again to suffocate.

"Where shall I drop you?"

"Here."

They were at the corner of Boulevard de Grenelle and Rue Saint-Charles.

"Shall I wait?"

"Wait for half an hour. If I'm not back by then, go to the office, or have lunch."

Janvier was curious, too, and watched the Chief Inspector's retreating silhouette with a quizzical look.

The sun was hitting the sidewalk where hot gusts and colder gusts alternated, as if the air as a whole had not yet had time to settle down to its spring temperature.

A small girl was selling violets outside a restaurant. From a long way off, Maigret spotted the corner bar, headed by the words *Le Metro*, which would be lit up in the evening. It was just an ordinary place, without personality, one of those tobacco bars where one goes to buy cigarettes, or have a drink at the counter, or else to sit and wait for a date.

His eyes traveled around the place, which had only about twenty tables on either side of the room, most of them unoccupied.

Of course his pickpocket of the day before was not there; the Chief Inspector went and sat down at the very back of the room, by the window, and ordered a beer.

In spite of himself he kept an eye on the door and the people who came up to it, pushed it open, went up to the cash desk behind which the cigarettes were stacked on the shelves.

He was beginning to wonder whether he had not been too gullible when he recognized the silhouette on the sidewalk, then the face. The young man was not looking in his direction; he headed for the copper bar, put his elbows on it, and ordered:

"A rum. . . ."

He was agitated. His hands moved restlessly. He didn't have the nerve to turn around, and he was waiting impatiently to be served, as he needed a drink badly.

Seizing his glass, he gestured to the bartender not to put the bottle back.

"Give me another. . . ."

This time, he turned in Maigret's direction. He knew, before going in, where he was. He must have spotted him from outside, or through the window of a nearby house.

He had an air of apology, as if saying that he had no choice, that he was coming over right away. With still trembling hands he counted out some small change and put it on the counter.

Finally he went over, seized a chair, and collapsed into it.

"Do you have a cigarette?"

"No. I only smoke . . ."

"A pipe, I know. I haven't got any cigarettes, or any money to buy them."

"Waiter! A pack of . . . What's your brand?"

"Gauloises."

"A pack of Gauloises and a glass of rum."

"No more rum. It makes me sick. . . ."

"A beer?"

"I don't know. I didn't eat anything this morning. . . ."

"A sandwich?"

There were several platters at the bar.

"Not just yet. I'm all in knots. You wouldn't understand. . . ."

He was well dressed, in gray flannel trousers and a tartan sports jacket. Like many young men, he was wearing no tie but had on a polo shirt.

"I don't know if you're at all the way one imagines you. . . ."

He was not looking Maigret in the face, but shot him a series of sidelong glances before fastening his gaze once more on the floor. It was tiring to follow the incessant movement of his long, thin fingers.

"Weren't you surprised to get the wallet?"

"After thirty years of detective work, one isn't easily surprised."

"And to find the money intact?"

"You needed it badly, didn't you?"

"Yes."

"How much did you have in your pocket?"

"About ten francs."

"Where did you you sleep last night?"

"I didn't sleep. I didn't eat either. I drank with my ten francs. You just saw me spend the last of the change. There wasn't enough left to get drunk on. . . ."

"And yet you live in Paris," Maigret observed.

"How do you know?"

"And in this very area."

There was nobody at the nearby tables, so they just spoke in muted voices. The sound of the door opening and shutting, nearly always for tobacco or matches, could be heard.

"But you didn't go home. . . ."

The other was silent for a moment, as on the telephone. He was pale, exhausted. One could feel that he was making a desperate effort to respond and trying, warily, to smell out any traps that might be set for him.

"Just as I thought," he grumbled, finally.

"What did you think?"

"That you would guess, that you'd get it more or less right the first time, and that once you were on the scent . . ."

"Go on. . . ."

He grew angry all of a sudden, raised his voice, forgetting that he was in a public place.

"And that once you were on the scent, I'd had it!"

He looked at the door, which had just opened, and for one moment the Chief Inspector thought he was going to bolt. He must have been tempted. There was a fleeting gleam in his dark pupils. Then he reached out to his glass of beer and emptied it in one gulp, his eyes fixed on the other man over his glass, as though sizing him up.

"Is that better?"

"I don't know yet."

"Let's get back to the wallet."

"Why?"

"Because that's what made you telephone me."

"Anyway, there wasn't enough."

"Not enough money? What for?"

"To get away. . . . To go anywhere, Belgium or Spain . . ."

And, overcome once again by suspicion:

"Did you come by yourself?"

"I don't drive. One of my inspectors brought me and he's waiting at the corner of Rue Saint-Charles."

The man lifted his head with a jerk.

"Did you identify me?"

"No. Your photograph isn't in our files."

"So you did have a look?"

"Of course."

"Why?"

"On account of my wallet, and even more on account of my badge."

"Why did you stop at the corner of Rue Saint-Charles?"

"Because it's just nearby and we were passing that way."

"You haven't had any report?"

"What about?"

"Nothing has happened in Rue Saint-Charles?"

Maigret was hard put to it to follow the successive expressions registered on the young man's face. Seldom had he seen anyone so anxious, so tortured, clinging to God knew what last hope.

He was afraid, obviously. But of what?

"Didn't the local police station alert you?"

"No."

"Do you swear that?"

"I only swear in the witness box."

The other's eyes seemed to bore into him.

"Why do you think I asked you to come?"

"Because you need me."

"Why do I need you?"

"Because you've got yourself into a mess and you don't know how to get out of it."

"That's not true."

The voice was sharp. The unidentified man raised his head, as though relieved.

"It's not I who am in trouble, and that—witness box or no witness box—I can swear to without hesitation. I'm innocent, do you understand!"

"Not so loud. . . ."

He glanced around. A young woman was putting some lipstick on, looking at herself in a mirror, then she turned toward the sidewalk in the hope of seeing the person she was waiting for. Two middle-aged men, hunched over a table, were talking in undertones, and from a few words he guessed at rather than actually heard, Maigret gathered the subject was racing.

"Tell me, instead, who you are and what you claim to be innocent of."

"Not here. Presently. . . ."

"Where?"

"At my house. May I have another beer? I will be in a position to pay you back presently, unless . . ."

"Unless what?"

"Unless her bag . . . Well . . . A beer?"

"Waiter! Two beers. . . . And the check."

The young man dabbed himself with a handkerchief which was still moderately clean.

"You're twenty-four?" the Chief Inspector asked him.

"Twenty-five."

"Have you been in Paris long?"

"Five years."

"Married?"

He was avoiding questions that would be too personal, too inflammatory.

"I was. Why do you ask that?"

"You don't wear a ring."

"Because I couldn't afford one when I got married."

He was lighting a second cigarette. He had smoked the first one inhaling deeply, and only now did he pause to savor the tobacco.

"The fact is, all the precautions I took are useless."

"What precautions?"

"As far as you are concerned. You've got me, neatly tied up, whatever I do. Even if I tried to make a break, now that you've seen me and know I come from around here . . ."

He had a bitter, ironical smile, an irony directed against himself.

"I always overdo everything. Your inspector with the car, is he still at the corner of Rue Saint-Charles?"

Maigret consulted the electric clock. It pointed to three minutes to twelve.

"Either he's just left, or else he's on the point of leaving; I told him to wait half an hour for me, and if I'm not back by then, to go and have lunch."

"It doesn't matter, does it?"

Maigret didn't answer, and when his companion rose, he followed. The two of them set off toward Rue Saint-Charles, on the corner of which stood a fairly new and modern apartment building. They took the pedestrian crossing and started down the street, but only covered about thirty yards.

The young man had stopped in the middle of the sidewalk. An open door led into the courtyard of the big building giving on Boulevard de Grenelle; under an arch, motorcycles and baby carriages were parked.

"Is this where you live?"

"Listen, Inspector . . ."

He was paler and more nervous than ever.

"Have you ever trusted a person, even when all the evidence was against him?"

"I've been known to."

"What do you think of me?"

"That you are rather complicated and there are too many pieces missing for me to judge you."

"Because you will be judging me?"

"That's not what I mean. Let's say, form an opinion."

"Do I look the part of a villain?"

"Certainly not."

"Or a man capable of . . . No . . . Come on . . . Best get it over quickly."

He took him into the courtyard and led him toward the left-hand wing, where, on the ground floor, a line of doors could be seen.

"That's what they call studios," he grumbled.

And he took a key from his pocket.

"If you force me to go in first . . . I'll do it. But if I pass out . . ."

He pushed the polished oak door. It opened onto a minute hall. An open door on the right revealed a bathroom with a hip bath. It was in a mess. Towels were strewn over the tiling.

"Open it, will you?"

The young man was indicating to Maigret the door directly in front, which was shut, and the Chief Inspector did what he asked.

His companion did not bolt. But the smell was nauseating, in spite of the open window.

Beside a couch which opened up into a bed at night, a woman was stretched on the multicolored Moroccan carpet, and bluebottles were circling and buzzing in the air around her.

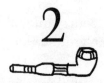

2

"HAVE YOU GOT a telephone?"

It was a ridiculous question, which Maigret put automatically, because he could see one on the floor in the middle of the room, about a yard from the body.

"I beg you . . ." muttered his companion, leaning for support against the door frame.

He was already at the end of his tether. For his part, the Chief Inspector was not sorry to leave this room where the smell of death had become unbearable.

He propelled the young man out, closed the door again behind him, and paused for a moment to readjust himself to the real world.

Children were returning from school, swinging their satchels, making their way to the various apartments. Most of the windows in the vast building were open. Several radios could be heard simultaneously, voices, music, women calling their husbands or their sons. On the first floor a canary fluttered about in its cage, and at another window there was some laundry hanging out to dry.

"Are you going to be sick?"

His companion shook his head but still did not dare open his mouth. He was clutching his chest with both hands, deathly pale, on the point of collapsing to judge by the near-convulsive movement of his fingers and the uncontrollable trembling of his lips.

"Take your time. . . . Don't try to talk. . . . Would you like to come and have a drink in the café on the corner?"

Again a shake of the head.

"It's your wife, isn't it?"

The man's eyes said that it was. Finally he opened his mouth to take a deep breath, but succeeded only after a long pause, as though his nerves were clamped in knots.

"Were you there when it happened?"

"No. . . ."

In spite of everything, he had managed to utter the single syllable.

"When did you see her last?"

"The day before yesterday. Wednesday. . . ."

"In the morning? In the evening?"

"Late in the evening. . . ."

They were walking, automatically, across the great sunbathed courtyard, all around which people were leading their daily lives in different compartments in the building. Most of them were eating, or just about to do so.

Fragments of sentences reached their ears:

"Did you wash your hands . . . ?"

"Watch out. . . . It's very hot."

Kitchen smells, particularly leeks, mingled here and there with the already springlike air.

"Do you know how she died?"

The young man nodded, short of breath once again.

"When I got back . . . "

"One moment. . . . You left the apartment late on Wednesday evening. Keep walking. Standing still won't do you any good. What time, roughly?"

"Eleven o'clock. . . ."

"Was your wife still alive? Was she in her dressing gown when you left her?"

"She hadn't undressed yet. . . ."

"Do you work at night?"

"No. I was going out to scurry up some money. . . . We were broke. . . ."

They both glanced unthinkingly at the open windows as they

passed by, and at some of them the occupants stared back, doubtless wondering what they were doing, walking about in this fashion.

"Where were you going to look for the money?"

"Friends' houses. . . . Anywhere. . . ."

"Did you succeed?"

"No. . . ."

"Did any of these friends see you?"

"At the Old Wine Press, yes. . . . I still had about thirty francs in my pocket. I looked in at various places where there was a chance of finding somebody I knew. . . ."

"On foot?"

"In my car. . . . I didn't abandon it until I ran out of gas, at the corner of Rue François-Premier and Rue Marboeuf. . . ."

"What did you do then?"

"I walked. . . ."

The young man Maigret had on his hands was exhausted, his nerves raw, like a person who has been flayed alive.

"How long have you been without food?"

"Yesterday I ate two hard-boiled eggs in a *bistrot*. . . ."

"Come with me. . . ."

"I'm not hungry. . . . If you are thinking of giving me lunch I may as well tell you right away . . ."

Maigret was not listening but made for Boulevard de Grenelle and went into a small restaurant where there were several unoccupied tables.

"Steak and chips for two," he ordered.

He wasn't hungry either, but his companion was in need of sustenance.

"What's your name?"

"Ricain. François Ricain. . . . Some people call me Francis. . . . It was my wife who . . ."

"Listen, Ricain. I've got to make a couple of telephone calls. . . ."

"To bring your men here?"

"Before I do anything else I've got to call the local Inspector, to let Headquarters know what's happening. Do you give your word you won't budge from here?"

"Where would I go?" Ricain replied bitterly. "In any case you'll arrest me and put me in prison. . . . I won't be able to stand it. . . . I would rather . . ."

He didn't finish, but his meaning was clear.

"A half bottle of Beaujolais, waiter. . . ."

Maigret went to the cashier to get some telephone counters. As he had expected, the local Inspector was out to lunch.

"Do you want me to get a message to him right away?"

"What time will he be back?"

"Around two o'clock. . . ."

"Tell him I'll be waiting for him at half past two in Rue Saint-Charles, by the entrance of the house on the corner of Boulevard de Grenelle. . . ."

At the Public Prosecutor's office, he only got through to a junior clerk.

"A crime has apparently been committed in Rue Saint-Charles. Take down the address. . . . When one of the officers on duty comes back, tell him I will be outside the entrance at a quarter past two. . . ."

Finally Police Headquarters, where Lapointe took the call:

"I'll expect you at Rue Saint-Charles in an hour. Alert Records. . . . Tell them to be at the same address around two o'clock. Tell them to bring something to disinfect a room where the smell is so strong you can't get in. Alert the pathologist. I don't know who's on duty today. See you there. . . ."

He went and sat down opposite Ricain, who had not moved and was looking around as if unable to believe that this commonplace spectacle was real.

It was a modest restaurant. Most of the customers worked in the neighborhood and ate alone, reading newspapers. The steaks were rare and the fried potatoes quite crisp.

"What's going to happen next?" asked the young man, automatically picking up his fork. "Did you alert everybody? Is the circus about to start?"

"Not before two o'clock. From now till then, we've got time to chat. . . ."

"I don't know anything. . . ."

"People always think they don't know anything. . . ."

He must not push him. After a few moments, as Maigret was putting a piece of meat in his mouth, François Ricain began, unconsciously, to cut his steak.

He had stated that he would be unable to eat. Not only was he eating, but he drank, and a few minutes later the Chief Inspector had to order a second half bottle.

"Even so you can't possibly understand. . . ."

"Of all the things people say, that's the one I've heard most often during my career. But nine times out of ten I have understood. . . ."

"I know. You'll be teaching me to blow my nose next. . . ."

"Does it need blowing?"

"It's not a laughing matter. You've seen, as I have . . ."

"The difference being that you had already seen it before. Isn't that right?"

"Certainly."

"When?"

"Yesterday, at about four o'clock in the morning?"

"Hold on a minute while I get this straight. The day before yesterday, that's to say Wednesday, you left your apartment at about eleven o'clock in the evening and your wife stayed behind. . . ."

"Sophie pressed me to take her too. I made her stay because I don't like begging for money in her presence. It would have looked as if I were using her. . . ."

"Right! You left by car. What sort of car?"

"A Triumph convertible."

"If you needed money so badly, why not sell it?"

"Because I wouldn't have got a hundred francs for it. It's an ancient car I bought secondhand, and it's passed through God knows how many hands. It hardly stands up on its four wheels. . . ."

"You looked for any friends who might be able to lend you money, and you didn't find any?"

"The ones I found were almost as broke as I was. . . ."

"You returned home, on foot, at four o'clock in the morning. Did you knock?"

"No. I opened the door with my key. . . ."

"Had you been drinking?"

"A certain amount, yes. At night, most of the people I see hang around bars or night clubs. . . ."

"Were you drunk?"

"Not to the point . . ."

"Depressed?"

"I was at my wits' end. . . ."

"Did your wife have any money?"

"No more than I did. There must have been twenty or thirty francs left in her bag."

"Go on. . . . Waiter! Some more chips, please. . . ."

"I found her on the floor. When I went over to her, I saw that half her face had sort of . . . gone. . . . I think I saw brains. . . ."

He pushed his plate away and drank down his fourth glass of wine in gulps.

"I'm sorry. I'd rather not talk about that. . . ."

"Was there a weapon in the room?"

Ricain stopped short, looking narrowly at Maigret, as though the crucial moment had come.

"A revolver? An automatic?"

"Yes."

"An automatic?"

"Mine. . . . A 6.35 Browning made in Hertal. . . ."

"How did you come to have this weapon in your possession?"

"I was waiting for that question. And you probably won't believe me. . . ."

"You didn't buy it at a gunsmith's?"

"No. I had no reason to buy a gun. . . . One night there were several of us, just friends, in a small restaurant in La Villette. We'd had a lot to drink. . . . We were showing off and pretending to be tough. . . ."

He had reddened.

"Especially me. . . . The others will bear me out. . . . It's a phobia of mine. When I drink, I think I'm really somebody. . . . Some people we didn't know attached themselves to us. You know how those things can go on into the small hours. It was in winter, two years ago. I was wearing a sheepskin jacket.

Sophie was with me. She had been drinking too, but she never completely loses her head. . . .

"Next day, around noon, when I went to put on my jacket, I found an automatic in the pocket. My wife told me I'd bought it the night before, in spite of her pleas. . . . I was insisting, apparently, that I absolutely had to kill someone who had a grudge against me. . . . I kept repeating:

" 'It's him or me, you see, old man!' "

Maigret had lit his pipe and was looking at his companion without betraying any sign of what he was thinking.

"Can *you* understand?"

"Go on. . . . We were at Thursday, four A.M. I suppose nobody saw you come home?"

"Of course not."

"And nobody saw you go out again?"

"Nobody."

"What did you do with the weapon?"

"How do you know I got rid of it?"

The Chief Inspector shrugged.

"I don't know why I did it. I realized I'd be accused. . . ."

"Why?"

Ricain looked at his questioner in amazement.

"It's obvious, isn't it? I was the only person with the key. . . . The weapon that was used belonged to me, and stayed in the chest of drawers. . . . We sometimes had fights, Sophie and I. . . . She wanted me to get a steady job."

"What is your profession?"

"If you can call it a profession. . . . I'm a journalist, without being attached to any particular paper. . . . In other words I place my copy where I can, mostly movie reviews. I'm also an assistant director, and sometimes a script writer. . . ."

"Did you throw the Browning into the Seine?"

"Just below the Bir-Hakeim bridge. Then I walked . . ."

"Did you go on trying to find your friends?"

"I didn't dare to any longer. Someone might have heard the shot and telephoned the police. I don't know . . . One isn't necessarily logical in moments like that. . . .

"I was about to be hunted down. . . . I would be accused and everything would be against me, even the fact that I had roamed about part of the night. . . . I had been drinking. . . . I was still in search of the first bar to open. . . . When I found one, in Rue Vaugirard, I drank three straight glasses of rum. . . .

"If anybody were to question me, I would be in no fit state to answer. I was sure to get muddled. They would shut me up in a cell. I suffer from claustrophobia, so badly that I cannot travel by subway. . . . The idea of prison, with huge bolts on the door . . ."

"Was it claustrophobia that gave you the idea of running away abroad?"

"You see! You don't believe me!"

"Perhaps I do."

"You have to have been in a situation like mine to know what goes on in one's head. . . . One doesn't work things out logically. I couldn't tell you what route I took. I needed to walk, to get away from the Grenelle neighborhood, where I pictured them already on my track. I remember noticing Montparnasse station, drinking white wine on Boulevard Saint-Michel . . . or perhaps it was in Montparnasse station. . . .

"My idea wasn't so much to run away. . . . It was to gain time, not to be interrogated in the state I was in. In Belgium, or somewhere else, I would have been able to wait. I would have followed the progress of the investigation in the papers. I would have found out details that I don't know about and which would have helped my defense. . . ."

Maigret could not help smiling at such a mixture of astuteness and naïveté.

"What were you doing in Place de la République?"

"Nothing. I wound up there, just as I might have wound up anywhere else. . . . I had one ten-franc note left in my pocket. I let three buses go by."

"Because they didn't have an open platform?"

"I don't know. . . . I swear, Inspector, that I don't know. I needed money to take the train. I got on the platform. There were a lot of people and we were packed tightly together. I saw you from behind. . . .

"At one moment you stepped back and you nearly lost your

balance. I noticed the wallet sticking out of your pocket. . . . I grabbed it, without thinking, and when I looked up I saw a woman looking straight at me. . . .

"I can't think why she didn't give the alarm there and then. I jumped from the bus as it was moving. Luckily, it was a very busy street, with a jumble of narrow streets all around it. I ran. . . . I walked. . . ."

"Two pastries, waiter. . . ."

It was half past one. In forty-five minutes, justice would don its usual trappings, and the studio in Rue Saint-Charles would be invaded by officials, while police outside would keep onlookers away.

"What are you going to do with me?"

Maigret didn't answer immediately, for the good reason that he had not yet made up his mind.

"Are you arresting me? I realize you can't do anything else, but I swear to you once more. . . ."

"Eat up. . . . Coffee?"

"What are you doing this for?"

"What am I doing that's so extraordinary?"

"You're making me eat, and drink. . . . You aren't pushing me around. On the contrary, you are patiently listening. . . . Surely that's not what you call grilling a person?"

Maigret smiled.

"Not exactly, no. . . . I'm just trying to get the facts into some sort of order."

"And get me talking. . . ."

"I haven't pressed you too much."

"Well, I do feel a bit better. . . ."

He had eaten his pastry seemingly without noticing, and he was lighting a cigarette. A little color had returned to his cheeks.

"Only, I couldn't go back there, and see . . . smell . . ."

"How about me?"

"That's your job. It isn't your wife. . . ."

He passed without transition from nonsense to sense, from blind panic to lucid reasoning.

"You're a strange creature. . . ."

"Because I'm straightforward?"

"I'm not anxious, either, to have you getting in my way when the Forensic Department descends, and I'm even less keen on reporters' pestering you with questions.

"When my inspectors arrive at Rue Saint-Charles—in fact, they must be there by now waiting for us—I'll get them to take you to Rue des Orfèvres. . . ."

"To the cells?"

"To my office, where you will wait for me quietly."

"And then? What happens after that?"

"That depends. . . ."

"What do you hope to find out?"

"I have no idea. . . . I have even less idea than you have, because I haven't studied the body closely and I haven't seen the weapon."

This whole conversation had been accompanied by the sound of glasses, knives and forks, the buzz of voices, the bustle of the waiters and the high-pitched tinkle of the cash-register bell.

The far side of the sidewalk was getting the sun, and the shadows of the passers-by were short and squat. Cars, taxis, buses came past, doors were slammed.

On leaving the restaurant the two men paused, as if hesitating. In their corner in the *bistrot*, they had been isolated for quite a time from other people, from the life that flowed by, from familiar noises, voices, and images.

"Do you believe me?"

Ricain put the question without daring to look at Maigret.

"The moment for believing or not believing hasn't come yet. Look! My men are here. . . ."

He could see one of the black cars of the Police Department in Rue Saint-Charles, and the truck of the Records Department, and he recognized Lapointe in the little group chatting on the sidewalk. The big Torrence was there too, and it was to him that the Chief Inspector entrusted his companion.

"Take him to the Quai. Make him wait in my office, stay with him, and don't be surprised if he falls asleep. He hasn't had a wink for two nights."

Shortly after two o'clock, a truck of the Paris City Health Department was seen arriving: Moers and his men did not have the necessary equipment.

Now there were groups of men in the courtyard waiting outside the studio door; the bystanders, kept at a distance by uniformed police, were observing them attentively.

On one side, Dréville, the Assistant Public Prosecutor, and
Camus, the Magistrate, were chatting with Chief Inspector Piget
of the XVth *Arrondissement.* All of them had come straight from
lunch, and a pretty substantial meal at that, and as the work of
disinfecting dragged on, they kept glancing at their watches.

The pathologist was Dr. Delaplanque, relatively new to the
job; Maigret liked him and was now asking a few questions.
Despite the smell and the flies, Delaplanque had not hesitated to
go into the room and make a preliminary examination.

"I'll be able to tell you a bit more presently. You mentioned a
6.35 pistol, which surprises me—I would have been willing to bet
the wound was made with a heavier weapon."

"How about the range?"

"On first inspection, there was no burn, no powder marks.
Death was instantaneous, or almost, as the woman lost very
little blood. Who is she, by the way?"

"The wife of a young journalist."

For everybody, Moers and the experts from Records, it was
routine work carried out without personal feeling. They had all
heard one of the men from the Health Department exclaiming, as
he went into the room: "My, that dame stinks!"

Some of the women had babies in their arms, others, strategi-
cally placed to see everything without having to move, were
leaning on their elbows at their windows, and their comments
were bandied from apartment to apartment.

"Are you sure it isn't the taller one?"

"No, I don't know the tall one. . . ."

They were referring to Lourtie. It was Maigret the two women
were watching for.

"There he is! The one smoking the pipe. . . ."

"Two of them are smoking pipes."

"Not the very young one, silly. The other one. . . . He's going
up to the men from the Ministry."

Dréville, the Assistant Prosecutor, was asking the Chief Inspector:

"Have you got any idea what it's all about?"

"The dead woman is a girl of twenty-two, Sophie Ricain, maiden name Le Gal, born in Concarneau, where her father is a watchmaker."

"Has he been notified?"

"Not yet. I'll see to that presently."

"Married?"

"For three years, to François Ricain, a young journalist who dabbles in the movies and is trying to make his way in Paris. . . ."

"Where is he?"

"In my office."

"Do you suspect him?"

"Not so far. He's in no condition to attend the Coroner's investigation, and he'd only get in our way."

"Where was he when the crime was committed?"

"Nobody knows the time of the crime."

"And you, Doctor, can't you establish it approximately?"

"Not for the moment. Perhaps after the autopsy, if you can tell me what time the victim had her last meal and what she ate."

"What about the neighbors?"

"You can see some of them watching us. I haven't questioned them yet, but I doubt whether they'll have anything interesting to tell us. And as you can see, you can get to these studios without passing the porter's lodge, which is at the Boulevard de Grenelle entrance."

A thankless task. They hung about. They talked aimlessly, and Lapointe followed in his master's steps, not opening his mouth, with the look and the demeanor of a faithful dog.

Now the disinfectant people were bringing out of the studio a flexible tube, painted gray, which they had taken in a quarter of an hour earlier. The foreman of the team, in a white smock, signaled that they could now go in.

"Don't stay inside the room too long," he advised Maigret. "There's still formol in the air."

Dr. Delaplanque knelt beside the body, which he examined with closer attention than he had done the first time.

"As far as I'm concerned, they can take it away."

"What about you, Maigret?"

"Maigret had seen all he had to see, a huddled corpse in a flowered silk dressing gown. A red slipper still clung to one foot. It was impossible to tell from her position in the room what the woman had been doing, or even exactly where she was standing when she was hit by the bullet.

As far as it was possible to judge, the face was fairly ordinary, moderately pretty. Her toenails were painted red but had not been attended to for quite a long time, because the varnish was cracked and the nails were not scrupulously clean.

The clerk was writing away beside his boss, as was the Chief Inspector's secretary.

"Bring the stretcher in. . . ."

They trod on dead flies. One by one, the people who were crowded in the room pulled out their handkerchiefs and put them to their eyes, because of the formol.

The body was taken away, while a respectful silence reigned for a few moments in the courtyard. The men from the Public Prosecutor's office left first, then Delaplanque, while Moers and the experts waited to begin their work.

"Do we look everywhere, Chief?"

"It's best. You never know."

Perhaps they were up against a mystery, and perhaps, on the other hand, it would turn out to be quite straightforward. It is always that way at the start of a case, or nearly always.

His eyes stinging, Maigret pulled open a drawer which contained a wide assortment of objects: an old pair of binoculars, some buttons, a broken pen, pencils, photographs taken during the making of a film, sun glasses, bills. . . .

He would come back when the smell had had time to dissipate, but despite it he still noted the way the studio was decorated. The floor was varnished black, and walls and ceilings were painted a bright red. The furniture, on the other hand, was chalky white, which gave an air of unreality to the whole room. It was like a stage set. Nothing seemed solid.

"What do you think of it, Lapointe? How would you like to live in a room like this?"

"It'd give me nightmares."

They went on. There were still some people lingering in the courtyard, and the police had let them come a little nearer.

"Didn't I tell you it was him? I wonder if he'll be back. They say he does it all himself, and as like as not he'll be questioning all of us."

The speaker, a washed-out blonde with a baby in her arms, was gazing at Maigret with a smile on her face that a film star might have inspired.

"I'm going to leave you Lourtie. Here is the key to the studio. When Moer's men have finished, shut the door again and start questioning the neighbors. The crime, if it is a crime, wasn't committed last night, but the night of Wednesday to Thursday. . . .

"Try to find out whether the neighbors heard any noises. Divide up the residents between Lourtie and yourself. Then question the local shopkeepers. There is a stack of bills in the drawer. You'll find the address of the stores where they did their shopping. . . .

"One more thing. . . . Will you make sure the telephone is still working? . . . I have a feeling that when I saw it at noon it was off the hook. . . ."

The telephone was working.

"Don't come back to the Quai, you two, without giving me a ring first. Keep your chins up. . . ."

Maigret went off in the direction of Boulevard de Grenelle and vanished into the Métro. Half an hour later he emerged into the fresh air and the sun, then went back to his office, where François Ricain was waiting patiently, while Torrence was reading a paper.

"Aren't you thirsty?" he asked Ricain, taking off his hat and opening the window a little wider. "Anything new, Torrence?"

"A reporter just phoned."

"I was surprised not to see them over there. Their tip-off system must be badly organized in the XVth *Arrondissement*. It's Lapointe who'll have them around his neck. . . ."

His eyes turned to Ricain, to his hands, and he said to the Inspector:

"Take him to the laboratory, just in case. . . . Have a paraffin test done. It isn't much use anyway, as it's almost two days since the crime was committed, but it will avoid awkward questions. . . ."

They would know, within a quarter of an hour, whether Ricain had powder marks on his fingers. The absence of them would not be conclusive proof that he had not fired the gun, but it would be a point in his favor.

"Hello! . . . Is that you? . . . I'm sorry. . . . Of course. If it hadn't been work, I would have been back for lunch. . . . Yes, I ate something, beefsteak and chips, with an overexcited young man. . . . I promised myself I'd ring you as we were going into the restaurant, then we got talking, and I must confess I simply forgot. . . . You aren't cross with me, are you? . . . No, I can't tell. . . . We'll have to see. . . ."

That evening he might or might not be home for dinner, he couldn't tell yet. Especially with a young man like François Ricain, who changed his mood within the space of a few seconds.

Maigret would have been hard put to it to formulate an opinion of him. Intelligent, that he certainly was, even keenly so, as some of his answers revealed. At the same time there was a rather naïve, or childish, side to him.

How should he judge him at that moment? He was in a lamentable physical and mental state, a nervous wreck, torn between conflicting emotions.

If he had not killed his wife, and if he really had toyed with the idea of fleeing to Belgium or somewhere else, it revealed a state of total inner confusion which the claustrophobia he suffered from was not by itself enough to explain.

Probably it was he who had thought up and done the decoration in the studio, the black flooring, the red walls and ceiling, the ghostly-pale furniture which stood out as though floating in space.

It gave the impression that the ground under one's feet was unstable, that the walls were going to advance or recede as in a movie set, that the chest of drawers, the couch, the table, the chairs, were fakes made of papier-mâché.

Did he not himself seem rather a fake? Maigret imagined the faces of the Assistant Prosecutor, or the Magistrate Camus, if they were to read, from beginning to end, the words the young man had spoken, first in the café at La-Motte-Picquet, and later in the little restaurant.

He would have been interested in Dr. Pardon's impression of him.

Ricain came back, followed by Torrence.

"Well?"

"Result negative. . . ."

"I've never fired a shot in my life, except at a fair. I'd have a hard time finding the safety catch. . . ."

"Sit down."

"Have you seen the Magistrate?"

"The Magistrate and the Assistant Prosecutor."

"What have they decided to do? Am I going to be arrested?"

"That's at least the tenth time I've heard you utter that word. . . . Up till now, I would have only one reason to make an arrest—the theft of my wallet—and I haven't brought a charge against you."

"I returned it to you. . . ."

"Precisely. Now we're going to try to clear up one or two things you have told me, and others which I don't yet know about. You may go, Torrence. Tell Janvier to come in. . . ."

A few moments later Janvier was settling down at the far end of the desk and taking a pencil from his pocket.

"Your name is François Ricain. You are twenty-five years old. Where were you born?"

"In Paris, in Rue Caulaincourt."

A bourgeois, almost provincial street, behind the Sacré-Coeur.

"Are your parents still alive?"

"My father. . . . He's a railroad mechanic."

"How long have you been married?"

"A little over three and a half years. Four years ago this June. . . . The seventeenth. . . ."

"So you were twenty-one and your wife was . . ."

"Eighteen. . . ."

"Was your father already a widower?"

"My mother died when I was fourteen. . . ."

"Did you go on living with your father?"

"For a few years. . . . At seventeen I left."

"Why?"

"Because we didn't get on. . . ."

"Was there any special reason?"

"No. I was bored. . . . He wanted me to go with the railroad, like him, and I refused. He thought I was wasting my time reading and studying. . . ."

"Did you pass your *baccalauréat* exam?"

"I left two years before . . ."

"What for? . . . Where did you live? . . . On what? . . ."

"You're rushing me," complained Ricain.

"I'm not rushing you. I'm asking you elementary questions."

"There were different periods. I sold newspapers in the street. Then I was an errand boy in a printing firm in Rue Montmartre. For a while I shared a room with a friend. . . ."

"His name and address. . . ."

"Bernard Fléchier. He had a room in Rue Coquillière. . . . I lost track of him."

"What did he do?"

"He drove a delivery truck."

"Next?"

"I worked for six months in a stationer's. I wrote short stories which I peddled to newspapers. One was accepted and I got a hundred francs. . . . The man I dealt with was surprised to see how young I was."

"Did he accept any other stories?"

"No. The others were rejected. . . ."

"What were you doing when you met your wife—I mean the girl who was to become your wife, Sophie Le Gal—that's right, isn't it?"

"I was third assistant director on a movie which the censors have banned, a film about war made by some young people. . . ."

"Did Sophie have a job?"

"Not regularly. She did walk-on parts. She sometimes did a bit of modeling. . . ."

"Was she living alone?"

"In a hotel room, Saint-Germain-des-Prés."

"Love at first sight?"

"No. We slept together, because after one wild party we wound up together in the street at three o'clock in the morning. She let me take her home. We stayed together for several months, then one fine day we had the idea of getting married. . . ."

"With her parents' consent?"

"They hadn't much to say. She went to Concarneau and came back with a letter from her father authorizing the marriage."

"And you?"

"I went to see my father, also."

"What did he say?"

"He shrugged. . . ."

"Didn't he go to the wedding?"

"No. Just friends, three or four. . . . In the evening we all ate together at the Central Market."

"Did Sophie have any affairs before meeting you?"

"I wasn't the first one, if that's what you mean."

"She didn't live for any length of time with a man who might have been enough in love with her to try to see her again?"

He seemed to be searching his memory.

"No. We did meet some former friends of hers, but nothing serious. You know, in four years we had time to mix in various different circles. Some people were our friends for six months, then dropped out of sight. Others took their place, and we saw them every now and then. You ask questions as if it was all clear-cut. They're writing down my answers. I've only got to make one mistake, or get muddled up or leave out some details, and you'll jump to God knows what conclusion. . . . You must admit it's not very fair."

"Would you rather be questioned in the presence of a lawyer?"

"Have I the right?"

"If you consider yourself to be a suspect. . . ."

"And you—what do you consider me to be?"

"The husband of a woman who has died, died a violent death. As a young man who panicked and stole my wallet and then returned it to me with its contents. As a very intelligent but not very stable character. . . ."

"If you'd just spent two nights as I have . . ."

"We'll come to that. So, you've held down different jobs, each one for a short time. . . ."

"It was only to earn my living while I was waiting . . ."

"Waiting to do what?"

"To start my career . . ."

"What career?"

He frowned and looked hard at Maigret, as if to make sure there was no trace of sarcasm in his voice.

"I'm still of two minds. . . . Perhaps I'll do both. Anyhow, I want to write, but I don't know if it will be in the form of movie scripts or novels. Directing tempts me, if I can do the whole film myself. . . ."

"Do you mix with movie people?"

"At the Old Wine Press, yes. You can meet people there who are at the bottom rung like myself, but a producer like Monsieur Carus isn't too grand to come and dine with us. . . ."

"Who is Monsieur Carus?"

"A producer, I told you. He lives in the Raphael Hotel, and his office is at 18b Rue de Bassano, off the Champs-Elysées. . . ."

"Has he financed any movies?"

"Three or four. . . . In co-production with the Germans and Italians. He travels a lot. . . ."

"What sort of age is this gentleman?"

"About forty."

"Married?"

"He lives with a young girl, Nora, who has been a model."

"Did he know your wife?"

"Of course. It's a very informal circle. . . ."

"Has Monsieur Carus got plenty of money?"

"He raises it for his movies."

"But he doesn't have a private income?"

"I told you he lives at the Raphael, where he has a suite. . . . It's pretty expensive. At night he goes to the smartest clubs."

"He wasn't the one you were looking for on the night of Wednesday to Thursday?"

Ricain blushed.

"Yes. Him or someone else. . . . Preferably him because he nearly always has wads of bank notes on him."

"Do you owe him money?"

"Yes. . . ."

"A lot?"

"Upwards of two thousand francs. . . ."

"Doesn't he ask for it back?"

"No. . . ."

A very slight change, hard to pinpoint, was taking place in the young man, and Maigret observed him more closely.

But he had to remain cautious, for he was still prepared to retreat into his shell at any moment.

3

WHEN MAIGRET GOT up, Ricain began to tremble and looked at him apprehensively, still apparently expecting some blow of fate, or a trick. The Chief Inspector went and stood for a moment by the open window, as if to steep himself in reality by watching the passers-by and the cars on the Saint-Michel bridge, and a tug with a big clover-leaf marking on its funnel.

"I'll be right back."

From the Inspectors' room, he asked for the Pathologists' Laboratory.

"This is Maigret. Would you please find out whether Dr. Delaplanque has finished the autopsy."

He had to wait quite a long time before he heard the pathologist's voice on the other end of the line.

"You've called at just the right moment, Inspector. I was going to call you. Have you been able to find out when exactly the young woman had her last meal, and what it consisted of?"

"I'll tell you in a moment. How about the wound?"

"As far as I can judge the shot was fired at a distance of, say, between a yard and a yard and a half."

"From the front?"

"From the side. The victim was standing up. She must have staggered back a step or two before falling on the carpet. The laboratory, which found patches of blood, will confirm this. And another thing. The woman had had a pregnancy which had been terminated toward the third or fourth month by the crudest possible methods. She smoked a lot, but was in quite good health."

"Do you mind holding on a moment?"

He went back to his office.

"Did you have dinner with your wife on Wednesday evening?"

"Around half past eight, at the Old Wine Press."

"Do you remember what she ate?"

"Wait. . . . I wasn't hungry. I just had some cold meat. Sophie ordered a fish soup which Rose recommended, then some beef. . . ."

"No dessert?"

"No. We drank a carafe of Beaujolais. . . . I had some coffee; Sophie didn't want any."

Maigret went into the next room and repeated the menu to Delaplanque.

"If she ate at half past eight, I can put the death at somewhere around eleven o'clock in the evening, because the food was almost completely digested. I'll tell you more after the chemical analysis, but it'll take a few days."

"Did you do the paraffin test?"

"Yes. I saw to that. There wasn't any trace of powder on the hands. You'll get my preliminary report in the morning."

Maigret went back again to his office and arranged the five or six pipes he kept there in order of size.

"I've got some more questions to put to you, Ricain, but I hesitate to do so today. You're worn out and you're only keeping going on your nerves."

"I'd rather get it over with now. . . ."

"As you wish. So, if I've understood you correctly, you've never, up till now, had any steady job or regular income?"

"There are tens of thousands of us in the same boat, I should think. . . ."

"Whom did you owe money?"

"All the shopkeepers. . . . Some of them won't let us have anything any more. . . . I owe another five hundred francs to Maki."

"Who's he?"

"A sculptor, who lives in the same block. He's abstract, but to make a bit of money he does portrait busts every now and then. This had happened a fortnight ago. He made four or five thousand francs and bought us dinner. Over the dessert I asked him to make me a small loan."

"Who else?"

"There's a stack of them!"

"Did you plan to pay them back?"

"I'm sure one day I'll make a lot of money. Most directors and well-known writers began like me."

"Let's turn to something else. Were you jealous?"

"Of whom?"

"I'm referring to your wife. I presume that sometimes some of your friends used to try to make up to her?"

Ricain fell silent, embarrassed, and shrugged his shoulders.

"I don't think you'll be able to understand. You belong to a different generation. . . . We young people don't attach so much importance to these things."

"Do you mean you allowed her to have intimate relations with other people?"

"It's difficult to reply to such a crude question."

"Even so, try."

"She posed in the nude for Maki. . . ."

"And nothing happened?"

"I never asked them."

"And Monsieur Carus?"

"Carus has as many girls as he wants, all the ones who want to get into the movies or television."

"Does he exploit the situation?"

"I believe so. . . ."

"Didn't your wife try to get into the movies?"

"She had a small speaking part three months ago."

"And you weren't jealous?"

"Not in the way you mean."

"You told me Carus had a mistress. . . ."

"Nora."

"Is she jealous?"

"That's not the same thing. Nora is an intelligent woman, and ambitious. . . . She looks down on the movies. What she cares about is becoming Madame Carus and having plenty of money at her disposal."

"Did she get on well with your wife?"

"As well as with anyone. She was condescending to all of us, men and women alike. . . . What are you driving at?"

"Nothing."

"Are you planning to interrogate everybody I was in touch with?"

"Possibly. Someone killed your wife. You say that it wasn't you, and until I have proof to the contrary I'm inclined to believe you.

"An unknown person got into your house on Wednesday evening, when you had just left. This person had no key, which leads one to suppose that your wife let him into the studio without being suspicious."

Maigret was keeping a close eye on the young man, who was becoming visibly impatient, trying to get a word in.

"One moment! Who, among your friends, knew of the existence of the gun?"

"Nearly all of them. In fact, all. . . ."

"Did you occasionally carry it on you?"

"No. But sometimes, when I was in funds, I would ask my friends around. . . . I would buy some cold cuts and salmon and things like that, and everybody brought a bottle of wine or whisky."

"What time did these little parties finish?"

"Late. We drank a great deal. . . . Sometimes people fell asleep and stayed till morning. Occasionally I would play with the gun, as a joke. . . ."

"Was it loaded?"

Ricain didn't answer at once, and at these moments it was difficult not to have suspicions about him.

"I don't know."

"Listen. You speak of parties when everyone was more or less drunk. You would grab a gun, just for fun, and now you tell me you didn't even know whether it was loaded. Earlier you told me you didn't know where the safety catch was. You could have killed any one of your friends without meaning to."

"It's possible. When one is drunk . . ."

"Were you often drunk, Ricain?"

"Quite often. Not so drunk I didn't know what I was doing, but I take my liquor neat, like most of my friends. When we meet, especially in clubs and cafés . . ."

"Where did you lock up the gun?"

"It wasn't locked up. It was kept in the top of the chest with old bits of string, nails, thumbtacks, bills, all the things we couldn't find a place for anywhere else."

"So that any one of the people who used to spend the evening with you could have taken the weapon and used it?"

"Yes."

"Do you have any suspicions?"

A moment's hesitation, once again, a sidelong glance.

"No. . . ."

"Nobody was deeply in love with your wife?"

"I was. . . ."

Why did he say it with a note of sarcasm in his voice?

"In love but not jealous?"

"I've already explained . . ."

"And Carus?"

"I told you . . ."

"Maki?"

"He's a big brute to look at, but he's as gentle as a lamb and women frighten him. . . ."

"Tell me about the others, the people you saw, the ones you met up with in the Old Wine Press and who used to round off their evenings with you, when you were solvent. . . ."

"Gérard Dramin. He's an assistant director. He was the one I worked with on a script, when I was third assistant on the picture."

"Married?"

"At the moment he's living apart from his wife. It isn't the first time. . . . After a few months they always go back to each other again."

"Where doe she live?"

"All over the place, always in hotels. He boasts openly of owning nothing except a suitcase and its contents. . . ."

"Are you taking this down, Janvier?"

"I'm with you, Chief."

"Who else, Ricain?"

"A photographer, Jacques Huguet, who lives in the same block as I, in the center building."

"How old?"

"Thirty."

"Married?"

"Twice. Divorced both times. He has one child by his first wife, two by the second. She lives on the same floor."

"Does he live by himself?"

"With Jocelyne, a nice girl, seven or eight months pregnant. . . ."

"That makes three women in his life. Does he still see the first two?"

"The girls get on well together."

"Go on."

"Go on with what?"

"The list of your friends, the regulars at the Old Wine Press."

"They keep changing, as I told you before. There's Pierre Louchard. . . ."

"What does he do?"

"He's over forty, he's a queer, and he runs an antique shop in Rue de Sèvres."

"What does he have in common with your group?"

"I don't know. He's a regular customer at the Old Wine Press. He follows us about. . . . He doesn't talk much, and seems to feel at home with us."

"Do you owe him money?"

"Not much. . . . Three hundred and fifty francs."

The telephone rang. Maigret picked up the receiver.

"Hello, Chief. Lapointe would like a word with you. Shall I put him through to your office?"

"No, I'll come around."

He went back into the Inspector's room.

"You asked me to call you when we were through, Chief. Lourtie and I have questioned all the neighbors who could have heard anything, especially the women, as most of the men are still at work.

"Nobody remembers a shot. They are accustomed to noises coming from the Ricains' apartment at night. Several of the tenants had complained to the janitor about it and were planning to write to the landlord.

"Once at about two o'clock in the morning an old lady who was suffering from tooth-ache was standing by her window when she saw a naked girl burst out of the studio and run into the courtyard pursued by a man.

"She wasn't the only one who said that there used to be orgies in the Ricains' studio."

"Did Sophie have visitors when her husband was away?"

"Well, the fact is, Chief, the women I spoke to weren't very precise. The terms that cropped up most often were: savages, people with no manners, or no morals. As for the concierge, she was waiting for their lease to expire to give them notice to quit: they were six months behind with the rent and the landlord had decided to get rid of them if they didn't pay up. What shall I do?"

"Stay at the studio until I get there. Keep Lourtie with you, as I may need him."

He went back to his office, where Janvier and Ricain were waiting in silence.

"Listen to me, Ricain. At this stage, I don't want to ask the Magistrate for a warrant against you. On the other hand, I don't suppose you want to sleep in Rue Saint-Charles tonight."

"I couldn't . . ."

"You haven't got any money. I would rather not see you let loose again in Paris trying to find a friend who'll lend you something."

"What are you going to do with me?"

"Inspector Janvier is going to take you to a small hotel, not far from here, on the Ile Saint-Louis. You can have food sent up to you. If you pass a drugstore or a pharmacy, buy yourself some soap, a razor, and a toothbrush. . . ."

The Chief Inspector gave Janvier a wink.

"I'd rather you didn't go out. Besides, I must warn you that if you should happen to . . ."

"I'll be followed. . . . I realized that. I'm innocent."

"So you said."

"Don't you trust me?"

"It's not my job to trust people. I'm content to wait. Good night."

Alone once again, Maigret paced his office for a few minutes, pausing every now and then in front of the window. Then he picked up the telephone to tell his wife that he would not be home for dinner.

A quarter of an hour later he was back in the subway on his way to Bir-Hakeim. He knocked on the studio door, and Lapointe let him in.

The smell of disinfectant still hung in the air. Lourtie, seated in the only armchair, was smoking a small, exceptionally strong cigar.

"Do you want to sit down, Chief?"

"No thank you. I presume you found nothing new?"

"Some photos. Here's one of the Ricains together on the beach. Another in front of their car. . . ."

Sophie wasn't bad-looking. She had that slightly sulky look that is fashionable among young people and a *bouffant* hair style. In the street one might have taken her for any one of thousands with the same mannerisms and the same way of dressing.

"No wine or liquor?"

"A bottle with some dregs of whisky in that cupboard."

An old, nondescript cupboard, like the cabinet and the chairs, but made original by the flat white paint which contrasted with the black floor and red walls.

Maigret, with his hat on, pipe in mouth, pulled open the doors and drawers. Very few clothes, three dresses altogether, cheap, garish. Some trousers, polo shirts. . . .

The kitchenette, next to the bathroom, was scarcely larger than a cupboard, with its gas ring and miniature refrigerator. In the latter he found an opened bottle of mineral water, a quarter of a pound of butter, three eggs, a cutlet in a congealed sauce.

Nothing was clean, neither the clothes nor the kitchen, nor the bathroom in which the dirty laundry was strewn about.

"Nobody called?"

"Not since we've been here."

By now the crime must have found its way into the evening papers, or would be doing so at any moment.

"Let Lourtie go and have a bite, then come back here and settle down as comfortably as possible. All right, Lourtie, old boy?"

"All right, Chief. Am I allowed a nap?"

As for Maigret and Lapointe, they set out on foot for the Old Wine Press.

"Have you arrested him?"

"No. Torrence has taken him off to the Stork, on the Ile Saint-Louis."

It was not the first time that they had put a customer they had been anxious to keep an eye on in there.

"Do you think he killed her?"

"He's both intelligent enough and stupid enough to have done it. On the other hand . . ."

Maigret struggled for words, but could not find them. He had seldom been so intrigued by a person as he was by this François Ricain. At first sight, he was just an ambitious young man of the kind one runs into every day in Paris or any other capital city.

A future failure? He was only twenty-five. Men who later became famous were still pounding the pavement at his age. At moments the Chief Inspector was inclined to trust him. Then, immediately afterwards, he would give a discouraged sigh.

"If I were his father . . ."

What would he do with a son like François? Try to bring him around, guide him back onto the rails?

He decided to go and see the father in Montmartre. Unless he came around to the Police Headquarters of his own accord when he read the papers.

Lapointe, who was walking beside him in silence, was little more than twenty-five years old. Maigret mentally compared the two men.

"I think it's there, Chief, on the other side of the boulevard, near the Air Terminal subway station."

They found themselves gazing at an entrance door flanked by two worm-eaten wine presses, with heavily curtained windows through which filtered the pink light of the lamps, which were already lit.

It was not time yet for apéritifs, much less for dinner, and there were only two people in the room, a woman, on the customers' side of the bar, perched on a high stool and drinking through a yellowish straw, and the boss on the other, bent over a newspaper.

The lights were pink, the bar was supported by wine presses, the massive tables were covered with checked cloths, and the walls were three-quarters paneled with dark woodwork.

Maigret, walking ahead of Lapointe, frowned as he caught sight of the man with the newspaper, as if he were trying to remember where he had seen him before.

The boss, for his part, raised his head, but it only took him an instant to recognize the Chief Inspector.

"What a coincidence," he remarked, tapping the still fresh print. "I was just reading that you were in charge of the case."

And, turning to the girl:

"Fernande, meet Chief Inspector Maigret in person. . . . Sit down, Inspector. What can I offer you?"

"I didn't know you had gone into the restaurant business."

"When you begin to get on a bit . . ."

It was true that Bob Mandille must have been about Maigret's age. He was much talked about in the old days, when he used to think up some new stunt every month, walking along the wing of an airplane in flight, parachuting over the Place de la Concorde and landing a few feet from the Obelisk, or leaping from a galloping horse into a racing car.

The movie industry had turned him into one of its most celebrated stunt men after trying in vain to make him a male lead. People had lost count of the accidents he had had, and his body must be a mass of scars.

He had kept his figure and his elegance. There was just a touch of stiffness in his movements, something mechanical. As for his face, it was just a little too smooth, with slightly too regular features, probably the result of plastic surgery.

"Scotch?"

"Beer."

"Same for you, young man?"

Lapointe was not at all pleased to be addressed in this way.

"You see, Monsieur Maigret, I've had enough. The insurance companies tell me I'm too old to be a good risk and all of a sudden they don't want me in the movies any more. So I married Rose and turned publican. . . . You're looking at my hair? Do you remember my picture, when I was scalped by the blades of a helicopter and my head was as bald as an egg? A wig, that's all it is. . . ."

He raised it, gallantly, as if it were a hat.

"You know Rose, don't you? She sang for a long time at the Trianon-Lyrique. Rose Delval, as she was called then. Her real name is Rose Vatan, which didn't sound right on a bill-board. . . .

"Well, what do you want to talk about?"

Maigret glanced in the direction of the girl called Fernande.

"Don't worry about her. She's part of the furniture. In two hours she'll be so drunk she won't be able to move and I'll put her into a taxi. . . ."

"You know Ricain, of course?"

"Of course. Your health. . . . I only drink water, so excuse me. . . . Ricain comes to dine here once or twice a week."

"With his wife?"

"With Sophie, naturally. It's unusual to see Francis without Sophie. . . ."

"When did you see them last?"

"Wait. . . . What day is it? Friday. . . . They came on Wednesday evening."

"With friends?"

"None of the gang were here that night. Except for Maki, if I'm not mistaken. . . . I seem to remember Maki eating in his corner."

"Did they sit down with him?"

"No. Francis just stuck his head in and asked me if I'd seen Carus and I said no, I hadn't seen him for two or three days."

"What time did they leave?"

"They didn't come in. They must have eaten somewhere else. Where is Francis now? I hope you haven't put him in . . ."

"Why do you ask?"

"I've just read in the paper that his wife was shot dead with a gun and that he's disappeared. . . ."

Maigret smiled. The news release of the local police station, where they didn't know the full story, had misled the reporters.

"Who told you about my restaurant?"

"Ricain."

"So he's not on the run?"

"No."

"Arrested?"

"Not arrested, either. Do you think he would have been capable of killing Sophie?"

"He's incapable of killing anything. If he was going to, it would be himself. . . ."

"Why?"

"Because there are times when he loses his self-confidence and starts hating himself. That's when he drinks. After a few glasses he becomes desperate, convinced that he's a failure who's going to let his wife down."

"Does he pay you regularly?"

"He's run up quite a bill. . . . If I listened to Rose, I'd have stopped giving him credit long ago. For Rose, business is business. True, her job is harder than mine, at the stove all day. . . . She's there now, and she'll still be there at ten o'clock tonight."

"Did Ricain come back that night?"

"Wait. I was busy with a table, later on . . . I felt a draft and I turned to the door. It was open and I thought I saw him there looking for someone. . . ."

"Did he find him?"

"No."

"What time was this?"

"Around eleven o'clock. You were right to press me. It was that evening that he came back a third time, later. . . . Sometimes, when the dinners are finished we stay on for a chat with the regulars. It was past midnight, on Wednesday, when he came back. He stayed by the door and signaled to me to come over. . . ."

"Did he know the customers you were with?"

"No. They were old friends of Rose, theater people, and Rose had joined us, in her apron. Francis is scared stiff of my wife. . . .

"He asked me if Carus had come. I told him he hadn't. And Gérard? . . . Gérard, that's Dramin, who's going to make a name for himself one day in the movies. . . . He hadn't come, either. Then he blurted out that he needed two thousand francs. I made it clear that I couldn't help. A few dinners, all right. A fifty- or a hundred-franc note every now and then when Rose is looking the other way, that I can manage. But two thousand francs . . ."

"He didn't say why he needed it so badly?"

"Because they were going to turn him out of the studio and sell everything he owned. . . ."

"Was it the first time?"

"No, and that's the point. Rose isn't so very wrong: he's a habitual sponger. But not a cynical one, if you see what I mean. He does it in good faith, always convinced that tomorrow or next week he will be signing a big contract. He's so ashamed of asking that one is ashamed of refusing."

"Is he a nervous person?"

"Have you seen him?"

"Of course."

"Nervous or calm?"

"A bundle of nerves."

"Well, I've never seen him any other way. Sometimes it's quite exhausting to watch. He clenches his fists, makes faces, flies into a fury over nothing, or else he's sorry for himself, or gets on his high horse. And yet, you know, Inspector, he's basically sound, and I wouldn't be surprised if he does something one day."

"What do you think of Sophie?"

"They say you mustn't speak ill of the dead. The Sophies of this world, you run into them by the dozen, if you see what I mean. . . ."

And with a glance he indicated the girl sitting at the bar, lost in contemplation of the bottles in front of her.

"I wonder what he saw in her. There are thousands of them, all dressed alike, with the same make-up, dirty feet, worn heels, wandering about in the mornings in slacks too tight for them and living on salads. All hoping to become models or film stars. . . . Jesus! . . ."

"She had a bit part."

"Ah yes, through Walter."

"Who is Walter?"

"Carus. If you totted up the number of girls who have earned their right to a bit part . . ."

"What sort of man is he?"

"Come and have dinner here and you'll probably be able to see for yourself. He sits at the same table one night in two, and there's always someone around to make the most of his hospitality. A producer. . . . You know how it goes. The man who finds the money to start a film, then the money to continue it, and then, after months or years, the money to finish it . . . He's half English and half Turkish, which is an interesting mixture. . . . A decent sort, straight, with a booming voice, always ready to buy a round of drinks and addressing everyone as 'tu' within five minutes of meeting them."

"Did he call Sophie 'tu'?"

"He addressed all women as 'tu' and calls them his baby, his sweetie, or his turtle dove as the fancy takes him."

"Do you think he slept with her?"

"I'd be surprised if he didn't. . . ."

"Wasn't Ricain jealous?"

"I expected that you were coming to that. . . . First of all, Carus wasn't the only one. I would think the others have all had a go at her. I could have, too, if I'd wanted, even though I could almost have been her grandfather. Leaving that aside . . . We had a few rows about that, Rose and I. . . .

"Question Rose and you'll find she hasn't a good word to say for him. She thinks he's a good-for-nothing, living by his wits and playing the big misunderstood act, but in spite of everything really just a little pimp. . . . That's my wife's opinion.

"It's true, of course, that she spends three-quarters of her time in the kitchen, so she doesn't know him as well as I do.

"I've tried to make her understand that Francis knew nothing of what was going on."

"Do you believe that?"

The retired acrobat had very pale blue eyes that reminded one of a child's. In spite of his age and his air of experience, he had still preserved a childlike enthusiasm and charm.

"Perhaps I'm a bit naïve, but I trust the boy. There have been times when I haven't been so sure, and then I've almost come around to Rose's way of thinking. . . . But I always come back to my original position: he's really in love. Enough for her to make him believe anything.

"The proof is the way he let himself be treated by her. . . . Some nights, when she had a drop too many, she told him, cynically, that he was nothing but a failure, a zero, that he had no guts, and, if you'll forgive me, no balls either, and that she was wasting her time on a half-portion like him. . . ."

"How did he take it?"

"He would withdraw into his shell, and you could see the beads of sweat on his forehead. Even so, he would force himself to smile:

"'Come on, Sophie. Come to bed. You're tired. . . .'"

At the back of the room a door opened. A small, very fat woman appeared, wiping her hands on a large apron.

"Well, well! The Chief Inspector. . . ."

And while Maigret was still trying to remember where he could have seen her before, since he had never been a regular customer at the Trianon-Lyrique, she reminded him:

"Twenty-two years ago . . . In your office. You arrested the character who lifted my jewels from my dressing room. I've put on a little weight since then. . . . In fact, it's thanks to those jewels that I was able to buy this restaurant. That's right, isn't it Bob? But why have you come here?"

Her husband explained, with a gesture toward the newspaper:

"Sophie's dead. . . ."

"Our Sophie, the little Ricain girl?"

"Yes."

"An accident? I'll bet it was him driving and . . ."

"She was murdered."

"What's he saying, Monsieur Maigret?"

"The truth."

"When did it happen?"

"Wednesday evening."

"They had dinner here."

Rose's face had lost not only her good humor, which was her trademark, as it were, but her cordiality.

"What have you been telling him?"

"I've been answering his questions. . . ."

"I bet you haven't had a good word for her. Listen, Inspector, Bob isn't a bad character and we get along quite well together. But on the subject of women, you mustn't listen to him. To hear him you'd think they're all tarts and men are their victims. Now, take this poor girl, for example . . .

"Look at me, Bob. Who was right . . . ? Was it him or her that caught it?"

She paused, glaring at them defiantly, her hands on her hips.

"Make it another, Bob," Fernande mumbled slackly.

And to speed her on her way, Mandille gave her a double portion.

"Were you fond of her, Madame?"

"How can I put it . . . ? She was brought up in the provinces. And moreover at Concarneau, where her father is a watchmaker. I'm sure her mother goes to mass every morning.

"So she comes to Paris and falls in with this gang who thinks they're geniuses because they work in the movies or on television. I've been in the theater myself, which is a far more difficult proposition. I've sung the whole repertoire but I never gave myself airs. While these little nitwits . . ."

"Which ones do you mean in particular?"

"Ricain, for a start. He considered himself the smartest of the lot. . . . When he managed to get an article into a magazine read by a few hundred imbeciles, he imagined he was going to rock the movie world to its foundations. . . .

"He took the girl over. Apparently they actually got married. He might at least have fed her properly, mightn't he? I don't know what they would have done for food if their friends hadn't invited them and if my half-wit of a husband hadn't given them credit. . . . How much does he owe you, Bob?"

"What's it matter?"

"You ass! And here I am, slaving away in the kitchen. . . ."

She was grumbling for the sake of grumbling, which did not prevent her from looking at her husband with a certain tenderness.

"Do you think she was Carus's mistress?"

"As if he needed her! He had enough on his hands with Nora. . . ."

"Is that his wife?"

"No. He wanted to marry her all right, but he has a wife in London and she won't hear of a divorce. Nora . . ."

"What's she like?"

"Don't you know her? That one, now, I wouldn't defend. You can see it isn't just prejudice. What do men see in her, I keep asking myself. . . .

"She's at least thirty, and if you cleaned all her make-up off, you'd probably guess nearer forty. She's thin, it's true, so thin you can count her bones. . . .

"Black and green around the eyes, to make them mysterious, it seems, but it only makes her look like a witch. No mouth, because she hides it under a layer of white stuff . . . And a greenish white on her cheeks. . . . That's Nora for you.

"As for her clothes . . . The other day she turned up in a silver *lamé* pajama affair so tight she had to come into the kitchen to get me to sew up the seam of the trousers. . . ."

"Does she work for the movies?"

"What do you take her for? She leaves that to the young girls who don't count. . . . Her dream is to become the wife of a big international producer, to be Madame the producer's wife one day."

"You're exaggerating," Mandille sighed.

"Less than you were a moment ago."

"Nora is intelligent, cultivated, much more cultivated than Carus, and without her he probably wouldn't be so successful."

From time to time, Maigret turned to Lapointe, who was

listening in silence, motionless by the bar, no doubt dumb-
founded by what he heard and by the atmosphere of the Old Wine
Press.

"Will you stay for dinner, Monsieur Maigret? If there isn't too
much of a rush perhaps I'll be able to come over now and then for
a chat. There's *mouclade*. . . . I never forget that I was born in
La Rochelle, where my mother sold fish, so I know some good
recipes. . . . Have you ever eaten *chaudrée fourrassienne?*"

Maigret rattled off, "Soup made of eel, baby sole, and
cuttlefish. . . ."

"Have you been there often?"

"To La Rochelle, yes, and to Fourras. . . ."

"Shall I put a *chaudrée* on for you?"

"Please. . . ."

When she had gone off, Maigret grunted:

"Your wife doesn't share your opinions about people. If I
listened to her I would be arresting François Ricain right away."

"I think you'd be making a mistake."

"Can you suggest anyone else?"

"As the guilty party? No. . . . Where was Francis at the time?"

"Here . . . in this neighborhood. . . . He claims he was running all over Paris looking for Carus or anybody who would lend
him some money. Wait now. He mentioned a club. . . ."

"The Zero Club, I'll bet. . . ."

"That's right. Near Rue Jacob."

"Carus often goes there. Some other customers of mine,
too. . . . It's one of the latest in-places to go to. The fashion
changes every two or three years. Sometimes they don't last as
long as that, just a few months. . . . It isn't the first time Francis
has been short of money, or that he's been around trying to cadge
the odd thousand-franc note, or notes. . . ."

"He didn't find Carus anywhere."

"Did he try his hotel?"

"I imagine so."

"Then he must have been at Enghien. Nora is a great gam-
bler. . . . Last year, at Cannes, he left her alone in the casino,
and when he went back for her she had sold her jewels and lost
the whole business. . . . Another beer? Wouldn't you prefer an
old port?"

"I'd rather have a beer. How about you, Lapointe?"

"A port," Lapointe mumbled, blushing.

"May I use the telephone?"

"In the back on the left. . . . Wait. I'll give you some counters."

He took a handful from the cash drawer and gave them to Maigret without counting them.

"Hello? . . . The Inspectors' room? . . . Who's speaking? Torrence? . . . Any news? . . . Nobody asked for me? . . . Moers? I'll call him when I've finished with you.

"Have you had a call from Janvier . . . ? He's still at the Stork? The boy's asleep? . . . Good. . . . Yes. . . . Good. . . . You're going to take over from him? . . . Okay, old man. . . . Good night. . . . Keep an eye open, though, even so. . . .

"If he wakes up there's no telling what he may get up to. . . . One second. . . . Could you telephone the River Police . . . ?

"Tomorrow morning they should send some frogmen to the Bir-Hakeim bridge. A little above it, a hundred feet at the most, they ought to find a revolver thrown from the bank. . . . Yes. Mention my name. . . ."

He rang off and dialed the laboratory.

"Moers . . . ? I gather you've been trying to get me. . . . You found the bullet in the wall? What . . . ? Probably a 6.35 . . . Well, send it to Gastinne-Renette. . . . It's possible we'll have a weapon to show them tomorrow. . . . And the prints? . . . I expect so. . . . Everywhere . . . on both of them. . . . And of several different people. . . . Men and women. . . . It doesn't surprise me, as they can't have cleaned the place very often. . . . Thank you, Moers. . . . See you tomorrow. . . ."

François Ricain was sleeping the sleep of exhaustion, in a small bedroom in the Ile Saint-Louis, as Maigret was about to settle down to a tasty *chaudrée* in the restaurant where the young couple used to meet their band of friends.

When he left the telephone booth, he could not help smiling as Fernande, who had suddenly come to life again, was making animated conversation with Lapointe, who did not know quite how to react.

4

IT WAS A strange evening of covert glances, whispers, of comings and goings around the confined floor space, with the pink light and the good smells from the Old Wine Press's kitchen.

Maigret had settled himself with Lapointe near the entrance in a sort of niche where there was a table for two.

"It's the table Ricain and Sophie used to take when they weren't with the others," Mandille had explained.

Lapointe had his back to the room, and every now and then, when the Chief Inspector pointed out something of interest, he would turn around, as discreetly as possible.

The *chaudrée* was good, and it was accompanied by a pleasing Charentes wine not usually sold commercially, the tart wine used to make cognac.

The one-time stunt man comported himself as master of the house, receiving his customers like guests and shepherding them from the door. He joked with them, kissed the women's hands, led them to their tables and, before the waiter had time, handed them the menu.

Almost always he would then come over to Maigret.

"An architect and his wife. . . . They come every Friday, sometimes with their son, who is studying law."

After the architect, two doctors and their wives, at a table for four, also regulars. One of the doctors was expecting a telephone call, and a few minutes later he collected his bag from the hat-check girl and made his apologies to his friends.

Maki the sculptor was eating by himself in his corner with a hearty appetite, helping himself with his fingers more freely than is usually considered good form.

It was eight o'clock when a sallow youth with unhealthy complexion came in and shook hands with him. He did not join him, but went and sat on a bench, spreading a mimeographed manuscript in front of him.

"Dramin," Bob announced. "He usually works while he eats. It's his latest movie script, which he's already had to start all over again two or three times. . . ."

Most of the customers knew one another, at least by sight, and exchanged discreet nods from a distance.

From the descriptions he had been given, Maigret at once recognized Carus and, even more easily, Nora, who would have had difficulty in passing unnoticed.

That evening she was not wearing *lamé* trousers but a dress in a material almost as transparent as cellophane, and so tight that she appeared to be naked.

Of the face, which was whitened like a clown's, one could only actually see the coal-black eyes, underlined not just with black and green but with gold specks which sparkled in the light.

There was something ghostlike about her face, her look, her manner, and the contrast was all the greater compared with the vitality of the portly Carus, with his solidly hewn features and his healthy smiling face.

While she followed Bob to the table, Carus shook hands with Maki, then Dramin, then the one remaining doctor and the two women.

When he in turn had sat down Bob leaned over to say a few words to him, and the producer's eyes looked around in search of Maigret, coming to rest on him with curiosity. He seemed about to get up to shake hands with Maigret, but first he looked over the menu which had been slipped into his hand, and began discussing it with Nora.

When Mandille came back to Maigret's corner, Maigret expressed his surprise.

"I thought the gang all sat together at the same table?"

"Sometimes they do. Some evenings they stay in their own

corners. Occasionally they get together over the coffee. Other days they all sit together. The customers make themselves at home here. We have very little space and we don't encourage . . ."

"Do they all know?"

"They've read the papers, or heard the news on the radio, of course. . . ."

"What are they saying?"

"Nothing. It's given them all quite a shock. Your presence here must make them feel uncomfortable. . . . What will you have after the *chaudrée*? My wife recommends the leg of lamb, which is real *pré-salé* meat. . . ."

"How about it, Lapointe? . . . Right, then, lamb for two. . . ."

"A carafe of red Bourdeaux?"

Through the curtain one could see the lights of the boulevard, the passers-by, some walking faster than others, the occasional couple walking arm-in-arm and stopping every few steps to kiss or lovingly look at each other.

Dramin, as Bob had predicted, ate with an eye on his manuscript, every now and then taking a pencil from his pocket to make a correction. He was the only one of Ricain's acquaintances not to appear concerned by the presence of the policemen.

He wore a dark suit, ready-made, a nondescript tie. He might have passed for an accountant or a cashier at the bank.

"Carus is debating whether to come and talk to me or not," Maigret said, who was observing the couple. "I don't know what Nora is whispering to him, but he doesn't agree."

He imagined the other evenings, with François Ricain and Sophie coming in, looking around for their friends, wondering whether anybody would invite them to sit with them, or whether they would have to eat alone in their corner. They must have seemed like poor relations.

"Are you planning to question them, Chief?"

"Not right now. After the lamb."

It was very hot. The doctor who had been called to the invalid's bedside was back already, and from his gestures they gathered that he was complaining that he had been disturbed for nothing.

Where had Fernande, the big girl propped against the bar, got to? Bob must have got rid of her. He was deep in conversation, with three or four customers who had taken her place. They were being very familiar and seemed in high spirits.

"The specter is trying to persuade her man to do something. . . ."

Nora was in fact talking to Carus in a low voice, without taking her eyes off Maigret, giving him advice. What advice?

"He is still hesitating. He is panting to come over and join us, but she's stopping him. I think I'll go over. . . ."

Maigret rose heavily, after wiping his lips with his napkin, and threaded his way between the tables. The couple watched him coming, Nora impassively, Carus with visible satisfaction.

"Am I disturbing you?"

The producer rose to his feet, wiped his mouth too, and held out his hand.

"Walter Carus . . . My wife . . ."

"Chief Inspector Maigret . . ."

"I know. . . . Please sit down. Will you have a glass of champagne with us? My wife drinks nothing else, and I must say I can't blame her for that. Joseph! A champagne glass for the Chief Inspector . . . !"

"Please, go on with your dinner."

"I hardly need tell you I know the reason for your presence. . . . I heard the news just now, on the radio, on my way to the hotel for a shower and a change. . . ."

"Did you know the Ricains well?"

"Quite well. Here we all know one another. . . . He more or less worked for me, in that I've got some money tied up in the film he's working on."

"Didn't his wife play a bit part in another of your pictures?"

"I've forgotten. More likely as an extra."

"Did she mean to make a career of it?"

"I don't think so. Not seriously. . . . At a certain age most girls want to see themselves on the screen."

"Was she talented?"

Maigret had the impression that Nora was kicking Carus under the table, as a warning.

"I must confess to you that I don't know. I don't think she even had a screen test. . . ."

"And Ricain?"

"Are you asking me whether he's talented?"

"What sort of a person is he, from a professional point of view?"

"What would you say, Nora?"

The reply came, icily:

"Zero. . . ."

The remark seemed to fall incongruously and Carus hastened to explain:

"Don't be surprised . . . Nora is a bit psychic. She has a kind of thing which puts her in instant contact with certain people. With others, it has the opposite effect. You can take my word for it or not, but this thing—I can't find any other word to describe it—has often been useful to me in business, even on the Stock Exchange. . . ."

Under the table, the foot was at work again.

"With Francis, contact was never established. . . . Personally, I find him intelligent, gifted, and I'd be willing to bet that he'll go far one day.

"Now take Dramin, for example, buried in his script over there. . . . There's a serious worker for you, who gets the job done as completely as you could wish. I've read some excellent dialogue of his. But unless I'm completely mistaken, he will never be a big-time director. He needs somebody, not only to guide him, but to inject the vital spark. . . ."

He was delighted with the words he had just found.

"The spark! . . . That's what is lacking most of the time, and that's essential, as much in the movies as in television. Hundreds of specialists come up with quite adequate work, a well-constructed story, dialogue that runs smoothly. But almost always, something is missing, and the result is flat and gray. The spark, if you see what I mean . . .

"Well now, you can't count on Francis to provide you with anything solid. His ideas are often preposterous. He has suggested thousands of ideas that would have ruined me. On the other hand, occasionally he has the spark. . . ."

"In what way?"

Carus scratched his nose, comically.

"That's just it. . . . You speak like Nora. . . . One evening, after dinner, he will talk with such conviction and such fire that you are sure you have a genius on your hands. Then, next day, you'll realize that what he was saying doesn't make sense. He's young. It'll all come out in the wash. . . ."

"Is he working for you at the moment?"

"Apart from his reviews, which are remarkable, although somewhat too sharp, he doesn't work for anybody. He's full of projects, fusses around with several films at the same time without ever finishing any of them."

"Does he ask you for advances?"

The feet, under the table, kept up their silent conversation.

"Look, Inspector, our profession isn't like other professions. We are all looking for talent, actors, script writers, and producers. . . . It doesn't pay to take a known director who will make you the same film over and over again, and as for stars, it's a question of finding new faces. . . .

"Also we are obliged to gamble on a certain number of promising young people. To gamble modestly, otherwise we'd be ruined overnight. A thousand francs here, a screen test, a word of encouragement . . ."

"In fact, if you lent considerable sums to Ricain it was because you hoped to get the money back someday. . . ."

"Without counting on it too much. . . ."

"And Sophie?"

"I was in no way involved with her career. . . ."

"Did she hope to become a star?"

"Don't make me say more than I already have. She was always with her husband and she didn't talk much. I think she was shy. . . ."

An ironical smile appeared on Nora's pale lips.

"My wife thinks otherwise, and, as I've more confidence in her judgment than I have in my own, don't attach too much weight to my opinions."

"How did Sophie and Francis get along?"

"How do you mean?"

He was feigning surprise.

"Did they seem to you to be very close?"

"You seldom saw one without the other, and I don't ever remember them quarreling in my presence."

Again there was an enigmatic smile on Nora's lips.

"Perhaps she was a bit impatient. . . ."

"In what sense?"

"He believed in his star, in the future, a future which he saw as brilliant, and just round the corner. I suppose that when she married him she imagined she was about to become the wife of a celebrity. Famous and rich . . . Now after more than three years, they were still living from hand to mouth and had nowhere to turn. . . ."

"Did she hold it against him?"

"Not in front of other people, as far as I know."

"Did she have any lovers?"

Nora turned to Carus, as if curious to hear his answer.

"You are asking a question which . . ."

"Why not tell the truth?"

For the first time, she was no longer content with signals under the table, and was breaking her silence.

"My wife is referring to an incident of no importance. . . ."

Nora interrupted, bitingly:

"It depends on whom . . ."

"One night we'd all been drinking. . . ."

"Where was this?"

"At the Raphael. We set off from here. . . . Maki was with us. Dramin, too. Then a photographer, Huguet, who works for an advertising firm. I think Bob came, too. . . .

"At the hotel I had some champagne and some whiskey sent up. Later I went into the bathroom and I had to pass through our room, where only the bedside lights were on.

"I found Sophie stretched out on one of the twin beds. Thinking she was ill, I bent over her . . ."

Nora's smile was growing more and more sarcastic.

"She was crying. . . . I had the greatest difficulty in getting a few words out of her. She eventually admitted to me that she was in despair, and wanted to kill herself."

"And how did I find the two of you?"

"I took her, automatically, into my arms, it's true, as I would to console a child. . . ."

"I asked you if she had any lovers. I wasn't thinking particularly of you."

"She posed in the nude for Maki, but I'm sure Maki wouldn't touch the wife of a friend. . . ."

"Was Ricain jealous?"

"You're asking too much of me, Monsieur Maigret. Your good health! . . . It all depends on what you mean by jealousy. . . . He wouldn't have liked to lose his hold over her, and see another man become more important to her. In that sense he was jealous of his friends as well. If, for example, I invited Dramin to come and have coffee at our table without asking him as well, he would sulk for the rest of the week."

"I think I understand."

"Have you had any dessert?"

"I hardly ever touch it."

"Nora doesn't either. Bob! . . . What do you recommend for dessert?"

"A pancake, *flambée*, with maraschino?"

Comically, Carus considered the rounded corners of his stomach.

"What's the difference? Pancakes it is. Two or three. . . . Armagnac rather than maraschino . . ."

All this time, Lapointe had been growing more and more bored in his corner, with his back to the room. Maki was picking his teeth with a match, doubtless asking himself whether his turn would come shortly to face the Chief Inspector across the table.

The doctors' table was the merriest, and from time to time one of the women burst into a piercing laugh which made Nora wince.

Rose abandoned her ovens for a while to make a tour of the tables, wiping her hand on her apron before offering it. Like the doctors, she too was in good spirits, which Sophie's death had done nothing to dampen.

"Well, Walter, you old rascal . . . How come you haven't been seen since Wednesday?"

"I had to fly to Frankfurt, to see a business associate, and from there I went on to London."

"Did you go with him, too, dear?"

"Not this trip. I had to go for a fitting. . . ."

"Aren't you afraid to let him travel by himself?"

She moved away with a laugh and stopped by another table, then another. Bob was cooking the pancakes on a grill.

"I gather that Ricain was looking for you during the night?"

"Why would he be looking for me?"

"It was the Inspector who told me just now. He needed two thousand francs urgently. On Wednesday he came around here and asked for you."

"I took the five o'clock plane. . . ."

"He came back twice. He wanted me to lend him the money, but it was too big a loan for me. Then he went on to the club."

"Why did he want two thousand francs?"

"The landlord was threatening to turn him out."

Carus turned to the Chief Inspector.

"Is that true?"

"That's what he told me."

"Have you arrested him?"

"No. Why?"

"I don't know. A stupid question, now I come to think of it. . . ."

"Do you think he could have killed Sophie?"

The feet, still those feet! It was possible literally to follow the conversation under the table, while all the time Nora's face remained frozen.

"I can't see him killing anybody. What weapon was used? The papers didn't say. The radio didn't mention it either. . . ."

"An automatic."

"But surely Francis never had a gun."

"Indeed he had!" the flat, precise voice of Nora cut in. "You saw it. That night in his place, and you were scared. He had had a lot to drink. He had just described a holdup scene to us. . . .

"He put one of Sophie's stockings over his head and he began threatening us with a gun, telling us to line up against the wall, with our hands in the air. Everyone obeyed, for fun.

"You were the only one who was frightened, and asked if the gun was loaded."

"You're quite right. It all comes back to me. . . . I hadn't thought about it again. I'd had a lot to drink, myself. . . ."

"In the end he put the gun back in the chest of drawers."

"Who was there?" asked Maigret.

"The whole gang. Maki, Dramin, Pochon . . . Dramin was with a girl I had never seen before and about whom I can remember nothing. She was ill and spent an hour in the bathroom."

"Jacques was there too."

"Yes, with his wife, who was already pregnant. . . ."

"Is anybody aware that last year Sophie was almost certainly pregnant as well?"

Why did Nora turn sharply to Carus? The latter looked at her in surprise.

"Did you know?"

"No. If she had a child . . . "

"She didn't have it," the Chief Inspector put in. "She had it aborted between the third and fourth months."

"Then it all went unnoticed."

Maki was coughing, in his corner, as if to call Maigret to order. It was quite a while since he had finished eating and he was becoming impatient.

"We've told you all we know, Inspector. If you need me, come around and see me in my office."

Did he really wink as he took a visiting card from his wallet and handed it to him?

Maigret had the impression that Carus had lots more to say, but that the presence of Nora was holding him back.

Settled in his corner once again, Maigret filled his pipe while Lapointe remarked, with a slight smile:

"He's still hesitating, but he'll be on his feet in a second."

He was referring to Maki. Unable to look directly into the room, to which his back was turned, the detective had spent his time observing the sculptor, the only person in his field of vision.

"At first, when you were sitting at Carus's table, he was

frowning, then he shrugged. He had a carafe of red wine in front of him. Less than five minutes later he had emptied it and signaled to the waiter to bring him another one.

"He didn't miss one of your gestures, or your movements. It was as if he was trying to read everyone's lips. . . .

"Soon he became impatient. At one moment he called the boss over and talked to him in a low voice. The two of them looked in your direction.

"Then he half rose to his feet, after a glance at his watch. I thought he was going to leave, but he ordered an armagnac which was brought to him in a big glass. He's coming over!"

Lapointe was not mistaken. Doubtless annoyed not to see Maigret make a move, Maki had decided to approach him instead. For a moment he stood, towering, between the two men.

"Excuse me," he murmured, putting his hand to his head in a sort of salute. "I wanted to let you know I was just leaving. . . ."

Maigret lit his pipe with a series of little puffs.

"Have a seat, Monsieur Maki. Is that your real name?"

Sitting down heavily, the man grumbled:

"Of course not. It's Lecoeur. . . . Not a name for a sculptor. . . . No one would have taken me seriously."

"Did you know I wanted a word with you?"

"Well, I'm a friend of Francis's too. . . ."

"How did you hear the news?"

"When I got here. I hadn't read the evening paper, and I never listen to the radio."

"Was it a shock?"

"I'm sorry for Francis. . . ."

"Not for Sophie?"

He was not drunk but his cheeks were flushed, his eyes shining, his gestures exaggerated.

"Sophie was a bitch."

He looked at them in turn as if defying them to deny it.

"What did he—Monsieur Carus—tell you?"

He pronounced the *Monsieur* ironically, as *Mossieu*, clowning it.

"Naturally, he knows nothing. What about you?"

"What do you expect me to know?"

"When did you last see Francis Ricain and his wife?"

"Him, Wednesday. . . ."

"Without her?"

"He was alone."

"What time?"

"Around half past six. He spoke to me before going off to find Bob. . . . I had finished my dinner and was just having my armagnac. . . ."

"What did he say to you?"

"He asked me whether I knew where Carus was. I must explain that I, too, work for that gentleman over there. Well, more or less. . . . He needed a clay model for some lousy film, a horror picture, and I knocked something together for him. . . ."

"Did he pay you?"

"Half the agreed-on price. . . . I was waiting for the other half."

"Did Francis tell you why he wanted to see Carus?"

"You know very well. He needed a couple of thousand francs. . . . I hadn't got it. I offered him a drink and he went off. . . ."

"And you haven't seen him since?"

"Neither him nor her. What did that Nora tell you?"

"Not much. . . . She doesn't seem to have a very soft spot for Sophie."

"She never had a soft spot for anybody. . . . Perhaps that's because she's so flat-chested. I beg your pardon. That wasn't very witty. I can't stand the sight of her. Nor him, either, for all his smiles and his handshakes. . . . At first sight they make a very odd couple, he all honey, and she all vinegar, but underneath they're both the same.

"When somebody can be of use to them, they squeeze him dry, then they chuck him away like an old orange peel. . . ."

"Which is what happened to you?"

"What did they tell you about Francis? You haven't answered me."

"Carus seems to think highly of him."

"And she?"

"She doesn't like him."

"Did they mention Sophie?"

"They told me about what happened in the bedroom one night when everybody had been drinking in the Raphael."

"I was there."

"It seems that nothing happened between Carus and Sophie. . . ."

"My eye!"

"Did you see them?"

"I went into the room twice, to go to the lavatory, and they didn't even notice. She tried once with me, too. She wanted me to model her in the nude—me, an abstract. . . . I ended up by giving in to be rid of her."

"Were you her lover?"

"I had to sleep with her, out of courtesy. She would have held it against me if I hadn't done it. I didn't feel very pleased with myself, because of Francis. . . . He didn't deserve to be married to a tramp."

"Did she talk about suicide to you as well?"

"Suicide? She? In the first place, when a woman talks about it, you can be sure she will never do it. She play-acted. With everybody. . . . With a different role for each person."

"Did Francis know?"

Maigret was starting to call him Francis, as well, as if he were gradually becoming intimately acquainted with Ricain.

"If you want my opinion, he suspected it. He shut his eyes to it, but it infuriated him. Did he really love her? . . . There are times when I wonder. . . . He pretended to. He had taken her on and he didn't want to let her go. She must have convinced him that she would kill herself if he left her. . . ."

"Do you think he's talented?"

"More than talented. Of all of us, he's the only one who will do something really important. I'm not bad in my field, but I know my limitations . . . He—well, the day he really gets down to it . . ."

"Thank you, Monsieur Maki."

"Just plain Maki. It's a name that doesn't go with Monsieur. . . ."

"Good night, Maki."

"Good night, Inspector. And this, I presume, is one of your detectives? . . . Good night to you, too."

He went off, with a heavy tread, after a wave to Bob.

Maigret mopped his brow.

"There's only one left: Dramin, with his nose in his script, but I've had enough for tonight."

He looked around for the waiter, asked for the bill. It was Mandille who came running over:

"Allow me to consider both of you as my guests. . . ."

"Impossible," said Maigret with a sigh.

"Will you at least accept a glass of old armagnac?"

They had to go through with it.

"Have you got the information you wanted?"

"I've begun to find my way around the group."

"They aren't all here. And the atmosphere changes from day to day. Some evenings it's very gay, even wild. . . . Haven't you spoken to Gérard?"

He was referring to Dramin, who was heading for the door, script in hand.

"Hey! Gérard . . . Let me introduce Chief Inspector Maigret and one of his detectives. . . . Will you have a drink with us?"

Very short-sighted, he wore thick glasses and held his head bent forward.

"How do you do? Please excuse me. . . . I have some work to finish. By the way, has Francis been arrested?"

"No. Why?"

"I don't know. Excuse me. . . ."

He unhooked his hat from the hat peg, opened the door, and set off along the sidewalk.

"You mustn't pay any attention to him. He's always like that. I think it's a pose, a way of making himself seem important . . . He does his absent-minded act, the loner . . . Perhaps he resents it that you didn't go and seek him out. I bet he hasn't read a line all evening. . . ."

"Your good health," murmured Maigret. "For myself, I'll be glad to get to bed. . . ."

Even so, he went by Rue Saint-Charles with Lapointe, and rapped on the studio door. Lourtie opened it. He had taken off his jacket and his hair was disheveled from sleeping in the armchair. The room was lit only by a night light, and the smell of the disinfectant had still not gone.

"Has nobody called?"

"Two reporters. I didn't tell them anything, except to apply to the Quai. . . ."

"No telephone calls?"

"There were a couple."

"Who?"

"I don't know. I heard the phone ring, I picked it up and said 'Hello'. . . . I heard breathing at the other end, but the caller said nothing and soon hung up. . . ."

"Both times?"

"Both times."

"About what time was it?"

"The first time around ten past eight, the second a few moments ago. . . ."

A few minutes later, Maigret was dozing in the small black car taking him home.

"I'm exhausted," he confessed to his wife as he started to undress.

"I hope you had a proper dinner."

"Too much so. . . . I must take you to that restaurant. It's kept by an old comic-opera singer who has turned her hand to cooking. She makes a *chaudrée* such as . . ."

"What time tomorrow?"

"Seven o'clock."

"That early?"

That early; in fact, it was seven o'clock immediately, with no transition. Maigret did not even have the sensation of having been asleep before he could smell coffee and his wife was touching him on the shoulder on her way over to draw back the curtains.

The sun was clear and mild. It was a delight to open the window once you were out of bed and to hear the sparrows chattering.

"I suppose I shouldn't expect you at lunchtime?"

"I probably won't have time to come back to eat. It's a strange case. Strange people. . . . I'm in the movie world, and, as in the movies, everything started with a gag, with the theft of my wallet. . . ."

"Do you think he was the killer?"

Madame Maigret, too, who knew the case only from the newspapers and the radio, was annoyed with herself for having asked the question.

"I'm sorry."

"In any case, it would be hard for me to give you an answer."

"Aren't you going to wear your light coat?"

"No. The weather is the same as yesterday's, and yesterday I wasn't cold. Not even on my way home last night. . . ."

He didn't wait for the bus but hailed a taxi and had himself dropped on the Ile Saint-Louis. Opposite the Stork there was a *bistrot* surrounded by piles of wood and sacks of coal. Torrence, his face drawn with fatigue, was drinking coffee when the Chief Inspector joined him.

"How did the night go?"

"Like all night watches. Nothing happened, except that I know just when everyone turns out his lights. . . . Someone must be ill, on the fourth floor, to the right, because there was light in the window until six o'clock in the morning.

"Your friend Ricain didn't go out. . . . Some of the guests came back. . . . A taxi came for a couple of travelers. . . . A dog attached itself to me and followed me about most of the night. . . . That's about it."

"You can go home and sleep."

"What about my report?"

"You can do it tomorrow."

He went into the hotel, where he had known the proprietor for thirty years. It was a modest establishment which seldom took in anybody but regulars, almost all of them from eastern France, since the owner was from Alsace.

"Is my guest awake?"

"He rang just ten minutes ago to ask for a cup of coffee to be sent up and some croissants. . . . They've just been taken in to him."

"What did he eat last night?"

"Nothing. He must have gone to sleep right away, because when we knocked on his door at about seven o'clock there was no answer. What is he—an important witness? A suspect?"

There was no elevator. Maigret, after climbing the four flights, reached the landing breathing hard, and paused for a moment before knocking at number 43.

"Who is it?"

"Maigret."

"Come in."

Pushing aside the tray on the blanket, Francis emerged from the bed, his thin chest bare, his face covered with a bluish beard, his eyes feverish. He still had a croissant in one hand.

"Excuse my not getting up, but I haven't any pajamas. . . ."

"Did you sleep well?"

"Like a log. I slept so soundly that my head is still heavy. What's the time?"

"A quarter past eight."

The room, small and ill furnished, overlooked the courtyard and the roofs. Voices from the neighboring houses, cries of children from a school playground, came in through the half-open window.

"Have you found out anything?"

"I had dinner at the Old Wine Press."

Ricain was watching him closely, already on the defensive, and one could sense that he felt the whole world thought he was a liar.

"Were they there?"

"The Caruses were. . . ."

"What did he have to say?"

"He swears you're some kind of genius."

"I presume Nora took the trouble to point out that I'm actually an imbecile?"

"More or less. . . . She certainly likes you less than he does."

"And she liked Sophie even less!"

"Maki was there too."

"Drunk?"

"Only toward the end; then he became a little unsteady."

"He's all right."

"He's sure you will be somebody one day, too."

"Which means that I am nobody. . . ."

He did not finish his croissant. Maigret's arrival seemed to have killed his appetite.

"What do they think happened? That I killed Sophie?"

"To tell the truth, nobody thinks you're guilty. However, some of them imagine that the police think differently, and everyone asked me whether I had arrested you."

"What did you say?"

"The truth."

"That is . . ."

"That you're free."

"Do you really think that's the truth? What am I doing here? You may as well admit it, you had a man on duty all night outside the hotel."

"Did you see him?"

"No, but I know how it goes. . . . And now what are you planning to do with me?"

Maigret was asking himself exactly the same question. He did not want to let Ricain wander freely about Paris, and on the other hand he did not have sufficient grounds to arrest him.

"First of all I am going to ask you to come with me to the Quai des Orfèvres."

"Again?"

"I may have several questions to put to you. Between now and then the frogmen of the River Police may have found your gun."

"What difference does it make whether they find it or not?"

"You have a razor and some soap. There is a shower at the end of the corridor. I will be waiting for you downstairs, or outside. . . ."

A new day was beginning, as clear, as balmy as the day before and the day before that, but it was too early yet to know what it would bring.

François Ricain made the Chief Inspector very curious, and the opinions he had gathered the day before did nothing to make him less fascinating.

By any standards, he was a youth out of the ordinary, and Carus had been impressed by his possibilities. But then didn't Carus become carried away every time he was confronted with an artist, only to let him drop a few months or a few weeks later?

Maigret resolved to go to see him in his office, to which the producer had given him an enigmatic invitation. He had something to say to him, something he did not want to talk about in front of Nora. She had sensed it, and the Chief Inspector wondered whether Carus would be at Rue de Bassano that morning or whether his mistress would prevent him from going.

So far, he had only touched the periphery of a circle of which there are thousands, tens of thousands, in Paris, composed of friends, relatives, colleagues, lovers and mistresses, regular customers at a café or restaurant, little groups which form, cling together for a while, and disperse to form into other more or less homogeneous little groups.

What was the name of the photographer who had been married twice, had had children by both wives, and had just given another to a new mistress?

He was still confusing the names and places corresponding to each of them. The fact was, Sophie's murder had been committed by someone intimately acquainted with the household—or with the young woman herself. Otherwise, she would not have opened the door.

Unless someone else had a key?

He was pacing to and fro as Torrence had done all night, but he had the good fortune to be walking in the sun. The street was teeming with housewives who turned around to look at this figure who was walking up and down, hands behind his back, like a schoolmaster supervising a school break.

Yes, he had plenty of questions to put to Francis. And no doubt he was about to be faced once again by a moody creature, in turns bridling and calming down, suspicious, impatient, suddenly giving a roar. . . .

"I'm ready."

Maigret pointed to the *bistrot* with the sacks of coal.

"Do you want a drink?"

"No, thank you."

A shame, since Maigret would have been very pleased to start this spring day with a glass of white wine.

5

IT WAS A bad stretch to get through. In nearly all of his cases, Maigret came to this period of floating, during which, as his colleagues used to whisper, he appeared to be brooding.

In the first stage—that is to say when he suddenly found himself face to face with a new world, with people he knew nothing about—it was as if he were breathing in the life around him, mechanically, and filling himself with it like a sponge.

He had done this the day before at the Old Wine Press, his memory registering, as it were subconsciously, the smallest details of the atmosphere, the gestures, the facial quirks of each person.

If he had not felt himself flagging, he would have gone on afterwards to the Zero Club, which some members of the circle frequented.

At the moment he had absorbed a quantity of impressions, a whole jumble of images, of phrases, of words of varying importance, of startled looks, but he did not yet know what to do with them all.

His close acquaintances knew that it was best not to ask him questions nor to question him by looks, as he would quickly become irritable.

As he expected, a note, on his desk, asked him to call Camus, the Magistrate.

"Hello! . . . This is Maigret."

He had seldom worked with this magistrate, whom he classed

neither among the outright meddlers nor among those who prudently leave the police time to get on with their work.

"I asked you to phone me because I had a call from the Public Prosecutor's office. . . . He is impatient to know where the inquiry has got to. . . ."

The Chief Inspector almost growled:

"Nowhere."

Which was true. A crime does not pose a mathematical problem. It involves human beings, unknown the day before, who were just passers-by among the rest. And now, all of a sudden, each one of their gestures, their words, takes on weight, and their entire life is gone over with a fine-tooth comb.

"The inquiry is going ahead," he said instead. "It's likely that we'll have the murder weapon in our hands within an hour or two. The frogmen are scouring the bottom of the Seine for it."

"What have you done with the husband?"

"He's here, in the icebox."

He corrected himself, as that was an expression which could mean something only to the detectives in his unit. When they did not know what to do with a witness, but still wanted to keep him on a string, or when they had a suspect who was not being co-operative, the put him in the "glacière."

They would tell them, as they showed them into the long glass-partitioned waiting room which ran along one side of the corridor:

"Just wait in here a moment, please."

It was always filled with people who were waiting: nervous women, some weeping and dabbing their eyes with their handkerchiefs, would-be tough customers trying to put on a bold front, some honest citizens who waited patiently, staring at the pale green walls, wondering whether their existence had been forgotten.

An hour or two in the glacière was often enough to make people talkative. Witnesses who were determined to say nothing became more amenable.

Sometimes they were "forgotten" for more than half a day, and they would keep watching the door, half rising to their feet every time the attendant came over, hoping it was their turn at last.

They could see the inspectors going off at noon, and would take their courage in both hands to go and ask Joseph:

"Are you sure the Chief Inspector knows that I'm here?"

"He's still in conference."

For want of a better solution, Maigret had put Ricain in the *glacière*.

He translated, for the Magistrate:

"He's in the waiting room. I'll be interrogating him again, as soon as I have more information."

"What is your impression? Guilty?"

Another question which the Magistrate would not have asked if he had worked longer with Maigret.

"I have no impressions."

It was true. He was waiting as long as possible before forming an opinion. And he still had not started "forming." He was keeping his mind free until he had some substantive evidence or until his prisoner broke down.

"Do you think it will be a long business?"

"I hope not."

"Have you discarded the possibility of a simple sordid crime?"

As though all crimes weren't sordid! They didn't speak the same language, they didn't have the same concept of a human being at the Law Courts as they did at Police Headquarters.

It was difficult to believe that an unknown man, looking for money, would have presented himself at Rue Saint-Charles after ten-o'clock at night, and that Sophie Ricain, already in her nightgown, would have let him into the studio without being suspicious.

Either her killer had a key, or else it was somebody she knew and trusted. Especially if the murderer had had to open the drawer in the chest in her presence and take out the gun.

"Kindly keep me informed. Don't leave me too long without news. The Prosecutor's office is getting impatient."

All right! The Prosecutor's office is always impatient. Gentlemen who live comfortably in their offices and who see crime only in terms of legal texts and statistics. A telephone call from the Ministry makes them tremble in their shoes.

"Why has nobody been arrested yet?"

The Prosecutor himself was under pressure from the newspapers. A good crime is good business for them, particularly if it presents a spectacular new angle every day. If the reader is kept in ignorance too long, he forgets about the case. And some nice front-page headlines are gone to waste.

"Certainly, Judge. . . . Yes, Judge. . . . I'll be calling you, Judge. . . ."

He winked at Janvier.

"Go and take an occasional look in the waiting room to see how he's reacting. He's the kind that'll either have a nervous breakdown or come and beat on my door."

In spite of it all he went through his mail and attended the morning conference, where he saw his colleagues and where they discussed unemotionally several of the current cases.

"Anything new, Maigret?"

"Nothing new, Director."

Here, they did not insist. You were among professionals.

When the Chief Inspector returned to his office, just before ten o'clock, the River Police were asking for him.

"Did you find the weapon?"

"Fortunately, the current has not been strong these days and the Seine was dragged at this point last autumn. My men found the weapon almost immediately, at about ten yards from the left bank, a 6.35 Belgian-made automatic. There were still five bullets left."

"Send it around to Gastinne-Renette, will you?"

And, to Janvier:

"Take care of it, will you—he's got the bullet already."

"Right, Chief."

Maigret was on the point of calling up Rue de Bassano, decided not to announce himself, and set off for the main staircase, taking care not to look toward the waiting room.

His departure could not have escaped the notice of Ricain, who must have wondered where he was going. He ran into Lapointe on his way out and instead of taking a taxi, as he had intended, he had himself driven to the building where Carus had his offices.

He paused to read the copper nameplates in the entrance arch, noting that there was a movie company on almost every floor. The company he was concerned with was called Carrossoc, and its reception rooms were on the first floor.

"Shall I come with you?"

"I'd rather you did."

Not only was it his way of doing things, but it was recommended in the manual of instructions for officers of the Police Department.

They entered a somewhat dark hall, with a single window overlooking the courtyard, where a chauffeur could be seen polishing a Rolls-Royce. A red-headed secretary was at the switchboard.

"Monsieur Carus, please."

"I don't know if he's in."

As if he did not have to pass her to reach the other offices!

"Whom shall I announce? Do you have an appointment?"

"Chief Inspector Maigret."

She got up, endeavoring to lead them to the anteroom, to put them, in their turn, in the *glacière*.

"Thank you. We'll wait here. . . ."

She was obviously not pleased. Instead of calling her boss, she disappeared through a padded door and was gone for three or four minutes.

She was not the first person to come back. Instead, it was Carus himself, in light gray worsted, freshly shaved and exuding a smell of lavender.

Evidently he had just come from his barber, and no doubt he had had a face massage. He was just the type to take his ease every morning for a good half hour in the reclining chair.

"How are you, my friend?"

He held out a cordial hand to the good friend he had not even known at six o'clock the previous evening.

"Come right in, please. You too, young man. . . . I presume this is one of your colleagues?"

"Inspector Lapointe."

"You may leave us, Mademoiselle. . . . I'm not in to anybody and I won't take any calls, except from New York."

He explained, with a smile:

"I hate to be interrupted by the telephone. . . ."

There were nonetheless three of them on his desk. The room was enormous, the walls decorated with beige leather to match the armchairs, the thick pile carpet a very soft chestnut color.

As for the immense Brazilian rosewood desk, it was piled high with enough files to keep a dozen secretaries busy.

"Sit down, please. What may I offer you?"

He went over to a low piece of furniture which proved to be a sizable bar.

"It's a little early for an apéritif, perhaps, but I happened to notice that you are a connoisseur of beer . . . So am I. I have some excellent beer, which I have sent directly from Munich . . ."

He was being even more expansive than the day before, perhaps because he did not have to bother about Nora's reactions.

"Yesterday, you caught me off base. . . . I was not expecting to meet you. I had had two or three whiskies before I got to the restaurant, and what with the champagne . . . I wasn't drunk. I never am. Even so, I have only a rather dim recollection this morning of certain details of our conversation. My wife reproached me for talking too much and too enthusiastically. . . . Your good health! I hope that's not the impression I gave you?"

"You seem to consider François Ricain somebody worthwhile, with every chance of becoming one of our leading movie directors. . . ."

"I must have said that, yes. . . . It's in my nature to be open to young people, and I'm easily carried away. . . ."

"You are no longer of the same opinion?"

"Oh, of course, of course! But with certain qualifications. I find a tendency, in this young man, toward disorder, toward anarchy. At one moment he will show too much self-confidence, and at the next he has none at all. . . ."

"If I remember your words correctly, in your opinion they were a very devoted couple."

Carus had settled down in one of the armchairs with his legs crossed, glass in one hand, cigar in the other.

"Did I say that?"

Suddenly changing his mind, he sprang to his feet, put the glass down on a console table, took several puffs at his cigar, and started pacing the carpet.

"Listen, Inspector, I was hoping you would come around this morning. . . ."

"So I gathered."

"Nora is an exceptional woman. Although she never so much as sets foot in my offices, I could describe her as the best business associate I have. . . ."

"You mentioned her gifts as a . . . medium."

He waved a hand as if to erase words written on an invisible blackboard.

"That's what I say in her presence, because it pleases her. . . . The truth is that she's got solid common sense and is seldom wrong in her appraisal of people. Personally, I get carried away. . . . I trust people too easily."

"She's a sort of safety catch?"

"Something like it . . . I've made up my mind quite definitely to marry her, when my divorce has gone through. It's already as if . . ."

He was obviously getting into difficulties, searching for words, while his eyes remained fixed on the ash of his cigar.

"Well . . . How can I put it? Although Nora's a superior woman, she still can't help being jealous. That's why yesterday, in her presence, I was obliged to lie to you. . . ."

"The bedroom incident?"

"Precisely. It didn't happen as I recounted it, of course. It is true that Sophie ran away to the bedroom to cry after Nora had said a lot of mean things to her. I don't remember exactly what they were, as we had all been drinking. In short, I went to comfort her. . . ."

"Was she your mistress?"

"If you insist on the word. . . . She flung herself into my arms, one thing led to another, and we were careless, very careless. . . ."

"And your wife caught you at it?"

"A Chief Inspector would not have hesitated to corroborate a charge of adultery. . . ."

He smiled, with a touch of satisfaction.

"Tell me, Monsieur Carus. I presume pretty girls must pass through your offices every day. Most of them are ready to do anything to land a part."

"That's correct."

"I believe I am right in thinking that you have been known to take advantage of this circumstance."

"I make no secret of it. . . ."

"Even from Nora?"

"Let me explain. . . . If I take advantage, as you put it, of a pretty girl now and then, Nora doesn't let it upset her too much on condition that there is no future. . . . It's part of the job. All men do the same, unless they don't have the opportunity. Even you yourself, Chief Inspector . . ."

Maigret looked at him stonily, unsmiling.

"Excuse me, if I have shocked you. . . . Where was I? . . . I am not unaware that you have questioned some of my friends and that you will continue to do so. I prefer to be quite straight with you. You have heard the way Nora talks about Sophie. . . .

"I would rather you didn't form an impression of the girl from what she said. . . .

"She wasn't ambitious, quite the contrary, and she wasn't the girl to sleep with just anybody. . . .

"She had been drawn to Ricain on an impulse when she was still a kid, and it was bound to happen, he has a kind of magnetism. . . . Women are impressed by men who are tortured, ambitious, bitter, violent. . . ."

"Is that your picture of him?"

"What about you?"

"I don't know yet."

"In short, he married her. She put her trust in him. . . . She followed him about like a well-trained little dog, keeping her mouth shut when he didn't want her to talk, taking up as little space as possible so as not to get in his way, and accepting the precarious life he led."

"Was she unhappy?"

"She suffered, but she took care to hide it. . . . Well, he needed her, her passive presence, but there were moments when he became irritated with her, complaining that she was a dead weight, an obstacle to his career, accusing her of being a dumb animal. . . ."

"Did she tell you this?"

"I had already guessed it, from remarks made in my presence. . . ."

"Did you become her confidant?"

"If you want to put it that way. . . . In spite of myself, I assure you. She felt herself lost in a world too harsh for her, and she had nobody to turn to. . . ."

"At what period did you become her lover?"

"Another word I dislike. . . . It was mostly pity, tenderness which I felt for her. My intention was to help her. . . ."

"To have a career in the movies?"

"I'm going to surprise you, but it was my idea and she resisted it. . . . She was not a striking beauty, one of those traffic-stoppers like Nora. . . .

"I have a pretty good instinct for the public's tastes. If I hadn't, I wouldn't be doing the job I do. With her somewhat ordinary face, and her small, rather fragile body, Sophie was exactly the picture of the young girl as most people imagine her to be.

"Parents would have seen their daughter in her, young people their cousin or their girl friend. . . . Do you see what I mean?"

"Did you have plans to launch her?"

"Let's say I was thinking about it. . . ."

"Did you tell her?"

"Not in so many words. I sounded her out discreetly. . . ."

"Where did your meetings take place?"

"That is an unpleasant question, but I am obliged to answer it, am I not?"

"Especially since I would find out for myself."

"Well, I've rented a furnished studio, quite chic, quite comfortable, in a new apartment house in Rue François-Premier. To be exact, it's the one on the corner of Avenue Georges V. I only have three hundred yards to walk from here. . . ."

"One second. This studio—was it intended exclusively for your rendezvous with Sophie, or was it for others as well?"

"In theory, it was for Sophie. . . . It was difficult for us to have any privacy here, and I couldn't go to her house either. . . ."

"You never went there when her husband was away?"

"Once or twice. . . ."

"Recently?"

"The last time was a fortnight ago. She hadn't telephoned me as she usually did. I didn't see her in Rue François-Premier either. I called her at home and she told me she wasn't feeling well. . . ."

"Was she ill?"

"Depressed. Francis was becoming more and more irritable. . . . Sometimes he was even violent. . . . She was at the end of her tether and wanted to go away, anywhere, work as a salesgirl in the first store she came across. . . ."

"Did you not advise her to do anything?"

"I gave her the address of one of my lawyers to consult about the possibility of a divorce. It would have been better for both of them. . . ."

"Had she made up her mind?"

"She was hesitating. She felt sorry for Francis. She felt it her duty to stay with him, until he achieved some success. . . ."

"Did she talk to him about it?"

"Certainly not. . . ."

"How can you be so sure?"

"Because he would have reacted violently. . . ."

"I would like to ask you a question, Monsieur Carus. Think carefully before answering, because I won't hide from you the fact that it is important. You knew that, about a year ago, Sophie was pregnant?"

He flushed scarlet all of a sudden, nervously stubbed out his cigar in the glass ashtray.

"Yes, I knew," he muttered, sitting down again. "But I can tell you right away, I can swear by all that's dear to me in this world, that the child was not mine. . . . I noticed that she was upset, preoccupied. I mentioned it to her. She admitted that she was expecting a child and that Francis would be furious. . . ."

"Why?"

"Because it would be another burden, another obstacle to his career. He was on the dole. With a child . . . In short, she was sure he would never forgive her, and she asked me for the address of a midwife or an obliging doctor. . . ."

"Did you help her?"

"I have to admit that I transgressed the law."

"It's a bit late now to pretend anything else."

"I did her that small service. . . ."

"Francis knew nothing about it?"

"No. He's too wrapped up in himself to notice what is going on around him, even when it concerns his wife. . . ."

He rose hesitantly and, no doubt to restore his composure, went to fetch some fresh bottles from the bar.

Everyone called him Monsicur Gaston, with a respectful familiarity, for he was a conscientious and worthy man, aware of the weighty responsibilities of the concierge of a great hotel. He had spotted Maigret before he had even entered the revolving doors, and had puckered his brows while he quickly passed in mental review the faces of the hotel guests who might have caused this visit from the police.

"Wait here for me a moment, Lapointe."

He had to wait, himself, for an old lady to check the time of arrival of an airplane from Buenos Aires before discreetly shaking Monsieur Gaston's hand.

"Don't worry. Nothing unpleasant."

"When I see you coming, I can't help wondering. . . ."

"If I am not mistaken, Monsieur Carus has a suite here, on the fourth floor?"

"That's right. With Madame Carus. . . ."

"Is she registered in that name?"

"Well, it's what we call her here. . . ."

The shadow of a smile sufficed to make Monsieur Gaston's meaning clear.

"Is she upstairs?"

He glanced at the key board.

"I don't know why I look. A habit . . . At this hour she'll certainly be having her breakfast. . . ."

"Monsieur Carus has been away this week, hasn't he?"

"Wednesday and Thursday. . . ."

"Did he go alone?"

"His chauffeur took him to Orly around five o'clock. . . . I think he had to take the Frankfurt plane."

"When did he come back?"

"Yesterday afternoon, from London."

"Although you aren't here at night yourself, perhaps you have a way of finding out if Madame Carus went out on Wednesday evening and at what time she came home?"

"That's easy. . . ."

He leafed through the pages of a big register bound in black.

"When they come home in the evening, the guests usually stop for a moment to tell my colleague on the night shift what time they want to be called and what they will have for breakfast.

"Madame Carus never fails. We don't note the time they come in, but it's possible to fix an approximate time by the order in which the names are listed on the page.

"Wait now. There are only a dozen names for Wednesday, before hers. . . . Miss Trever . . . An early bedder, an old lady who always comes home before ten o'clock. The Maxwells . . . At first glance, I would say she came back before midnight, say between ten o'clock and midnight. At any rate, before the theaters were out. I'll ask the night porter to confirm it. . . ."

"Thank you. Would you announce me?"

"Do you want to see her? Do you know her?"

"I had coffee last evening with her and her husband. Let's say it's a courtesy visit."

"Put me through to 403, please. . . . Hello? . . . Madame Carus? . . . This is the concierge. . . . Chief Inspector Maigret is asking if he may come up. . . . Yes. . . . Right. . . . I'll tell him. . . ."

And, to Maigret:

"She wants you to wait ten minutes."

Was it to finish that fearful and elaborate ritual of making herself up, or was it to telephone Rue de Bassano?

The Chief Inspector went back to Lapointe, and the two of them wandered in silence from showcase to showcase, admiring the stones exhibited by the leading Parisian jewelers, as well as the fur coats and the linens.

"Are you thirsty?"

"No, thank you."

They had the unpleasant sensation of attracting attention, and it was a relief when the ten minutes were up and they went into one of the elevators.

"Fourth floor."

Nora, who herself let them in, was wearing a pale green satin dressing gown that matched her eyes, and her hair seemed more bleached than the day before, almost white.

The sitting room was enormous, with light coming in from two bay windows, one of which opened onto a balcony.

"I wasn't expecting your visit, and you caught me as I was getting up. . . ."

"I hope we are not interrupting your breakfast?"

The tray was not in the room, but was probably next door.

"It's not my husband you want to see? . . . He left for the office quite some time ago. . . ."

"I was passing by, and I wanted to ask you a few questions. Of course, there's no obligation to answer. First of all, a question I am putting, as a matter of routine, to everybody who knew Sophie Ricain. Don't read anything into it. Where were you on Wednesday night?"

Without flinching, she sat down in a white armchair and asked:

"At what time?"

"Where did you have dinner?"

"Just a moment. Wednesday? . . . Yesterday, you were with us. . . . On Thursday I dined alone at Fouquet's, not in the first-floor dining room, which is where I go when I'm with Carus, but on the ground floor, at a small table. . . . Wednesday . . . On Wednesday, I didn't have dinner, that's all there is to it. . . .

"I should tell you that except for a light breakfast I usually only have one other meal a day. If I have lunch, I don't dine. . . . So, if I dine it's because I didn't have lunch. On Wednesday we lunched at the Berkeley with friends. . . .

"In the afternoon I had a fitting, just around the corner from here. . . . Then I had a drink at Jean's, in Rue Marboeuf. . . . I must have come home around nine o'clock."

"Did you go straight up to your suite?"

"That's right. I read until one o'clock in the morning, as I can't get to sleep early. . . . Before that I watched television. . . ."

There was a set in a corner of the room.

"Don't ask me what program it was. All I know is that there were young singers, boys and girls. . . . Do you want me to call the floor waiter? . . . True, it's not the same. . . . But tonight you can question the night waiter. . . ."

"Did you order anything?"

"A champagne split. . . ."

"At what time?"

"I don't know. . . . Shortly before getting ready for bed. . . . Do you suspect me of going to Rue Saint-Charles and murdering that wretched Sophie?"

"I don't suspect anybody. I am only doing my duty, and in the process trying to be as unobtrusive as possible. Last evening you referred to Sophie Ricain in terms which implied a lack of warmth between the two of you."

"I made no effort to hide it. . . ."

"There was talk of an evening here, when you found her in your husband's arms. . . ."

"I oughtn't to have brought it up. . . . It was just to show you that she would throw herself at any man who came along, and that she wasn't the little white lamb or the timid little slave that certain people have doubtless described. . . ."

"Of whom are you thinking?"

"I don't know. . . . Men tend to let themselves be taken in by that sort of act. Most of the people we mix with probably take me for a cold, ambitious, calculating woman. Go on, admit it!"

"Nobody has spoken to me in such terms."

"I'm sure that's what they think. . . . Even a person like Bob, who ought to know better . . . Little Sophie, on the other hand, all sweet and submissive, is the misunderstood girl everybody is sorry for. . . . You can think what you like. . . . I'm telling you the truth."

"Was Carus her lover?"

"Who says so?"

"You told me yourself that you had surprised them . . ."

"I said she had thrown herself into his arms, that she was sniveling to get sympathy, but I never said Carus was her lover. . . ."

"All the others were, weren't they? Isn't that what I'm meant to understand?"

"Ask them. We'll see if they dare to deny it. . . . "

"And Ricain?"

"You put me in an awkward position. . . . It's not up to me to pass final judgment on people we mix with and who are not necessarily friends. Did I say Francis knew what was going on? It's possible. . . . I don't remember. . . . I get carried away."

"Carus was flattered by the boy, and insisted that he had a fantastic future before him. . . . Personally, I regard him as a little sponger posing as an artist. . . . You can take your pick."

Maigret rose, pulling his pipe from his pocket.

"That's all I wanted to ask you. Ah! Just one small question. Sophie had become pregnant, a year ago now."

"I know. . . ."

"Did she tell you about it?"

"She was two or three months pregnant, I forget which. Francis didn't want a child, because of his career. . . . So she asked me if I knew an address . . . She had heard about Switzerland, but was hesitating to make the journey. . . ."

"Were you able to help her?"

"I told her I knew no one. . . . I was not keen for Carus and myself to become involved in that sort of thing. . . ."

"How did it end?"

"Well, no doubt, from her point of view, since she made no further mention of it and she didn't have a child. . . ."

"Thank you."

"Have you been to Carus's office?"

Maigret answered the question with another:

"Hasn't he telephoned?"

He was making sure, in this way, that once she was by herself the young woman would ring Rue de Bassano.

"Thank you, Gaston," he said, as he passed the concierge.

Out on the sidewalk he took a deep breath.

"If it ends up with a general confrontation of witnesses, it should be quite an exciting event."

As though to wash out his mouth, he went and drank a glass of white wine in the first bar he passed. He had been wanting one all morning, ever since the events of Rue Saint-Louis-en-L'Ile, and Carus's beer had not removed the urge.

"To the Quai, Lapointe, young man. I'm curious to see what sort of state our Francis is in."

He was not in the *glaciére,* which contained only an old lady together with a very young man with a broken nose. In his office he found Janvier, who gestured toward Ricain, fuming in a chair.

"I had to let him in here, Chief. He was making such a racket in the corridor, demanding to see the Director, threatening to tell all the newspapers. . . ."

"I'm within my right . . . !" stormed the youth. "I've had enough of being treated like an imbecile or a criminal. . . . My wife has been killed and it's I who am being watched, as if I were trying to escape. I'm not left one moment's peace, and . . ."

"Do you want a lawyer?"

Francis looked him in the eyes, hesitantly, his pupils dilated with hatred.

"You . . . you . . ."

His anger was preventing him from finding words.

"You give yourself fatherly airs. You must love yourself for being so kind, so patient, so understanding. . . . I thought that way too. . . . Now I see that everything they say about you is just hot air."

He was becoming carried away, his words tumbling on top of one another, his speech getting faster and faster.

"How much do you pay them, the newspapermen, to flatter you? What a damn fool I was. When I saw your name in the wallet I thought I was saved, that at last I had found someone who would understand.

"I called you. . . . For without my telephone call you wouldn't have found me. With your money, I'd have been able. . . . When I think I didn't even take the price of a meal. . . .

"And what's the result? You shut me up in a crummy hotel bedroom. With a detective standing guard on the sidewalk. . . .

"Then you put me into your rat trap and every now and then your men come and take a peek at me through the glass. . . . I totted up at least twelve who gave themselves this little treat. . . .

"All this, because my wife was killed in my absence and the police are powerless to protect citizens. Because the next thing is, instead of looking for the real culprit, they have to seize on the obvious suspect, the husband who was unfortunate enough to take fright. . . ."

Maigret was puffing slowly at his pipe, facing Francis, in full spate now, standing in the middle of the room waving his clenched fists.

"Have you finished?"

He put the question in a calm voice, without any trace of impatience or irony.

"Do you still not want to call a lawyer?"

"I am quite capable of defending myself. And when the time comes and you realize your mistake and let me go, you'll have to . . ."

"You're free to go."

"What do you mean?"

His fury abated all of a sudden, and he stood there, his arms dangling, staring in disbelief at the Chief Inspector.

"You've been free all along, as you know perfectly well. If I provided you with a roof over your head last night it's because you had no money and you did not, or so I presume, want to sleep in the studio in Rue Saint-Charles."

Maigret had pulled his wallet from his pocket, the same wallet that Francis had stolen from him on the platform of the bus. He took out two ten-franc notes.

"Here is something to buy a snack and get you back to Rue de Grenelle. One of your friends will lend you a little money to tide you over. I should inform you that I have had a telegram sent to your wife's parents in Concarneau, and that her father arrives in Paris at six o'clock this evening. I don't know whether he will get in touch with you. I didn't speak to him on the telephone myself, but it seems he wants to take his daughter's body back to Brittany."

Ricain no longer spoke of leaving. He was trying to understand.

"Of course, you're the husband, and it's up to you to decide."

"What do you advise me to do?"

"Funerals are expensive. I don't suppose you will often have time to visit the cemetery. So if the family are very anxious . . ."

"I'll have to think about it. . . ."

Maigret had opened the door of his cupboard, where he always kept a bottle of brandy and some glasses, a precaution which had often proved useful.

He filled a single glass, and offered it to the young man.

"Drink that."

"What about you?"

"No thank you."

Francis drank the brandy down in one gulp.

"Why are you giving me liquor?"

"To steady you."

"I suppose I'll be followed?"

"Not even that. On condition you let me know where I can get in touch with you. Are you planning to return to Rue Saint-Charles?"

"Where else could I go?"

"One of my Inspectors is there at the moment. By the way, last evening the telephone rang twice in the studio. The Inspector picked up the receiver and both times nobody answered."

"It couldn't have been I, because . . ."

"I'm not asking if it was you. Somebody called the studio. Somebody who had not read the newspapers. What I am wondering is whether that man or that woman was expecting to hear your voice or your wife's."

"I have no idea. . . ."

"Hasn't it ever happened that you have picked up the receiver and only heard breathing?"

"What are you driving at?"

"Suppose they thought you were out, and wanted to talk to Sophie?"

"That again? What have they been telling you, all the people you were questioning last evening and this morning? What scraps of scandal are you trying to . . . to . . ."

"One question, Francis."

The latter started, surprised to hear himself addressed in this way.

"What did you do, about a year and a half ago, when you found out that Sophie was pregnant?"

"She's never been pregnant."

"Has the medical report arrived, Janvier?"

"Here it is, Chief. Delaplanque has just sent it through."

Maigret ran his eye over it.

"There! You can see for yourself that I'm not making false allegations, and that I am simply referring to medical facts."

Ricain was looking savagely at him once more.

"And what's all this about, for God's sake? Anyone would think you had sworn to drive me out of my mind. First you accuse me of killing my wife, then . . ."

"I have never accused you."

"It's just as if . . . You insinuate . . . Then, to calm me down . . ."

He seized the glass which had contained the brandy, and dashed it violently to the floor.

"I ought to get to know your tricks better! What a fine movie that would make! But the Ministry would take care to stop it. . . . So, Sophie was pregnant a year ago? And, of course, as we had no children, I presume we took ourselves to an abortionist. Is that right? So that's the new charge that's been dreamed up for me, because you couldn't make the other one stick!"

"I never pretended you were aware of what was happening. I asked if your wife mentioned it to you. In fact she went to someone else."

"Because it had to do with someone besides me, the husband?"

"She wanted to spare you the worry, perhaps a battle with your conscience. She imagined a child would be a handicap at this point in your career."

"And so?"

"She confided in one of your friends."

"But who, for God's sake?"

"Carus."

"What? You want me to believe that Carus . . ."

"He told me so this morning. Nora confirmed it half an hour later, with just one variation. According to her, Sophie was not alone when she spoke of being a mother. You were both there."

"She was lying. . . ."

"Quite possibly."

"Do you believe her?"

"For the time being, I believe nobody."

"Me included."

"You included, Francis. But even so, you're free to go."

Maigret lit his pipe, sat at his desk, and began thumbing through some papers.

6

Ricain had left hesitantly, awkwardly, suspicious like a bird that sees its cage open, and Janvier had shot an inquiring glance at his Chief. Was he really being let loose, without any kind of tail being put on him?

Pretending not to understand the mute question, Maigret went on thumbing through his papers, finally got up and went and stood at the window.

He was morose. Janvier had returned to the Inspectors' room and was exchanging views in an undertone with Lapointe when the Chief Inspector came in. Instinctively the two men separated, but it made no difference. Maigret seemed not to have seen them.

He was pacing back and forth between offices as if he did not know what to do with his heavy body, pausing by a typewriter, a telephone, or an empty chair, shuffling papers for no particular reason.

Finally he grumbled:

"Tell my wife I won't be home for dinner."

He didn't call her himself, which was significant. Nobody dared to speak to him, far less ask questions. In the Inspectors' room, everybody was in a state of suspense. He sensed it, and with a shrug he returned to his office and picked up his hat.

He said nothing, neither where he was going nor when he would be back, left no instructions, as if all of a sudden he had lost interest in the case.

On the big dusty staircase he emptied his pipe, tapping it against his heel, then crossed the courtyard and nodded vaguely in the direction of the porter, and set off toward Place Dauphine.

Perhaps it was not really where he wanted to go. His mind was elsewhere, in an area which was not familiar to him, Boulevard de Grenelle, Rue Saint-Charles, Avenue de La-Motte-Picquet.

He could see the dark outline of the elevated, which cut a diagonal in the sky, thought he could hear the muted rumble of carriages. . . . The padded, somewhat syrupy atmosphere of the Old Wine Press, the liveliness of Rose, who never stopped wiping her hands on her apron, the waxlike face of the former stunt man, with its ironical smile . . .

Maki, huge and gentle in his corner, his eye growing darker and more bleary as he drank . . . Gérard Dramin, with his ascetic face, ceaselessly correcting his script . . . Carus, who took so much trouble to be friendly with everyone, and Nora, artificial from dyed hair to fingertips . . .

One would have said his feet were carrying him, without his knowledge, by force of habit, to the Dauphine, and he greeted the proprietor, sniffed the restaurant's warm smell, and went over to his corner, where he had sat on the bench thousands of times before.

"There's *andouillette*, Inspector."

"With mashed potatoes?"

"And to start with?"

"Anything. A carafe of Sancerre."

His colleague from Records was eating in another corner with someone from the Ministry of the Interior whom Maigret knew only by sight. The other customers were nearly all regulars, lawyers who would get through their meals quickly and then go across the square to plead their cases, a magistrate, a Gaming Act Inspector.

The proprietor, too, realized that this was not the moment to start a conversation, and Maigret ate slowly, with concentration, as if it were an important act.

Half an hour later he was walking around the Law Courts, his hands behind his back, slowly, like a lonely man exercising his dog, then he was back once more on the great staircase, and finally pushing open his office door.

A note from Gastinne-Renette was waiting for him. It was not the final report. The gun found in the Seine was indeed the one which had fired the bullet in Rue Saint-Charles.

He shrugged his shoulders again, for he had known it all along. At moments he felt himself submerged under these secondary questions, these reports, these telephone calls, these routine activities.

Joseph, the ancient attendant, knocked on his door and as usual came in without waiting for an answer.

"There's a gentleman to see you. . . ."

Maigret put out a hand, glanced at the form:

"Show him in."

The man was in black, which emphasized his ruddy complexion and the shock of gray hair on his head.

"Sit down, Monsieur Le Gal. Let me offer my condolences. . . ."

The man had had time for weeping on the train, and it seemed that he had had a few drinks to give himself courage. His eyes were hazy, and his words came with difficulty.

"What have they done with her . . .? I didn't want to go to her place, in case I should meet that man, for I think I would strangle him with my bare hands. . . ."

How many times had Maigret witnessed this same reaction from families?

"In any case, Monsieur Le Gal, the body is no longer in Rue Saint-Charles. It's in the Police Pathological Department. . . ."

"Where's that?"

"Near Austerlitz bridge, on the river. I'll have you driven over, because you must make an official identification of your daughter."

"Did she suffer?"

He was clenching his fists, but it was not a convincing gesture. It was as though his impetus had evaporated on the way, together with his rage, so that he was merely repeating words he no longer believed in.

"I hope you have arrested him?"

"There is no proof against her husband."

"But, Inspector, from the day she first spoke to me about this man, I predicted it would all end badly. . . ."

"Did she take him to see you?"

"I never saw him. I only know him from a bad photograph. She didn't want to introduce him to us. . . . From the moment she met him the family no longer meant anything to her. . . .

"All she wanted was to get married as quickly as possible. She had even drawn up the letter of consent, which I had to sign. . . . Her mother wanted to stop me. In the end I gave in, so now I hold myself partly responsible for what happened. . . ."

Wasn't there always this side of things in every case, at once sordid and moving?

"Was she your only child?"

"Fortunately, we have a son of fifteen."

Actually, Sophie had vanished from their lives a long time before.

"Could I take the body back to Concarneau?"

"As far as we are concerned the formalities have been completed."

He had said "formalities."

"You mean they've . . . I mean, there was a . . ."

"A post-mortem, yes. As for transportation, I advise you to get in touch with an undertaker's who will see to the arrangements."

"And him?"

"I've spoken to him. He has no objection to her being buried in Concarneau."

"I hope he isn't thinking of coming? Because if he does, I won't be answerable for what happens. There are people in our part of the world who have less self-control than I have. . . ."

"I know. I'll see to it that he stays in Paris."

"It's he, isn't it?"

"I assure you I do not know."

"Who else would have killed her? She only saw through his eyes. He had literally hypnotized her. Since her marriage she hasn't written three times, and she didn't even take the trouble to send us a New Year card. . . .

"I found out her knew address through the newspapers. I

thought she was still in the little hotel in Montmartre where they lived after their marriage. A funny sort of wedding, with no relatives, no friends! . . . Do *you* think that's a promising start?"

Maigret heard him out, nodding sympathetically, then closed the door behind his visitor, whose breath reeked of alcohol.

And Ricain's father? Wouldn't he, too, be making an appearance? The Chief Inspector was expecting him. He had sent one detective to Orly, another to the Raphael to photograph the page in the registry which the concierge had shown him.

"There are two reporters, Chief Inspector. . . ."

"Turn them over to Janvier."

Janvier came in a moment later.

"What do I tell them?"

"Anything. That we're coming along with our inquiries."

"They thought they would find Ricain here, and they brought a photographer along with them."

"Let them look. Let them go and knock on the Rue Saint-Charles door if they like."

He was laboriously following a train of thought, or rather several trains of contradictory thoughts. Had he been right to let Francis go, in the overwrought state he was in?

He would not get far with the twenty francs the Chief Inspector had given him. He would be forced to start his begging rounds again, knocking on doors, calling on friends.

"Well, it's not my fault if . . ."

Anybody would have thought Maigret had an uneasy conscience, that he had something with which to reproach himself. He kept returning to the starting point of the affair, the very beginning: the platform of the bus.

He could see in his mind's eye the woman with the blank face whose shopping bag bumped against his legs. A chicken, some butter, eggs, leeks, some leafy celery. He had wondered why she was doing her shopping so far afield.

A young man was smoking a pipe that was too short and too heavy. His fair hair was as pale as Nora's dyed hair.

At the time, he still had not met Carus's mistress, who passed herself off, at the Raphael and elsewhere, as his wife.

For a moment he had lost his balance and somebody had neatly extracted his wallet from his pocket.

Somehow he would have liked to dissect that instant of time, which seemed to him to be the most important one of all. The unknown man leaving the moving bus, in Rue du Temple, and hurrying away, zigzagging among the housewives, toward the narrow streets of the Marais . . .

His face was clear in the Chief Inspector's memory. He had been certain he would recognize him, because the thief had turned around. . . .

Why had he turned around? And why, on discovering Maigret's identity from the contents of the wallet, had he put it in a brown envelope and sent it back?

At the time, the time of the theft, he thought he was being followed. He was convinced that he would be accused of his wife's murder and that they would come and shut him up. He had given a curious reason for not wanting to let himself be arrested. Claustrophobia . . .

It was the first time, in the thirty years of his career, that he had heard a suspect give this as a reason for flight. On reflection, however, Maigret was forced to concede that sometimes it was perhaps the case. He did not take the subway himself, except when there was no other means of transportation, because he felt suffocated in it.

And here in his office, what about this compulsive jumping to his feet every few seconds and standing by the window?

Sometimes people, especially people from the Prosecutor's office, criticized him for doing the Inspectors' work for them, for going and interrogating witnesses on the spot instead of summoning them, for returning to the scene of a crime without any concrete reason, even for taking over watches himself, in sunshine and rain alike.

He liked his office, but he could never stay there for two hours at a stretch without feeling an urge to escape. When a case was on he would have liked to be everywhere at the same time.

Bob Mandille must be having his siesta now, for the Old Wine Press shut late at night. Did Rose take a siesta too? What would she have told him if they had sat down together at a table in the deserted restaurant?

They all had different opinions about Ricain and Sophie. Some of them, like Carus, did not mind changing their opinions and contradicting themselves after a lapse of a few hours.

Who was Sophie? One of those teen-agers who throw themselves at every man they meet? An ambitious girl who had believed that Francis would launch her on a film star's career?

She used to meet the producer in a hideaway in Rue François-Premier. That is, if Carus was telling the truth.

They had talked about Ricain's jealousy, and how he virtually never left his wife. On the other hand, he did not hesitate to borrow money from her lover.

Did he know? Did he close his eyes?

"Show him in. . . ."

He had expected it. It was the father. Ricain's, this time, a large, powerful man, with a youthful look despite his iron-gray hair, which he wore in a crewcut.

"I hesitated to come. . . ."

"Sit down, Monsieur Ricain."

"Is he here?"

"No. He was this morning, but he's gone."

The man had strongly etched features, pale eyes, a thoughtful expression.

"I would have come earlier, but I was on duty as engineer on the Ventimiglia-Paris . . ."

"When did you last see Francis?"

Surprised, he echoed:

"Francis?"

"That's what most of his friends call him."

"At home we called him François. Wait now. . . . He came to see me just before Christmas. . . ."

"Had you remained on good terms?"

"I saw very little of him."

"And his wife?"

"He introduced her to me days before the marriage."

"How old was he when his mother died?"

"Fifteen. . . . He was a good boy, but he was already beginning to be difficult and he couldn't stand being corrected. . . .It was no use trying to stop him from doing what he wanted. . . . I wanted him to join the railway . . . Not necessarily as a worker. . . . He would have got a good desk job. . . ."

"Why did he go and see you before Christmas?"

"To ask for money, of course. . . . He never came for anything else. He had no real job. He scribbled a bit and said one day he'd be famous.

"I did my best. But I couldn't hold on to him. Sometimes I was away three days on end. . . . It wasn't much fun for him to come back to an empty place and get his own meals. What do you think yourself, Chief Inspector?"

"I don't know."

The man showed surprise. That a senior functionary of the police should have no definite opinion was beyond his understanding.

"Don't you think he's guilty?"

"So far there's nothing to prove it, any more than there's anything to prove the contrary."

"Do you think this woman has been good for him? She didn't even take the trouble to put on a dress when he introduced us; she came in slacks, with shoes that were more like clogs. . . . She hadn't even combed her hair. . . . It's true, one sees others like that in the streets. . . ."

There was a lengthy pause while Monsieur Ricain shot hesitant glances at the Chief Inspector. Finally he pulled a worn wallet from his pocket and took several hundred-franc notes from it.

"It will be best if I don't go and see him myself. If he wants to see me, he knows where I live. . . . I suppose he still has no money. He might need some to get himself a good lawyer. . . ."

A pause. A question.

"Have you any children, Chief Inspector?"

"Unfortunately, no."

"He mustn't feel abandoned. Whatever he's done, if he's done anything wrong, he isn't responsible. . . . Tell him that's what I think. Tell him he can come to the house any time he wants. I don't insist. . . . I understand. . . ."

Moved, Maigret looked at the bank notes that a broad calloused hand with square fingernails was pushing across the desk.

"Well . . ." sighed the father, as he rose, crumpling his hat in his hands. "If I understand you right, I can still hope he's innocent. Mind you, I'm sure of it. . . . The papers can say what they like, I cannot bring myself to believe that he's done such a thing. . . ."

The Chief Inspector accompanied him to the door, shook the hand that was offered hesitantly.

"Can I keep on hoping?"

"One must never despair."

Alone once again, he was on the point of telephoning Doctor Pardon. He would have liked to chat, to put various questions to him. Pardon was no psychiatrist, to be sure, nor was he a professional psychologist.

But in his career as a general practitioner he had seen all kinds, and often his advice had reinforced Maigret in his opinions.

At that time Pardon would be in his office, with a score of patients lined up in the waiting room. Their monthly dinner was not due until the following week.

It was curious: suddenly, for no precise reason, he had a painful sensation of loneliness.

He was no more than a cog in the complicated machinery of justice, and he had at his disposal specialists, inspectors, the telephone, the telegraph, all kinds of desirable services; above him there were the Public Prosecutor, the Magistrate, and, in the last resort, the judges and juries of the Court of Assizes.

Why, at that point, did he feel responsible? It seemed to him that the fate of a human being depended on him, he still did not know which one—the man or woman who had taken the gun from the drawer in the white painted chest and fired it at Sophie.

A detail had struck him, from the outset, that he had not yet managed to explain. It is rare in the course of a dispute, or in a moment of emotion, for a person to aim at the head.

The reflex action, even in self-defense, is to shoot at the chest, and only professionals shoot at the stomach, knowing that victims of stomach wounds rarely recover.

From the distance of about three feet, the murderer had aimed at the head. . . . To make it look like suicide?

He had left the weapon in the studio. At least if Ricain was to be believed. . . .

The couple came home, at about ten o'clock. He needed money. Francis left his wife behind in Rue Saint-Charles, which was unusual for him, while he set off in search of Carus or some other friend who might be able to lend him two thousand francs. . . .

Why wait until that night if the money had to be handed over next morning?

He went back to the Old Wine Press, half opened the door to see whether the producer had arrived. . . .

At that time Carus was already in Frankfurt, a fact they were just cross-checking at Orly. He hadn't mentioned his journey to Bob or any other member of the little group. . . .

Nora, on the other hand, was in Paris. . . . Not in her suite at the Raphael, as she had claimed that morning, since the concierge's register contradicted her story. . . .

Why had she lied? Did Carus know she was absent from the hotel? Hadn't he telephoned her, on arriving at Frankfurt?

The telephone rang.

"Hello. . . . Doctor Delaplanque. . . . Shall I put him through? . . ."

"Please do. . . . Hello!"

"Maigret? Sorry to disturb you, but there's something that's been bothering me since this morning. . . . I didn't mention it in my report because it's rather vague. In the course of the autopsy, I came across faint marks on the wrists of the corpse, as if someone had grasped them with some force. You couldn't call them bruises, properly speaking. . . ."

"I'm listening."

"That's all. . . . While I can't positively say there was a struggle, I wouldn't be surprised if there had been. I picture the aggressor seizing the victim by the wrists and pushing her. . . . She might have fallen against the couch, recovered, and it would have been just before she was upright again that the shot was fired. . . . That would explain why the bullet was taken from the wall three feet and ten inches from the door, whereas if the girl had been standing upright . . ."

"I follow. . . . Are the marks very light?"

"There's one more pronounced than the others. It could be a thumb, but I can't say anything for sure. That's why I can't record it officially. You may be able to make something of it. . . ."

"The way things are at the moment I'm ready to try to make something of anything that's available. Thank you, Doctor."

Janvier was standing, silent, in the doorway.

He had returned to the neighborhood by himself this time, with an obstinate expression, as if it were a matter to be settled between Boulevard de Grenelle and himself. He had walked along the banks of the Seine, and paused forty yards upstream from the Bir-Hakeim Bridge, at the spot where the gun had been thrown in and fished out of the river, then he set off in the direction of the big new apartment house in Boulevard de Grenelle.

Eventually he had gone in and rapped on the glass-fronted porter's lodge. The girl inside was young and alluring, and she had a small, well-lighted sitting room.

After showing her his badge he asked:

"Is it your job to collect the rents?"

"Yes, Inspector."

"You know François Ricain, I presume?"

"They live on the courtyard and they seldom pass by here. . . . I mean, seldom *used* to pass by here. . . . But she . . . I knew them, of course, but it wasn't pleasant always having to dun them for money. In January they asked for a month to pay, then on the fifteenth of February they asked another delay. The landlord had decided to put them out if they hadn't paid the two outstanding amounts by the fifteenth of March. . . ."

"And they didn't?"

"That was the day before yesterday, the fifteenth. . . ."

Wednesday. . . .

"Weren't you concerned when you didn't see them?"

"I didn't expect them to pay. In the morning he didn't come for his mail, and I said to myself he didn't want to face me. Anyway, they didn't get many letters. . . . Mostly prospectuses and magazines he subscribed to. In the afternoon I went and knocked on their door and nobody answered. . . .

"On Thursday I knocked again, and as there still was no answer I asked a tenant whether she had heard anything. It even occurred to me that they might have bolted. It would be easy for them because of the entrance on Rue Saint-Charles, which is always open. . . ."

"What's your opinion of Ricain?"

"I didn't pay much attention to him. . . . Every so often the tenants complained that they had been having a row or had guests in till all hours, but there are others in the building who don't exactly creep about on tiptoe either, especially the young ones. . . . He looked like some sort of artist. . . ."

"And she?"

"What do you expect me to say? They were skating on thin ice. It's not much of a life. . . . Are you sure she didn't kill herself?"

He was learning nothing new, nor really seeking to learn anything. He was prowling, taking in the streets of the neighborhood, the houses, the open windows, the interiors of the shops.

At seven o'clock he pushed open the door of the Old Wine Press and was almost disappointed not to see Fernande perched on her bar stool.

Bob Mandille was reading the evening paper at one of the tables, while the waiter was finishing setting the tables, arranging a glass vase with a rose on each of the checked tablecloths.

"Hello! The Chief Inspector. . . ."

Bob rose and came over to shake hands with Maigret.

"Well? What have you found out? The newspapers aren't too happy. . . . They say you're clamming up and keeping them at arm's length. . . ."

"Simply because we have nothing to tell them."

"Is it true you have released Francis?"

"He was never detained and he is free to come and go. Who's been talking to you about it?"

"Huguet, the photographer, who lives in the same building on the fourth floor. That's the one who's already had two wives, and has given a child to a third. He saw Francis in the courtyard as he was coming back home. I'm surprised he hasn't been in to see me. . . . Tell me, has he got any money?"

"I gave him twenty francs for a bite to eat and a bus fare."

"In that case it won't be long now before he's here. Unless he's called at his newspaper and by a miracle there was some spare cash in the till. It does happen sometimes. . . ."

"You didn't see Nora Wednesday night?"

"No, she didn't come in. Besides, I can't remember ever seeing her without Carus. He was on a trip. . . ."

"In Germany, yes. She went out alone. I wonder where she could have gone."

"Didn't she say?"

"She claims she went back to the Raphael around nine o'clock."

"Isn't it true?"

"The concierge's register says it was more like eleven."

"Strange. . . ."

Bob's thin, ironical smile made a sort of crack in the fixed mask of his face.

"Does it amuse you?"

"You must admit that Carus would not have let such an opportunity slip! He took advantage of every occasion without any inhibitions. . . . It would be funny if Nora, for her part . . . But somehow I can't believe it of her. . . ."

"Because she's in love with him?"

"No. Because she is too intelligent and too level-headed. She would not risk losing everything, just when she was so near to achieving her objective, for the sake of an adventure, even with the most attractive man in the world."

"Perhaps she wasn't so near to achieving her objective as you think."

"What do you mean?"

"Carus used to meet Sophie regularly in an apartment in Rue François-Premier specially rented for the purpose."

"Was it as serious as that?"

"So he claims. He even says she was star material and that she would soon have become one."

"Are you serious? Carus, who . . . But she was just a mere girl, the kind you find thirteen to the dozen. . . . You've only got to walk down the Champs-Elysées and you can pick up enough like her to cover all the screens in the world. . . ."

"Nora knew about their liaison."

"Well, that beats me. . . . It's true, if I were to believe all I hear every time a customer pours his heart out to me, I would have ulcers. Go and tell my wife about it. She'd be upset if you didn't pop in to pass the time of day. She's got a soft spot for you. . . . How about a drink?"

"Not right now. . . ."

The kitchen was bigger, more modern than he had supposed. As he expected, Rose wiped her hand before offering it to him.

"So, you've decided to let him go?"

"Are you surprised?"

"I really don't know. . . . Everybody who comes in here has a version of his own. For some, Francis did it out of jealousy. For others, it's a lover she wanted to get rid of. . . . And for others still, a woman was having her revenge. . . ."

"Nora?"

"Who told you that?"

"Carus was having a serious affair with Sophie. Nora knew about it. He was planning to launch her. . . ."

"Is that true, or are you just making it up to get me talking?"

"It's true. Does it surprise you?"

"Me? It's a long time now since I was surprised by anything. If you were in this business like me . . ."

The idea never occurred to her that one acquires a certain experience of human beings in Police Headquarters.

"But if it's Nora who did it you'll have trouble proving it. She's sharp enough to outwit the whole bunch of you. . . ."

"Will you be eating here? I've got duck à l'orange. . . . As a first course I can offer you two or three dozen scallops just in from La Rochelle. My mother sent them. . . . Ah, yes. . . . She's turned seventy-five and she goes every morning to the market. . . ."

Huguet, the photographer, arrived with his companion. Huguet was a pink youth with an innocent face and jovial expression, and he looked as if he was proud to be seen with a woman seven months pregnant.

"Do you know each other? Chief Inspector Maigret . . . Jacques Huguet . . . His girl friend. . . ."

"Jocelyne," Huguet put in, as if it were important or as if it gave him pleasure to pronounce this poetic name.

And, with exaggerated attentiveness, almost as though he were making fun of her:

"What's your drink, my darling?"

He smothered her with little attentions, enveloped her with warm and tender glances, as if to say to the others:

"As you can see, I am in love and I am not ashamed. . . . We have made love. . . . We are expecting a child. . . . We are happy. . . . And it makes no difference to us if you find us ridiculous."

"What will you have, my children?"

"A fruit juice for Jocelyne. A port for me. . . ."

"And what about you, Monsieur Maigret?"

"A glass of beer."

"Hasn't Francis come yet?"

"Have you a date with him here?"

"No, but it strikes me he would probably like to see his friends again. If only to show them that he's free, and that you couldn't keep him there. . . . He's like that."

"Did you have the impression that we intended to keep him locked up?"

"I don't know. It's difficult to tell what the police are going to do. . . ."

"Do you think he killed his wife?"

"What difference does it make whether it was he or someone else! She's dead, isn't she? If Francis killed her, it's because he had good reason. . . ."

"What reasons, in your opinion?"

"I don't know. . . . He'd got fed up with her, perhaps? Or else she made scenes? Or perhaps she was deceiving him? One must let people lead the lives they want, mustn't we, my pet?"

Some customers came in, not regulars, and hesitated to go to a table.

"Three?"

It was a middle-aged couple and a young girl.

"This way. . . ."

This was Bob's big moment: the menu, the whispered advice, the praise for the Charentes wine, for the *chaudrée* . . .

Occasionally he addressed a wink to his companions who had remained at the bar.

It was then that Ricain came in, stopped in his tracks on seeing the Chief Inspector with Huguet and the pregnant girl.

"So there you are!" cried the photographer. "Well, what happened? . . . We thought you were in the darkest depths of some prison."

Francis forced a smile.

"As you see, I'm here. Good evening, Jocelyne. Have you come for me, Inspector?"

"Just now, for the duck *à l'orange*. . . ."

"What will you have?" Bob came over to ask after passing on the order to the waiter.

"Is that port?"

He hesitated.

"No . . . a Scotch. Unless I've run out of credit . . ."

"Today I'll give you credit."

"And tomorrow?"

"That depends on the Chief Inspector."

Maigret was a little put out by the tone of the conversation, but he supposed this was a special brand of humor peculiar to the group.

"Did you go to the newspaper?" he asked Ricain.

"Yes. . . . How did you know?"

"Because you needed money. . . ."

"I just managed to get an advance of a hundred francs against what they owe me. . . ."

"And Carus?"

"I didn't call on him."

"But you were looking for him everywhere on Wednesday evening, and nearly all the night as well."

"It's not Wednesday any more. . . ."

"By the way," the photographer put in, "I've seen Carus. I went to the studio and he was giving some girl I don't know a screen test. . . . He even asked me to take some pictures.''

Maigret wondered whether he had had some taken of Sophie as well.

"He's dining here. At least, that was his intention at three o'clock this afternoon, but with him you never know. . . . Especially with Nora. . . . By the way, I ran into Nora too.''

"Today?''

"Two or three days ago. In a place where I never expected to see her. . . . A small night club in Saint-Germain-des-Prés, where you see nothing but teen-agers. . . .''

"When was this?'' asked Maigret, suddenly attentive.

"Wait now. . . . It's Saturday. . . . Friday. . . . Thursday. . . . No, on Thursday I was at the opening of the ballet. It was Wednesday. I was looking for pictures to illustrate an article on teen-agers. I had been told about this club. . . .''

"What time was that?''

"Around ten o'clock. . . . Yes, I must have got there at ten o'clock. . . . Jocelyne was with me. What do you think, sweetie? It was ten o'clock, wasn't it? A crummy place, but picturesque, with all the boys wearing hair down to their collars. . . .''

"Did she see you?''

"I don't think so. She was in a corner, with a beefy character who certainly wasn't a teen-ager. . . . I suspect he was the proprietor, and they looked as if they were talking seriously about something.''

"Did she stay long?''

"I fought my way into the two or three rooms where almost everybody was dancing. Well, if you can call that dancing. . . . They were doing their best, glued together. . . .

"I got another glimpse or two of her, between the heads and the shoulders. She was still deep in conversation. The character had taken a pencil from his pocket and was writing figures on a piece of paper. . . .

"It's funny, now that I think about it. . . . As it is, she doesn't look quite real. But there, in that crazy atmosphere, it would have been worth a photograph. . . .''

"Didn't you take one?"

"I'm not such an idiot! I don't want trouble with Papa Carus. I rely on him for a good half of my meal ticket. . . ."

They heard Maigret order:

"Another beer, Bob. . . ."

His voice, his manner, were no longer quite the same.

"Could you reserve the table I had yesterday?"

"Aren't you going to eat with us?" asked the photographer in surprise.

"Another time."

He needed to be alone, to reflect. Once again, by chance, the pieces that he had carefully fitted together had been thoroughly scrambled, and nothing held together any more.

Francis was covertly watching him, with an anxious expression. Bob, too, was aware of the change.

"You look as if you were surprised to learn that Nora would go to a place like that. . . ."

But the Chief Inspector had turned to Huguet:

"What's the club called?"

"Do you want to make a study of beatniks, too? Wait. . . . It's not a very original name. . . . It must date from the time when it was just a *bistrot* for tramps. The Ace of Spades. . . . Yes. On the left as you go up. . . ."

Maigret emptied his glass.

"Keep my corner for me," he repeated.

A few moments later, a taxi was taking him to the other side of the river.

The place, by day, was colorless. There were only three long-haired customers to be seen and a girl in a man's jacket and trousers smoking a small cigar. A character in a cardigan hustled in from the second room and took up his place behind the bar, a suspicious look in his eye.

"What'll it be?"

"A beer," said Maigret mechanically.

"And after that?"

"Nothing."

"No questions?"

"What do you mean?"

"That I wasn't born yesterday, and that if Chief Inspector Maigret comes here it isn't because he's thirsty. So I'm waiting for the commercial."

Playfully, the man poured himself a short drink.

"Somebody came in to see you on Wednesday evening. . . ."

"Hundreds of somebodies, if you will permit me to correct you."

"I'm referring to a woman, with whom you spent a long time in conversation."

"Half of the people were women and I was in conversation, as you put it, with quite a lot of them."

"Nora."

"Now we're talking. Well . . .?"

"What was she doing here?"

"What she comes to do here once a month, on the average."

"That is to say . . . ?"

"Look at the books."

"Because . . . ?"

Astounded, Maigret guessed the truth before the man told him.

"Because she's the boss, that's why, Inspector. She doesn't shout about it. . . . I'm not even sure Papa Carus is in the picture. Everyone has the right to do what they like with their money, haven't they?

"I haven't said anything, you know. . . . You tell me a story and I don't say yes or no. . . . Even if you ask me if she owns any other night clubs of the same sort . . ."

Maigret looked at him, questioningly, and the man flickered his eyelids affirmatively.

"There are some people who know which way the wind blows," he concluded lightly. "It's not always the ones who think themselves clever who make the best investments. With three clubs like this, for just one year, I'd retire to the Riviera. . . .

"So, with a dozen, and some of them in the Pigalle area and one on the Champs-Elysées . . ."

7

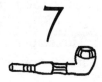

W**HEN MAIGRET RETURNED** to the Old Wine Press, they had placed three tables end to end and started to eat their dinner all together. On seeing him, Carus rose to his feet and came over, checked napkin in hand.

"I trust you will give us the pleasure of joining us?"

"Please don't be offended if I prefer to eat alone in my corner."

"Are you afraid to have dinner with somebody you will be forced to arrest sooner or later?"

He looked him in the eyes.

"There's every chance, isn't there, that poor Sophie's murderer is among us this evening? Well! . . . As you wish. But we shall ask you at least to have a glass of armagnac with us."

Bob had shown him to his table, in the corner by the revolving door, and he had ordered the scallops and *caneton á l'orange* that Rose had recommended.

He could see them side-view, in two rows. It was obvious, from first glance, that Carus was the dominant figure. His manner, his bearing, his gestures, his voice, his look had the self-assurance of a man of importance.

Ricain had taken a place opposite him unwillingly, it seemed, and only joined half-heartedly in the conversation. As for Dramin, he was with a young girl whom Maigret had not yet met, a rather dim creature with scarcely any make-up, soberly dressed, whom Bob later described as a film cutter.

Maki ate a lot, drank his liquor neat, looked at his companions one after another, and replied to their questions with grunts.

It was Huguet, the photographer, who talked back to the producer most of the time. He seemed to be in top form and kept gazing with proprietary satisfaction at the belly of the placid Jocelyne.

It was not possible, from a distance, to follow the conversation. But from odds and ends of phrases, from exclamations and facial expressions, Maigret managed more or less to follow the sense.

"We'll soon see whose turn is next . . ." the facetious photographer had said, or words to that effect.

And his eyes looked for a moment in Maigret's direction.

"He's watching us. He's peeling off our skins. . . . Now that he's got all he can from Francis, he'll turn on someone else. . . . If you go on making such a sour face, Dramin, he'll pick on you. . . ."

Several lone diners, watching from a distance, envied their merriment. Carus had ordered champagne, and there were two bottles cooling in silver buckets. Bob himself went over to pour it.

Ricain was drinking heavily. It was he who was drinking the most, and he did not smile once at the photographer's cracks, not all of which were in the best of taste.

"Look natural, Francis. Don't forget that the eye of God is fastened upon you. . . ."

Maigret was the butt of his humor. Were they funnier on other evenings when they got together?

Carus was doing his best to help Huguet ease the tension. As for Nora, she turned her cold eyes on each of them in turn.

Beneath it all, the dinner was a gloomy affair and nobody was behaving quite naturally, perhaps partly because they were all reacting to the Chief Inspector's presence.

"I bet you'll turn out a script one day that our good friend Carus will produce. . . . All tragedies end that way."

"Shut up, will you?"

"I'm sorry. I didn't know you would . . ."

It was worse when they were silent. In reality there was no

friendship between them. It was not free choice that brought them together. Each one had an ulterior motive.

Weren't they all dependent on Carus? Above all Nora, who extracted from him the means to buy her night clubs. She had no guarantee that he would marry her one day, and she chose to take precautions.

Did he suspect anything? Did he imagine that he was loved for himself?

It was unlikely. He was a realist. He needed a companion, and for the time being she filled the bill well enough. He was probably pleased that her appearance was striking enough to attract attention wherever they went together.

"That's Carus and his friend Nora. . . . Isn't she stunning?"

Why not? He had none the less become Sophie's lover, and was planning to make a star of her.

This presupposed that he would get rid of Nora. He had had others before her. He would have others after. . . .

Dramin lived in a world of unfinished scripts to which Carus had the power to give life. So long as he believed in his talent . . .

Francis was in the same boat, with the difference that he was less humble, less patient, that he was readily aggressive, especially when he had had a few drinks. . . .

As for Maki, he kept his thoughts to himself. His sculpture did not sell, yet . . . While he was waiting for the dealers to show some interest, he painted scenery, good or bad, for Carus and anybody else, content when he did not have to pay for his dinner, eating twice as much on such occasions and ordering the most expensive dishes on the menu.

The photographer, now . . . Maigret found it less easy to read his character in his face. At first sight he did not seem to matter. In nearly all groups which get together frequently, one finds this sort of simpleton character, with big, frank eyes, who plays the role of buffoon. His transparent honesty allowed him to put his foot in his mouth, and every now and then to come out with a home truth nobody else would have got away with.

His very job indicated someone of no consequences. . . . They laughed at him and his ever pregnant women.

Rose, wiping her hands, came out to make sure that everybody was satisfied and, without sitting down, accepted a glass of champagne.

Every now and then Bob went and stood beside Maigret.

"They are doing their best," he whispered knowingly.

Sophie was missing. Everyone felt it. How had Sophie behaved on these occasions?

Sulkily, no doubt, or shyly, but with the knowledge, all the same, that she was the one the rich man of the crowd, Carus, favored. In all probability she had met him that same afternoon in the hideaway in Rue François-Premier.

Carus needed them, too. It was through launching young people that he made most of his money. To be thus surrounded by a sort of court at the Old Wine Press gave him more of a sense of importance than dining with financiers who were richer and more influential than himself.

A wink to Bob, who brought two fresh bottles to the big table. Ricain, exasperated by the photographer's gibes, answered him curtly. One could see the moment approaching when, goaded beyond endurance, he would jump to his feet and stalk out. He did not yet dare to do so, but he was straining at the leash.

True, one of them had probably killed Sophie, and Maigret studied their faces, while the heat made the blood rise to his head.

Carus was in Frankfurt on Wednesday evening, of that they had confirmation from Orly. Nora was talking figures between ten and eleven o'clock in the hectic atmosphere of the Ace of Spades.

Maki? . . . But why would Maki want to kill her? . . . He had slept with Sophie, by chance, because she expected it, or so it appeared, of all their friends. It was a way of reassuring herself, of proving she had some charms, that she was not just any other girl caught up in the movies.

Huguet? . . . He already had three women. . . . It seemed to be a mania, like giving them children. It was a wonder he managed to feed all his different broods. . . .

As for Francis . . .

Again Maigret went over Ricain's movements. The return to Rue Saint-Charles, around ten o'clock. . . . The urgent need of money. . . . He had hoped to find Carus at the Old Wine Press, but Carus was not there. . . . Bob had balked at the amount. . . .

He had left Sophie at home. . . .

Why, when he usually took his wife everywhere with him?

"No!" cried the photographer in a loud voice. "Not here, Jocelyne. This is not the time to go to sleep. . . ."

And he explained that since she had been pregnant she had taken to dropping off to sleep, anywhere, any time.

"Some of them crave pickles, some go for pig's feet or calf's head. She sleeps. Not only does she sleep, she snores. . . ."

Maigret attached no importance to the incident, and went on trying to reconstruct Ricain's comings and goings up to the moment when the latter had stolen his wallet, in Rue du Temple, on the platform of the bus.

Ricain, who had not kept a *centime* for himself . . . Ricain, who had telephoned to tell him . . .

He filled his pipe, lit it. Anybody might have thought that he, too, was dozing off in his corner over his coffee.

"Won't you come and have one for the road with us, Inspector?"

Carus again. Maigret decided to accept, and sit with them for a moment.

"Well," laughed Huguet, "whom are you going to arrest? . . . It's impressive enough to know you're there, watching all our expressions. . . . Every now and then I even begin to feel guilty myself."

Ricain looked so ill that nobody was surprised when he suddenly got to his feet and headed for the lavatory.

"There should be a drinking license, like a driving license," said Maki dreamily.

The sculptor would certainly have got one at the drop of a hat, for he had drained glass after glass and the only effect was to make his eyes shine and his face turn brick red.

"It's always the same with him. . . ."

"Your health, Monsieur Maigret," Carus was saying, holding up his glass. "I was going to say, to the success of your inquiry, since we are all eager for you to find out the truth. . . ."

"All except one!" the photographer corrected him.

"Except one, perhaps. Unless it is not one of us. . . ."

When Francis returned, his eyelids were red and his face had lost its composure. Without being asked, Bob brought a glass of water.

"Do you feel better now?"

"Alcohol doesn't agree with me. . . ."

He was avoiding Maigret's eyes.

"I think I'm going home to bed. . . ."

"Won't you wait for us?"

"You forget I haven't had much sleep these past three days. . . ."

He looked younger, in his physical disarray, much like an overgrown schoolboy ashamed of being made ill by his first cigar.

"Good night. . . ."

They watched Carus get up, follow him over to the door, speak to him in a low voice. Then the producer sat at the table which Maigret had occupied, pushed away a coffee cup, and made out a check while Francis waited, his eyes averted.

"I couldn't leave him in the lurch. If I had been in Paris on Wednesday, perhaps nothing would have happened. I would have had dinner here. He would have asked me for his rent money and he wouldn't have had to leave Sophie. . . ."

Maigret started, turned the phrase over in his mind, looked at each of them in turn.

"If you will excuse me, I will leave you now."

He needed to be out of doors; he was beginning to suffocate. Perhaps he had drunk too much, too? In any case, he did not finish the enormous glass of armagnac.

Without any precise aim, and with his hands in his pockets, he wandered along the sidewalks where several shop windows remained lit. Couples, mainly, were stopping to stare at the washing machines and television sets. Young couples dreaming, making calculations.

"Hundred-franc monthly installments, Louis . . ."

"Plus two hundred and fifty on the car . . ."

Francis and Sophie must have walked like this, arm in arm, in this neighborhood.

Did they dream of washing machine and television set?

They did have a car, the battered old Triumph which Ricain

had abandoned somewhere during that fateful Wednesday night. Had he gone back to get it?

With the check he had just received he had enough to pay his rent. . . . Did he intend to live by himself in the studio where his wife had been murdered?

Maigret crossed the boulevard. An old man was sleeping on a bench. The big new building towered in front of him, with about half of its windows lit.

The other tenants were at the movies, or else they were lingering on, as they were at the Old Wine Press, at restaurant tables.

The air remained balmy, but some large clouds would shortly be passing in front of the full moon.

Maigret turned the corner of Rue Saint-Charles and went into the courtyard. Light could be seen in a small window with frosted glass beside Ricain's door, the window of the bathroom with the hip bath.

Other doors, other windows, also lit, both on the studio side and in the main building. . . .

The courtyard was deserted, silent, the trash cans in place, a cat making its way stealthily along the wall. . . .

Now and then a window would shut, and a light would go out. Early bedders. Then, on the fourth floor, a window lit up. It was a little like the stars which suddenly begin to shine brightly or disappear in the sky.

He thought he could make out, behind the blind, the voluminous silhouette of Jocelyne, and the outline of the photographer's disheveled hair.

Then his eye traveled from the fourth floor to the ground floor. "At about ten o'clock . . ."

He knew the timetable of that night by heart. The Huguets had dined at the Old Wine Press, and as they had been sitting by themselves the meal must have been brief. What time had they come home?

As for Ricain and Sophie, they had opened the studio door and switched on the lights somewhere near ten o'clock. Then, almost immediately afterwards, Francis had gone out. . . .

Maigret could still see the human shapes, high up, coming and going. Then there was only one, the photographer's. . . . The man opened the window, looked at the sky for a moment. . . . Just as he was about to go off, his eye fell upon the courtyard. He must have seen the lighted studio window and, in the center of the empty space, Maigret's silhouette etched in the moonlight. . . .

The Chief Inspector emptied his pipe against his heel and went into the building. Coming from the courtyard, he did not have to pass in front of the porter's lodge. He went into the elevator, pushed the button for the fourth floor, and a moment later found himself once again in a hallway.

When he knocked on the door, it was as if Huguet had been waiting for him, for he opened at once.

"It's you!" he said with a curious smile. "My wife is getting ready for bed. . . . Will you come in, or would you rather I came out with you?"

"Perhaps it would be better if we went downstairs."

"One moment. . . . I'll tell her and get my cigarettes."

An untidy sitting room was half visible, with the dress Jocelyne had been wearing that evening thrown on an armchair.

"No. . . . No. . . . I promise I'll be back in a moment. . . ."

Then he lowered his voice. She was whispering. The bedroom door remained ajar.

"Are you sure?"

"Don't worry. See you in a moment."

He never wore a hat. He did not take a coat.

"Let's go. . . ."

The elevator was still there. They took it.

"Which side? The street or the courtyard?"

"The courtyard."

They reached it, walked side by side in the dark. When Huguet raised his head, he saw his wife looking out of the window, and signaled her to go back.

There was still light in Ricain's bathroom. Was his stomach turning over again?

"Have you guessed?" asked the photographer finally, after a cough.

"I'm just wondering."

"It's not a pleasant situation, you know. Ever since it happened, I've been trying to be smart. Just now, at dinner, I spent the most disagreeable night of my life. . . . "

"It was quite obvious."

"Have you got a match?"

Maigret handed him his matches and began slowly to fill one of the two pipes he had in his pocket.

8

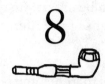

"DID RICAIN AND his wife have dinner at the Old Wine Press on Wednesday evening?"

"No. . . . The fact is, they only ate there when they happened to be in funds, or when they could find someone to invite them. They went by at about half past eight. Only Francis went in. . . . Often, in the evenings, he only half opened the door. If Carus was there, he would go on in, with Sophie following, and sit at his table. . . ."

"Whom did he speak to, on Wednesday?"

"When I saw him, he only exchanged a couple of words with Bob. He asked: 'Is Carus here?'"

"And when he was told no, he left. . . ."

"He didn't try to borrow money?"

"Not then. . . ."

"If he was counting on Carus to invite him to dinner, does it mean they hadn't eaten?"

"They must have gone for a snack to a self-service place in Avenue de La-Motte-Picquet. They often used to go there."

"Did you and your wife stay long?"

"We left the Old Wine Press at about nine. We strolled for about a quarter of an hour. We went home and Jocelyne undressed immediately. Since she's been pregnant she's always tired. . . ."

"So I heard."

The photographer looked puzzled.

"You talked about it at dinner. It seems she even snores."

"Both my other two did, as well. . . . I think all women snore when they are a few months pregnant. I said that to tease her. . . ."

They were talking in an undertone, in a silence broken only by the sound of cars in Boulevard de Grenelle, on the far side of the building. Rue Saint-Charles, beyond the open gate, was empty; only at long intervals would the silhouette of a man going by come into view, or a girl tripping past on her high heels.

"What did you do?"

"I saw her to bed and went to say good night to my children. . . ."

His first two wives lived in the same building, one with two children, the other with one.

"Do you do that every night?"

"Nearly every night. Unless I get home too late. . . ."

"Are you welcome?"

"Why not? They have nothing against me. . . . They know me. They know that's the way I am. . . ."

"In other words, one day or other you will leave Jocelyne for somebody else?"

"If it comes to the point. . . . You know, for myself, I don't attach any importance to it. I adore children . . . the greatest man in history was Abraham. . . ."

It was hard not to smile, especially when, as now, he was talking sincerely. Beneath the contrived jokes, there really was a core of genuineness.

"I stayed with Nicole for a moment. . . . Nicole, that's the second one. Sometimes we have a little reunion for old times' sake. . . ."

"Does Jocelyne know?"

"It doesn't bother her. If I wasn't made like that, she wouldn't be with me."

"Did you make love?"

"No. I thought about it. . . . The child started to talk in its sleep and I tiptoed out."

"What time was this?"

"I didn't look at my watch. I went back home. I changed the

film in one of my cameras, because I had to take some pictures early the next morning. Then I went to the window and opened it. . . .

"I open it every night, wide at first, to get rid of the cigarette smoke, then halfway, because, winter or summer, I can't sleep all shut in. . . ."

"Next?"

"I smoked a last cigarette. There was a moon, like tonight. . . . I saw a couple crossing the courtyard and I recognized Francis and his wife. They were not holding hands, as they usually did, and they were having a heated conversation."

"Did you hear anything?"

"Just one thing which Sophie said in a piercing voice, which made me think she was in a furious temper."

"Did she often get that way?"

"No. She said: *'Don't play the innocent. . . . You knew perfectly well . . .'*"

"Did he answer?"

"No. He seized her by the arm and dragged her toward the door. . . ."

"You still don't know what time this was?"

"Yes, I do. I heard the church clock strike ten. A light went on in the bathroom window. I lit another cigarette. . . ."

"Were you curious?"

"I just wasn't sleepy, that's all. I poured myself a glass of calvados. . . ."

"Were you in the living room?"

"Yes. The bedroom door was open and I had put out the lights so Jocelyne could sleep. . . ."

"How long did all this take?"

"The time it took me to finish the cigarette I had lit in my first wife's place, then the one I lit by the window. . . . A little over five minutes? Less than ten, anyway. . . ."

"Did you hear anything?"

"No. I saw Francis leave and go quickly toward the gate. He always kept his car in Rue Saint-Charles. . . . After a while the motor coughed, then, a few moments later, it started."

"When did you go down?"

"A quarter of an hour later. . . ."

"Why?"

"I told you. . . . I wasn't sleepy. I wanted a chat."

"Just a chat?"

"Perhaps a bit more. . . ."

"Had you previously had relations with Sophie?"

"You want to know if I had slept with her. . . . Once. Francis was drunk and as there was nothing left in the house he had gone out to fetch a bottle from a *bistrot* that was still open. . . ."

"Was she willing?"

"It seemed perfectly natural to her. . . ."

"And afterwards?"

"Afterwards, nothing. . . . Ricain came back without the bottle—they had refused to sell him one. We put him to bed. . . . The next few days there was no question of anything more happening. . . ."

"Let's get back to Wednesday evening. You went down . . ."

"I went to the door. I knocked. And so as not to scare Sophie, I whispered: 'It's Jacques. . . .'"

"Nobody answered?"

"No. There wasn't a sound inside. . . ."

"Didn't this strike you as odd?"

"I told myself she had had a row with Francis and didn't want to see anybody. I assumed she was in bed, furious, or in tears. . . ."

"Did you go on trying?"

"I knocked two or three times, then I went upstairs again to my place. . . ."

"Did you go back to the window?"

"When I had got into my pajamas, I looked down into the courtyard. . . . It was empty. The light was still on in the Ricains' bathroom. I climbed into bed and went to sleep. . . ."

"Go on. . . ."

"I got up at eight, made myself some coffee while Jocelyne was still sleeping. . . . I opened the window wide, and I noticed that the light was still on in Francis' bathroom. . . ."

"Didn't it strike you as funny?"

"Not really. These things happen. I went to the studio, where I worked until one o'clock, then I had a bite to eat with a friend. I had a date at the Ritz with an American movie star who kept me cooling my heels for an hour, and then hardly gave me enough time to take pictures of him. What with one thing and another, it was four o'clock before I got back. . . ."

"Hadn't your wife gone out?"

"To do her shopping, yes. After breakfast she had gone back to bed. She was asleep."

He was aware of the comic side to this leitmotif.

"Was there still. . . ."

"A light on? Yes. . . ."

"Did you go down and knock on the door?"

"No. I telephoned. Nobody answered. Ricain must have gone back, slept, gone out with his wife, forgetting to turn out the light."

"Did that happen sometimes?"

"It happens to everybody. Let's see . . . Jocelyne and I went to a movie in the Champs-Elysées. . . ."

Maigret just managed to stop himself from asking:

"Did she fall asleep?"

The cat came and rubbed itself against his trouser leg and looked at him as if demanding to be stroked. But when Maigret bent down, it moved quickly away and miaowed at him from a few feet farther on.

"Whom does it belong to?"

"I don't know. . . . Everybody. . . . People throw it scraps of meat from the window and it lives outdoors."

"What time did you come back on Thursday evening?"

"Around ten thirty. After the movies we had a drink in a *brasserie* and I met a friend. . . ."

"The light?"

"Of course. But there was nothing surprising about that because the Ricains might well have been back. Even so, I phoned. I admit I was a bit worried when I didn't get an answer. . . ."

"Only a bit?"

"Well, I didn't suspect the truth. If one were to imagine a murder every time somebody forgets to switch off the light. . . ."

"In short . . ."

"Look! He hasn't put out his light now, either. I don't think he can be working. . . ."

"Next morning?"

"Of course I telephoned again, and twice more during the day, until I learned from the newspaper that Sophie was dead. I was at Joinville, in the studios, taking stills for a film being made . . ."

"Did someone answer?"

"Yes. A voice I don't know. I decided to say nothing and hung up after waiting a few moments. . . ."

"You didn't try to get hold of Ricain?"

Huguet said nothing. Then he shrugged his shoulders and resumed his comic expression.

"Look, I don't work at the Quai des Orfèvres!"

Maigret, who was staring idly at the light diffused by the frosted glass, suddenly started toward the studio door. Thinking he understood, the photographer went after him.

"While we were busy chatting . . ."

If Francis wasn't working, if he wasn't sleeping, if the light was still on, that night . . .

He hammered violently on the door.

"Open up! It's Maigret. . . ."

He was making so much noise that a neighbor appeared at his door in pajamas. He looked at the two men in astonishment.

"Now what's going on? Can't one have a moment's peace?"

"Run to the concierge. Ask her if she has a passkey."

"She hasn't."

"How do you know?"

"Because I already asked her, one evening when I had forgotten my key. I had to call a locksmith. . . ."

For a man who made himself out to be simple, Huguet did not lose his head. Wrapping his handkerchief around his fist, he delivered a blow at the frosted glass, which splintered into fragments.

"We must act fast," he panted, as he looked in.

Maigret looked, too. Fully dressed, Ricain was seated in the bath which was too small for him to lie in. Water was flowing from the tap. The bath was overflowing and the water was pink.

"Have you got a strong screwdriver, a jack, anything heavy?"

"In my car. . . . Wait."

The neighbor went off to put on a dressing gown, and he emerged followed by a barrage of questions from his wife. He went out of the main door, and there was the sound of a car trunk being opened.

As the woman herself appeared, Maigret shouted:

"Call a doctor. The nearest one."

"What's going on? Isn't it enough for . . . ?"

She went off, grumbling, while her husband came back with a jack. He was taller, broader, and heavier than the Chief Inspector.

"Let me do it. As long as I don't have to worry about the damage . . ."

The wood resisted at first, then cracked. Another two heaves, one lower, then one higher up, and the door suddenly yielded, while the man had to stop himself from falling in.

The rest was confusion. Other neighbors had heard the noise, and there were soon several of them in the narrow entrance. Maigret had pulled Francis out of the bath and dragged him over to the divan bed. He remembered the drawer in the chest, and its assortment of contents.

He found some string. With the aid of a large blue pencil he improvised a tourniquet. He had scarcely finished it when a young doctor shouldered him aside. He lived in the building, and had hastily pulled on a pair of trousers.

"How long ago?"

"We've just found him. . . ."

"Telephone for an ambulance."

"Is there any chance of . . . ?"

"For God's sake, don't ask questions!"

The ambulance pulled up in the courtyard five minutes later. Maigret climbed in front beside the driver. At the hospital, he had to wait in the corridor while the acting house surgeon performed a blood transfusion.

He was surprised to see Huguet appear.

"Will he pull out of it?"

"They don't know yet."

"Do you think he really meant to commit suicide?"

It was apparent that he had his doubts. So did Maigret. Cornered, Francis had had to make a theatrical gesture.

"Why do you think he would have done a thing like that?"

The Chief Inspector took the question in the wrong sense.

"Because he considered himself too intelligent."

Naturally, the photographer did not understand and stared at him with some bewilderment.

It was not Sophie's death that Maigret had in mind at that precise moment. It was an event much less serious, but perhaps of greater consequence for Ricain's future: the theft of his wallet.

9

HE HAD SLEPT until ten o'clock, but he had not been able to have his breakfast by the open window as he had been promising himself, for there was a downpour of fine rain.

Before going to the bathroom, which had no window, frosted or otherwise, giving onto the courtyard, he telephoned the hospital and had the greatest difficulty in getting through to the doctor on duty.

"Ricain? . . . What is it? . . . An emergency? . . . We had eight emergencies last night, and if I had to remember all their names . . . Good. . . . Blood transfusion . . . Attempted suicide. . . . Hm! . . . If the artery had been cut he wouldn't be here, or else we'd have laid him out in the basement. . . . He's all right, yes. . . . He has not opened his mouth. . . . No. . . . Not one word. . . . There's a cop outside his door. . . . Obviously you know all about it. . . ."

At eleven o'clock Maigret was in his office. His feet were hurting him once more. He had decided to put his new shoes on again, since he had to break them in sometime.

Seated opposite Lapointe and Janvier, he began automatically to arrange his pipes in order of size, then he chose one, the longest, and filled it carefully.

"As I was saying, he is too intelligent. Sometimes it's as dangerous as being too stupid. An intelligence not applied along with a certain force of character. No matter! I know what I want to say, even if I can't find the words to express it.

"Besides, it isn't my concern. The doctors and psychiatrists will take care of all that.

"I'm almost sure he was an idealist, an idealist incapable of living up to his ideal. Do you see what I mean?"

Not too clearly, perhaps. Maigret had seldom been so prolix and so confused all at once.

"He would have liked, above all, to be exceptional in all things. To succeed very fast, as he was burning with impatience, but all the while remaining pure. . . ."

He was losing heart, his words lagging far behind his thought.

"The best and the worst. He must have hated Carus, because he needed him. That didn't stop him from accepting the dinners the producer stood him, and he didn't think twice about touching him for a loan.

"He was ashamed of himself. He was angry with himself.

"He was not so naïve that he didn't realize that Sophie hadn't turned into the wife he thought he could see in her. But he needed her, too. He even took advantage, it must be conceded, of her affair with Carus.

"He will refuse to admit it. He can't admit it.

"And that's just the reason he shot his wife. They were already quarreling, on Wednesday evening, as they came into the court-yard. What it was about doesn't matter. She must have been exasperated, watching his two-faced game, and probably spat out the truth in his face.

"I wouldn't be surprised if she called him a pimp. Perhaps the drawer was partly open. At any rate, he could not tolerate hearing a truth of that sort being voiced.

"He shot her. Then he stopped in his tracks, frightened by what he had just done, and by the consequences.

"I'm convinced that from this moment he made up his mind that he would not let himself be convicted, and while he roamed the streets his brain began to work, to concoct a complicated plan.

"So complicated, in fact, that it almost worked.

"He goes back to the Old Wine Press. He asks for Carus. He needs two thousand francs right away, and he knows Bob isn't the man to lend him a sum like that.

"He has thrown the weapon into the Seine, so as to get around the question of fingerprints.

"He shows his face several times at the Zero Club—'Hasn't Carus got here yet?'—He drinks, walks about ceaselessly adding little touches to his plan.

"True, he hasn't enough money to leave the country, but even if he had it wouldn't be of any use to him, because sooner or later he would be extradited.

"He must get back to Rue Saint-Charles, make a pretense of discovering the body, and alert the police.

"And so he thinks of me.

"He's about to pull an act on me that no normal person would even have dreamed of. The details begin to fall into place. His wanderings are starting to pay dividends.

"He watches me, from early morning, at the door of my house. If I don't take the bus, doubtless he has some alternative solution.

"He steals my wallet. He calls me up, plays his part in such a way as to lead suspicion away from himself.

"And that's just it—he overdoes it! He gives me the menu of Sophie's nonexistent dinner at the Old Wine Press. He lacks stability, simple common sense. He can invent an extravagant story and make it plausible, but he doesn't think of the simplest and most mundane details."

"Do you think his case will ever get to the courts, Chief?" asked Lapointe.

"That depends on the psychiatrists."

"What would you decide, yourself?"

"The courts."

And, as his two colleagues showed surprise at such a definite reply, so uncharacteristic of what they knew of the Chief Inspector, Maigret observed:

"He would be too unhappy to be thought mad, or even only partially responsible. In the dock, on the other hand, he will be able to play the role of the exceptional being, a sort of hero."

He shrugged, smiled sadly, went over to the window, and gazed at the rain.

MAIGRET
AND THE
TOY VILLAGE

1

PEG LEG'S FUNERAL

IT PROBABLY DID not last more than a second, but the impression it made upon Maigret was quite extraordinary. It was like one of those dreams that, we are told, pass in a flash but seem to go on forever. Years later, Maigret could still have pointed to the exact spot where it happened, the paving stone on which he had been standing, the stone wall on which his shadow had been projected. He would be able to remember not only every detail of the scene, but also the various smells in the air and the feel of the breeze, all of which vividly recalled his childhood.

It was the first time that year that he had ventured out without his overcoat, his first sight of the countryside at ten o'clock in the morning. Even his pipe, an unusually large one, seemed to taste of spring. There was a lingering nip in the air. Maigret walked along with a heavy tread, his hands in his trouser pockets. Félicie walked beside him, or, rather, a little ahead of him, since in order to keep up with him, she had to take two steps for every one of his.

Together, they drew level with a brand-new building of pink brick. In the window were displayed a few vegetables, two or three cheeses, and a string of blood sausages on a ceramic plate.

Félicie quickened her step, stretched out her hand, and pushed open the glass door of the shop. And it was then, evoked, no doubt, by the sound of the bell, that Maigret experienced the sensation that he was never to forget.

The shop bell was no ordinary bell. A cluster of thin metal

tubes was suspended above the door, which, when opened, created a draft that caused the tubes to collide and emit a carillon of tinkling chimes.

Long ago, in Maigret's childhood, the pork butcher in his home village had completed the redecoration of his shop by installing just such a carillon.

And this was why, at this moment, for Maigret the present seemed suddenly in abeyance. How long this feeling lasted it was impossible to tell, but while it did, Maigret was genuinely transported to another time and place. It was as if he no longer inhabited the body of the thickset Chief Superintendent obediently trailing along behind Félicie.

The long-lost village boy, it seemed, was there on the spot, hiding somewhere, invisible, looking on, with laughter bubbling up inside him.

Well, really! It was all too ridiculous, wasn't it? Could anything be more out of place than that solemn, bulky figure of a man in the company of that caricature of a woman out of a children's book wearing that absurd red hat? And in such surroundings, too, flimsy and insubstantial as a toy village.

What was he doing there? Conducting an inquiry? Investigating a murder? Here and now, among brick cottages, pink as sugared almonds, with the air full of the twittering of small birds, the fields sprouting tender young green shoots, buds bursting into bloom all over the place, and even the leeks in the shopwindow looking as pretty as flowers?

Yes, he was often to recall this moment in the years to come, and not always with equanimity. For years and years afterward, one or other of his colleagues at the Quai des Orfèvres would pick on a brisk spring morning to remark, half seriously, half teasingly:

"I say, Maigret . . ."

"What is it?"

"Félicie is here!"

And he could almost imagine her standing there, with her slim figure, her quaint clothes, her big blue eyes, her supercilious nose, and, above all, her hat, that outrageous scarlet confection, perched on the top of her head and trimmed with a stiff, iridescent green feather.

"Félicie is here!"

Grrr! It was well known that the name Félicie had only to be spoken for Maigret to growl like a bear. And this was not to be wondered at, since Félicie had given him more trouble than all the hardened criminals brought to justice by the Chief Superintendent in his long career.

On this particular May morning, Félicie really was there, standing at the door of the little grocer's shop. The sign, MÉLANIE CHOCHOI, ÉPICIÈRE, in yellow lettering, was just legible beneath a couple of transparent stickers advertising a brand of starch and a metal polish. Félicie stood waiting for the Chief Superintendent to be so obliging as to rouse himself from his reverie.

At long last, he stirred, found himself back in the real world, and gathered up the threads of his inquiry into the murder of Jules Lapie, nicknamed Peg Leg.

Her sharp features overspread with an expression of mingled hostility and irony, Félicie was braced to meet his questions, as she had been since early that morning. Behind the counter stood Mélanie Chochoi, a pleasant little woman, with hands folded on a bulging stomach, contemplating the Chief Superintendent of the Police Judiciaire and Peg Leg's servant. And a very odd couple they must have seemed to her.

Maigret, puffing gently at his pipe, looked about him. His eyes wandered from the cans of food on the shelves to the unfinished street beyond the glass door, with its newly planted, spindly little trees. Taking his watch from his waistcoat pocket, he finally murmured, with a sigh:

"You came in here at a quarter past ten, I think you said? That's right, isn't it? How can you be so sure about the time?"

Félicie's lips twitched in a little patronizing smile.

"Come over here," she said.

He went across to her, and she pointed to the room behind the shop, which served as a kitchen for Mélanie Chochoi. In the dim interior could be seen a cane armchair, on which lay a ginger cat rolled up in a ball on a red cushion, and just above it, on a shelf, an alarm clock with the hands standing at ten-seventeen.

Félicie had been right. She always was. As for the little shop-keeper, she was wondering what on earth these people had come for.

"What did you buy?"

"A pound of butter. Give me a pound of butter, please, Madame Chochoi. The Chief Superintendent wishes me to do exactly as I did the day before yesterday. Now then, *demi-sel* next, wasn't it? And then . . . let me think. . . . A package of pepper, a can of tomatoes, and two cutlets . . . Put them in my string bag, will you?"

Everything seemed strange to Maigret that morning. He could not shake off the feeling that he was as out of place in this little world as a giant in a toy village.

A few miles from Paris, he had diverged from the route along the Seine. At Poissy, he had climbed the hill, and then suddenly, surrounded by real fields and orchards, there before him was this isolated little community. Its name, proclaimed a signboard beside the newly built road, was JEANNEVILLE ESTATE.

A few years earlier, this must have been an area of fields, meadows, and thickets, like the surrounding countryside, until the advent of a property developer with a wife or mistress named Jeanne, after whom, no doubt, this embryo village had been named.

Streets had been mapped out, the avenues of the future, and lined with immature trees, their thin trunks packed with straw to protect them from frost.

Here and there, houses and cottages had been built. It was neither a village nor a town, but something different from either. It was unfinished, with gaps between the houses, a great deal of scaffolding, and patches of empty ground, and, in the streets, useless standard gas lamps, an absurd refinement, since the streets could barely be said to exist apart from the blue plaques inscribed with their names.

DREAM HOUSE, WORLD'S END, OPEN HOUSE—every cottage had its name on a board, surrounded by scrollwork, and down there below was Poissy, the silver ribbon of the Seine dotted with real coal barges, and railroad tracks used by real trains. On the plateau beyond could be seen the farms and bell tower of Orgeval.

Here, only the little old shopkeeper, Mélanie Chochoi, seemed real. She had been lured away from a nearby market town by the promise of a fine new shop, to supply the needs of the new housing development.

"Anything else, dear?"

"Let me think. . . . What else did I buy on Monday? Ah! Yes, hairpins."

Mélanie sold everything, from toothbrushes to face powder, from kerosene to postcards.

"I think that was all, wasn't it?"

Maigret noted that neither Peg Leg's cottage nor the approach to it could be seen from the shop.

"My milk!" exclaimed Félicie. "I nearly forgot my milk!"

And, in her usual condescending manner, she explained to Maigret:

"I was so confused with all your questions that I forgot to bring my milk jug. . . . Anyway, I had it with me on Monday. . . . Today, I left it behind. It's in the kitchen. . . . A blue jug with white spots . . . You'll find it next to the stove. . . . That's right, isn't it, Madame Chochoi?"

She spoke in the manner of a queen bestowing a great boon upon a lowly subject, while at the same time implying that she, like Caesar's wife, was above suspicion.

She was most insistent that nothing should be overlooked.

"What did we talk about on Monday, Madame Chochoi?"

"I believe you pointed out that my Zouzou must have worms, seeing that he would keep eating his fur."

Zouzou, presumably, was the tomcat which lay dozing on the red cushion in the armchair.

"Let me see. . . . You collected your *Ciné-Journal* and bought a paperback novel for twenty-five sous."

Spread out on the counter was a variety of cheap novels and magazines with garish covers, but Félicie ignored them and shrugged.

"How much do I owe you? Hurry, please, because the Chief

Superintendent wants everything done exactly as it was on Monday, and I wasn't in here as long as this."

"Tell me, Madame Chochoi," interposed Maigret, "while we're on the subject of last Monday morning . . . did you, by any chance, happen to hear a car go by while you were serving Mademoiselle Félicie?"

The shopkeeper gazed out at the sunlit street beyond the glass door.

"I don't know. . . . Let me think. . . . Not that we see many cars around here, though one hears them going past on the main road . . . Monday, did you say? . . . I remember seeing a little red car go past the back entrance to the Sébiles' house. . . . But what day that was, I really couldn't say. . . ."

Just to be on the safe side, Maigret wrote in his notebook: *Red car, Sébile.*

And he and Félicie went out into the street again. Félicie, with her coat draped over her shoulders and her sleeves flapping, swayed as she walked.

"This way. I always take the shortcut home."

A narrow pathway with vegetable gardens on either side.

"Did you meet anyone on the way?"

"You'll see in a minute."

And she was right. He did see. As they emerged into another street, the postman, who had just ridden up the hill, passed by on his bicycle and, turning toward them, called out:

"Nothing for you, Mademoiselle Félicie."

She looked at Maigret.

"He saw me here on Monday at this same time, as he does almost every morning."

The path they were on skirted a hideous pale-blue roughcast cottage, surrounded by a tiny garden in which there stood, beneath the hedge, a row of clay animal sculptures. Félicie went through the gate, her trailing coat brushing against a row of gooseberry bushes as she did so.

"Here we are. This, as you see, is the garden. In a minute, you'll see the summerhouse."

It had been a few minutes short of ten o'clock when they had set out from the cottage, using the front door, which opened onto an avenue. In going to the grocer's and back, they had described a more or less complete circle. They walked beside a border of carnations which would shortly be coming into flower, and then past several beds of tender young green lettuce.

"This is where I expected him to be," stated Félicie, pointing to a length of string stretched taut above a shallow trench. "He'd just started pricking out his tomatoes. As you see, this row is half done. When I saw that *he* wasn't here, I assumed he must have gone indoors for a drop of *vin rosé*."

"Did he drink a lot?"

"Only when he was thirsty . . . As you will see, he always kept a glass standing bottom up on the barrel in the cellar."

The carefully tended garden of a man of modest means, a cottage such as almost anyone in straitened circumstances might dream of building for his retirement. They passed from the sunlit garden into the bluish shade of the adjoining terrace. There was the little summerhouse on the right, furnished with a table, on which stood a half-bottle of brandy and a little glass with a very thick base.

"You saw the bottle and the glass. Now you told me this morning that your employer never drank alcohol, especially that particular kind, except when he had company."

She looked at him defiantly, meeting his eyes with her own clear blue gaze, as if to proclaim emphatically that she had absolutely nothing to hide.

Yet she could not resist retorting:

"He was not my employer."

"I know. . . . You told me. . . ."

Heavens above! People like Félicie really were maddening to have to deal with. What else was it she had said in that shrill voice of hers that so irritated Maigret? Ah, yes. She had said:

"It would be a breach of trust on my part to reveal secrets that concern others besides myself. Some people, no doubt, look upon me as a servant. . . . But the time will come, I daresay, when they will see things in a different light, when they will discover . . ."

"What will they discover?"

"Nothing."

"Are you insinuating that you were Peg Leg's mistress?"

"What do you take me for?"

"His daughter, then?" Maigret had ventured to suggest.

"I refuse to answer. One day, perhaps . . ."

This was the cross he had to bear. Félicie! Stubborn as a mule, acid-tongued, full of strange fancies, her sharp-featured face clumsily daubed with powder and rouge, a little servant girl, given to putting on queenly airs in the local dance hall. And, every now and then, that disturbing, fixed gaze, and at other times that odd, fleeting smile, tinged with irony, if not contempt.

"What if he did take a nip by himself? That's no concern of mine."

But old Jules Lapie, nicknamed Peg Leg, had not been alone; Maigret was convinced of it. A man at work in his garden, wearing clogs and a straw hat, does not suddenly put down his tools to go indoors and fetch a bottle of old brandy from the sideboard, and bring it out to the summerhouse to drink it.

At some stage, there must have been another glass on that green-painted garden table. Someone had removed it. Was it Félicie?

"You say you expected to find Lapie at work in the garden. When you saw that he was not there, what did you do?"

"Nothing. I went into the kitchen, lit the gas to heat the milk, and went to the pump to get some water to wash the vegetables."

"And then?"

"I climbed up on the old chair I keep for the purpose and changed the flypaper."

"Still wearing your hat? You always wear a hat to go shopping, don't you?"

"I'm not a slattern."

"When did you take your hat off?"

"When the milk was ready. I went upstairs. . . ."

Everything in the house, to which the old man had given the name Cape Horn, was fresh and new. The pine staircase smelled of varnish. The stairs creaked.

"Go on up. I'll follow you."

She opened the door of her bedroom, with its chintz-covered

mattress that served as a couch and its walls covered with photographs of film stars.

"Here we are. I took off my hat. . . . I thought:

"Oh! I forgot to open Monsieur Jule's bedroom window. . . .

"I crossed the landing. . . . I opened the door, and I cried out. . . ."

Maigret, who had refilled his pipe in the garden, was still puffing at it. He was looking down at the polished floor, gazing at the chalk outline of Peg Leg's body as it had been found lying there on Monday morning.

"And the revolver?" he asked.

"There was no revolver. You know very well there wasn't. It was all in the police report. And don't tell me you haven't read it!"

On the mantelpiece stood a scale model of a three-masted schooner, and the walls were covered with pictures, all of sailing ships, for all the world as if the dead man had been a retired seaman. But the head of the local police, who had handled the case in its early stages, had told Maigret of Peg Leg's one extraordinary adventure.

Jules Lapie had never been a seaman, but had been employed as bookkeeper by a firm in Fécamp, a ship chandler, supplier of sails, rope, winches, and all kinds of ships' stores and provisions.

A bachelor, thickset, persnickety almost to the point of mania, a colorless man, with a brother who was a ship's carpenter.

One morning, Jules Lapie, then about forty, went aboard the *Sainte-Thérèse*, a three-masted schooner due to sail that same day for Chile, to oversee the loading of a cargo of phosphates. Lapie's duties were prosaic enough. It was his task to check that nothing was missing from the consignment as ordered, and to receive payment from the captain.

What precisely had gone wrong? The sailors of Fécamp were never backward in making fun of the persnickety bookkeeper who always seemed so ill at ease when compelled by his duties to set foot on board a ship. Drinks were poured and glasses clinked, as was the custom. He was plied with drink, though God knows what manner of drink it was to make him so very, very drunk.

Be that as it may, when, at high tide, the *Sainte-Thérèse* glided out between the piers of the little harbor of that small port in Normandy, Jules Lapie, who everyone believed, or pretended to believe, had gone ashore, was huddled, dead drunk and snoring, in a corner of the hold.

They battened down the hatches. It was not until they had been two days out at sea that they found him. The captain refused to turn back, to deviate from his course, and thus it came about that Lapie, who in those days still had both his legs, found himself aboard a ship bound for Cape Horn.

This episode was to cost him a leg, when he was thrown through a skylight during a fight.

Years later, he was to be killed by a revolver shot, one Monday in spring, having been lured away from his tomato plants, while Félicie was out getting her supplies from Mélanie Chochoi's brand-new grocery.

"Shall we go downstairs?" murmured Maigret, with a sigh.

The house was so peaceful, so pleasant to be in, with its dollhouse cleanliness and its wholesome smells. The dining room, on the right, had been transformed into a mortuary chapel. The Chief Superintendent opened the door a crack. The shutters were closed, and the room was in darkness except for the thin slivers of light showing through the slats. The coffin was lying on the table, which was covered with a cloth. Beside it was a bowl of holy water, with a sprig of rosemary in it.

Félicie stood waiting for him at the kitchen door.

"In other words, you know nothing, you saw nothing, you haven't the remotest idea who your employer—sorry! Jules Lapie—could possibly have been entertaining during your absence."

She met his glance unwaveringly, but said nothing.

"And you are quite sure that, when you returned, there was only one glass on the garden table?"

"I saw only one. . . . But if you say there were two . . ."

"Did Lapie have many visitors?"

Maigret sat down next to the stove, reflecting that a drink would be most welcome, preferably a glass of that *vin rosé* mentioned by Félicie. He had seen the barrel down there in the cool, dark cellar. The sun was rising higher in the sky, and, in its heat, the morning dew was gradually evaporating.

"He didn't welcome callers."

Quite a character, this fellow, whose whole life must have been turned upside down by that trip around the Horn! On his return to Fécamp, where, in spite of the loss of his leg, his strange adventure was viewed with some mirth, he withdrew still further into himself, and devoted his energy to a prolonged lawsuit against the owners of the *Sainte-Thérèse*. He claimed that, since he had been detained aboard against his will, the shipping company was at fault, and was therefore liable to pay compensation. He set the highest possible value on his amputated leg, won his case, and was awarded substantial damages.

The people of Fécamp thought him a figure of fun. He shunned them and, having come to hate the sea, moved inland, and was one of the first to succumb to the lure of the dazzling prospects held out by the developer of Jeanneville.

He engaged a girl whom he had known as a child in Fécamp to come and keep house for him.

"How long have you lived in this house?"

"Seven years."

"You are now twenty-four . . . so you were seventeen when . . ."

Allowing his thoughts to drift at will, he suddenly asked:

"Have you got a steady boyfriend?"

She looked at him, but did not answer.

"I asked you if you had a steady boyfriend."

"My private life is no concern of yours."

"Does he visit you here?"

"I don't have to answer that."

She deserved a good slap, she really did. It was not the first time that Maigret had been tempted to administer one, or at least to take her by the shoulders and shake her.

"No matter. I'll soon find out."

"You won't find anything out."

"Oh? That's what you think, is it?"

He pulled himself up. It was really too absurd. He was not

going to demean himself by having an argument with this chit of
a girl.

"Are you sure you have nothing more to tell me? Think it over
while there is still time."

"I've done all the thinking that's necessary."

"Sure you're not hiding something from me?"

"If you're as clever as they say, how could I hide anything from
you?"

"Well, we'll just have to wait and see."

"I wish you luck."

"What are you planning to do after Jules Lapie's funeral? His
family will be coming here, I presume."

"I don't know. I hadn't thought."

"Will you be staying here?"

"I might."

"Are you expecting to inherit his property?"

"I think it's very likely."

Maigret did not wholly succeed in controlling his irritation.

"At all events, my dear, I want you to remember one thing. As
long as I am investigating this case, I forbid you to leave the area
without informing the police."

"Are you putting me under house arrest?"

"No!"

"And what if I should feel like going off somewhere?"

"You will apply to me for permission."

"Do you think I killed him?"

"My thoughts are my own, and I have no intention of sharing
them with you."

He had had enough. He was furious, mainly for having allowed
himself to get into such a state over a nonentity like Félicie.
Twenty-four, was she? It seemed hardly possible. The way she
was carrying on, one would take her for a youngster of twelve or
thirteen, solemnly playing out some juvenile fantasy or other of
her own.

"Good-bye."

"Good-bye."

"Oh, by the way, what are you having for lunch?"

"Don't worry about me. I won't starve."

She could say that again! He could just see her, after he had gone, sitting down at the kitchen table, nibbling at whatever came to hand, and, at the same time, reading one of those paperback romances on sale in Madame Chochoi's shop.

Maigret was still furious. To be made a fool of in front of everyone, and, worse, to be made a fool of by a poisonous little shrew like Félicie!

It was Thursday. The Lapie family had turned up in force. There was his brother, Ernest Lapie, the ship's carpenter from Fécamp, an uncouth man with close-cropped, bristling hair and pockmarked face; his wife, a huge woman with a hairy upper lip; and a couple of children she herded along like geese in a field. Then there was a youth of nineteen, a nephew of the dead man, named Jacques Pétillon, who had come from Paris. He seemed nervous and sickly, and was viewed with suspicion by the Lapie contingent.

There was as yet no cemetery in Jeanneville. The procession had set out for Orgeval, of which the new development was a suburb. Félicie created quite a sensation by appearing in a crepe veil. Where on earth could she have got hold of it? Maigret was to learn later that she had borrowed it from Mélanie Chochoi.

Félicie, without waiting to be invited, took her place at the head of the procession. She walked, stiff as a ramrod, in front of the family, the very embodiment of grief, dabbing her eyes with a black-edged handkerchief, also no doubt borrowed from Mélanie, which she had sprayed with cheap eau de Cologne.

Sergeant Lucas, who had spent the night in Jeanneville, was at Maigret's side. Both were walking at the rear of the procession along the dusty road, listening to the larks singing in the clear sky.

"She knows something, that's for sure. She's so sharp, she'll cut herself one of these days. . . ."

Lucas nodded in agreement. The doors of the little church were left open throughout the service, so that the scents of springtime were even more pervasive than the incense. It was not far from the church to the graveside.

After the ceremony, the family were to return to the cottage, to deal with the matter of the will.

"Why did my brother have to make a will?" exclaimed Ernest Lapie in surprise. "We don't go in for that kind of thing in our family."

"According to Félicie . . ."

"Félicie! Félicie! I'm sick of the sound of her name."

Involuntarily, Maigret shrugged.

And there she was, shouldering her way to the front, making sure of being the first to throw a spadeful of earth on the coffin. And having done so, she left the graveside in floods of tears, walking so fast that it seemed she was almost bound to trip and fall.

"Stay with her, Lucas."

She walked and walked at a very brisk pace, taking advantage of the twists and turns of the streets and lanes of Orgeval. Lucas followed, barely fifty yards behind her, but eventually, coming out into a more or less deserted street, he saw the back of a delivery truck disappearing around a corner, and realized that he had lost her.

He went into the nearest café.

"Tell me . . . that truck that's just driven off . . ."

"Yes . . . It belongs to the car mechanic, Louvet. He just looked in for a quick one. . . ."

"Did he give a lift to anyone?"

"I don't know. . . . I don't think so. . . . I didn't see him leave."

"Do you know where he's bound for?"

"Paris. He always goes there on Thursdays."

Lucas hurried over to the post office, which, by a lucky chance, was just across the street.

"Hello . . . Yes . . . Lucas speaking . . . This is urgent. . . . A delivery truck, rather battered . . . Hang on a minute. . . ."

He turned to the postmistress.

"Do you happen to know the license number of Monsieur Louvet's truck?"

"No . . . but I do remember that the last figure is an eight."

"Hello . . . The last figure is eight. A young woman dressed in mourning . . . Hello . . . Don't hang up. . . . No, I don't want her arrested. Just followed . . . understand? . . . You'll be hearing further from the Chief Superintendent himself."

He returned to join Maigret, who was walking alone behind the family on the Orgeval-Jeanneville road.

"She got away."

"What do you mean?"

"She must have jumped into the delivery truck as soon as it stopped. . . . By the time I turned the corner, it was too late. I called the Quai des Orfèvres. They're putting out an all-points alert. They're keeping watch on all roads into Paris."

So, Félicie had vanished! Without fuss, in broad daylight, under the very noses of Maigret and his most trusted assistant! She had vanished, in spite of that voluminous mourning veil, which made her conspicuous a mile off.

The family mourners kept looking back at the two policemen, wondering where on earth Félicie could have got to. She had taken the front-door key with her. They had to go in through the garden. Maigret opened the dining-room shutters. The table was still covered with a sheet, the sprig of rosemary had been left lying there, and the whole place smelled of candle grease.

"I could do with a drink," said Ernest Lapie, sighing. "Etienne! Julie! Keep off the flower beds! There must be some wine somewhere."

"In the cellar," Maigret told him.

Lapie's wife had gone to Mélanie's shop to buy some cookies for the children, and, while she was about it, she got enough for everyone.

"My brother had no reason whatsoever to make a will, Chief Superintendent. I realize that he was eccentric. . . . He was unsociable, to say the least, and didn't bother to keep in touch. . . . All the same . . ."

Maigret was rummaging through the drawers of the little desk that stood in a corner of the room. He took out several bundles of bills and receipts neatly fastened together, and there underneath lay an old gray wallet. It contained nothing but a single buff envelope.

To be opened after my death.

"Well, gentlemen, this is what we are looking for, I think."

I, Jules Lapie, the undersigned, being sound in mind and body, do hereby declare, in the presence of Ernest Forrentin and François Lepape, both residing in Jeanneville, in the district of Orgeval . . .

As Maigret read on, his voice took on a graver tone.

"Félicie was right!" he said, when he had finished. "It is she who inherits the house and all its contents."

The relatives were quite simply thunderstruck. The will contained one phrase that they would not readily forget:

Having regard to the attitude that my brother and his wife saw fit to adopt at the time of my accident . . .

"All I said was that I couldn't see the point of moving heaven and earth just because . . . " expostulated Ernest Lapie.

In view of the conduct of my nephew, Jacques Pétillon . . .

The sickly young man from Paris wore the hangdog expression of an undistinguished schoolboy on Prize Day.

All to no avail. Félicie was the heir. And Félicie, for God knows what reason, had vanished.

2

IN THE MÉTRO

MAIGRET, WITH HIS hands in his trouser pockets, stood facing the bamboo coatrack in the entryway, with its lozenge-shaped mirror beneath the pegs. The sight of his face reflected in this mirror might well have brought a smile to his lips, for he was reminded of a shamefaced child longing to gratify an unreasonable whim. Yet Maigret did not smile, but, after some hesitation, stretched out his hand, seized the wide-brimmed straw hat that was hanging from one of the pegs, and put it on his head.

Well, well! Old Peg Leg had had an even bigger head than the Chief Superintendent, who always had difficulty finding a hat large enough to fit him. Deep in thought, still wearing the straw hat, he went into the dining room, to take another look at the photograph of Jules Lapie that he had found in a drawer.

Once, on being asked to comment on Maigret's methods by a visiting criminologist, the Chief Commissioner of the Police Judiciaire had replied, with an enigmatic smile:

"Maigret? How can I put it? He settles into a case as if it were a pair of comfortable old slippers."

Today, it would not have taken much to induce the Chief Superintendent to step not into the victim's slippers so much as into his clogs. For there they stood, inside the door on the right, obviously just where they were supposed to be. There was a place for everything, and everything was in its place. Except for the absence of Félicie, Maigret would have been prepared to believe that life was going on just as usual in the house, that he himself was Lapie, on the point of making his slow way into the garden, to finish picking out his row of tomatoes.

Behind the freshly painted cottages that could be seen from the garden, the sky was filled with the glorious colors of sunset. Ernest Lapie, the dead man's brother, had sent his family back to Fécamp, announcing that he himself was proposing to spend the night in Poissy. The others, the neighbors and the few farm workers from Orgeval who had attended the funeral, had doubt-less returned to their homes, or dropped into the Anneau d'Or, the local inn, for a drink.

Sergeant Lucas was also at the inn, Maigret having instructed him to take his suitcase there, and to stay within reach of the telephone, pending further news from Paris.

Peg Leg had had a huge head, a square jaw, thick gray eyebrows, and gray bristles all over his face, since it was his habit to shave only once a week. He had been mean with money. One only had to glance through his bills. It was obvious that, as far as he was concerned, every penny counted. His brother had admitted:

"To be sure, he was careful. . . ."

And in Normandy, when one man says of another that he is "careful" . . .

It was a mild evening. The sky was visibly changing from rose to violet. Fresh breezes were blowing in from the countryside, and Maigret, his pipe clenched between his teeth, caught himself stooping a little, as Lapie had done. More than that, as he made for the cellar, he found that he was dragging his left leg. He turned on the tap of the barrel of *vin rosé*, rinsed the glass, and helped himself. At this hour, Félicie would normally be at work in the kitchen, and the smell of simmering stew would no doubt be drifting out into the garden. This surely was the time of day for watering the plants. He could see people out with their watering cans in the neighboring gardens. Dusk was spreading through the rooms of Cape Horn, where, no doubt, in the old man's time, the lighting of the lamps was delayed until the last possible moment.

Why had he been killed? Maigret could not help reflecting that he, too, would one day retire to a little house in the country, with a garden, a broad-brimmed straw hat. . . .

Theft could not have been the motive, since, according to his brother, Peg Leg possessed almost nothing apart from the quarterly payment of his famous damages. A savings-bank book had been found in the house, along with an envelope containing two thousand francs, and a few premium bonds. His gold watch had also been found.

Oh, well! They would have to look elsewhere. But first, he would have to dig deeper into the old man's character. He had been grumpy, churlish, taciturn, persnickety. A loner. The smallest disruption of his settled habits must have infuriated him. He had never even entertained the thought of marriage and a family, and, as far as was known, had never had a love affair of any description.

What had Félicie been hinting at? No, really! Félicie was a liar. Lying was as natural to her as breathing. Or, at least, bending the truth to suit herself. Being just a servant to the old man was altogether too humdrum. So she chose to let it be understood that the reason he sent for her to come and live with him . . .

Maigret turned toward the kitchen window. How had they got along together, those two lonely souls, so cut off from the rest of the world? Maigret had a feeling—no, a conviction—that they had fought like cat and dog.

Suddenly . . . Maigret gave a start . . . He had just come from the cellar, having helped himself to a second glass of wine. There he stood, in the dusk, with the straw hat on his head. For a moment, he thought he must be dreaming. A light had been switched on behind the lace curtains in the kitchen, gleaming saucepans sprang into view on glossy painted shelves. The phut of a gas jet could be heard. The Chief Superintendent glanced at his watch. It was ten to eight.

He opened the door, and there was Félicie, who had already taken off her hat and veil and hung them on the coatrack, putting a pan of water on to boil.

"Oh! So you're back!"

She did not seem surprised, but merely looked him up and down, taking in the straw hat, which Maigret had by now forgotten.

He sat down near the window in what must have been the old man's chair, and stretched out his legs. Félicie went about her business as if he were not there. She set the table for her dinner, and fetched butter, bread, and sausage from the cupboard.

"Tell me, my dear . . ."

"I'm not your dear."

"Tell me, Félicie . . ."

"Mademoiselle Félicie, if you don't mind."

Heavens above! Why did she have to be so disagreeable? It was maddening, like trying to get hold of some slithering wild creature, such as a lizard or a grass snake. It bothered him to have to take her seriously, but he felt he had no choice, since it was only through her that he could hope to arrive at the truth.

"I asked you not to leave Jeanneville."

She smiled smugly, as if to say:

"Well, you couldn't stop me, could you? So there!"

"What did you go to Paris for, may I ask?"

"Just for the ride."

"Indeed? I may as well tell you that, any time now, I shall be getting a detailed report on where you went and what you did."

"I know. Don't think I didn't see that great oaf you had tail me."

"What great oaf?"

"He was tall, with red hair. I changed trains six times on the Métro, but I couldn't shake him off."

Inspector Janvier, no doubt. He must have got on her track as soon as the mechanic put her down at Porte Maillot.

"Who did you go to see?"

"No one."

She sat down to eat. What is more, she put one of her paperback romances on the table in front of her—she had marked her place with a knife—and settled down for a quiet read.

"Tell me, Félicie."

She had a forehead like a nanny goat's. The Chief Superintendent had been struck by it the very first time he saw her. A high, stubborn forehead, butting away obstinately at anything that stood in its path.

"Do you intend to spend the night alone in this house?"

"What about you? Are you planning to stay?"

She ate, she read. Smothering his exasperation, he looked at her quizzically, and tried to sound as fatherly as he could.

"You told me this morning that you were sure he had made you his heir. . . ."

"Well! What of it?"

"How did you know?"

"I just did, that's all."

She had made coffee, and she now poured herself a cup. She obviously liked her coffee, and she lingered over it, savoring it, but she did not offer any to Maigret.

"I'll come and see you tomorrow."

"Suit yourself."

"By then, I hope you will have had time to reconsider."

She looked him boldly in the eye, giving him the full benefit of her clear, inscrutable gaze, shrugged, and murmured:

"What is there to reconsider?"

Outside the front door of Cape Horn, Maigret found Inspector Janvier waiting for him. He had followed his quarry all the way back to Jeanneville. His cigarette glowed in the dark. It was a fine, starlit night. The only sound was the croaking of frogs.

"I knew her at once, Chief, from the description Lucas gave me over the telephone. When the truck drove up to the city gate, the young lady was sitting in front with the driver, all very friendly. Then she got out. She walked up Avenue de la Grande-Armée, looking in the shopwindows. On the corner of Rue Villaret-de-Joyeuse she went into a patisserie, and ate half a dozen cream puffs and drank a glass of port."

"Did she spot you?"

"I don't think so."

"I know she did."

Janvier looked somewhat abashed.

"Next, she went into the Métro. She bought a second-class ticket. She kept moving from one line to another—the trains were almost empty at that hour. She changed first at Place de la Concorde, then at Gare Saint-Lazare. . . . She had a paperback novel in her bag, and she read it between stops. . . . We changed five times in all."

"Did she speak to anyone?"

"No one . . . As time went on, the cars began to fill up. By six o'clock, with all the shops and offices closing, they were jammed tight. . . . You know how it is. . . ."

"Go on."

"At Place des Ternes, we were so jostled by the crowd that we found ourselves almost shoulder to shoulder. I confess it was only then that I realized she knew she was being followed. She looked straight at me. I had the impression, Chief . . . How shall I put it? . . . For a few seconds her face seemed to change completely. It was as if she was afraid. . . . I'm convinced that for those few seconds she was afraid, of me or of something. . . . It was over in a flash, and she was elbowing her way onto the platform."

"Are you sure she didn't speak to anyone?"

"Quite sure. She waited on the platform for the train to come in, and peered into the most crowded car."

"Did she show any particular interest in any of the passengers?"

"I couldn't really tell. What I do know is that she had quite recovered from her momentary panic, and that, as the train disappeared into the darkness of the tunnel, she couldn't resist turning to me with a look of triumph. Then she hurried up the steps to the exit. . . . I don't think she knew quite where she was. . . . She had an apéritif in a bar on the corner of Avenue des Ternes, then consulted a railroad timetable and took a taxi to Gare Saint-Lazare. And that's all. I took the same train as she did to Poissy, and then followed her up the hill on foot."

"Have you had anything to eat?"

"I managed to grab a sandwich at the station."

"Wait here. I'll send Lucas to relieve you."

Maigret set off for Orgeval, leaving Jeanneville to the peace of the night, with just a few windows here and there showing a rosy light. It was not long before he was reunited with Lucas in the Anneau d'Or at Orgeval. Lucas was not alone. His companion, wearing blue overalls, could be none other than the car mechanic, Louvet. The young man was in a very animated state, which was hardly surprising seeing that he already had four or five saucers piled up in front of him.

Lucas also had alcohol on his breath as he made the introductions.

"As I was telling the Sergeant, Chief Superintendent, I hadn't the least inkling when I set off in my jalopy . . . I go to Paris every Thursday afternoon to stock up with spare parts and things."

"Always at the same time of day?"

"More or less."

"Was Félicie aware of that?"

"To tell the truth, I hardly know her. . . . I've seen her around, but never to talk to. I did know Peg Leg, though, because he came in here every night for his game of cards with Forrentin and Lepape. Sometimes the landlord would make up a fourth, and sometimes I would. . . . As a matter of fact, Forrentin and Lepape are here now, over there in the corner, to the left, with the Mayor and the builder."

"When did you discover you had a passenger?"

"Just before I got to Saint-Germain . . . I heard a sigh behind me. At first I thought it was just the wind, because there was a bit of a breeze, and the tarpaulin was flapping. . . . Then, suddenly, there was this voice asking me if I had a light. . . . I turned around, and there she was, with her veil thrown back, and a cigarette in her mouth.

"She was in no laughing mood, I can tell you. She was as white as a sheet, and the cigarette shook between her lips.

"'What on earth are you doing here?' I asked.

"And then it all came pouring out. . . . She said she absolutely had to get to Paris. There was not a moment to lose. It was a matter of life and death. The people who killed Peg Leg were after her, and the police couldn't do a thing about it.

"I stopped the truck for a minute, so that she could get in the front beside me, because she was sitting on an old crate in the back, and it was none too clean. . . .

"'Later . . . later,' she kept repeating. 'When I've done what I have to do, I may tell you the whole story. . . . Anyway, I'll be eternally grateful to you for this. You have saved my life.'

"When we got to the city gate, she thanked me, and got out. Her manner was very grand, as if she was a princess or something."

Lucas and Maigret exchanged glances.

"Now, if it's all the same to you, we'll have one final drink. Oh, yes, I insist. It's my round. And I'll be off and have a bite to eat. This isn't going to get me into any trouble, is it? Cheers!"

Ten o'clock at night. Lucas was mounting guard outside Cape Horn, having relieved Janvier, who had gone back to Paris. The dining room of the Anneau d'Or was blue with smoke. Maigret had eaten too much, and was on his third or fourth drink of the local so-called marc.

Sitting astride a rush-seated chair, with his elbows on the back rail, he seemed at times to fall into a doze, with his eyes half shut and the smoke drifting upward from the bowl of his pipe.

Opposite him were four men playing cards on a table covered with a crimson cloth. Fingering the grubby cards as they talked, they answered questions and told an occasional anecdote. The landlord, Monsieur Joseph, was filling the gap left by old Lapie, and the mechanic, having had his supper, had returned to take the fourth hand.

"To put it in a nutshell," said Maigret, sighing, "he lived like a fighting cock. His social position was not unlike that of a respectable country parson, looked after by a faithful housekeeper. I daresay he wasn't averse to a bit of cosseting, and . . ."

Lepape, who was deputy mayor of Orgeval, winked at the others. His partner, Forrentin, was manager of the new development, and lived in the best house, overlooking the main road, not far from the billboard advertising the remaining plots for sale in Jeanneville.

"A parson and his housekeeper, that's rich!" sniggered the Deputy Mayor.

Forrentin contented himself with a sarcastic smile.

"Oh, come! You didn't know him. Anyone can see that," exclaimed the landlord, having called a run of three and *belote*. "Even though he's dead, there's no denying he was as pigheaded as they come."

"In what way?"

"Well, for one thing, he moaned and groaned from morning to night, about anything and everything. He was never satisfied. . . . Well! Take that business over the glasses. . . ."

He appealed to the others for confirmation.

"First, he complained that my liqueur glasses were too thick, and he went and rummaged on my shelves till he found an odd one right at the back that suited him. Then, one day, by pouring his drink from his own glass into one of the others, he found that they held exactly the same amount, and he was furious.

" 'Well, seeing you chose that particular glass yourself!' I protested.

"And the upshot was that he went into town and bought another glass, and brought it to me. And that one held nearly half as much again as mine did.

" 'I don't mind,' I said, 'so long as you pay me an extra twenty-five centimes.'

"After that, I didn't set eyes on him again for a whole week. Then one evening, there he was, standing in the doorway.

" 'Will you fill my glass?'

" 'For an extra twenty-five centimes,' I repeated.

"So he went away again. This went on for a whole month, and I was the one who had to give way in the end, because we needed him to make a fourth at cards.

"Doesn't that prove my point, that he was as pigheaded as they come? And he was the same with his servant girl. They were at loggerheads from morning to night. You could hear them at it for miles. Then one of them would sulk, and it would go on for weeks at a time. In the long run, though, I think she got the better of him, because, saving your presence, she's even more pigheaded than he was. Still, I would like to know who killed the poor fellow. He wasn't a bad man, at heart. . . . It was just the way he was made. He never played a hand at cards without complaining, at some point, that someone was cheating."

A little while later, Maigret asked:

"Did he often go to Paris?"

"Practically never. Just once a quarter, to collect his compensation. He used to go there and back in a day."

"And Félicie?"

"Say, fellows, do any of you know whether Félicie ever went to Paris?"

They had no information on this point. On the other hand, they knew that she often went dancing on Sunday at a dance hall on the waterfront at Poissy.

"Do you know what the old man called her? He always referred to her as his 'Poll Parrot,' because of the peculiar clothes she wears. You see, Chief Superintendent—this won't please my good friend Forrentin, but I speak as I find—everybody who lives in Jeanneville is more or less crazy. It's not a real community. It's full of poor devils who have scrimped and saved all their lives to buy a little place in the country for their retirement. Well, when the day comes, they fall for Forrentin's glowing sales talk. . . . Don't attempt to deny it, Forrentin. You know very well you're a wizard at gilding the pill. . . . So there they are at last in their earthly paradise, and it doesn't take them long to find out that all they have bought is damned boredom at a hundred francs an hour. . . .

"Only, by then it's too late. They've invested the whole of their miserable pittance in the place, and they have to find their fun where they can get it, or manufacture it as best they can. . . . One will go to law over the branch of a tree overhanging his garden, another because some dog has cocked its leg against his begonias . . . and some . . ."

Maigret was not asleep, and, to prove it, he stretched out his arm for his glass and raised it to his lips. But the heat had made him drowsy, and he allowed his thoughts to drift back gently to Jeanneville. Bit by bit, he reconstructed it in his mind, its unfinished avenues, its infant trees, its houses, seemingly built of boy bricks, its tiny, carefully tended gardens, its clay animals and glass witch balls.

"Did he never have any visitors?"

It didn't make sense. Such a quiet, uneventful, self-contained existence. If there had really been no more to his life than that, surely it was inconceivable that one morning, only last Monday, in fact, while Félicie was out doing her shopping at Mélanie Chochoi's grocery store, Peg Leg should suddenly have been impelled to abandon his tomato plants, go to the sideboard in the dining room, get out the bottle of brandy and a glass, and then sit all by himself in the summerhouse, sipping the brandy normally reserved for very special occasions. And, after that . . .

He had been wearing his gardening hat when he went upstairs to his bedroom, with its highly polished floor. What had he gone there for?

No one had heard the shot, and yet a revolver had been fired by someone, at point-blank range, someone who, according to the ballistics report, had been standing less than two feet away from the old man.

At least if the revolver had been found, it might have been supposed that Peg Leg had gone out of his mind and . . .

The Deputy Mayor, adding up his score, was troubled by no such doubts. He murmured, as if it explained everything:

"What is there to say? He was an eccentric."

Very true. But he was dead. Someone had killed him. And Félicie, looking as if butter wouldn't melt in her mouth, as usual, had given the police the slip right after the funeral, and hitched a lift to Paris, where she had gazed in the shopwindows, just as if nothing had happened, and eaten cream puffs, had a glass of port, and, to crown it all, gone for a joy ride on the Métro!

"I wonder who'll get the house?"

The cardplayers chatted intermittently. To Maigret, who was not listening, their voices provided a background murmur to his thoughts. He did not tell them that the house now belonged to Félicie. He was drifting. Impressions formed and dissolved. He had lost all sense of time and place. Félicie, by now, was probably in bed, reading. Being left all alone in the house where her employer had been murdered did not seem to worry her. . . . Ernest Lapie, the dead man's brother, chagrined by the terms of the will . . . He was not short of money, but it was beyond him why his brother . . .

"It's a well-built house. The best in the development."

Who had said that? Forrentin, probably.

"And what's more, it's got charm. It's a convenient size, too, spacious and yet compact."

Maigret recalled the gleaming staircase. Whatever might be

said of Félicie, no one could deny that she kept the place spotlessly clean. As Maigret's mother used to say, you could eat off the floor.

A door on the right . . . the old man's bedroom . . . A door on the left . . . Félicie's . . . Adjoining Félicie's bedroom, another room, much larger, crammed with furniture.

Maigret frowned. You couldn't call it a presentiment, still less an idea. It was no more than a vague feeling that there was something not quite right about the setup.

"In the young man's time . . ." Lepape remarked.

Maigret started.

"The nephew, do you mean?"

"Yes. He lived with his uncle for six months or more. . . . It must have been about a year ago. . . . He was in poor health. Apparently it was thought that a spell in the country might do him good, after living in Paris all that time."

"Where did he sleep?"

"Ah! There you have it. . . . It's sort of a joke, really."

Lepape winked. Forrentin looked disapproving. It was plain to see that the manager frowned on gossip concerning the development over which, in his own estimation, he held absolute dominion.

"That doesn't mean a thing," he protested.

"Well, was there or was there not anything between the old man and Félicie? See here, Chief Superintendent, you know the layout of the house. Upstairs on the right, there is one bedroom, the one occupied by Peg Leg. On the opposite side there are two rooms, but you have to go through the first one to get to the second. Well, when the young man moved in, his uncle put him in his own bedroom, and moved in across the way. In other words, to all intents and purposes, he moved in with Félicie. He slept in the first room, and she moved into the one beyond, which meant that to get to and from her own bedroom she had to go through the old man's. . . ."

Forrentin was affronted.

"Would it have been preferable, do you think, to put an eighteen-year-old youth in with the girl?"

"Not at all, not at all," protested Lepape, looking sly. "I'm not making any insinuations. All I'm saying is that the old man was sleeping next door to Félicie, while the nephew was well out of the way across the landing. As to any suggestion that there was something funny going on . . ."

Maigret, for his part, was not thinking along these lines. Not that he had any illusions about the proclivities of elderly or even quite old men. And besides, Peg Leg was only sixty, and a vigorous sixty at that.

It was just that the notion did not fit with the view he personally had formed of the man. He felt he was beginning to understand this cross-grained recluse, whose hat he had recently worn.

Whatever it was that was worrying him, it was not the old man's relationship with Félicie. What was it, then? It had something to do with the layout of the rooms.

He repeated to himself, like a schoolboy, memorizing a lesson:

"The nephew on the right . . . all alone . . . the uncle on the left, and then Félicie . . ."

So the uncle had interposed himself between the two of them. Had he wanted to prevent the young people from getting together behind his back? Had his idea been to keep Félicie on a tight rein? No, because as soon as his nephew left the house, he had returned to his former quarters, and left her to her own devices on the other side of the landing.

"Let it rest for tonight, Chief."

He stood up. He was going upstairs to bed. He could hardly wait for tomorrow, when he would return to the toy village and once more see the little brick cottages, rosy in the sunlight, and take another look at those three bedrooms. But first, he would put a call through to Janvier in Paris, to tell him to find out all he could about the young man.

Up to now, Maigret had scarcely given him a thought. No one had seen him in Jeanneville on the morning of the murder. He was a tall, thin youth, high-strung, unlikely to do much good, but Maigret could not see him committing a murder.

According to report, his mother, Lapie's sister, had married a violinist, who used to perform in cheap local restaurants. He had died young. In order to support her son, she had taken a job as a cashier with a textile firm on Rue du Sentier, and she, in her turn, had died, two years ago.

A few months after her death, Lapie had taken the young man into his home. They had not seen eye to eye, which was not surprising. Jacques Pétillon was a musician, like his father before him, and Peg Leg was not the man to put up with the scraping of a violin or the blaring of a saxophone in his house.

Now, Jacques Pétillon earned his living as a saxophone player in a nightclub on Rue Pigalle. He lived in a furnished room on the sixth floor of a boardinghouse on Rue Lepic.

Maigret sank into the soft feather mattress on his bed and fell asleep, with mice scampering about all night above his head. The room had a wholesome country smell, a compound of hay and mildew, and in the morning he awoke to the lowing of cows, and the wheezing of the local bus as it approached the Anneau d'Or. Then he breathed in the aroma of coffee laced with brandy.

About those bedrooms . . . But first he must telephone Janvier.

"Hello . . . The address is the Hotel Beauséjour, Rue Lepic. . . . Good hunting, old boy."

And he lumbered off to Jeanneville, whose rooftops seemed to grow out of an undulating sea of oats. As he ambled along, a very odd thing happened. He quickened his pace and peered ahead, eager for his first sight of the windows of Cape Horn, and for . . . Well, yes! It must be admitted. Eager for his first sight of Félicie. He could picture her already at work in her kitchen, with her sharp features and her nanny-goat forehead, receiving him as rudely as she knew how, and gazing at him out of her clear, inscrutable eyes.

Was he already beginning to miss her?

He understood, he guessed, he was certain that Peg Leg had needed this dear enemy as much as he had needed his glass of wine from the barrel, the air he breathed, his nightly game of cards, and his squabbles with his partners over a run of three or a trump.

In the distance, he could see Lucas stamping up and down in the lane. It must have been a chilly night for him, keeping watch out there. And then, through the open window of her bedroom, he saw tendrils of dark hair escaping from a turban of sorts, then a tense figure shaking out bedding. He had been seen. He had been recognized. Doubtless, the question of how he should be received was already being considered.

In spite of himself, he smiled. Félicie was there, all right!

3

THE DIARY

"Hello! is that you, Chief? . . . Janvier speaking . . ."

The day was oppressive. It was not just that there was thunder in the air, or that, every now and then, Maigret had to wipe a thin film of perspiration from his face, or that his fingers were twitching with impatience. It reminded him a little of the distress he used to feel as a child when he happened to be where he ought not to have been and knew perfectly well that he was wanted elsewhere.

"Where are you calling from?"

"Rue des Blancs-Manteaux. I'm speaking from a small watchmaker's shop. . . .Our friend is all alone in a filthy bistro opposite. He seems to be waiting for something or someone. He's just had another glass of brandy."

A pause. Maigret knew very well what the Inspector was going to say next.

"I was wondering, Chief . . . don't you think you'd better come yourself and . . . ?"

The pressure had been on him since early that morning, but Maigret had stubbornly continued to resist it.

"Carry on the good work. Call me if there are any new developments."

Was he doing the right thing, he wondered. Was this really the proper way to go about things? And yet he could not bring himself to leave Jeanneville. Something was holding him back, though just what it was, he could not say.

A very odd case this was turning out to be. Fortunately for him, the press had shown no interest in Peg Leg's death. At least twenty times he had caught himself muttering under his breath: "And yet the old man *was* murdered."

It was as if the murder was somehow of secondary importance, as if, in spite of himself, he was obsessed with quite a different problem. And that problem, needless to say, was Félicie.

The landlord of the Anneau d'Or had lent him an old bicycle. Astride it, Maigret looked like a performing bear. But it enabled him to go back and forth between Orgeval and the housing development as often as he pleased.

The weather was still glorious. Spring and sunshine would always be associated in his mind with this locality. Flowers growing all along the low garden walls, and in the beds and borders. Retired people whose hobby was gardening turning their heads indolently to watch the Chief Superintendent or Sergeant Lucas go by, for Maigret had decided to keep Lucas with him.

Lucas also was of the opinion that this was an odd way of going about things, but he kept his thoughts to himself. He was fed up with pacing up and down outside Cape Horn. What was he supposed to be doing there, anyway? Keeping an eye on Félicie? All the windows in the house were open. The girl could be plainly seen going about her business. She had gone out to do her shopping as usual. She knew that she was being followed. Was it thought that she might try to slip away again?

Lucas was puzzled, but he dared not say anything to Maigret. He just champed at the bit, smoked his pipe endlessly, and occasionally relieved his feelings by kicking a pebble.

And yet, since early this morning, it had seemed that the center of interest had shifted away from Jeanneville. The first phone call had come from Rue Lepic. Maigret had been waiting for it, seated on the terrace of the inn, beside a bay tree in a green-painted tub.

He had already established a routine, as he always did, wherever he happened to be. He had an arrangement with the postmistress that she would give him a shout from the window as soon as any call came through from Paris.

"Is that you, Chief? . . . Janvier speaking . . . I'm calling from a café on the corner of Rue Lepic. . . ."

Maigret could see it all: the steep little street, the pushcarts piled high with fruit and vegetables, the housewives in their down-at-heel slippers, the colorful hubbub of Place Blanche, and, wedged between two small shops, the Hotel Beauséjour, which he had had occasion to visit in the course of duty more than once in the past.

"Jacques Pétillon didn't get home until six o'clock this morning. He was exhausted. He threw himself on his bed fully dressed. I went to the Pélican, the dive where he works. He hadn't been there all night. What shall I do?"

"Stay where you are. . . . If he goes out, follow him."

Could it be that the nephew was less innocent than he seemed? In any case, Maigret would surely do better to give serious consideration to him instead of concentrating on Félicie. It was plain that this was Janvier's opinion. In the course of his second telephone call, he ventured to hint as much.

"Hello! Janvier speaking . . . The young man has just gone into the tobacconist's on Rue Fontaine. He's as white as a sheet, and he seems very jumpy and uneasy. . . . He keeps looking around, as if he suspected he was being followed, but I don't think he's spotted me. . . ."

So, Pétillon, after snatching a few brief hours of sleep, was on the move again. The tobacconist's shop on Rue Fontaine was the haunt of some pretty unsavory characters.

"What's he doing?"

"He hasn't spoken to anyone. . . . He's watching the door. . . . It looks as if he's waiting for someone. . . ."

"Keep at it. . . ."

In the meantime, Maigret had learned a few more facts about old Lapie's nephew. Why was it that he could not seem to work up an interest in this boy, whose ambition it was to become a famous soloist, and who barely managed to scrape a living by playing the saxophone in a nightclub in Montmartre?

Pétillon had been through some hard times. More than once, he had been forced to take on casual night work as a vegetable porter in Les Halles. Often, he had had to go hungry. And, several times, he had been reduced to pawning his violin.

"Don't you think it's odd, Chief, that he should have been out the whole night, and not set foot in the Pélican, and that now . . . ? I wish you could see him. . . . You ought to see him. . . . He's in torment. He's terrified. You can feel it. . . . Maybe if you could get here . . ."

But Maigret's answer was always the same.

"Keep at it!"

Maigret, in the meantime, perched on his bicycle, plied to and fro between the terrace of the Anneau d'Or, where he sat waiting for phone calls, and Félicie's blue cottage.

He wandered about the place as if he owned it. Félicie went on with her housework, pretending to ignore him. She cooked her meal, having bought what she needed in the morning at Mélanie Chochoi's shop. Sometimes her eyes would meet those of the Chief Superintendent, but he still found it impossible to tell what her feelings were.

As Maigret saw it, she was the one who ought to be afraid. She had been altogether too sure of herself, right from the start. Unless she had something to hide, her attitude simply didn't make sense, and he was watching her for the first cracks to appear.

"And yet, the old man *was* murdered."

He could not get her out of his mind. She held the vital clue, and he was determined to wrest it from her. He roamed around the garden. Five or six times he went to the cellar and helped himself to a glass of *vin rosé*. This, too, had become a part of his routine. He had made a discovery. Poking about with a fork in the compost heap near the hedge, he had unearthed a liqueur glass similar to the one he had seen that first day on the table in the summerhouse. He had shown it to Félicie.

"All you have to do is have it tested for fingerprints," she had remarked contemptuously, as if it were no concern of hers.

When he went upstairs to the bedrooms, she did not follow him. He made a thorough search of Lapie's room, and then crossed the landing and began looking through Félicie's drawers.

No doubt she could hear him moving about from downstairs. Was she at all apprehensive?

The weather was still perfect, very mild, with a gentle, sweet-scented breeze and bird song coming in through the windows.

Presently, searching through an untidy jumble of stockings and underclothes at the bottom of Félicie's wardrobe, he came upon a diary. He could see why Peg Leg had called her his Poll Parrot. Even her underclothes were in garish colors, shocking pink and acid green, with six-inch insertions of imitation lace.

Hoping by so doing to provoke her, Maigret went down to the kitchen with the diary in his hand. It was dated the previous year. Félicie was engaged in peeling potatoes into a blue enamel basin.

"*13 January*. Why doesn't he come?

"*15 January*. Implored him.

"*19 January*. Tortured by uncertainty. Is it his wife?

"*20 January*. Misery.

"*23 January*. At last!

"*24 January*. Bliss!

"*25 January*. More bliss!

"*26 January*. Him again. His lips, heaven!

"*27 January*. Life is unfair.

"*29 January*. Oh, to escape—to escape!"

Every now and then, Maigret looked up from his reading, but Félicie pretended to ignore him.

Maigret affected to laugh. It was a laugh that sounded false in his ears and made him feel like a hotel guest fumbling with the chambermaid and covering it up with a lewd jest.

"What's his name?"

"It's none of your business."

"Married, is he?"

A savage look, like a cat defending its kittens.

"The grand passion, was it?"

She did not reply, but he kept on, feeling ashamed of himself for his persistence. He told himself that it was wrong. He thought of Rue Lepic and Rue Fontaine, and the terrified young man who, ever since last night, had been scurrying hither and thither.

"Now then, my dear, you may as well tell me. Did this man come to visit you here?"

"Why shouldn't he?"

"Was your employer aware of it?"

No! He had had enough of this. The girl was making a fool of him. Not that he expected to fare much better with Mélanie Chochoi, but still, she was next on his list. He propped his bicycle against the front of the shop and waited until Mélanie had finished serving a woman who wanted a can of peas.

"By the way, Madame Chochoi, do you happen to know if Monsieur Lapie's housekeeper had many men friends?"

"I suppose so."

"What do you mean by that?"

"Well, she told me so at any rate. . . . And there was one in particular. . . . But it's not really my business, is it? She seemed very unhappy a lot of the time, poor girl. . . ."

"Was he a married man?"

"Very likely . . . She was always hinting at obstacles. . . . She didn't tell me much, really. . . . If she confided in anyone, it would have been Monsieur Forrentin's maid, Léontine."

A man had been murdered, and here was Maigret, a mature, serious-minded man, concerning himself with the love life of a silly, romantic girl! How foolishly romantic, the entries in her diary showed all too plainly.

"*17 June.* Misery.

"*18 June.* Feeling very blue.

"*21 June.* Happiness is a delusion. There is not enough in the world to go around.

"*22 June.* I love him.

"*23 June.* I love him."

Maigret went to Forrentin's house and rang the doorbell. The development manager's maid, Léontine, was a moon-faced girl in her twenties. She was scared at the very sight of him. The last thing she wanted was to get her friend into trouble.

"Of course, she always told everything. Everything she wanted to tell me, that is . . . She often stopped by to see me, just for a quick visit. . . ."

He could see the two of them so clearly, Léontine with her

mouth hanging open in wonder, and Félicie with her coat draped negligently over her shoulders.

"Are you alone? If only you knew."

She would talk and talk, as girls do among themselves.

"I've seen him. . . . I'm so happy."

Poor Léontine was thrown into confusion by Maigret's questions.

"I won't say a thing against her. . . . Félicie has suffered so much!"

"On account of a man?"

"Several times she threatened to kill herself."

"Didn't he return her affection?"

"I don't know. . . . Please don't badger me."

"Do you know his name?"

"She never told me."

"Did you ever see him?"

"No."

"Where did they meet?"

"I don't know."

"Was she his mistress?"

Léontine blushed, and stammered:

"She did say, once, that if she ever had a child . . . What has all this got to do with the old man being murdered?"

Maigret kept going, but he was more and more conscious of a vague, unhappy feeling that he had blundered.

Oh, what the hell! Here he was back on the terrace of the Anneau d'Or. The postmistress called out to him:

"There have been two calls for you from Paris already. I'm expecting them to call back again any minute."

Janvier again. But no, it was not his voice. It was a voice the Chief Superintendent did not recognize.

"Hello! Is that Monsieur Maigret?"

So it could not be anyone from the Quai des Orfèvres.

"I'm a waiter in the buffet at the Gare Saint-Lazare. . . . I'm calling on behalf of a gentleman who asked me to tell you . . . Wait a minute. . . . His name escapes me. . . . It was the name of a month. . . . Février . . ."

"Janvier."

"That's it. . . . He's on his way by train to Rouen. He couldn't wait to speak to you himself. . . . He wondered whether you could possibly meet his train at Rouen. He said if you were to hire a car . . ."

"Any other message?"

"No, sir. I've told you what he said. There wasn't anything else."

It could mean only one thing. If Janvier has decided on the spur of the moment to take the train to Rouen, it must be because Pétillon is on it. Hastily emerging from the telephone booth, which was stifling, he mopped his face and stood as if uncertain what to do next, under the inquisitive eyes of the postmistress. A car . . . He might manage to get hold of one. . . .

"No, damn it all," he grumbled. "Janvier can figure it out for himself."

Searching the three bedrooms had yielded nothing, apart from Félicie's diary. Poor Lucas, bored and disgusted, was still kicking his heels outside Cape Horn, peered at by the neighbors behind their net curtains.

Instead of rushing off to track down the mysterious nephew, Maigret sat down to a meal on the terrace of the inn, sipped his coffee, washed it down with a glass of old brandy, and then, with a sigh, remounted his bicycle. He stopped at the cottage to slip Lucas a package of sandwiches, and then rode down the hill to Poissy.

It did not take him long to locate the dance hall where Félicie spent most of her free Sundays. It was a wooden building overlooking the Seine. At this time of day it was deserted, and it was the proprietor himself, an Indian in a sweater, who came out to ask him his business. Five minutes later, seated at a table over a couple of drinks, the two men realized that they had met before. It was a familiar experience for Maigret. The man who now made his living by running a Sunday dance hall had formerly been a fairground wrestler, and had got into trouble with the police. He recognized the Chief Superintendent first.

"You're not here on my account, I trust. As you can see, it's all open and aboveboard here."

"I don't doubt it," said Maigret, with a smile.

"As for the customers . . . No, Chief Superintendent, I doubt if you'll find anything to interest you here. . . . Salesgirls, housemaids, decent young boys . . ."

"Do you know a girl named Félicie?"

"Who's she?"

"An odd sort of girl, thin as a stick, with a pointed nose and a forehead like a nanny goat's, always decked out in all the colors of the rainbow, like a ship dressed for a review . . ."

"You mean the Parakeet!"

Well, of course. Lapie's name for Félicie had been Poll Parrot.

"What has she done?"

"Nothing . . . I just wanted to know about the people she came into contact with here."

"I can't think of anyone really. My wife . . . No, you won't ever have heard of her; she's on the level. . . . My wife, as I was saying, called her the Princess, on account of her la-di-da airs and ways. Who exactly is she, anyway? I never could find out. . . . She really did carry on as if she was royalty. When she danced, she held herself as stiff as a poker. When she was asked about herself, she let it be understood that she was not what she seemed, but that she wished to remain incognito. A load of crap, in other words . . . Come to think of it, she always sat at this table, all by herself. She always sipped her drink with her little finger stuck out. . . . Her ladyship wouldn't dream of dancing with just anybody who . . . Last Sunday . . . Bless my soul! I've just remembered. . . ."

Maigret could picture the crowded dance floor and the bouncing wooden planks, the loud strains of the accordion, and the proprietor standing with his hands on his hips, waiting to go around the tables collecting the money.

"She danced with a fellow I'd seen somewhere before, though I can't for the life of me remember where. . . . He was short and thickset, with a crooked nose. . . . But that's not the point. . . . What I did notice was that he held her very close. Then suddenly, right there in the middle of the dance floor, she slapped his face. I thought there was going to be trouble, and I was going to intervene. But not at all. The fellow just slunk off without a word of protest, and her ladyship, all high and mighty, returned to her seat and proceeded to powder her nose. . . ."

By now, Janvier must have been in Rouen for some hours. Maigret propped his bicycle against the terrace of the Anneau d'Or and went across the road to speak to the postmistress. It was refreshingly cool in there.

"Any calls for me?"

"Just one message, asking you to call Police Headquarters in Rouen. Shall I get them for you?"

It was not Janvier who answered, but one of the local inspectors.

"Chief Superintendent Maigret? I have a message for you. The young man, after wandering in and out of a dozen or so bars in Montmartre, took the train to Rouen. Apparently, he spoke to no one, although he seemed to be looking for someone wherever he went. When he got to Rouen, he made straight for the Barracks. He went into a brasserie nearby, a place frequented by prostitutes. . . . I daresay you know of it, the Tivoli. . . . He stayed there about half an hour, then wandered about for a while, and finally ended up at the station. He seemed more and more worn out and discouraged. . . . At present, he's waiting for the train to Paris, and Inspector Janvier is still tailing him."

Maigret gave the usual instructions: the proprietress of the brasserie was to be questioned as to which particular girl Pétillon had come to see, what his business with her had been, and so forth. . . . While he was still in the telephone booth, he heard a rumbling sound, which he took to be a passing bus, but which he realized, when he came out, was distant thunder.

"Are you expecting any more calls?" asked the postmistress, who had never experienced such hustle and bustle in all her uneventful life.

"Very possibly. My sergeant will be taking over for me."

"How fascinating police work must be! We've never seen anything like it, in this quiet little backwater of ours."

He smiled absently, suppressing the temptation to shrug his shoulders, and was soon back once more on the unfinished road leading to the development.

"Sooner or later she'll talk; she must!" he repeated to himself along the way.

There was a storm brewing. Menacing purple clouds were massing on the horizon, the slanting sunbeams seemed to have narrowed, and the atmosphere was oppressive.

"Go back to the Anneau d'Or, Lucas, and wait there in case there are any telephone messages. . . ."

His expression, as he opened the door of Cape Horn, was resolute. He had been put upon long enough. He had reached his limit! He was going to confront that miserable girl once and for all and, if necessary, shake her until her eyes popped out of her head.

"This is it, my dear! Playtime is over!"

She was there all right. He knew she was. He had seen the ground-floor curtain twitch while he was giving Lucas his instructions. He went in. Silence. In the kitchen, a pot of coffee was percolating. In the garden, no one. He frowned.

"Félicie," he called softly. "Félicie."

Then angrily, on a rising note, he shouted:

"Félicie!"

For an instant, he was almost persuaded that she had got the better of him again, and slipped through his fingers a second time. But no, he could hear a faint sound upstairs, not unlike the cry of a tiny baby. He took the stairs two at a time and came to a halt in the doorway of Félicie's bedroom when he saw her lying full-length on her couch.

She was crying, with her face buried in the pillow, and at that same moment big raindrops began to fall, and a door, somewhere in the house, was slammed shut by a sudden gust of wind.

"What's the matter?" he growled.

She did not move. Her back shook with sobs. He touched her on the shoulder.

"What's wrong, child?"

"Leave me alone. . . . For God's sake, leave me alone!"

It crossed his mind that this was all just an act, that Félicie had picked her moment, and even arranged herself in this touching attitude, with her dress artfully hitched up well above her bony knees. But he dismissed the thought.

"Get up, my dear."

Well, well! She was actually doing as she was told. The last thing he expected from Félicie was meek, unprotesting obedience. And here she was, sitting on the edge of the couch, her eyes brimming with tears, her face streaked with rouge, gazing at him with such a miserable, weary expression that it made him feel like an absolute brute.

"What's the matter? Come on, now. Tell me all about it."

She shook her head. She was incapable of speech. She made him understand that she would be only too willing to talk if only she could, and then, once more, buried her face in her hands.

Standing looming over her in this small room, he felt disproportionately massive, so he drew up a chair, sat down at the foot of her couch, and considered taking hold of her hands and pulling them away from her tear-stained face. For he did not yet quite trust her. It would not altogether have surprised him to discover that, behind those nervously cupped hands, she was smiling sarcastically.

But her tears were genuine. She was crying like a child, unmindful of the ravages to her face. And when at last she spoke, she sounded like a child as well:

"Why are you so horrid to me?"

"Me, horrid! Not at all, child . . . Take it easy, now. Don't you see that I only want what's best for you?"

She shook her head.

"Heavens above! Can't you realize that a murder has been committed, and that you are the only person familiar enough with the ways of this house to . . . I'm not for a moment suggesting that you killed your employer. . . ."

"He wasn't my employer!"

"I know. You told me. . . . Let's say your father, then. . . . Because that's what you've been hinting at all along, isn't it? Very well, let us suppose that old Lapie committed an indiscretion years ago, and later made up for it by taking you into his home. . . . You are his sole heir. . . . You are the only one to benefit from his death."

He was forcing the pace too much. She sprang to her feet and stood straight and stiff as a ramrod, the very embodiment of righteous indignation.

"But it is so, child. Come on now, sit down. On the face of it, you ought to be under arrest."

"I'm quite ready."

Good God! How impossible she was! Maigret would have been happier with the most hardened of hardened criminals, the most intransigent of recidivists. How could one possibly tell when she was playacting and when she was genuine? Was she ever wholly genuine? Even now he could feel that she was watching him the whole time, watching him with quite terrifying penetration.

"That's beside the point. What we need is your help. The man who took advantage of your absence to kill your employer— sorry, to kill Jules Lapie, I mean—must have known enough about your household routine to . . ."

Wearily, she had sat down again on the edge of the couch. She murmured:

"I'm listening."

"And besides, Lapie would never have taken a complete stranger up to his bedroom. . . . He was killed in his bedroom. . . . What could he possibly have been doing there at that hour of the morning? He was working in his garden. He had offered a drink to his visitor, in spite of his known stinginess in such matters. . . ."

Every now and then Maigret almost had to shout to be heard above the noise of the thunder. Then, after an especially loud clap, she put out her hand instinctively, and grasped him by the wrist.

"I'm scared."

She was trembling. She really was trembling.

"You have nothing to fear. I'm here."

What an idiotic thing to say! He realized it almost before the words were out of his mouth. Quick to sense his sympathy, she took full advantage of it, assumed a piteous expression, and bleated:

"You have hurt me so! And now you're going to hurt me again. I'm so unhappy. . . . Dear God! How miserable I am! . . . And you . . . you . . ."

She gazed at him in wide-eyed supplication.

"You keep picking on me because I'm a weak, defenseless girl with no one to protect me. . . . You've had a man out there all night and all day, and he'll be back again tonight."

"What is the name of the man whose face you slapped at the dance hall last Sunday?"

For an instant she looked put out, then she sniggered.

"You see!"

"What's that supposed to mean?"

"It's always me. . . . You bully me and bully me, as if . . . as if you hated me. . . . What have I ever done to you? Yes, I beg you, tell me what harm I have ever done to you?"

At this point Maigret ought to have stood up, asserted himself, and put an end to all this nonsense once and for all. He had had every intention of doing so, thankful at least that there were no witnesses to his absurd scene. But he missed his chance. He was half out of his chair when another roll of thunder gave Félicie an excuse for a fresh outburst of hysteria. She threw herself into his arms and, with her face so close to his that he could feel her hot breath on his cheek, she cried:

"Is it because I'm a woman? Are you another of those men like Forrentin?"

"What's wrong with Forrentin?"

"He wants me. . . . He pesters me. . . . He says that sooner or later he will have his way, and that, in the end, I . . ."

There might be some truth in it. Maigret recalled the manager's face, his furtive smile, his coarse, sensual hands.

"If that's what you want, say so! I'd rather that than . . ."

"No, child, no."

This time he did manage to get to his feet. He pushed her away from him.

"Let's go downstairs, shall we? There's no point in staying up here."

"You came of your own accord. . . ."

"That doesn't mean that I have to stay, still less that I have any ill intentions such as you suggest. . . . Come on, let's go."

"Just give me time to tidy up."

She went over to the mirror and dabbed her face with powder, sniveling.

"Something terrible is going to happen—I can feel it—and it will be all your fault!"

"What, for instance?"

"I don't know. . . . But I warn you, if they find me dead . . ."

"Don't be so silly. . . . Come along. . . ."

He made her lead the way. The sky was so overcast that he had to switch on the kitchen light. The coffee was simmering on the stove.

"I think I'd be better off away from here," declared Félicie, turning off the gas.

"Where would you go?"

"Anywhere . . . I don't know. . . . Yes, I'll go right away, somewhere where no one will ever find me. . . . I ought never to have come back."

"You'll stay here."

She muttered something between clenched teeth. He was not sure that he had heard her correctly, but he fancied that what she had said was:

"We'll see about that!"

Taking a shot at random, he said:

"If you're thinking of joining young Pétillon, I'd better tell you right away that he is at this moment in Rouen, in a brasserie frequented by prostitutes."

"It's not . . ."

Then, changing her tack:

"What's that to me?"

"Is it he?"

"Is what he? What do you mean?"

"Is he your lover?"

She smiled disdainfully.

"A kid like him! Why, he's barely twenty!"

"At any rate, my poor child, he's the one you're trying to shield."

"I'm not trying to shield anyone. . . . And what's more, I'm not answering any more questions. . . . You've no right to harass me from morning to night, and nag and nag at me. . . . I'll lodge a complaint."

"Go ahead."

"You think you're so clever, don't you? And you're so strong. Well, any fool can bully a poor, helpless girl with no one to protect her."

He put on his hat, having made up his mind that, in spite of the rain, he was going back to the Anneau d'Or. He made for the door, without even bothering to tell her he was leaving. He had had enough. He had got it all wrong. He would have to go right back to the beginning again, and examine the facts from a fresh angle.

To hell with the rain! He took a resolute step forward, only to find Félicie clinging to his arm.

"Please don't go!"

"Why ever not?"

"You know why. . . . Don't go. . . . I'm terrified of thunder."

And it was true. For once, she was not lying. She was trembling from head to foot. Once again, she begged him to stay, and when he did reluctantly return with her to the kitchen and sit down, glowering, but sitting down all the same, she seemed genuinely grateful, and to prove it, she said:

"Would you like a cup of coffee? Can I get you a little glass of something?"

And, with a forced smile, she repeated, as she poured his coffee:

"Why are you so unkind to me? I've never done you any harm. . . ."

4

THE TAXI

MAIGRET WALKED ALONG Rue Pigalle at a leisurely pace, with his hands deep in his coat pockets. It was past midnight, and, following the storm, there was quite a chill in the air, and the streets were still wet in places. By the light of the neon signs the nightclub doormen were quick to recognize him, and the customers standing at the horseshoe-shaped counter of the tobacconist's shop on the corner of Rue Notre-Dame-de-Lorette exchanged inquiring glances. An outsider would have noticed nothing amiss. And yet an almost imperceptible tremor ran through the night spots of Montmartre from end to end, like the breeze on a pond that presages a gale.

Maigret was aware of it. It gave him considerable satisfaction. Here at least was something more manageable than a weeping, defiant girl. He was conscious of shadowy figures slinking past, knew that the word was being passed at lightning speed throughout the cabarets of the district, and that here and there lavatory attendants were hastily concealing little envelopes of "snow."

There to his left was the Pélican, with its blue neon sign and its black doorman. Someone loomed up in front of him out of the shadows, and a voice whispered:

"Am I glad to see you!"

It was Janvier. He went on to say, in those flat tones of his which to some seemed to denote callousness, but which, in fact, were merely a mannerism:

"It's in the bag, Chief. There was just one thing worrying

me . . . that he would crack too soon. . . . He's at the end of his rope."

The two men stood together on the edge of the sidewalk, savoring the night air with apparent enjoyment, and Maigret refilled his pipe.

"Even before we left Rouen, I could see what a state he was in. While we were waiting for the train in the buffet, I kept expecting him to come up and buttonhole me, and get it all off his chest. . . . If ever I saw a loser, he's it. . . ."

Nothing of what was going on around him escaped Maigret. His mere presence there in the street, he knew, was having its effect. How many people with uneasy consciences were quietly making themselves scarce, or finding hiding places for things they did not want found?

"On the train, he collapsed into a heap. . . . When we got to Gare Saint-Lazare, he didn't seem to know what to do next. And besides, he was pretty drunk by then, because he'd been drinking heavily ever since yesterday. . . . Finally he went back to his place on Rue Lepic. Presumably he washed up. Anyway, he changed into his dinner jacket. . . . He picked at some food in a crummy little restaurant on Place Blanche, and then he went to work. Are you going in there? Do you want me with you?"

"Be off with you, and get some sleep, my dear fellow."

If Maigret should have need of anyone, he could always call on the two men he had kept on duty at the Quai des Orfèvres.

"Here goes!" He sighed.

As he went into the Pélican, the doorman rushed up to him, grinning from ear to ear. He shrugged. All this bogus civility was nothing new to him. He refused to surrender his coat to the coatroom attendant. Velvet curtains divided the vestibule from the cabaret. He could already hear the strains of jazz inside. A small bar on the left. Two women yawning, a drunken youth, the proprietor, bowing and scraping.

"Good evening," grunted the Chief Superintendent.

The proprietor, needless to say, was looking uneasy.

"What's up? No unpleasantness, I trust."

"No, no, of course not."

And Maigret, pushing him aside, went across and sat at a corner table not far from the band.

"Would you care for a whisky?"

"Just a small beer, thanks."

"You know very well we don't serve beer."

"A brandy-and-water, then."

It was a sorry sight that met his eyes! Such an exchange of furtive glances. Was there a single genuine customer in the whole of that cramped little room, where shaded lights cast a reddish glow that turned to violet when the band was playing a tango? There were plenty of dance hostesses. Now that they had recognized the new arrival, they were no longer bothering to dance together. One of them even went as far as to get out her crochetwork.

On stage, Pétillon, in his dinner jacket, looked even younger and thinner than he really was. His face was as white as a sheet beneath his long fair hair, and his eyelids were red from fatigue and anxiety. Try as he would, he could not keep his eyes off the Chief Superintendent, waiting patiently in his corner.

Janvier was right; it was in the bag. The signs were unmistakable. Here was a man who had reached the end of his rope. He was falling apart. His head was swimming. There was only one thing he wanted now: to unburden himself of the load on his conscience, and the sooner the better. So much so that at one point it really looked as if Jacques Pétillon was about to lay down his saxophone and hasten to Maigret's side.

It was not a pretty sight, a man convulsed with terror. He was not the first whom Maigret had seen in this state. At times, he himself had cunningly manipulated an interrogation—which might last for twenty hours or more—to induce in his suspect, or, one could almost say, his patient, just such a condition of physical and moral collapse.

In this case he was in no way responsible. As a suspect, Pétillon had not interested him. Instinctively, he had felt that he was of no account. He had ignored him, mesmerized instead by that enigmatic girl, Félicie, whom he could still not get out of his mind.

He sipped his drink. His air of unconcern must have astonished

Pétillon. His hands, with their long thin fingers, were shaking, and the other members of the band were watching him, and exchanging sidelong glances.

What had he been searching for in the past tumultuous forty-eight hours? What desperate hope had he clung to? What face had he expected to see as he watched the comings and goings in a bar or a café, his feverish gaze riveted on the door? Time and time again, he had been disappointed and gone elsewhere to resume his search, finally ending up in Rouen, in a brasserie near the Barracks frequented by prostitutes.

He was squeezed dry. If Maigret had not come for him, he would have given himself up, stumbling up the dusty staircase of Police Headquarters, and demanding to be given a hearing.

This was it! The band was taking a few minutes off. The accordion player went across to the bar for a drink. The others chatted in undertones. Pétillon laid down his instrument and came down the two steps leading from the stage.

"I must talk to you!" he stammered.

The Chief Superintendent replied, sounding very kind and gentle:

"I know, young fellow."

Here? Maigret looked around at the revolting décor. The last thing he wanted was for the poor boy to make a spectacle of himself in public, especially since he was so obviously close to tears.

"Thirsty?"

Pétillon shook his head.

"In that case, let's get out of here."

Maigret paid for his drink, in spite of the proprietor's protests that it was on the house.

"Look, I think the band will have to do without you for the rest of the night. You and I are going to take a little walk, just the two of us. . . . Get your hat and coat, Pétillon."

"I haven't got a coat."

As soon as they were outside, he took a deep breath, as if about to execute a high dive, and began:

"Listen, Chief Superintendent . . . I'll tell you the whole story. . . . I've had about as much as I can take. . . ."

He was trembling from head to foot. The streetlights were no doubt swimming before his eyes. The proprietor of the Pélican and the doorman watched as they walked away.

"Take your time, son."

He was taking him to the Quai des Orfèvres. It would make it easier for both of them. Maigret could not count the number of times he had known a case to end like this, late at night, in his own office, after everyone had gone home except for one man on duty at the desk in the hall. He could not remember how often he had seen the eerie light of his green-shaded lamp reflected on the face of a broken man.

This one was just a boy. Maigret felt disgruntled, reflecting that the characters in this particular drama were a decidedly feeble lot.

"We're going in here. . . ."

He nudged him toward a brasserie on Place Pigalle, feeling badly in need of a glass of beer before hailing a taxi to take them to the Quai des Orfèvres.

"What will you have?"

"Anything. It doesn't matter. . . . I swear to you, Chief Superintendent, that I didn't . . ."

"I know. . . . I know. . . . You'll tell me all about it later. . . . Waiter! Two beers."

Maigret shrugged. Two more people had recognized him, and had abandoned their *soupe à l'oignon* to get away from him.

The hunched back of one of them could be seen in the telephone booth as he called for a taxi.

"Is she your mistress?"

"Who?"

Well, well! The boy really had no idea what he was talking about. There was no mistaking the genuineness of his bewilderment.

"Félicie."

And Pètillon, as if confronted for the first time with a notion that had never even crossed his mind, repeated:

"Félicie, my mistress?"

He was utterly at sea. He had been on the very brink of a sensational confession, and here was this fellow Maigret, who had set half the police force of Paris on his track, and who held his fate in his hands, babbling about his uncle's servant girl!

"I swear to you, Chief Superintendent . . ."

"Good . . . Let's be going, anyway. . . ."

Ears were flapping. Two women nearby, while pretending to repair their make-up, were listening for all they were worth. They would be better off without an audience.

They were out in the street once more. A few yards away, in darkened Place Pigalle, was a taxi stand. Maigret started to raise his arm to summon one. Close by, a policeman on foot patrol gazed absently into space.

And at that precise second, a shot rang out. The Chief Superintendent was conscious, at almost the same moment, of another sound, that of a taxi driving off toward Boulevard Rochechouart.

It all happened so quickly that he did not immediately register the fact that his companion's hand had flown to his chest, and that he was swaying on his feet, groping with his other hand for something to hold on to. Mechanically, he asked:

"Are you hit?"

The policeman hurried off toward the taxi stand. He opened the door of the first cab, sprang into the driver's seat, and drove off fast. The taxi driver, taking it in the right spirit, leaped onto the running board.

Pétillon, his hand pressed to his starched shirt front, fell to the ground. He attempted to cry out, but the only sound he managed to produce was an odd, pitifully faint little gurgle.

Next morning, the newspapers reported the incident baldly in a paragraph inconspicuously tucked away:

Last night, in Place Pigalle, Jacques P., a jazz musician, was shot in the chest by an unknown assailant, who escaped in a taxi. A policeman on duty at the time immediately gave chase, but was unable to catch up with the gunman.

It is presumed that the motive was either revenge or jealousy.

The wounded man, whose condition is said to be serious, was taken to Beaujon Hospital. The police are continuing their inquiries.

It was not wholly accurate. Police handouts to the press seldom are. It was true that Jacques Pétillon was in Beaujon Hospital. It was true that his condition was serious, so serious that it might not be possible to save his life. His left lung had been perforated by a large bullet.

As to the story of the police giving chase, that was a different matter. At the daily briefing that morning, Maigret had sounded bitter when he discussed the matter with the Chief Commissioner.

"I blame myself, Chief. . . . I was dying for a beer, and I persuaded myself that it would give the boy a chance to pull himself together before I brought him here. . . . He was on the verge of collapse. He hadn't had a minute's respite all day. . . . I was wrong, of course. . . .

"The man must have seen his chance, and wasted no time. He wasn't born yesterday, you can be sure of that.

"When I heard the shot, I had no thought but for the boy. . . . I left it to the foot policeman to give chase. . . . Have you read his report? The taxi led him on a wild-goose chase to Place d'Italie, right at the other side of Paris. Then it came to an abrupt stop, and it turned out that there was no one in it but the driver.

"The driver, protesting his innocence, was brought in for questioning. . . . Oh, well, however you look at it, I was well and truly led by the nose. . . ."

Irately, he glanced through the taxi driver's statement.

"I was in my cab at the stand in Place Pigalle when I was approached by a man I didn't know, who offered me two hundred francs to help him play a joke on a friend. That's what he said, anyway. He was to set off a firecracker—his exact words again—and the bang was to be the signal for me to drive at full speed as far as Place d'Italie. . . ."

A little too forthcoming for a taxi driver on the night shift! Still, it would be difficult to prove that he was lying.

"I couldn't see the man very clearly. I was parked in the shadow of the trees, and besides, he was careful to keep his head down. He was broad-shouldered and was wearing a dark suit and a gray hat."

A description that would fit almost anyone!

"I won't forget that setup in a hurry, I can promise you,"

grumbled Maigret. "I can't deny that it was ingenious. The fellow had only to keep out of sight, crouched between two taxis, or in any patch of shade. . . . He shoots. . . . And instantly, the taxi moves off, and, as is to be expected, everyone assumes that the murderer is inside. The policeman on the spot sets off in pursuit, leaving our villain at leisure to slink away or melt into the crowd, as he chooses. . . . The other drivers at the stand have been questioned. None of them saw anything. . . . Except one old fellow—I've known him for years—who thinks he spotted a shadowy figure lurking near the fountain."

And to think that the saxophone player had been ready to talk, willing to tell the whole story, right there in the Pélican, and it had been Maigret himself who had shut him up! Now, God alone could tell when, if ever, it would be possible to take a statement from him.

"What are you proposing to do?"

There was a standard procedure in such cases. The incident had occurred in Montmartre, within a narrowly circumscribed area. The next step was to pull in for questioning some fifty men, all of them known to the police, who had been seen in the locality on the night in question, and who had scurried hither and thither like scalded cats the moment word had got around that Chief Superintendent Maigret was in the vicinity of Place Pigalle.

Some of these men were hardened criminals. Lean on them a little, threaten them with closer investigation into their affairs, and they would be only too willing to tell what they knew.

"I'll put a couple of men on it, Chief. As for myself . . ."

He could not help himself; his thoughts were elsewhere. Right from the start! Ever since he had first set foot in that cardboard cutout of a place called Jeanneville.

Surely his reluctance to leave the vicinity of Cape Horn and Félicie, with all her inconsistencies, had amounted almost to a presentiment?

Events had proved him wrong. It now seemed almost certain that it was in the area of Place Pigalle that the solution to the mystery of old Lapie's death was to be found.

"All the same, I'm going back there."

Pétillon had had time to tell him just one thing: Félicie was not his mistress. He had been flabbergasted at the very suggestion, as if such a thought had never so much as entered his mind.

It was half past eight. Maigret telephoned his wife.

"Is that you? . . . No, nothing special . . . I don't know when I'll be back."

His erratic comings and goings were nothing new to her. He fished a bundle of reports out of his pocket. Among them was one from Rouen, which included the life history of all the women who plied their trade at the Tivoli. Pétillon had not "gone upstairs" with any of them. He had gone into the brasserie and sat down on one of the corner benches upholstered in crimson velvet. Presently, two of the women had gone over to him and sat down on either side of him.

"I'm looking for a girl by the name of Adèle," he had said.

"You've left it a bit late, love. Adèle hasn't worked here for ages. You do mean the little dark one with pear-shaped tits, don't you?"

He didn't know. All he knew was that he was looking for a girl named Adèle who had worked there about a year ago. But she had left some months before, and no one knew where she had gone. It would be a hopeless undertaking to try to track down every Adèle in every brothel in France.

An inspector would be detailed to make a thorough search of the saxophone player's room in Rue Lepic. Janvier, who would not be able to get as much rest as he would have liked, would spend the day combing the Place Pigalle area.

As for Maigret, he took the train once more from Gare Saint-Lazare, got off at Poissy, and toiled up the hill to Jeanneville.

After last night's storm, the grass looked even greener, and the sky a softer blue. Soon the colored houses came into view, and, as he went past her shop, he waved to Mélanie Chochoi, who was looking vacantly out the window.

He was going to see Félicie. He was looking forward to it with pleasure. Why, he wondered. Involuntarily, his pace quickened. He smiled as he thought of Lucas, who was no doubt fed up again after a night spent on guard outside Cape Horn. He could see him in the distance, sitting on the grass verge, with an unlit pipe in his mouth. He must be longing for some sleep and something to eat.

"Well, how are things, my poor Lucas?"

"Dead quiet, Chief. I could do with a cup of coffee and a few hours in bed. . . . But first, coffee."

His eyes were puffy from lack of sleep, his coat crumpled, and his shoes and the bottoms of his trousers spattered with reddish mud.

"It's back to the Anneau d'Or for you. . . . There's been a new development."

"What's happened?"

"The saxophone player has been shot in the chest."

The Chief Superintendent sounded indifferent, but Sergeant Lucas was not deceived, and he went off shaking his head.

Well, here he was! Maigret looked around him with the satisfaction engendered by familiar surroundings, and went toward the front door of the cottage. But, on second thought, no. He decided he would prefer to go around to the back and in through the garden. He opened the gate. The kitchen door stood open.

Then he stood stock still and gaped stupidly, feeling well-nigh uncontrollable laughter rising in his throat. At the sound of his footsteps, Félicie had come to the door, and she stood there in the doorway, her back very straight, looking at him with a severe expression on her face.

But, good God, what was wrong with her? What had she done to her face? Her eyes were swollen and her cheeks streaked with red, but, this time, not from weeping.

As he came nearer, she said, sounding even more acid than usual:

"Well, I hope you're satisfied now."

"What happened? Did you fall downstairs?"

"A fat lot of good it did, leaving a policeman on guard night and day outside the house! Some watchdog! He was asleep at the time, I daresay!"

"See here, Félicie, you'd better stop talking in riddles. You're not trying to tell me . . ."

"That the murderer came here and attacked me? Yes! Isn't that what you wanted?"

Maigret had meant to tell her about the attempted murder of

Pétillon, but he decided to postpone it until he had learned more about what had been happening at Cape Horn.

"Come and sit down. . . . Out here in the garden, yes . . . Don't look like that! Stop glowering at me, do , and just tell me, as calmly as you can, exactly what happened. Last night, when I left here, you were in a highly nervous state. What did you do?"

Contemptuously, she replied:

"Nothing."

"Very well. You had your dinner, I presume. Then you locked up the house and went up to bed. That's right, isn't it? Are you sure you locked all the doors?"

"I always lock the doors before I go to bed."

"So you went to bed. What time was that?"

"I stayed downstairs until the storm was over."

It was true that he had been heartless enough to walk out on her, knowing full well how terrified she was of thunder and lightning.

"Did you have anything to drink?"

"Just some coffee."

"To help you sleep, no doubt! And then?"

"I read."

"For how long?"

"I don't know. Maybe till about midnight. I put the light out. I was sure something dreadful was going to happen. I warned you!"

"Well, now you can tell me all about it."

"You're making fun of me. . . . But I don't care. . . . You think you're so clever, don't you? . . . Sometime later, I heard a sort of scratching sound in Monsieur Lapie's bedroom. . . ."

Maigret did not believe a word of her story, and as he listened, watching her face all the while, he was wondering what she hoped to gain by this new pack of lies. For lying came as naturally to her as breathing. In response to his inquiries, the Superintendent of Police in Fécamp had supplied him over the telephone with certain facts.

Maigret now knew that Félicie's sly hints about her relationship with Jules Lapie were pure invention. She had a perfectly good father and mother of her own. Her mother was a washerwoman, and her father a drunken good-for-nothing, who loafed about the waterfront, doing odd jobs here and there, especially if there was any free drink being handed out. Questioning the neighbors had yielded no results. Even the most blatant gossips could suggest no link between old Lapie and the washerwoman. It was simply that, hearing that his brother was looking for a girl to keep house for him, the ship's carpenter had recommended Félicie, who was employed by him to help part time with the housework.

"You were saying, my child, that you heard a scratching sound. So, naturally, you went straight to the window and called for help to the policeman outside. . . ."

Her only response to this heavy sarcasm was a shake of her head.

"Why ever not?"

"Because."

"Because, I presume, you thought you knew who was in the room next door, and you didn't want him arrested?"

"Maybe."

"Go on."

"I crept out of bed without making a sound."

"And without turning on the light, I don't doubt. Because if you had, Sergeant Lucas would have spotted it. The shutters don't quite meet in the middle. . . . Anyway, you got out of bed. . . . Weren't you frightened? Or is it only thunder and lightning you're afraid of? . . . What happened next? Did you come out of your room?"

"Not right away. I put my ear to the door and listened. I could hear someone moving about across the landing. . . . I heard a chair scrape, and then what sounded like a muffled oath. . . . I realized that the man, whoever it was, had not found what he was looking for, and that he was getting ready to leave."

"Had you locked your bedroom door?"

"Yes."

"And then you opened it and, without any sort of weapon to protect yourself, you flew out to confront the intruder, who might well be the man who had murdered Jules Lapie?"

"Yes."

She spoke defiantly. He gave an admiring little whistle.

"I take it, then, that you were quite confident that he wouldn't harm you? Needless to say, you couldn't possibly have guessed that, at the material time, young Pétillon was miles away in Paris."

Involuntarily she exclaimed:

"What do you know about it?"

"Let's see . . . what time would this have been?"

"I didn't look at the time until *afterward*. By then, it was half past three in the morning. . . . How do you know that Jacques . . . ?"

"Oh, so you're on first-name terms, are you?"

"Oh, for heaven's sake, stop it! If you don't believe me, go away and leave me alone."

"Sorry. I won't interrupt you again. . . . You were very brave. You came out of your room armed only with your courage, and . . ."

"He smashed his fist into my face!"

"And then took to his heels?"

"He ran out through the garden gate. . . . That's how he got in."

Maigret was sorely tempted to say, in spite of the bruises on her face:

"Well, my dear, you might as well know that I don't believe a word of it."

If he had been told that she had inflicted the injuries on herself, he would have been quite prepared to believe it. Why?

But, no sooner had the thought crossed his mind than his eye was caught by something in a flower bed. Following his glance, she saw what he had seen, footprints in the still-damp earth.

Her lips twitched in a little smile, as she said:

"My footprints, would you say?"

He stood up.

"Come with me."

He went into the house. More muddy footprints were clearly to be seen on the highly polished treads of the staircase. He went into the old man's bedroom.

"Did you come in here at all?"

"Yes, but I didn't touch anything."

"This chair here—was it in this same position last night?"

"No. It was over by the window."

It was now pushed up against the huge walnut wardrobe, and besides, mudstains were clearly visible on the rush matting on the floor.

So Félicie had been telling the truth, after all. A man really had broken into Cape Horn in the night, and that man could not possibly have been Pétillon, since he, poor fellow, at the time had been lying on an operating table in Beaujon Hospital.

If Maigret needed further proof, he found it when he got up on the chair and examined the top of the wardrobe, where the thick coating of dust was crisscrossed with finger marks. Maigret noted also that one of the boards had been loosened with a tool of some sort.

He would have to get the Forensic Laboratory people on to it, to take photographs and test for fingerprints, if any.

Looking pensive and wearing a troubled frown, Maigret murmured, as if to himself:

"And you didn't call for help! You knew that there was a policeman right under your window, and you didn't utter a sound. You even took care not to turn on any lights."

"I did in the kitchen, when I went down there to bathe my face in cold water."

"Ah! But then, the kitchen light couldn't be seen from the street, could it? In other words, you deliberately failed to give the alarm. In spite of the fact that he attacked you, you were determined to give your assailant enough time to get away. This morning you got up as usual, as if nothing had happened, and still you said not a word to the Sergeant."

"I knew very well that you would come back!"

In an odd sort of way—he knew that it was childish of him, and was a little ashamed of himself—he felt flattered that she should have waited for him to arrive, rather than turn to Lucas for help. He was even secretly touched by her words:

"I knew very well that you would come back!"

He went out of the room, locking the door behind him. At all events, the mysterious intruder had not extended his search from the top of the wardrobe. No drawers had been opened. Nothing had been disarranged. Which must mean that he knew . . .

When they returned to the kitchen, Félicie glanced at her bruised face in the mirror.

"You told me just now that you were with Jacques last night."

He looked at her searchingly. She was really upset, no doubt about it. She waited in anguish for him to speak. When at last he did, he said, making it sound as casual as he could:

"You assured me yesterday that he was not your lover, that to you he was just a kid. . . ."

She did not reply.

"Last night there was an accident. . . . Some unknown person shot at him in the street."

She gave a cry.

"Is he dead? Tell me! Is Jacques dead?"

He was sorely tempted. When had she ever scrupled to lie to him? In police work, surely everything was permissible in the interests of bringing the criminal to justice? It was on the tip of his tongue to say "yes." How would she react? Who could tell but that . . . ?

But he hadn't the heart to go through with it. She was upset enough already. Turning his head away, he mumbled:

"No, don't distress yourself. . . . He's not dead. Only wounded . . ."

She began sobbing. With her hands to her forehead and her eyes wild, she wailed distractedly:

"Jacques! Jacques! Oh, my darling Jacques!"

In a sudden burst of fury, she turned on this imperturbable man, who persisted in avoiding her eyes:

"And you were there with him, weren't you? And you let it happen! I hate you, do you hear? I hate you. It's all because of you, yes, because of you. . . ."

She collapsed into a chair, and went on sobbing, slumped over the kitchen table with her head against the coffee grinder.

Every now and then, she repeated:

"Jacques! My darling Jacques!"

Was Maigret really as hard-hearted as she supposed? Be that as it may, he stood for a while in the doorway, hardly knowing where to look, then went out into the deserted garden, prowled around for a minute or two, hesitated, peered at his shadow on the ground, and finally went into the cellar and poured himself a glass of wine.

This was not the first time he had seen Félicie cry. But her tears today were of a different kind.

5

NUMBER 13

MAIGRET'S PATIENCE, THAT morning, was inexhaustible. All the same! He had not been able to prevent Félicie from wearing her full mourning outfit, including the absurd flat black hat with the crepe veil, which floated like the draperies on a Grecian frieze. And what on earth had she done to her face? Had she merely tried to cover up her bruises? It was impossible to tell with her, her sense of the dramatic being so highly developed. Whatever the reason, her face was dead white, as thickly daubed with grease and powder as the face of a clown. In the train on the way to Paris she sat motionless, like a priestess, her melancholy gaze fixed on distant horizons, the whole effect deliberately contrived to evoke the response:

"Good God! How she must be suffering! . . . And what admirable self-control! She is the very embodiment of anguish. Our Lady of Sorrows in the flesh!"

And yet, not once did Maigret permit himself so much as the ghost of a smile. When they came to a grocer's in Rue du Faubourg-Saint Honoré, and she wanted to go in, he murmured kindly:

"I don't think he's in a fit condition to eat anything, my dear."

Was he being obtuse, then? No, he understood and, seeing that she persisted, let her have her way. She bought a bunch of the finest Spanish grapes, some oranges, and a bottle of champagne. She insisted on buying flowers as well, a huge bunch of white lilac, and she staggered along, carrying it all herself, and still looking like the Tragic Muse incarnate.

Maigret trotted along at her heels, resigned and indulgent, like any fond papa. He was relieved to find, when they arrived at Beaujon Hospital, that visitors were not admitted at this hour, for, looking the way she did, Félicie would have given the patients a shock. He was, however, able to persuade the house surgeon to arrange for her to catch a glimpse of Jacques Pétillon in his cubicle, which was right at the end of a long corridor, gleaming with glossy paint and filled with stale smells, with open doors at either side, through which could be seen rows of beds, wan faces, and white walls, white linen, and white equipment, too much white altogether, for white, in this place, was the color of pain.

They were kept waiting for some considerable time, and all the while she just stood there, clutching her parcels. At long last, a nurse appeared. She looked at Félicie, gave a little start, and exclaimed:

"I'll take all that stuff. . . . It will do for the children's ward. . . . Shh! You mustn't talk. Don't make a sound."

She opened the door the merest crack, so that Félicie could see little in the darkened cubicle but the dim figure of Pétillon, motionless as a corpse.

Then the nurse shut the door again, whereupon Félicie saw fit to say:

"You will save him, won't you? I beg you, I implore you, do everything you can to save his life."

"But, mademoiselle . . ."

"Spare no expense. . . . Here . . ."

Maigret did not laugh, he did not even smile, when she took a thousand-franc note, folded over many times, and held it out to the nurse.

"If it's a question of money, whatever the amount . . ."

Even though she had never appeared more extravagantly ridiculous, she was no longer a figure of fun to Maigret. More than that, he felt positively protective toward her. As they went back down the corridor, with Félicie's black veil floating luxuriantly behind her, a child stepped into her path. She bent down to kiss the little patient, and sighed.

"Poor little mite!"

Surely the suffering of others is especially painful to those who have themselves suffered? Close by stood a young nurse with platinum-blonde hair, wearing an outrageously tight and reveal-ing coverall. She watched the scene with a barely stifled giggle, and called out to a colleague in one of the wards to come and see the fun.

"You ought to be ashamed of yourself, young woman!" admon-ished Maigret. And he stalked off with Félicie like a hen with one chick. Félicie had heard the reprimand, and she was grateful to him. Outside in the sunlit street, she was visibly more relaxed. She seemed to feel that there was a kind of bond between them, and he took advantage of this to murmur:

"You know the whole truth, don't you?"

She did not deny it. Shamefacedly, she averted her eyes.

"Come on."

It was a little short of midday. Maigret decided to take a turning to the right and join the noisy and colorful throng in Place des Ternes. She followed him, teetering on her excessively high heels.

"But you won't get anything out of me," she said a few mo-ments later.

"I know."

By now, he knew a great many things. He did not yet know the name of old Lapie's murderer, or of the man who had shot the saxophone player the previous night, but that was only a matter of time.

What he did know was that Félicie . . . How could he express it? On the train, for instance, the other people in the car, observ-ing her theatrical pose of frozen grief, had thought her absurd; in the hospital, the pert little nurse had giggled helplessly; the proprietor of the dance hall in Poissy had nick-named her the Parakeet; others called her the Princess; and Lapie had called her his Poll Parrot. Maigret himself had been thoroughly irritated by her childish posturing.

Even now, people were turning around to look at them, and

they certainly did make an odd couple. And when Maigret ushered her into a little restaurant, mostly patronized by regulars, but empty at this time of day, he caught the waiter winking at the proprietor, seated behind the cash desk.

What Maigret had discovered was quite simply that under even the most preposterous exterior, there beats a human heart.

"What do you say to having a nice, quiet lunch with me?"

Mechanically, she repeated:

"I won't tell you anything, just the same."

"I understand, child. You won't tell me anything. What will you have to eat?"

The little restaurant was cozy and rather shabby, with yellowing white walls, and a number of large, somewhat tarnished mirrors. Here and there stood globular nickel-plated receptacles, in which the waiter disposed of the dirty table linen. Behind the cash desk were pigeonholes, painted to look like wood, in which the regular customers' table napkins were kept. The plat du jour, which was *Navarin printanier*, was chalked up on the wall. On the menu, supplementary prices had been written in next to almost all the dishes.

Maigret gave the order. Félicie flung back her veil, and its weight pulled back the hair on her forehead.

"Were you very miserable in Fécamp?"

He knew what he was doing. He was quite prepared for the tremor of her lips, and the defiant expression on her face, which was almost second nature to her.

"Why should I have been?"

Of course! Why should she? He knew Fécamp well, with its mean, cramped little terraced houses huddled at the foot of the cliffs, upstream from the estuary, its streets awash with dirty water, and its children playing amid the sickening stench of fish.

"How many brothers and sisters have you?"

"Seven."

The drink-sodden father. The mother at her washtub from morning till night. He could imagine her, an overgrown, skinny child with thin legs and bare feet. She had been put to work as a menial in a little waterfront restaurant, Chez Arsène, where she was housed in the attic. She had been dismissed because she had pinched a few sous from the till. Subsequently, she had been employed as a daily help by Ernest Lapie, the ship's carpenter.

She was eating now, very daintily, though not actually with her little finger stuck out. Maigret felt no inclination to laugh.

"I could have married the son of a shipowner, if I'd wanted to."

"I'm sure you could, child. But you refused him, is that it?"

"I don't like redheads. And besides, his father made a pass at me. Men are such pigs. . . ."

It was an odd thing, but from some angles she looked so much younger than her twenty-four years, more like a high-strung twelve-year-old, and it was difficult to imagine how anyone could take her seriously.

"Tell me, Félicie. Was your employer—sorry, Peg Leg, I should say—was Peg Leg of a jealous disposition?"

He felt very pleased with himself. She was reacting as he had expected, chin up, eyes blazing with anger, a look of mingled surprise and anxiety.

"There was never anything between us."

"I know, child. But that didn't prevent him from being jealous, did it? I bet you anything you like that he forbade you to go dancing in Poissy on your Sundays off, and that you had to slip away without telling him."

She did not reply. Doubtless, she was wondering how he could possibly have found out about the old man's perverse jealousy, which drove him to spy on her, to go to meet her on her way back on Sunday nights, and to make the most frightful scenes.

"You led him to believe that you had more than one lover. . . ."

"Why shouldn't I have lovers?"

"Why not, indeed! And you told him all about them. And he called you every name under the sun. I wonder he didn't take a strap to you."

"He wouldn't have dared touch me. . . ."

She was lying. Maigret could just see the two of them. They were as cut off from the rest of the world, in the newly built cottage in the middle of the Jeanneville Estate, as if they had been shipwrecked together on a desert island. Neither had any ties elsewhere. From morning to night, they spied on each other, and quarreled and fought, because they needed each other. In fact, they were everything to one another.

The only escape for Peg Leg was his nightly game of cards at the Anneau d'Or, but Félicie's bids for freedom were altogether noisier and more spectacular.

The old man was forced to lock her in her room and stand guard under her window to prevent her from slipping away to the dance hall in Poissy on Sundays, to play the part of a princess in disguise. Every other free moment she could get was spent in pouring out the secrets of her heart to her bosom friend, Léontine.

It was all so simple, really. One after another, the humble, hard-working regular patrons of the restaurant came in to have their lunch and read their newspapers. But there was not one who did not gape in bewilderment at the extravagant creature who looked so much out of place in these familiar surroundings, not one who, glancing covertly at Félicie from time to time, was not tempted to smile and exchange a wink with the waiter.

And yet she was just a woman, or, rather, a child on the brink of womanhood. This was what Maigret had seen in her, which was why his manner toward her was now so gentle, so indulgent, so affectionate.

Around her, he was beginning to reconstruct the daily life of Cape Horn. Had old Lapie still been alive, Maigret would certainly not have scrupled to scandalize the old man by accusing him outright:

"You're eaten up with jealousy where that girl is concerned!"

Jealous! How could he be jealous, when he had never even been in love in his whole life? But jealous he was, nonetheless, because she was a part of his world, such a narrow little world that to deprive him of so much as a fragment of it would mean a fearful loss to him.

When had he ever sold his surplus vegetables, or the fruit from his orchard? Or even given them away? Never! They were his property. Félicie, too, was his property. Strangers were not made welcome in his house. He and he alone had drunk the wine in his cellar.

"How did he come to invite his nephew to stay?"

"He went to see him in Paris. . . . He had wanted him to come to Cape Horn after his sister died. But Jacques wouldn't hear of it. . . . He had his pride. . . ."

"And one day, when Lapie was on one of his quarterly visits to Paris to collect his compensation, he went to see his nephew, and found him in a pitiful state, isn't that so?"

"What do you mean by that?"

"Pétillon had been reduced to unloading vegetables in Les Halles."

"There's nothing to be ashamed of in that!"

"Of course not. Nothing whatever. Quite the reverse. Anyway, he brought him home. He gave up his own room to him, because . . ."

She was outraged.

"It wasn't like that at all!"

"All the same, he did keep a very close eye on you both. . . . What did he find out?"

"Nothing."

"Were you Pétillon's mistress?"

She looked down at her plate, neither confirming nor denying it.

"Be that as it may, the fact is that life became impossible for Pétillon, and he left the house."

"He and his uncle didn't see eye to eye. . . ."

"That's what I'm saying."

Maigret felt a glow of contentment. He would always remember this simple meal in the restful, commonplace surroundings of the little restaurant, mainly patronized by regulars. A slanting sunbeam flickered on the tablecloth and on the carafe of red wine. A pleasant, almost cordial intimacy had developed between himself and Félicie. He knew well enough that if he ventured to refer to it, she would resume her disdainful manner, and deny it vehemently. Yet she was enjoying herself as much as he was, thankful for a respite from her solitary life, and the chaotic fantasies with which she filled it.

"It will all sort itself out in the end. You'll see."

She was almost ready to believe him. But her mistrustful nature was too strong for her. She was still afraid of stumbling into some sort of trap. Every now and then—but alas, not for long—she seemed on the point of letting go, and behaving normally, like any other girl. She was within a hair's breadth of relaxing completely, of looking at Maigret without affectation, and saying what she really felt. Tears welled up in her eyes; a softer, more resigned expression spread over her features.

She was about to confide in him, and he was only too willing to help her, to be a father to her. . . .

But at the very last minute, her wariness got the upper hand again. She looked more stubborn then ever, and she said, in her most acid tones:

"You needn't think I don't know what you're up to."

She felt so alone. Only she was burdened with the whole weight of the tragedy. She was right at the very center of things. Surely the fact that a chief superintendent of the Police Judiciaire, a celebrity like Maigret, spent all his time harassing her and her alone was proof enough of that!

Little did she suspect that her companion, even now, was pulling a great many other strings. He had inspectors digging away in Place Pigalle and thereabouts. At the Quai des Orfèvres, a number of dubious characters, hustled out of bed in their sleazy lodgings in the small hours, were being interrogated. In various provincial towns, officers of the Vice Squad were searching for a girl named Adèle, who had recently spent several months working in a brasserie in Rouen.

All this was standard police procedure, and was bound, in the end, to yield results.

But sitting here in this little restaurant, where the regulars greeted one another with no more than a discreet nod—for, although they had seen each other every single day at lunchtime for years, they had not been introduced—the Chief Superintendent was not concerned with the mechanics of detection, but with the essential nature of the crime.

"Do you like strawberries?"

There were several punnets of them on the sideboard, packed in cotton wool, the first of the season.

"Waiter . . . bring us some strawberries."

It amused him to see how she relished them. It was not so

much that she was greedy as that expensive delicacies appealed to her imagination. It was of little consequence that Jacques Pétillon was in no condition to enjoy grapes, oranges, or champagne. It was the gesture that was important, and the sight of the big purple fruit and the gold cap on the bottle. She might or might not like strawberries, but she was certainly eating them with enjoyment.

"What's wrong child?"

"Nothing."

She had suddenly turned very pale, and this time it was not an act. She had had a shock. She choked on a mouthful of fruit, and seemed on the point of scrambling to her feet and bolting. She coughed and hid her face in her handkerchief, pretending that all that was amiss was that something had gone down the wrong way.

"What on earth . . . ?"

Turning around, Maigret saw a small man wearing, in spite of the mildness of the weather, a heavy overcoat and a muffler. The man took them off, hung them on a coat peg, and collected a rolled table napkin from the pigeonhole numbered thirteen.

He was middle-aged, graying, ordinary, one of those colorless people so often to be found in large towns, lonely, fussy, touchy characters, widowers or hardened bachelors, whose lives consisted of a succession of familiar little rituals. The waiter served him without showing him a menu, and brought him an open bottle of mineral water. The man, just as he was about to open his newspaper, caught sight of Félicie, and frowned, as if trying to remember, asking himself . . .

"Aren't you going to finish your strawberries?"

"I've had enough. Let's go."

She had already put her napkin down on the table. Her hand was trembling.

"Calm down, my dear."

"Me? I'm perfectly calm. Why ever shouldn't I be?"

From where he was sitting, Maigret was able to see the man's reflection in the mirror opposite. His face was still working as he tried to place the vaguely familiar features. Was it . . . ? No . . . Had she . . . ? No, that wasn't it. . . . Come on! He went on trying to figure it out. He was almost there. . . . There! He had it! His eyes widened. It had quite shaken him. He seemed to be saying to himself:

"Good heavens! What an extraordinary coincidence!"

But he did not move from his seat. He did not nod or smile, or show any outward sign of recognition. Where had they met? And in what circumstance? The man was staring searchingly at Maigret. He summoned the waiter, and whispered something to him. The waiter must have said that he didn't know, that he had never seen either of them before.

And while all this was going on, Félicie, sick with apprehension, had suddenly got to her feet and stumbled off to the ladies' room. Had she received such a shock that she was going to bring up the strawberries, which, so short a time ago, she had been savoring with such refined enjoyment?

During her absence, Maigret and the unknown man looked at one another with undisguised curiosity. Number 13 looked as if he were sorely tempted to go across and speak to Félicie's companion.

The frosted-glass door leading to the rest rooms also led to the kitchens. The waiter came and went constantly. He had red hair. Like the shipowner's son in Fécamp who had wanted to marry Félicie. Maigret could not help smiling. Everything she saw was fuel for her imagination. She had seen a redheaded waiter. Then Maigret had asked her if she had been very miserable in Fécamp. At lightning speed, her imagination had transformed the waiter into the shipowner's son who . . .

She had been away a long time, and Maigret was beginning to feel uneasy. The waiter, too, had been absent longer than usual. Number 13 was looking very thoughtful, like a man on the brink of a momentous decision.

At long last, she reappeared. She was almost smiling. As she came toward him, she pulled her veil down over her face. She did not sit down.

"Shall we go?"

"I've ordered coffee. You like coffee, don't you?"

"Not now. It's bad for my nerves."

Pretending to be taken in, he summoned the waiter, and, as he was paying the bill, subjected him to a searching glance. The waiter flushed a little. It was all so obvious. Clearly, she had entrusted him with a message for Number 13. Probably she had scribbled a note on a scrap of paper and told him not to hand it to the man until after they had left the restaurant.

On the way out, the Chief Superintendent glanced absently at the thick overcoat, with its bulging pockets, hanging on the coat peg.

"We can go back to Jeanneville now, can't we?"

She took his arm in what might have been a spontaneous manner.

"I'm so tired. . . . It's all been so distressing."

Seeing him standing irresolutely on the edge of the sidewalk, as if undecided as to what to do next, she could scarcely conceal her impatience.

"Why are you just standing there? What're you thinking? The next train leaves in half an hour."

She was absolutely terrified. Her hand shook on Maigret's arm. Suddenly, strangely, all that mattered to Maigret was to reassure her. He shrugged.

"What the hell! Taxi! Gare Saint-Lazare, Suburban Line."

He could only guess at the enormity of the weight that he had lifted from her shoulders. There in the open taxi, with the sunlight streaming in, words poured out:

"You promised you wouldn't leave me. . . . That's what you said, wasn't it? You're not afraid of being compromised, are you? Are you married? How stupid of me; of course you are, otherwise you wouldn't be wearing a wedding ring."

A little tremor of fear at the station. He had bought only one ticket. Did he mean to bundle her into the train, and stay behind in Paris himself? She had forgotten that he carried an official travel pass. He slumped down beside her on the seat and looked at her with a faint stirring of remorse.

As to the elderly gentleman whom he thought of as Number 13, he could lay hands on him whenever he chose, seeing that he was one of the regulars at the little restaurant. The train moved off, and Félicie believed herself out of danger. In Poissy, as they walked past the dance hall together, the proprietor, standing outside the rickety wooden building, recognized Maigret, and winked at him.

The Chief Superintendent succumbed to an irresistible urge to tease Félicie a little.

"D'you know, I think I'd like a word with him. I want to ask him whether he ever caught Peg Leg spying on you while you were dancing."

She tugged impatiently at his arm.

"You can save yourself the trouble. He followed me here several times."

"You see! I said he was of a jealous disposition, didn't I?"

They walked up the hill. As they went past Mélanie Chochoi's shop, Maigret had another little dig at her:

"What if I were to go in and ask her how often she had seen you and Jacques Pétillon roaming about together at night?"

"She never saw us!"

This time, she spoke with absolute conviction.

"You took good care she shouldn't, is that what you mean?"

They were now in sight of the house. One of the big trucks from the Forensic Laboratory was just driving away, and Lucas was standing alone at the front door, looking as if he owned the place.

"What was that truck doing here?"

"It belongs to the photographers and technicians."

"Oh, yes, fingerprints."

She would know about fingerprints, of course. She was always reading novels, detective stories among them, no doubt.

"Well, my dear Lucas?"

"Nothing much, Chief. As you thought, the fellow wore rubber gloves. All they could do was to make casts of his footprints. He was wearing brand-new shoes. Probably hadn't had them more than two or three days."

Félicie had gone up to her bedroom, to take off her veil and mourning garments.

"Have you any news, Chief? I get the feeling . . ."

He knew him so well. Maigret, in his present expansive and receptive mood, seemed to breathe life in at every pore. He looked about him. These surroundings, which had become so familiar to him that, without realizing it, he was beginning to take on some of the mannerisms of the people who lived there . . .

"What would you say to a drink?"

He went to the sideboard in the dining room, got out the bottle of brandy, which was not quite empty, filled two little glasses, and went and stood in the doorway, looking out into the garden.

"Cheers! Félicie, my dear, I wonder . . ."

She had reappeared, wearing an apron, and was looking about her to make sure that the technicians from the Forensic Laboratory had not messed up her kitchen.

"I wonder if you would be so kind as to make a cup of coffee for my friend Lucas? I have business at the Anneau d'Or myself, but the Sergeant will take good care of you. See you this evening."

She gave him a look of mingled anxiety and mistrust, as was only to be expected.

"I really am going to the Anneau d'Or, I promise you."

And so he was, but not for long. Since there was no taxi to be had in Orgeval, he asked Louvet, the mechanic, to drive him to Paris in his truck.

"To Place des Ternes, please . . . The best way is via Rue du Faubourg-Saint-Honoré."

When he got there, he found the restaurant deserted. The waiter must have been having a nap somewhere behind the scenes, because, when he finally appeared, his hair was standing up in spikes and he was yawning.

"Do you happen to know the home address of the gentleman who was lunching here today, and to whom you gave a note from the lady who was with me?"

The silly fool, mistaking Maigret for a jealous lover or a possessive father, denied having done any such thing. The Chief Superintendent produced his card.

"Honest to God, I don't know his name. I don't think he lives around here, because he only ever comes in for lunch. . . ."

Maigret was not prepared to wait another day.

"Do you know where he works?"

"Let me think. . . . I seem to remember hearing him say something about it to the boss. . . . I'll just go and see if he's in."

The waiter, it seemed, was not the only one to have been taking a nap. The proprietor appeared without a collar and smoothing his rumpled hair.

"Number 13? He's in leather goods. . . . He mentioned it one day, I remember, when we were chatting about this and that. . . . He works for a firm on Avenue de Wagram."

It did not take the Chief Superintendent long to locate the firm by means of the classified directory: Gellet and Mautoison, leather goods, import and export, 17B Avenue de Wagram. He went straight there. The offices were dark, with greenish windows, on which the name of the firm could be read backward, as in a mirror. He could hear the chatter of typewriters.

"The man you want to see is Monsieur Charles. . . . Just a minute . . ."

He was conducted through a maze of corridors and staircases smelling of animal skins to a little cubbyhole right at the back of the building, with a plate inscribed STATIONERY affixed to the door.

The man was Number 13, all right, looking grayer than ever in the long gray coverall he wore at work. The appearance of Maigret in his little sanctum gave him a considerable start.

"Sir?"

"I am from the Police Judiciaire. . . . You have nothing to fear. . . . I am merely seeking information."

"I don't see . . ."

"Oh, yes, you do, Monsieur Charles. You see very well. Be so good as to show me the note handed to you by the waiter in the restaurant earlier today."

"I swear to you . . ."

"I wouldn't do that if I were you, unless you want me to arrest you as an accessory to murder."

The man blew his nose noisily, not merely to gain time, but because he had a permanent cold in the head, which explained the heavy overcoat and muffler.

"You put me in a very awkward position."

"Not nearly as awkward as if you refuse to answer my questions."

Maigret had assumed his most hectoring tone. He was playing it rough, as Madame Maigret would have said. It always made her smile, knowing, as she alone did, what he was really like inside.

"Look here, Chief Superintendent, I had no idea . . ."

"To begin with, I want to see that note."

Instead of feeling for it in his pockets, as might have been expected, the man climbed a ladder and reached up to the very top shelf, where he had hidden it behind a stack of letterhead. He produced not only the note but also a revolver, which he handled gingerly, like someone terrified of firearms.

"For heaven's sake, whatever happens, say nothing. Throw you-know-what into the Seine. *It is a matter of life and death.*"

Maigret smiled at the last words, which were Félicie all over. Had she not said the same thing to Louvet, the mechanic from Orgeval?

"When I realized . . ."

"When you realized that someone had planted a revolver in your coat pocket—is that what you were going to say?"

"You knew about it?"

"You had just entered the Métro. In the crush, you were jostled by a young woman dressed in deep mourning, and you realized, as she made off toward the exit, that she had slipped something heavy into your pocket. . . ."

"It wasn't until later that I realized . . ."

"And you were very much alarmed. . . ."

"I've never handled a gun in my life. I couldn't even tell if it was loaded. I still don't know. . . ."

To the utter horror of the stationery clerk, Maigret removed the clip, from which one bullet was missing.

"But because there was something about that young woman in deep mourning . . ."

"I had every intention, at first, of handing in this . . . this object to the police. . . ."

Number 13 was looking distressed.

"You're a sensitive man, Monsieur Charles. You have a somewhat romantic view of women, have you not? I don't imagine you have had many amorous adventures in your life. . . ."

The sound of a bell. The poor man, terrified, looked up at a board above his desk.

"That's the boss wanting me. May I . . . ?"

"Run along! You've told me all I wanted to know."

"But that young lady . . . tell me . . . did she really . . . ?"

Maigret's brow darkened.

"As to that, only time will tell, Monsieur Charles. . . . Hurry, now. It wouldn't do to keep the boss waiting."

For the bell was ringing again, with imperious insistence.

Presently, having hailed a taxi in the street, the Chief Superintendent instructed the driver to take him to Gastinne-Renette, the gunsmith.

So, for three whole days, Félicie, well aware that she herself was under surveillance, and that every inch of the house and garden was likely to be searched, had kept the gun hidden on her person. He could just see her sitting beside the driver of the truck, realizing that there were too many cars around, and that the truck was probably being followed. If she were to throw the gun out, Louvet might see her doing it. In Paris . . .

From the time she got out at Porte Maillot, she was aware that there was an inspector following her. To give herself time to think, she went into a patisserie and stuffed herself with cream puffs. She drank a glass of port. Possibly she didn't much care for port, but it represented gracious living to her, like the grapes and champagne that she had taken to the hospital. The Métro . . . There were too few people about at that time of day. She waited. The Inspector waited also, never taking his eyes off her.

Six o'clock, at long last. Crowds jostling on all the platforms, a solid mass of people. And one of them, providentially, wearing an overcoat with gaping pockets.

It was a pity that Félicie was not there to see Maigret as the taxi drove him to the gunsmith's. If she had been, self-satisfaction might well have triumphed over misery for a few seconds at the expression of admiration on the Chief Superintendent's face.

6

MAIGRET
STAYS PUT

How many thousands of times had Maigret, with heavy tread, climbed the wide, dusty staircase of Police Headquarters, the steps always creaking a little underfoot, and, in winter, an icy draft swirling in the air? Maigret was a creature of habit. For instance, when he was almost at the top, he would invariably glance over his shoulder at the stairwell below. Invariably, also, when he reached the vast corridor of the floor occupied by the Police Judiciaire, he would stand for a moment gazing absently into the room generally known as the "aquarium." This room, immediately to the left of the staircase, was none other than the glass-walled waiting room, with its table covered in green baize, its chairs upholstered in green, and its walls hung with black frames, filled with small disk-shaped photographs of policemen killed in the line of duty.

Today, although it was already half past five, the waiting room was crowded. Maigret was so wrapped up in his own thoughts that he did not realize at first that most of these people were here at his behest. There were several familiar faces among them. One man sprang to his feet and accosted him:

"I say, Chief Superintendent, how much longer are we to be kept waiting? You wouldn't consider seeing me first, as a personal favor, would you?"

All the craziest characters of Place Pigalle were there, rounded up, on his orders, by one of his inspectors.

"You know me, don't you? You know I'm on the level. I

wouldn't dream of getting mixed up in a sordid business like that. I've been kicking my heels here all afternoon. . . ."

Maigret's broad back receded. Seemingly at random, he put his head around two or three of the office doorways that lined the corridor as far as the eye could see. The whole department was seething with activity. It was all so familiar to him. People were being interrogated all over the place, even in his own office, where Rondonnet, a recent addition to his staff, was sitting in Maigret's personal chair, and smoking a pipe just like the Chief's. In his eagerness to emulate Maigret, he had gone even further, and ordered glasses of beer to be sent across from the Brasserie Dauphine. In the chair opposite sat one of the waiters from the Pélican. Rondonnet winked at the Chief and, temporarily leaving his "patient" to his own devices, went out with him into the corridor, where such private interchanges so often took place.

"There's something in the wind, all right, Chief. I'm not quite sure what, yet. . . . You know how these things go. . . . I deliberately left them to stew in the aquarium. . . . Word has got around. One can feel it. They know something. . . . Have you seen the Chief Commissioner? Apparently he's been calling around, trying to get hold of you, for the last hour. Oh, and by the way . . . there's a message for you."

He went to fetch it from Maigret's desk. It was from Madame Maigret.

"Elise has arrived from Epinal with her husband and the children. I've asked them all to stay to dinner. I do hope you'll be able to join us. They've brought us some *cèpes*."

Maigret would not be joining them. He had too much on his mind. There was something he wanted to check, an idea that had occurred to him a short time ago, while he was waiting at the gunsmith's for Monsieur Gastinne-Renette's ballistics report. He had been pacing up and down in the shooting gallery in the basement, idly watching a young married couple, who were about to leave for Africa on their honeymoon, trying out some extremely powerful guns.

His thoughts, as usual, had returned to Peg Leg's cottage. Once again, he saw himself climbing the gleaming stairs, and then suddenly—the picture was absolutely clear in his mind—he saw himself hesitating on the landing, looking from one door to the other. And then he remembered the three bed-rooms.

"Well, I'll be damned!"

And from then on, he had only one thought: to get back there as soon as possible, to confirm what he felt to be virtually a certainty. As to the ballistics report, he knew in advance what it would contain, for there was no doubt in his mind that the revolver on Avenue de Wagram was the one used in the killing of old Lapie. A Smith & Wesson. Not a toy, by any means. Not the sort of weapon favored by amateurs, but the real thing, a professional killer's gun.

A quarter of an hour later, old Monsieur Gastinne-Renette confirmed his theory.

"You were right, Chief Superintendent. It is the same gun. I'll send you my detailed written report tonight, with the enlarged photographs."

Maigret had decided, nevertheless, to look in at the Quai, to find out if there had been any new developments. He was now standing outside the Chief Commissioner's padded door. He knocked.

"Ah! There you are, Maigret! I was afraid you might not get my message. Was it you who sent Dunan to Rue Lepic?"

Maigret had forgotten all about it, but yes, he had. Just on the off chance. He had instructed Dunan to make a thorough search of the room Jacques Pétillon had occupied in the Hotel Beauséjour.

"He telephoned in a short time ago. It seems someone had been there before him. He'd like a word with you as soon as possible. Will you be going there?"

He nodded, feeling gloomy and oppressed. He hated having his train of thought interrupted, and his mind was filled with Jeanneville, not with Rue Lepic.

As he was leaving the building, he was stopped in his tracks by another of the characters who had been rounded up and left to stew in the aquarium.

"Could you possibly arrange for me to be seen right away? I have a pile of things to attend to. . . ."

He shrugged. A little later, as he got out of his taxi in Place

Blanche, he felt suddenly dizzy. The whole square was bathed in sunlight. The wide terrace of one of the big cafés was crowded with people, as if there were nothing more to life than sitting at a table, drinking a cold beer or an apéritif, and ogling the pretty women as they went by.

Maigret experienced a fleeting pang of envy. He thought of his wife, who, at this very moment, was entertaining her sister and brother-in-law in their apartment on Boulevard Richard-Lenoir. He thought of the *cèpes*, simmering on the stove, and exuding an appetizing smell of garlic and damp woodland. He adored *cépes*.

He wished he had the leisure to join the throng on the terrace. It was several days since he had last had a decent night's sleep, and he had eaten nothing but odd snacks, with a snatched drink here and there of whatever he could get. It seemed to him that he was compelled, by virtue of his wretched calling, to live the lives of a whole lot of other people, instead of quietly getting on with his own. Oh, well, thank goodness, he would be retiring in a few years' time, and then, with a broad-brimmed straw hat on his head, he would cultivate his garden, a carefully tended garden like old Lapie's, and, like Lapie, he would resort to the cellar, from time to time, for a refreshing glass of wine.

"Bring me a small beer . . . and hurry."

He had barely had time to sit down when he caught sight of Inspector Dunan, who had been watching for him.

"I was hoping you'd come, Chief. . . . Wait till you see . . ."

Away in Jeanneville, Félicie would be busy cooking her evening meal on the gas stove, with the kitchen door wide open, and the kitchen garden bathed in the golden glow of the setting sun.

The Hotel Beauséjour was wedged between a shoeshop and a pork butcher's. They went in. At the reception desk, which was glassed in, a monstrously fat man sat in a high-backed chair, with his grossly swollen feet immersed in an enamel basin of water. Beside him was a wooden panel, on which hung the keys of the bedrooms.

"I assure you, I am not to blame. You have only to ask Ernest. He was the one who showed them upstairs. . . ."

Ernest, the porter, who looked even sleepier than Maigret, because he was on duty night and day and seldom managed to snatch more than two hours' sleep at a stretch, explained in a drowsy voice:

"It was early this afternoon. . . . At that time of day, we get no one in but *casuals*, if you get my meaning. That's all the rooms on the first floor are used for. . . . The women are mostly regulars. . . . They usually just call out on their way up:

" 'I'm going up to Number 8,' or whatever.

"And when they come down again, they collect their commission. . . . They get five francs a time, you understand.

"I mentioned at the time that I didn't recognize that one. . . . A dark girl, rather less shopworn than most of them . . . She waited here in the lobby to be given a key."

"What about the man with her?" asked Maigret.

"I couldn't say. . . . We never look at them too closely, you know, because they don't like it. It embarrasses them. Some deliberately turn their backs, or pretend to blow their noses, and in winter they wear their coat collars turned up. . . . He was just a man like any other. I didn't notice anything special about him. . . . I took them up to Number 5, which happened to be available at the time. . . ."

A couple came up to the desk. The girl asked:

"Is Number 9 free, Ernest?"

The bloated old man glanced at the board, and replied with a nod and a grunt.

"That's Jaja. . . . She's one of the regulars, all right! What was I saying? Oh, yes . . . The man came down first, after about a quarter of an hour. . . . That's the usual thing. . . . I didn't see the woman leave. But anyway, about ten minutes later I went up to the room, found it empty, and tidied up.

"I must have missed her as she went out, I said to myself.

"Then things got busy, and I forgot all about it, and it must have been half an hour later or more when, to my amazement, I caught sight of the woman slinking out behind my back. . . .

"That's odd! I said to myself. Where has she been hiding?

"After that, I didn't give it another thought until your inspector, who had borrowed the key to the saxophone player's room, came down again and started asking questions."

"You say you'd never seen her before?"

"No . . . I couldn't say that. All I know for sure is that she wasn't a regular. . . . And yet there was something vaguely familiar about her. . . . I had the feeling that I had seen her somewhere before."

"How long have you been working here?"

"Five years."

"So you might possibly have seen her here sometime in the past?"

"It's possible. . . . We get many of them in and out, you know. They turn up regularly for a time, a fortnight or a month, perhaps, and then they move to some other district, or to the provinces, or get pulled in by your fellows. . . ."

With heavy tread, Maigret went upstairs with the Inspector. Pétillon's room was high up, on the fifth floor. The lock had not been forced. It was a very ordinary lock, and could have been opened with the commonest type of passkey.

Maigret looked about him and whistled, for whoever had ransacked the room had certainly made a good job of it. There was not much furniture, but what there was had been turned inside out. Pétillon's gray suit was lying on the rug with the pockets hanging out. All the drawers were open, and their contents scattered about. To top it all, the young woman had slit open the mattress, the pillow, and the eiderdown with a pair of scissors, and the floor was covered in a snowdrift of down and wadding.

"What do you make of it, Chief?"

"Any fingerprints?"

"The people from Criminal Records have already been. I took the liberty of calling them myself. They sent along Moers, but he didn't find anything. What on earth could they have been looking for, to turn the place upside down like this?"

That was not what interested Maigret. What they had been looking for, as Dunan put it, suggesting that there was more than one person involved, was far less significant than the thoroughness and determination of the search. And, what was more, there had not been a single blunder!

The revolver that had killed Jules Lapie was a Smith& Wesson, a weapon favored by the hard core of the criminal fraternity.

What had been the sequence of events following the old man's death? Pétillon had lost his head. He had dashed madly from one sleazy Montmartre dive to another, in search of someone who was not to be found. Even the knowledge that the police were after him had not stopped him. He had pressed on with his search, traveling all the way to Rouen to inquire for a girl named Adèle, who had worked at the Tivoli brasserie until a few months before.

It was at this point that he had visibly lost heart. He had reached the end of his rope. He had given up the struggle. Maigret had only to pick him up, and he would talk.

And it was then that he was shot full in the chest, right out in the open, in the middle of a busy street. One thing was certain: his assailant was no novice at the game.

Surely it was this same man who, wasting no time, had made straight for Jeanneville?

In Place Pigalle, Pétillon had been accompanied by no less a person than the Chief Superintendent himself, but that had not deterred his would-be murderer.

Lapie's house had been under constant surveillance. The man must have been aware of this, or at least suspected it, but, still undeterred, he had broken into the bedroom, pushed a chair up against the wardrobe, and wrenched off one of the planks at the top.

Had he found what he was looking for? Interrupted by Félicie, he had knocked her down and fled, leaving no traces other than a few unhelpful footprints, made by brand-new shoes.

This last incident had taken place between three and four in the morning, and already, by this afternoon, Pétillon's room had been ransacked.

This time, the culprit was a woman. A dark, reasonably attractive woman, like Adèle from the brasserie in Rouen. She had not slipped up in any way. According to the hall porter, the renting of rooms by the hour for the purposes of prostitution was so commonplace that if she had brought an accomplice in with her instead of a client, no one would have noticed. But she could not be sure that the Hotel Beauséjour was not also under surveillance. So she decided to play it straight. She picked up a man in the usual way, and requested the use of a room. But, when he had left, instead of going out after him, she had slunk upstairs to the fifth floor, knowing that the upper floors were deserted at that time of day, and searched every inch of the room.

What conclusion was to be drawn from this ever more rapid succession of events? That time was running out for *them*. That *they* had to find what they were looking for in the shortest possible time. It therefore followed that whatever it was, *they* had not yet found it.

And, on this account, Maigret, too, was seized with a feverish sense that time was running out. It was a feeling that seemed to overwhelm him every time he abandoned his surveillance of Cape Horn. It was as if he had some premonition of disaster.

He snapped back the elastic band of his notebook, scribbled a note, and tore out the page. It read:

Institute exhaustive search of the Ninth and Eighteenth Ar-rondissements tonight.

"Take this to Superintendent Piaulet. He will understand."

Out in the street once more, his glance returned to the café terrace, crowded with people who had nothing to do but enjoy themselves and savor the spring weather. What the hell! Surely there was time for another quick beer? With froth still clinging to his trim mustache, he bundled into a taxi and sat slumped in his seat.

"First, take me to Poissy. . . . I'll give you directions from there."

Manfully, he struggled against waves of drowsiness. With half-closed eyes, he promised himself that as soon as this case was over he would sleep for twenty-four hours at a stretch. He could picture his bedroom, with the windows wide open, and the sunlight flickering on the counterpane, the familiar sounds of home, Madame Maigret tiptoeing about, and shushing the delivery boys if they made too much noise.

But, as the popular song has it, that day would never come. It was just a dream, an empty promise, a hollow resolution. When the time came, the wretched telephone would ring, that telephone that Madame Maigret always longed to stifle with a pillow, as if it were some malevolent living thing.

"Hello. Yes . . ."

And Maigret would be off on his travels again.

"Where to now, sir?"

"Turn left up the hill. . . . I'll tell you when to stop."

Drowsy as he was, he was nevertheless impatient of delay. The thought had occurred to him at the gunsmith's, and he had been obsessed with it ever since. Why had it not struck him sooner? Still, he felt he had finally hit the jackpot, as they say in gambling circles. From the start, he had been intrigued by the layout of the three bedrooms. And then he had allowed himself to be led astray by notions of the old man's jealous disposition.

"It's on the right. . . . Yes . . . The third cottage . . . Look here, I've half a mind to keep you here for the night. . . . Have you had dinner? No? Hold on . . . Lucas! Come over here a minute, old fellow. . . . Any new developments? Is Félicie here? . . . What's that? She invited you in for a cup of coffee and a drop of brandy? . . . No, no! You're wrong about that. It's not because she's scared. It's because I told off a pert little hospital nurse this morning for making fun of her. She's showing her gratitude to me by being decent to you, that's all. . . . Make the most of it while you can. . . . Be off with you now to the Anneau d'Or. . . . Have some dinner, and see that the driver does, too. . . . Keep in touch with the postmistress. I've warned her to expect calls all through the night. . . . Is my bike here?"

"It's in the garden, propped up against the wall of the cellar."

Félicie was standing in the doorway, watching them. When the car drove off, Maigret went toward her, and saw that she was, once again, bristling with mistrust.

"So you went back to Paris, *in spite of everything!*"

He knew what she was thinking. Had he gone back to the little restaurant where they had had lunch, and found the gentleman with the overcoat and muffler, and had he talked, in spite of her pathetic little note?

"Come with me, Félicie. This is no time for playing games."

"Where are you going?"

"Upstairs . . . Come along."

He opened the door of old Lapie's bedroom.

"Now, I want you to think carefully. . . . Jacques spent several months in this room, if I'm not mistaken. . . . Can you tell me exactly how the room was furnished at that time?"

The question took her by surprise. She looked around, trying to remember.

"To begin with, there was the brass bed, which is now in the storeroom—at least that's what I call it. . . . It's the room next to mine, which I slept in for several months. . . . Since then, it's been used for storing all the old junk in the house, and the apples are stored there in the autumn."

"The bed . . . That's one thing. . . . And what else? What about the dressing table?"

"No, it's the same one."

"What about chairs?"

"Let me think. There were a couple of chairs with leather seats. . . . They're in the dining room now. . . ."

"And the wardrobe?"

He had deliberately left it till last, and he was so tense that he bit right through the ebonite mouthpiece of his pipe.

"It's the same one."

It was a fearful letdown. He had hurried back all the way from Paris, only to find that he was up against a brick wall, or, even worse, a gaping void.

"No, I'm wrong. . . . It was the same as this, but not the same one. There are two of these wardrobes, exactly alike, in the house. He bought them at an auction three or four years ago. I can't remember exactly when. . . . I was a bit upset about it, because I wanted a wardrobe with a mirror. There isn't a single full-length mirror in the house. . . ."

Phew! If she only knew what a load she had just taken off his mind! Leaving her standing, almost forgetting her existence, he ran headlong into Félicie's bedroom, and through to the adjoining room, where he opened the window and flung back the wooden shutters with a clatter.

Why had he not thought of it sooner? The room was crammed

with stuff, a roll of linoleum, old rugs, chairs stacked one on top of the other, as in a café after closing time. There were unpainted deal shelves, used, no doubt, for storing apples in winter, an old pump in a crate, two tables, and finally, right at the back, behind all this bric-à-brac, a wardrobe identical with the one in the old man's bedroom.

Maigret was in such a hurry that he knocked over the dismantled sections of the brass bedstead, which were stacked against the wall. He pushed one of the tables up against the wardrobe, climbed onto it, and felt along the dusty boards behind the cornice.

"Could you get me some sort of tool?"

"What kind of tool?"

"A screwdriver, scissors, pliers, anything . . ."

The dust drifted down on his hair like powder. Félicie had gone downstairs. He could hear her footsteps on the garden path. She went into the cellar, and returned at long last with a hammer and chisel.

"What are you going to do?"

Pry up the boards, of course, what else? And besides, it was easy enough. One of them was loose already. Underneath it, Maigret felt a wad of paper. He pulled out what proved to be a small package wrapped in an old newspaper.

He looked at Félicie, whose face was lifted up to his. She was pale and tense.

"What's in this parcel?"

"I haven't the remotest idea."

Her voice had the old, familiar sharp edge; her expression was defiant.

He climbed down from the table.

"We'll soon find out, won't we? Are you sure you don't know what's in it?"

Did he believe her, or did he not? He seemed to be playing cat and mouse. He took his time, subjecting her to a long look, before unwrapping the parcel.

"The newspaper is more than a year old. . . . Well, well! Félicie, my dear, did you know that there was a fortune hidden in the house?"

For the parcel that he had just opened contained a thick wad of thousand-franc notes.

"Careful! Don't touch!"

He climbed back onto the table and loosened all the other boards on top of the wardrobe, to make sure that nothing else was hidden there.

"We'll be more comfortable downstairs. Come along. . . ."

Feeling very pleased with himself, he sat down at the kitchen table. Maigret had always had a weakness for kitchens, with their appetizing smells and piles of good things to eat, plump vegetables, juicy meat, poultry waiting to be plucked. The half-bottle of brandy from which Félicie had poured a glass for Lucas was still there, and he helped himself to a drop or two before settling down to count the money, which he did conscientiously, like a professional cashier.

"Two hundred and ten . . . eleven . . . twelve . . . Wait a minute, there are two stuck together here. . . . Thirteen, fourteen . . . Two hundred and twenty-three, four . . . seven, eight . . ."

He looked at her. She was staring fixedly at the notes, her face drained of color, so that the bruises she had received the night before stood out in sharp contrast.

"Two hundred and twenty-nine thousand francs, Félicie, my love . . . What do you say to that? There were two hundred and twenty-nine thousand-franc notes hidden in your little friend Pétillon's bedroom. . . .

"Because that, undoubtedly, is where the money was hidden, don't you see? The gentleman who is at present so urgently in need of money knew exactly where to look. . . . There was just one thing he didn't know, which was that there were two identical wardrobes in the house. . . . And, anyway, even if he had known, it would never have occurred to him that Lapie was such an old fusspot that when he moved back into his own room, he would insist on taking his own wardrobe with him."

"Where does that get you?" she said, in a strained voice.

"Well, for one thing, it explains why you were knocked down last night, and also why, a few hours later, your friend Jacques's hotel bedroom on Rue Lepic was ransacked. . . ."

He stood up. He needed to stretch his legs. He was not entirely happy. To have achieved one object was not enough. Now that he had found what he had been looking for, and been vindicated by the results—he had a vivid mental picture of Gastinne-Renette's shooting gallery, where the notion had suddenly struck him— now that he had resolved one problem, others were coming to the fore. He paced up and down the garden, straightened the bent stem of a rose bush, and absently picked up the seeder which Lapie, better known as Peg Leg, had dropped a few minutes before going meekly upstairs to his bedroom to die.

Through the open window the Chief Superintendent could see Félicie standing motionless as a statue. A faint smile played about his lips. And why not? He shrugged, as if to say:

"Well, there's no harm in trying!"

And, fidgeting with the seeder, to which lumps of soil were still clinging, he spoke to her through the window:

"You see, child, I am becoming more and more convinced that, strange as it may seem to you, Jacques Pétillon did not kill his uncle. I'll go further, and say that I don't believe he played any significant part in the whole dreadful business."

She looked at him, but did not stir. He could see not the slightest tremor of relief on her drawn features.

"What do you say to that? You must be pleased, surely?"

She forced herself to smile, but it was a pathetic effort, no more than a slight twitching of her thin lips.

"I am pleased. Thank you."

He was in an ebullient mood, but with an effort was able to restrain himself.

"I can see you're pleased, very pleased. And I'm sure that now you will do everything you can to help me prove the innocence of the boy you love. . . . You do love him, don't you?"

She turned her head away, doubtless so that he would not see her quivering mouth and tear-filled eyes.

"Come now, of course you love him. There's nothing to be ashamed of in that. I'm sure he's going to pull through, and when he does, he'll receive you with open arms, in gratitude for all you've done for him."

"I haven't done anything for him."

"Well, let that pass. . . . It doesn't matter. I still say I'm convinced you'll marry him, and have lots of children."

As he had expected, she blew up. Was not this precisely what he had been aiming at?

"You're a brute! A brute! You're the cruelest, the most . . . the most . . ."

"Because I tell you that Jacques is innocent?"

Those few simple words got through to her at last, in the very midst of her outburst of rage. She knew that she was in the wrong, but it was too late. She did not know what to say; she was miserable and, at the same time, utterly at sea.

"You know very well you don't believe that. . . . It's just a trick to make me talk. . . . From the very first moment you set foot in this house . . ."

"When was the last time you saw Pétillon?"

Her presence of mind had not wholly deserted her.

"This morning," she quickly retorted.

"Before that, I mean."

She did not reply, and Maigret ostentatiously turned his back on her, gazing across the garden at the summerhouse, where, on that fateful morning, a half-bottle of brandy and two glasses had been set out on the green table. Her eyes followed his gaze. She knew what he was thinking.

"I'm not saying anything."

"I know. You have already told me so at least twenty times. It's beginning to sound like the chorus of a song. . . . It's lucky for us that we found the money."

"What do you mean?"

"Oh, so you are interested after all? When Pétillon left Cape Horn, a year ago, it was because he had quarreled with his uncle—isn't that so?"

"They didn't get on, but . . ."

"So, after that, he never came back. . . ."

She was trying to figure out what he was getting at now. Her face was working with the effort.

"And you never saw him again!" said Maigret at last. "Or, rather, you never saw him to speak to again. If you had, you would no doubt have told him that the wardrobes had been switched."

She was quick to sense the danger in these insidious questions and statements. Good heavens, how could a defenseless girl hope to outwit this imperturbable man, standing there smoking his pipe and beaming at her like an indulgent father? She hated him. Yes, she hated him. Never in all her life had she been made to suffer as this Chief Superintendent had made her suffer, not allowing her a moment's peace, puffing away at his pipe, and making the most disconcerting remarks as casually as if he were passing the time of day.

"You were never his mistress, Félicie?"

Ought she to say yes? Ought she to say no? What was all this leading up to?

"If you had been his mistress, you and he would have gone on meeting, because the row with his uncle had nothing to do with your relationship. You would have had plenty of opportunities to tell him about the old man moving back to his own room. Pétillon would have known that the money was no longer there, but in the storeroom. You see what I'm getting at? Knowing that, he would have had no occasion to go into his uncle's bedroom, and there, for whatever reason, kill the old man. . . ."

"It's not true. . . ."

"So you were not his mistress."

"No."

"Was there ever anything at all between you?"

"No."

"In other words, he didn't know you were in love with him?"

"That's right."

A complacent smile spread over Maigret's features.

"Well, my dear, I do believe that, at last, for the first time since the beginning of this case, you are telling the truth. . . . As to your feelings for the boy, I was never in any doubt. I knew all about that right from the start. . . . You've never had much fun out of life, my poor child. So, having little that was real to draw on, you lived in a world of dreams. You saw yourself not as little Félicie, old Monsieur Lapie's servant girl, but as all the glamorous heroines of romantic fiction rolled into one.

"In your dream world, Peg Leg was no longer your cantankerous employer, but, as in all the best popular novels, your natural father. There's no need to blush. You had to have a romantic history, if only for something to tell your friend Léontine, and to write in your diary.

"The first man to cross the threshold of this house was transformed in your imagination into your lover. It was the grand romantic passion, though I'm as sure as I am of anything that the poor boy hadn't an inkling of what was going on in your mind. I am equally sure that the manager of this development, Forrentin, never made a pass at you, but that, on account of his goaty beard, you transformed him into a satyr."

As he said this, a fleeting smile played about Félicie's lips. But it was soon gone, to be replaced by her customary hostile expression.

"What is all this leading up to?"

"I don't know yet," he admitted, "but I soon will, thanks to the money we've found. Now, I'm going to ask you a favor. The people who are searching for that money, and who need it so desperately that they are prepared to take such risks as they have done in the past few days, are not likely to give up at this late stage. . . . The simple idea that occurred to me, that there were two identical wardrobes and that they had been switched, could also occur to them. . . . I would be much easier in my mind if I knew you were not going to be left all alone here tonight. I know you hate me, but even so, I'd be obliged if you would agree to my spending the night here. You can lock your bedroom door. What have you got for dinner?"

"Blood sausage, and I was thinking of making mashed potatoes to go with it."

"Splendid. May I invite myself to dinner? I just have to pop over to Orgeval to see to a couple of things, and then I'll be back. Agreed?"

"Whatever you say."

"Come on, now, let me see you smile."

"No . . ."

He stuffed the bank notes into his pocket and went to fetch his bicycle, which was propped up against the cellar wall. While he was there, he thought he might as well pour himself a glass of wine. Having drunk it, he mounted the bicycle, and was just about to ride off, when she called out to him.

"Just the same, I still hate you!"

Turning around with a beaming smile, he retorted:

"And I, my dear Félicie, adore you!"

7

A LOBSTER DINNER

HALF PAST SIX in the evening. That was about the time when Maigret, astride his bicycle outside Cape Horn, had turned around to call out to Félicie, standing in the cottage doorway:

"And I adore you!"

At Béziers, the telephone was ringing in the Superintendent's office at Police Headquarters. The window was wide open. The office was empty. Arsène Vadibert, the Superintendent's secretary, was watching a game of bowls in his shirt sleeves under the plane trees. He turned toward the barred window, through which the shrill, insistent ringing could be heard.

"Coming! Coming!" he called out, sounding more than a little reluctant. His thick, nasal regional accent was difficult to understand over the telephone.

"Coming! Coming! Hello! . . . Paris, did you say? . . . Eh? What? This is Béziers . . . Béziers, yes, spelled as it's pronounced. The Police Judiciaire? . . . We received your note. . . . I said your *nottttte.* Don't you people in Paris understand French? . . . Your note on the subject of a girl named Adèle . . . Well, I think we may have something for you."

He leaned forward a little to watch Grêlé, wearing a white shirt, crouching in preparation for a spectacular throw.

"It happened last week—Thursday it was—in the *maison.*" (Needless to say, he pronounced it *maisong.*) . . . "What did you say? . . . Which *maisong?* . . . *The maisong,* of course . . . The one here is called the Paradon. . . . A girl by the name of

Adèle . . . a little, dark girl . . . What? . . . Pear-shaped breasts? . . . As to that, *mossieu,* I couldn't say; I've never seen her breasts. . . . And besides, she's run off. . . . If you'd only listen, you'd know the answer to that. . . . I have enough on my plate already. . . . As I was saying, this girl Adèle decided to move out, and asked to be paid off. The assistant manageress sent for the proprietor. Apparently she wasn't entitled to leave just like that. She had to give a month's notice. Anyway, he refused to give her the money owing to her, and she went berserk, and started smashing bottles and ripping up cushions. There was a hell of a rumpus, but in the end she left anyway, though, not having a sou to bless herself with, she had to borrow some money from one of the other girls. . . . She was bound for Paris. . . . What? . . . I haven't the vaguest idea. . . . You asked for an Adèle, and I've given you one. . . . So long, chum . . ."

Thirty-five minutes past six. The Anneau d'Or in Orgeval. A grayish-white façade with an open door in the middle. A bench on either side of the door. At the end of each bench, a bay tree in a tub. Benches and tubs painted dark green. Half the street sunlit, the other half in shadow. A truck drew up outside the inn, and the butcher got out, wearing a blue-and-white-checked coverall.

In the bar, where it was cool and dark, the landlord, Forrentin, Lepape, and the driver of Maigret's taxi were playing cards. Lucas stood watching them, nonchalantly smoking his pipe, his manner consciously modeled on that of the Chief Superintendent. The landlord's wife was rinsing glasses.

"Good evening, everybody!" called out the butcher. "A pint for me, Madame Jeanne . . . By the way, could you make use of a fine lobster? I've just been given two in town, and I'm the only one at home who eats lobster, because my old woman claims it makes her break out in a rash."

He went out to fetch the live lobster from his truck, and returned carrying it by one claw. Across the way, a window was flung open, a hand was seen to wave, and a voice called out:

"Telephone, Monsieur Lucas."

"One minute, Monsieur Lucas, before you go. Do you like lobster?"

Did he like lobster!

"Germaine! Get a court bouillon ready, would you, as soon as you can. I have a lobster here, waiting to be cooked."

"Hello! Lucas speaking, yes . . . The Chief should be here any moment now. . . . What? From Béziers? Adèle? Thursday?"

Maigret arrived on his bicycle just as the butcher's truck drove off. Lucas was still on the telephone. He went into the bar and stood watching the cardplayers. The lobster was crawling about clumsily on the tiled floor near the bar counter.

"Tell me, madame, is that lobster yours? Could you bear to part with it, I wonder?"

"I was just about to cook it for your sergeant and the driver."

"They can make do with something else. If you don't mind, I'll take this back with me."

Lucas came across the road.

"I think they've found Adèle, Chief. . . . In Béziers . . . She left there suddenly for Paris on Thursday."

The cardplayers glanced at them every now and then, trying to catch what they were saying.

Ten minutes to seven. Inspector Rondonnet and Chief Superintendent Piaulet were talking in one of the offices of Police Headquarters. The high windows looked out on the Seine, where a tug could be heard chugging wheezily.

"Hello! Is that Orgeval? . . . I'd be much obliged, mademoiselle, if you would call Chief Superintendent Maigret to speak to me."

The waving hand appeared once more at the window. Lucas ran across the street. Maigret, carrying the lobster, was just about to remount his bike.

"It's for you, Chief."

"Hello! Piaulet? Any developments?"

"Rondonnet thinks he may be on to something. According to the doorman of the Sancho, which is just opposite the Pélican, the proprietor of the Pélican was seen to make a phone call from the café on the corner last night while you were in his place. . . . Hello? . . . Yes . . . Not long after that, a taxi showed up. No one got out. The proprietor talked in a whisper to someone inside. . . . Do you see what I'm getting at? . . . Sounds fishy, don't you think? . . . And another thing: on Saturday night, there was a row in the tobacconist's on Rue Fontaine. It's hard to say, exactly. . . . The man involved wasn't a regular. . . ."

"Ouch!" exclaimed Maigret.

"What?"

"It's nothing. . . . Just the lobster . . . Go on."

"That's about all, really. . . . We're continuing the interrogations. . . . I have the feeling that some of them know a lot more than they're telling."

"All that can wait till I get back. . . . Hello? . . . By the way, I want some information from Criminal Records. . . . Something that happened about thirteen months ago—I'm not quite sure what. A holdup, maybe, or a case of fraud . . . I want to know whether any of the Place Pigalle fraternity was living with a girl named Adèle about that time. . . . Lucas will be within reach all night, so it doesn't matter how late you call back. . . . What's going on?"

"One moment . . . Rondonnet, who has been listening on the extension, wants to say something. I'll put him on."

"Hello, is that you, Chief? I don't know if it's of any significance, but I've suddenly remembered something. . . . Anyway, the date fits. . . . It happened in April of last year. . . . I was on the case myself. It was on Rue Blanche, remember? Pedro, the proprietor of the Chamois . . ."

Seeing that the lobster would not keep still, Maigret put it gently down on the floor, and growled:

"Don't move."

"What?"

"It's the lobster. . . . Pedro . . . No . . . Sorry, it doesn't ring a bell."

"He ran a small nightclub, not unlike the Pélican, but even sleazier, on Rue Blanche. . . . He was tall and thin, very pale, with a white streak, just one, in his black hair. . . ."

"I'm with you."

"It was three in the morning. He was just about to close when a car drew up, and five men got out, leaving the motor running.

The headwaiter was already putting up the shutters. . . . They shoved him aside. . . ."

"I have a vague recollection of it."

"They bundled Pedro into a little back room behind the bar. A few minutes later, there was a volley of shots, and a lot of splintered glass and flying bottles. Then the whole place suddenly went dark. I happened to be in the neighborhood at the time. . . . By a miracle, we reached the spot in time to catch four of the villains, including the Fly, who had fled to the roof. . . . Pedro was dead, with five or six bullets in him. . . . Only one of the killers got away, and it took us several days to find out who he was. It was Albert Babeau, the Musician. The one they call Midget, because he really is undersized, and wears platform soles to increase his height. . . . Hold on. Piaulet is saying something. . . . No . . . He wants to speak to you."

"Hello, Maigret . . . I remember the case, too. . . . I have the file in my office. Would you like me to . . . ?"

"There's no need. It's all coming back to me. . . . The Musician was arrested at Le Havre, wasn't he? How long after the incident?"

"About a week . . . We got an anonymous tip."

"How many years did he get?"

"I'd have to look up his record for that. . . . The Fly was the one they came down on hardest, because three shots had been fired from his revolver. . . . Twenty years he got, if I'm not mistaken. The others got between one and five years. . . . Pedro was reputed to keep large sums of money on the premises, but nothing was found. . . . Do you think there could be any connection? . . . Look, couldn't you come and see me here, and we could talk it over?"

Maigret hesitated. His foot knocked against the lobster.

"I can't make it just now. . . . Listen . . . What needs to be done is this. Lucas will be on call all through the night. . . ."

As he came out of the phone booth, he remarked to the postmistress:

"I warned you that you probably wouldn't get much sleep tonight. It now looks as if you won't get any."

He had a brief word with Lucas, who eyed the lobster gloomily.

"Very good, Chief . . . I've got it, Chief. . . . What about the taxi?"

"Better keep it, for the time being."

The sky was splashed with the glorious colors of a splendid sunset as Maigret returned along the road he had taken so many times in the past few days. Affectionately, he contemplated the toy cottages of Jeanneville, knowing that, before long, this now familiar landscape would be nothing more than a memory.

The soil smelled good, the grass was lush, the crickets were beginning to chirp, and, he thought, there was no sight on earth more soothing and innocent than a row of neatly tended vegetable gardens, with their owners, in straw hats, peaceably plying their hoses.

"It's I!" he called out, stepping into the hallway of Cape Horn, which was filled with the smell of frying blood sausage.

And, hiding the lobster behind his back:

"Tell me, Félicie . . . This is important, mind. . . ."

She was instantly on the defensive.

"Do you know how to make mayonnaise, at least?"

A disdainful smile.

"Very well, then, get on with it, and meanwhile put this gentleman here on to boil."

He was in high good humor. He rubbed his hands. Then, noticing that the dining-room door was open, he went in. The table, he saw, was laid for one, with a red-and-white-checked cloth, a glass, silver cutlery, and an attractively arranged basket of bread. He frowned, but said nothing.

He waited, little suspecting that this lobster, even now turning red in the pot of boiling water, was to be the subject of endless teasing by his wife. Madame Maigret was not of a jealous disposition, or so she claimed.

"Jealous of what, for heaven's sake?" she would often exclaim, with a little forced laugh.

Which did not prevent her from seizing every opportunity, when the subject of Maigret's work came up among relations or friends, of saying:

"It's not all hard work, you know. It has its compensations. One might, for instance, in the course of an inquiry, find oneself dining on lobster with a girl named Félicie, and spending the night with her afterward. . . ."

Poor Félicie! Good heavens, the last thing on her mind was an amorous adventure! As she came and went, her stubborn Norman mind, behind that bulging nanny-goat forehead of hers, was filled with anxious, if not desperate, thoughts. The coming of dusk brought her only deepening sadness and uneasiness. Through the open window, she watched Maigret pacing back and forth. Perhaps she, like Our Lord, was wondering whether this cup would ever be taken from her.

He had picked a bunch of flowers and was arranging them in a vase.

"By the way, Félicie, where did poor old Lapie have his meals?"

"In the kitchen. Why? It wasn't worth messing up the dining room, just for him alone."

"Indeed!"

And there he was, scooping up the cutlery and the cloth, and setting a place for himself at the table near the stove, while she stirred the mayonnaise feverishly, convinced that it was about to curdle.

"If all goes well, and if you behave yourself, I may have some good news for you tomorrow morning."

"What news?"

"How can I tell you, since I won't know until the morning?"

Anxious though he might be to spare her feelings, he could not help himself.

He knew that she was unhappy and distraught, and strained almost to the breaking point, and yet he could not refrain from teasing her. It was as if he felt impelled to get back at her in some way.

Was it perhaps because he had a slightly guilty conscience about being here instead of in Paris, conducting operations in preparation for the grand climax that was building up around and about Place Pigalle?

"The front line is no place for a general."

True enough. But ought he to be skulking quite so far in the rear, with a chain of messages buzzing to and fro, keeping the postmistress up all night, and making that good fellow Lucas trot back and forth between Orgeval and Jeanneville as if he were nothing better than a village postman?

The man who broke in, looking for the money, might think of the changing around of the furniture and come back. And this time, he might do worse than merely stun Félicie with a blow of his fist.

All of which, needless to say, was perfectly true. Still, it was not Maigret's real reason for staying. If the truth were told, he had stayed because he liked it here. It was so peaceful in this comic little fairy-tale village, even though, all the while, he was directing operations in another far-off, much more real and violent world.

"Why have you brought all that stuff in here?"

"Because I want us to have dinner together. . . . I said so, remember, when I invited myself. This is the first and probably the last meal we shall be sharing, unless . . ."

He smiled.

"Unless what?" she asked.

"Nothing. You will hear all about it tomorrow morning, child, and then, if we have time, we can also add up all the lies you've told me. . . . Here, have this claw. . . . Yes, I insist. . . ."

And, all of a sudden, as he was eating under the ceiling light, the thought came unbidden into his head:

Still and all, Peg Leg *was* murdered!

Poor old Peg Leg. What a strange history his had been! He who had so shrunk from any kind of adventure that he had shunned even marriage, the commonest adventure of all, had yet not been able to avoid losing his leg on a three-masted schooner, at Cape Horn, right on the other side of the world.

His longing for peace and quiet had brought him to Jeanneville, from which all human passion seemed excluded, with its houses like dollhouses, and its trees seemingly made of painted wood, like the trees of a toy farm.

And yet, even here, adventure had once more found him out. It had come in sinister guise from a place where he had never so much as set foot, and whose horrors he could barely have imagined. It had come from Place Pigalle, a world apart, a sort of metropolitan jungle, in which the tigers grease their hair and carry Smith & Wessons in their pockets.

One morning, just like any other, with the soft watercolors of sky and landscape all about him, he was gardening, with his straw hat on his head, pricking out his harmless tomato shoots, already seeing them in his mind's eye, perhaps, laden with heavy red fruit, their thin skins splitting in the sunshine, and then, a few minutes later, he was lying dead in his bedroom, which was filled with the wholesome rural smell of polish.

As was her habit, Félicie was eating off the edge of the table, bobbing up every few seconds to take a look at a saucepan simmering on the stove, or to pour boiling water into the coffee percolator. The window was wide open on the deep, velvety blue of a night peppered with stars. Unseen, the crickets chirped to one another, and the frogs croaked in concert. Down in the valley, a train chugged by. In the Anneau d'Or a game of cards was in progress, and good, faithful Lucas was eating cutlets instead of lobster.

"What are you doing?"

"Washing up."

"Not now, child. You're worn out. Do me a favor, will you, and go straight up to bed. . . . Yes! I insist. And don't forget to lock your door."

"I couldn't sleep."

"Is that so? Very well, I'll give you something to help you sleep. . . . Give me a glass of water. . . . I'll just dissolve these two tablets. . . . There . . . Drink up, now. . . . There's nothing to be afraid of. I've no intention of poisoning you."

She drank the draught, to prove to him that she was not afraid. But, irked by Maigret's paternal manner, she felt impelled to reiterate:

"Just the same, I still hate you. One day you'll be sorry for the way you've treated me. . . . Anyway, it doesn't matter, because tomorrow I'm going away."

"Where to?"

"Anywhere . . . I don't ever want to set eyes on you again. I want to get away from this house, and when I've gone, you can do whatever you like."

"As you please. Tomorrow . . ."

"Where are you going?"

"I'm seeing you up to your room. I want to make quite sure you're safely locked in. . . . Oh, good, I see you've closed the shutters. . . . Good night, Félicie."

He returned to the kitchen, to find the carcass of the lobster still lying on a pottery plate. It would remain there, staring at him all through the night.

The hands of the alarm clock on the black mantelpiece stood at half past nine when Maigret took off his shoes and crept silently upstairs, to check that Félicie, under the influence of the Seconol, was sleeping peacefully.

A quarter to ten. Maigret was sitting in Peg Leg's cane armchair. He was smoking his pipe with eyes half shut. The sound of a car coming up the hill. The slam of a door. An oath from Lucas, who had bumped into the bamboo coatrack in the darkness of the hall.

"They've just been on the phone, Chief. . . ."

"Ssh! Keep your voice down. She's asleep."

Lucas looked at the remains of the lobster with the merest hint of resentment.

"The Musician had a girl friend who used the name Adèle. From her file it appears that her real name is Jeanne Grosbois. She was born somewhere near Moulins. . . ."

"Go on."

"At the time of the Chamois holdup, she was working in the Tivoli brasserie in Rouen. She left there the day after Pedro was murdered. . . ."

"Presumably she went to join the Musician in Le Havre. What happened next?"

"She spent several months in Toulon, in the Floralies, then she moved to Béziers. . . . She made no secret of the fact that her man was doing time in the Santé."

"Has she been seen in Paris?"

"Yes. Last Sunday . . . One of her old friends spotted her in Place Clichy. She announced that she would soon be leaving for Brazil."

"Is that all?"

"No. The Musician was released last Friday."

All this was just routine, as Maigret called it. At this very moment, police cars were being deployed in the deserted side streets surrounding Place Pigalle. At the Quai, the protesting gentlemen of the fraternity were still being questioned, and were beginning to realize that they had stepped in something very nasty.

"Call and ask them to let us have a photograph of the Musician as soon as possible. There's sure to be one in Records. No, better still, call them and send the taxi to fetch it."

"Anything else, Chief?"

"Yes. When the driver gets back with the photograph, go with it to Poissy, and show it to the man who owns the dance hall near the bridge. It will be closed, of course, so you'll have to wake up the proprietor. . . . He's an ex-con. . . . Show him the photograph and ask him if it's the same man who got into a scuffle with Félicie at his place last Sunday night."

The car drove off. Silence reigned once more. The night was still. Maigret poured brandy into one of the little glasses, warmed it in his hand, and sipped it slowly, glancing up at the ceiling from time to time as he did so.

Every time Félicie turned over in her sleep, the bedspring creaked. Was she dreaming? He wondered whether her dreams were as extravagant as her daytime fantasies.

Eleven o'clock. A clerk in a gray coverall up in the attics of the Palais de Justice extracted two photographs from a file, one taken in profile, the other full face, the features in both pictures being too sharply defined. The clerk handed them to the driver, who had been instructed to take them back to Lucas.

In the neighborhood of Place Pigalle, crowds were pouring out of the Montmartre movie houses and, over their heads, the luminous sails of the Moulin-Rouge rotated. The buses edged their way through the crowds with difficulty. The doormen, in blue, red, and green livery, some dressed as Cossacks, others with black faces, were at their posts outside the various nightclubs, while Superintendent Piaulet, inconspicuous under the trees in the middle of the square, directed operations. All around, unseen by the crowds, his instructions were being carried out.

Janvier was seated at the bar of the Pélican, while the members of the band were taking their instruments out of their cases. In spite of the poor lighting, it did not escape Janvier's notice when a terrified-looking waiter dashed across to the proprietor and dragged him off to the rest room.

Montmartre was full of decent, honest people who had come there for an enjoyable evening out, and were now crowding the café terraces, sipping one last beer before going home to bed. But, on the fringe, the other Montmartre was just beginning to come to life. There, rumors and whispers were rife, and fear was in the air. The proprietor came back from the rest room, smiled at Janvier, went across to a woman sitting alone in a corner, and began talking to her in an undertone.

"I think I'll make an early night of it," she announced. "I'm worn out."

She was only one of many who, on hearing that police cars were closing in, preferred not to linger in the danger area. But all the exits were already sealed. On Boulevard Rochechouart, Rue de Douai, Rue Notre-Dame-de-Lorette, dim figures loomed out of the shadows.

"Your papers, please."

What happened next largely depended on the whim of those manning the roadblocks.

"You may go. . . ."

But more often it was:

"Get in. . . ."

Into the dimly lit Black Marias strung out all along the streets.

Had the trap closed yet on the Musician and Adèle, or would they succeed in slipping through the net? Word had certainly reached them. Even if they were cowering in an attic somewhere, some kind soul would have taken the trouble to warn them.

A quarter to twelve. Lucas, who was playing dominoes with the landlord of the Anneau d'Or, to pass the time—only one feeble light had been left on in the deserted bar—heard the taxi draw up outside and got to his feet.

"I shouldn't be gone more than half an hour," he said. "Just time enough to see someone in Poissy, and have a word with the Chief Superintendent afterward."

The dance hall was all in darkness. Lucas's knocks reverberated in the silent night. The first person to appear was a woman in curlers, who poked her head out of a window.

"Fernand . . . it's for you."

Lights, footsteps, grumbling. The door opened a crack.

"Eh? What's that? . . . I thought that little fracas might land me in trouble. . . . I run a respectable business. I've sunk a lot of money in it. The last thing I want is to be mixed up . . ."

He shambled over to the bar, his suspenders dangling, his hair umcombed, and studied the two photographs.

"I see. . . . Well, what do you want to know?"

"Is that the man who was put in his place by Félicie?"

"And if it was?"

"Nothing. That's all. Did you know him?"

"Never set eyes on him before or since . . . What's he done?"

Midnight. Lucas got out of the taxi, and Maigret started up out of his armchair like a man roused from sleep. He did not seem greatly interested in what the Sergeant had to tell him.

"I thought as much."

With those jokers, tough nuts though they might be, it was usually plain sailing. One knew the sort of person one was dealing with. One could tell in advance what they would do. Not like that amazing girl Félicie. She was more trouble than the whole lot of them put together.

"What am I to do now, Chief?"

"Go back to Orgeval, and play dominoes while you wait for phone calls."

"Who told you I'd been playing dominoes?"

"You and the proprietor are all alone there, and you don't play cards."

"Are you expecting anything to happen here?"

He shrugged. He didn't know. It didn't matter.

"Good night."

One o'clock in the morning. Félicie was talking in her sleep. Maigret put his ear to her door and tried to hear what she was saying, but was unable to do so. Mechanically he turned the doorknob, and the latch gave.

He smiled. He was touched. She trusted him, after all, it

seemed, since she had not troubled to lock her door. He stood for a moment listening to her breathing, and to the words that tumbled out like the babbling of a child. All he could see was the bed, like a milky stain, and her black hair on the pillow. He shut the door softly and returned downstairs on tiptoe.

The shrill blast of a whistle in Place Pigalle. This was the signal. All the exits were sealed. The uniformed police, advancing shoulder to shoulder, scooped up men and women, who were pouring in from all directions in the hope of slipping through the cordon. One policeman was badly bitten on the finger by a fat redhead in evening dress. The Black Marias were filling up.

The proprietor of the Pélican, standing in the doorway of his nightclub, puffing nervously at a cigarette, protested feebly:

"I give you my word, gentlemen, you won't find anything here, other than a few Americans doing the town. . . ."

Young Inspector Dunan, whom Maigret had seen earlier that day in the Hotel Beauséjour, felt someone tugging at his sleeve, and was surprised to recognize the hall porter of the hotel. Come to see the fun, no doubt.

"Hurry! It's her. . . ."

He pointed to the glass door of a café, which was empty except for the proprietor standing behind the bar. At the back of the room a door closed, but not before the Inspector had time to catch a shadowy glimpse of a woman.

"She's the one who came in with a man."

Adèle . . . The Inspector summoned two policemen. They made swiftly for the door at the back, went past the deserted rest rooms and down a narrow staircase, which smelled of damp, stale wine, and urine.

"Open up."

A cellar door. It was locked. One of the men smashed it open with a blow of his shoulder.

"Hands up, whoever is in there."

The beam of a flashlight played over casks, bottles in racks, and crates containing apéritifs. Not a sound was to be heard. Yet as they stood motionless, in response to an order from the Inspector, they sensed, if they did not actually hear, a gasp of indrawn breath and the frantic beating of a heart.

"Get up, Adèle."

She sprang to her feet like a Fury from behind a pile of crates. Knowing that she was trapped, she nevertheless struggled frantically to escape, so that it took all the strength of the three men to fasten handcuffs on her.

"Where's your boyfriend?"

"Don't know."

"What were you doing in this neighborhood?"

"Don't know."

She sniggered.

"It's easier to rough up a defenseless woman than to lay hands on the Musician, isn't it?"

They took her bag from her. In the bar, they opened it, and found nothing but a grubby visiting card, a few small coins, and some letters written in pencil, no doubt those she had received from the Musician during his jail term, since they were addressed to her in Béziers.

The first of the Black Marias, with as many people as it could hold, had driven off toward the Central Police Station. The cells there would soon be overcrowded. Many of the gentlemen were in dinner jackets and the ladies in evening dresses. There were also a number of waiters, and doormen in livery.

"Well, we've got his woman anyway, Superintendent."

Superintendent Piaulet, none too hopeful of getting results, questioned her.

"Sure you won't talk? Where is he?"

"Where you'll never find him."

"Take her away. Not to the cells. Hand her over to Rondon-net."

In the many dubious one-night hotels, police were going from room to room, asking to see everyone's papers. The men, wearing nothing but their shirts, were highly embarrassed at being found there, especially because they were not alone.

"All I ask is that my wife should not hear of this. . . ."

But, of course, of course!

"Hello! Is that you, Lucas? Would you tell Maigret that we've got Adèle. . . . Yes . . . Needless to say, she won't talk. . . .

No, no news of the Musician . . . She's being interrogated, yes. . . . The whole area is still sealed off. . . ."

Now that most of the big fish were in the net, things had quieted down a good deal around Place Pigalle. It was like the flat calm after a storm. The streets were quieter than usual, and late-night revelers coming in from the center of the city were puzzled to find the atmosphere so muted, with even the touts having seemingly lost heart.

Four o'clock. For the third time that night, Lucas went to Cape Horn, to find Maigret divested of his collar and tie.

"You don't happen to have any tobacco on you, do you? I used up the last of mine half an hour ago."

"They've got Adèle. . . ."

"What about him?"

He could still not be absolutely sure that he was right, and yet . . . One fact was incontrovertible: the Musician hadn't a sou to bless himself with. On the night of his release from prison, Adèle had been forced to leave Béziers without the money due her. He had come to Poissy. That was on Sunday. Possibly, he had even come as far as Jeanneville, and followed Félicie to the dance hall. Surely, the easiest way would be to seduce the little, garishly dressed servant girl? He could gain access to the house through her. . . .

But instead, she had slapped his face!

And the following day, Monday, old Lapie was murdered in his bedroom. The Musician had been compelled to flee, empty-handed.

"When did they arrest Adèle?"

"Half an hour ago. They called us immediately."

"You'd better go now, and take the taxi with you."

"Do you think he'll . . . ?"

"Hurry! You must go at once, I tell you."

Maigret shut the door carefully behind him and returned to the kitchen. The red carcass of the lobster was still there on the table. He put out the light and sat down in his chair by the window.

8

A CUP OF COFFEE
FOR FÉLICIE

SHE LOOKED ABOUT her, wide-eyed. She had no idea what time it was. She had forgotten to set her alarm clock as usual the previous night. It was dark in the bedroom, except for the streaks of silvery daylight showing through the slats of the shutters.

Félicie listened. Her mind was a blank. She still felt dazed and weary, as one does on waking from a very deep sleep. At first, she was unable to distinguish between dream and reality. She had had an argument, a vehement argument, culminating in an actual physical struggle with that detestable, imperturbable man who was bent on destroying her. Oh, how she hated him!

Who had opened the door in the night? Someone had, she was sure. She had lain still, waiting, uneasy. It had been dark. A patch of yellowish light had streamed in from the landing. Then the door had closed. The purring of a car engine . . . All night long, she had heard that sound in her sleep.

She lay very still. She dared not move. She felt that some danger threatened her. There was a weight on her stomach. The lobster. She remembered now. She had eaten too much lobster. She had been drugged. He had forced her to swallow some drug or other.

She listened. What was that? Someone was moving about in the kitchen. She recognized the familiar sound of the coffee grinder. She must be dreaming. Who on earth could possibly be grinding coffee down there?

She gazed down at the floor, all her senses alert. Someone was

253

pouring boiling water. The aroma of freshly made coffee drifted up the staircase right into her room. The clink of china. Another very familiar sound, the sugar canister being opened, and then the slam of a cupboard door.

Someone was coming up the stairs. She suddenly remembered that she had not locked her door last night. Why had she not turned the key? Because her pride would not let her. Yes! She had wanted to show that man that she was not afraid. She had intended to creep out of bed later, after he had gone downstairs, and turn the key without making a sound, but she had fallen asleep as soon as her head had touched the pillow.

Someone was knocking at her door. She raised herself on one elbow. She gazed at the door in anguish, her nerves stretched to breaking point. The knocking was repeated.

"Who's there?"

"Your breakfast."

Frowning, she felt about for her dressing gown, but could not find it, so she quickly slid back into bed and pulled the sheet up to her chin. The door opened, and a tray appeared, with a cloth on it, and a blue-spotted cup.

"Did you sleep well?"

And there was Maigret, looking more imperturbable than ever. He seemed scarcely to be aware that he was in a young girl's bedroom, and that she was still in bed.

"What do you want?"

He put the tray down on the bedside table. He was looking very clean and spruce. Where had he cleaned up? In the kitchen, no doubt, or at the pump. His hair was still damp.

"You do take coffee with milk for breakfast, don't you? Unfortunately, I wasn't able to get to Mélanie Chochoi's for fresh bread. . . . Eat up, child. . . . Here's your dressing gown. I'll turn my back while you put it on."

In spite of herself, she did as she was bidden, and drank a scalding mouthful of coffee. Then, with the cup suspended in midair, she froze.

"Who's that downstairs?"

Someone had moved down there, she was sure of it.

"Who's that downstairs? Tell me!"

"The murderer."

"What did you say?"

She sprang out of bed.

"What's your game this time? You're determined to drive me right around the bend, aren't you? And I'm utterly defenseless. I have no one. . . ."

He sat down on the edge of the bed, watched her helpless flutterings, shook his head and sighed.

"The murderer really is downstairs, you can take my word for it. . . . I was sure he would be back. . . . In his predicament, he had no choice but to take the gamble. . . . Besides which, he thought I was safely out of the way in Paris, directing operations from there. He never dreamed that I was stubbornly determined to keep watch in this house."

"And did he come?"

She stopped short. She was completely at sea. Grasping Maigret by the wrist, she cried:

"But who? Who is he? Surely it isn't possible that . . . ?"

Her eagerness to learn the truth was so great that she dashed out alone to the landing, pale, thin, and shivering in her vivid-blue dressing gown, intending to go and see for herself. But, suddenly in the grip of fear, she got no farther than the head of the stairs.

"Who is he?"

"Do you still hate me?"

"Yes . . . I don't know. . . ."

"Why did you lie to me?"

"Because!"

"Listen to me, Félicie. . . ."

"I'm not going to listen to any more from you. . . . I'm going to open the window and shout for help."

"Why did you never tell me that, when you returned to the house on Monday morning, you saw Jacques Pétillon coming out of the garden? Oh, yes, you did see him. He must just have come through the gate in the hedge. It was on his account that the old man had fetched the bottle of brandy and the two glasses from the sideboard. He thought his nephew had come to make peace, to apologize or something. . . ."

She listened to him in frozen silence, unprotesting.

"And you thought that it was Jacques who had killed his uncle. You found the revolver in the bedroom, and you carried it on your person for three days, before getting rid of it by planting it on a stranger in the Métro. You saw yourself as a heroine of a romance. At all costs, you would save the man you loved—though he, poor fellow, knew nothing about it! And the long and the short of it is that you and your lies very nearly got him arrested for a murder he didn't commit."

"How do you know?"

"Because the real murderer is downstairs."

"Who is he?"

"No one you know."

"You're just trying to trick me again. But I won't say another word, do you hear, not one single word! And now you can take yourself out of here. I want to get dressed. . . . No . . . Stay . . . What could have brought Jacques here, that Monday of all days?"

"He came to oblige the Musician."

"What musician?"

"A buddy of his. You know how it is in Paris. One meets all sorts, some good, some bad. . . . Especially if one happens to play the saxophone in a nightclub . . . If you don't drink your coffee soon, it will be stone cold."

He had opened the shutters earlier. He now went across and looked out the window.

"Hello! There's your friend Léontine on her way to buy her bread. She's looking this way. . . . Little does she know what tales you have to tell her!"

"I won't tell her anything."

"Do you want to bet?"

"I wouldn't dream of such a thing."

"Do you still hate me?"

"Is it true that Jacques is innocent?"

"If I say yes, you won't hate me any longer. If I say no, you'll hate me worse than ever. . . . What a girl! Very well, then. Jacques is guilty of only one thing. One night, a little over a year ago, when he was still living in this house as his uncle's guest, he was guilty, I repeat, of giving shelter for a night, or possibly several nights, to someone whose acquaintance he had made in Montmartre. The man's name was Albert Babeau, alias the Musician, alias Midget. . . ."

"Why Midget?"

"You wouldn't understand. . . . Following a holdup in a nightclub called the Chamois, the Musician, on the run from the police, remembered his friend Pétillon, who had gone to live with an elderly uncle in the country. A splendid hideout for a man on the run . . ."

"I remember now," she exclaimed suddenly.

"What?"

"The only time Jacques . . . the only time he was ever rude to me . . . I had gone into his room without knocking. And I heard a sound, as if something was being hastily pushed out of sight. . . ."

"It wasn't something, it was someone, someone who ought not to have been there. And that someone, before he made his escape from this house, had found an ideal hiding place for his loot, in that same room, under one of the boards on top of the wardrobe. Soon after, he was arrested, and was sentenced to a year in prison. . . . What are you looking at me like that for?"

"It's nothing. . . . Go on."

She was blushing. She looked away, so that the Chief Superintendent would not see the involuntary sparkle of hero worship that had come into her eyes.

"Needless to say, when he was released, penniless, it was imperative for him to lay hands on his loot. His original plan was to gain access to the house by making up to you. . . ."

"Me! Surely you don't imagine that I . . ."

"You slapped his face. . . . His next move was to seek out Pétillon and spin him heaven knows what yarn. Probably that he'd left something he valued behind in the house and needed Pétillon's assistance to get it back. . . . So, while Pétillon was chatting with old Lapie in the garden . . ."

"I see!"

"And about time."

"Thank you very much!"

"It's my pleasure. Peg Leg must have heard something. . . . I daresay he had pretty sharp ears. . . ."

"And how!"

"He went up to his bedroom, and surprised the Musician in the act of climbing on a chair. The man lost his head and shot him at point-blank range. Pétillon, hearing the shot, took to his heels in terror. Meanwhile, the Musician had also fled, but in a different direction. You saw Jacques, your own beloved Jacques, as you would express it, all in capitals, I daresay, but you failed to spot the Musician.

"And that's the whole story. Needless to say, Jacques said not a word. When he realized that he was under suspicion, he lost his head, like the boy that he is. . . ."

"It's not true!"

"Are you suggesting that he's not just a boy? So be it. Then he's an idiot. Instead of coming to me with the whole story, he got it into his head that he must seek out the Musician and demand an explanation. He went looking for him in every sleazy dive he could think of. At last, in despair, he even went as far as Rouen, in the hope of getting some information out of the man's mistress. . . ."

"How did he come to know a woman like that?" interrupted Félicie, stung by jealousy.

"That I can't tell you, my dear. In Paris, you know . . . Anyway, he had worked himself up into a fearful state. He was at the end of his rope. . . . That night, he had reached the point where he had to tell someone or burst, but before he could do so, the Musician, who had friends to keep him informed, shot him, to teach him to keep his mouth shut."

"Don't talk like that."

"That same night, the Musician came back here, hoping that this time he would find what he was looking for. You can't imagine the predicament of a man on the run without money. He searched the cavity on top of the wardrobe, but found nothing. . . . You, on the other hand, were left with a tangible memento of his visit. . . . He reasoned that, if the money was not here, then Pétillon must have found it, which explains why he sent Adèle to search his room on Rue Lepic.

"But nothing was found there either. . . . That same night, Montmartre was completely sealed off by a police cordon. The man was trapped like a hunted animal. Adèle was caught.

"God alone knows how he did it, but the Musician managed to slip through the police cordon. By now, he was more desperate than ever, and there is no one more desperate than a hardened criminal on the run. He took a taxi to Poissy. He was so broke that, by way of payment, he coshed the taxi driver on the back of the head."

Félicie shivered. She was gazing at Maigret as if watching the breath-taking denouement of a suspense movie.

"Did he come here?"

"He did. . . . Very cautiously, without making a sound. He didn't so much as tread on a twig as he crossed the garden and crept past the open kitchen window, and . . ."

To her, Maigret had already become a hero of romance. She marveled at him.

"Did he attack you?"

"No. When he was least expecting it, he suddenly felt the cold steel of a revolver barrel against his temple."

"What did he do?"

"Nothing. He just said:

"'Hell! I've copped out!'"

She felt let down. But no, it couldn't possibly have been as easy as all that. Her old mistrust flooded back; her features sharpened.

"Are you sure you're not hurt?"

"I've just told you. . . ."

He was only saying that to reassure her! Of course there had been a struggle. He was a hero, and . . .

Suddenly she caught sight of the tray on the bedside table.

"And after all that, you quietly set about grinding the coffee. . . . You had the . . . the presence of mind to prepare my breakfast coffee, remembering that I took it with milk, and bring it up to me. . . ."

She was on the verge of crying. . . . Then she wept tears of gratitude and hero worship.

"You did all that, you! But why? Tell me why?"

"Why indeed? Because I hate you. I hate you so much that, as soon as Lucas gets here with the taxi, I will be off, taking my sausage with me. . . . Oh! I forgot to tell you that the Musician is tied up like a sausage. I had to borrow poor Lapie's gardening twine for the purpose."

"And what of me?"

It was all he could do to repress a smile at this cry, which, whether she knew it or not, came from the bottom of her heart.

It meant: What of me? Am I to be left all alone? Am I never again to know what it is to be taken seriously? Will there no longer be anyone to harass me with questions, and tease me and . . . ?

And what of me?

"You'll have to make do with Jacques. . . . That shop in the Faubourg-Saint-Honoré where you can buy grapes and oranges and champagne will still be there. . . . I can't remember now what the visiting hours are at the hospital, but you can easily find out. . . ."

The taxi, such a familiar sight in Paris but looking somewhat out of place on the winding roads of these parts, with fields on either side, came into view.

"You'd better hurry up and get dressed."

He went out to the landing, without so much as a backward glance, and as he began going downstairs, he heard her murmur:

"How can you be so horrid to me?"

A few seconds later, he was skirting old Lapie's armchair, in which the Musician was securely tied up. Overhead, footsteps came and went, water splashed, coat hangers rattled in a wardrobe, a shoe was dropped and picked up, and a voice could be heard muttering feverishly.

Félicie was there, all right!

L'Aiguillon-sur-Mer, 1942

MAIGRET'S
RIVAL

1

THE EVENING
LOCAL

MAIGRET SURVEYED HIS fellow passengers with wide-open, sullen eyes and, without meaning to, assumed that self-important look people put on when they have spent mindless hours in the compartment of a train.

Well before the train began to slow down as it approached a station, men in large, billowing overcoats started to emerge from their various cells, clutching a leather briefcase or a suitcase, in order to take up their positions in the corridor. There they would stand with one hand casually gripping the brass bar across the window, oblivious, or so it appeared, of their fellow travelers.

Huge raindrops were making horizontal streaks across this particular train window. Through the transparent, watery glass the Superintendent saw the light from a signal tower shatter into a thousand pointed beams, for it was now dark. Farther down, he glimpsed streets laid out in straight lines, glistening like canals, rows of houses that all looked exactly the same, windows, door-steps, sidewalks, and, in the midst of this universe, a solitary human figure, a man in a hooded coat hurrying somewhere or other.

Slowly and carefully, Maigret filled his pipe. In order to light it, he turned in the direction the train was going. Four or five passengers who, like himself, were waiting for the train to stop so that they could slip away into the deserted streets or quickly make their way to the station restaurant stood between him and the end of the corridor. Among them, he recognized a pale face, which immediately turned the other way.

Old Cadaver!

The Superintendent's immediate reaction was to groan:

"He's pretending he doesn't see me, the idiot."

Then he frowned. Why on earth would Inspector Cavre be going to Saint-Aubin-les-Marais?

The train slowed down and pulled into the station at Niort. Maigret stepped onto the cold and wet platform, and called to a porter:

"How do I get to Saint-Aubin?"

"Take the 6:17 train on Platform Three."

He had half an hour to wait. After a brief visit to the men's room, at the very end of the platform, he pushed open the door of the station restaurant and walked over to one of the many unoccupied tables. He then dropped wearily on a chair and settled down to wait in the dusty light.

Old Cadaver was there, at the other end of the room, sitting, as Maigret was, at a table with no cloth on it, and again he pretended not to have seen the Superintendent.

Cavre was his real name, Justin Cavre, but he had been known as Old Cadaver for twenty years, and everyone at the Police Judiciaire used this nickname when referring to him.

He was ridiculous, sitting stiffly in his corner with his constipated air, shifting uncomfortably in order to avoid meeting Maigret's eye. He knew the Superintendent had seen him; that was obvious. Skinny, sallow, with reddened eyelids, he made you think of the sort of schoolboys who skulk peevishly around the playground, although they long to join in the fun.

Cavre was just that kind of person. He was bright. He was probably the most intelligent man Maigret had come across in the police force. They were both about the same age. Actually, Cavre had a better educational background, and had he persevered, he could well have become a superintendent ahead of Maigret.

Why, even as a young man, had he given the impression of carrying the weight of some curse on his narrow shoulders? Why did he give them all black looks, as if he thought each and every one of them was out to get him?

"Old Cadaver has just started on his novena."

It was an expression often heard of at the Quai des Orfèvres some years ago. At the slightest provocation, or sometimes for no reason at all, Inspector Cavre would suddenly embark on a cure of silence and mistrust, a cure of hatred, one might say. For a week at a time he would not say a word to anyone. Sometimes, his colleagues would catch sight of him chuckling to himself, as though he had seen through their supposedly evil schemes.

Few people knew why he had suddenly left the police force. Maigret himself did not learn the facts until later, and had felt very sorry for him.

Cavre loved his wife with the jealous, consuming passion of a lover rather than with the feelings of a husband. What exactly he found so beguiling about that vulgar woman, who had all the aggressive mannerisms of a call girl or a phony movie star, one could only surmise. Nevertheless, the fact remained that it was because of her that he had got into serious trouble while on the force. A story of kickbacks had sealed his fate. One evening, Cavre had emerged from the Chief's office with his head down and his shoulders drooping. A few months later he was known to have set up a private detective agency above a stamp shop on Rue Drouot.

People were having dinner, each in his own aura of boredom and silence. Maigret finished his half-pint of beer, wiped his mouth, picked up his suitcase, and walked past his former colleague at a distance of less than two yards, but Cavre continued to stare down at a patch of spit on the floor.

The little train, looking black and wet, was already at Platform Three. Maigret climbed into a cold, damp compartment of the old-fashioned type and tried in vain to shut the window properly.

People were walking back and forth on the platform outside, and the Superintendent heard other familiar sounds. The compartment door opened two or three times and a head appeared. Each passenger was trying desperately to find an empty compartment. Whenever one of them caught sight of Maigret, the door shut again.

Once the train had started to move, the Superintendent went out into the corridor to close a window that was causing a draft. In the compartment next to his, he saw Inspector Cavre, who this time was pretending to be asleep.

There was nothing to be alarmed about. It was silly to keep brooding on this strange coincidence. The whole thing was non-sensical, and Maigret would have liked to simply shrug it off.

What difference did it make to him if Cavre was also going to Saint-Aubin?

Darkness sped by outside the windows, shot through from time to time with a flicker of light, the headlights of a car, or, more mysterious and inviting, the yellowish rectangle of a window.

Examining Magistrate Bréjon, a delightful, rather shy man of old-fashioned courtesy, had repeated over and over again:

"My brother-in-law, Naud, will meet you at the station. I've told him you're coming."

And Maigret kept thinking obsessively as he drew on his pipe: "What on earth can Old Cadaver be up to?"

The Superintendent was not on an official case. Bréjon, with whom he had worked so often, had sent him a short note asking him if he would be good enough to pop into his office for a few moments.

It was January, and raining in Paris, as it was in Niort. It had been raining for more than a week, and the sun had not once peeked out. The lamp on the desk in the Examining Magistrate's office had a green shade. While Monsieur Bréjon was talking, and constantly cleaning the lenses of his spectacles as he did so, Maigret reflected that he, too, had a green lampshade in his office, but that the one he was looking at now was ribbed like a melon.

"So sorry to bother you . . . especially since it's not a profes-sional matter. Do sit down. . . . But of course . . . A cigar? . . . You may perhaps know that my wife's maiden name is Lecat. . . . It doesn't matter. That's not what I want to discuss. . . . My sister, Louise Bréjon, became Madame Naud when she married. . . ."

It was late. People outside looking up at the gloomy façade of the forbidding Palais de Justice and seeing the light on in the Examining Magistrate's office would no doubt think that serious issues were being debated up there.

Maigret's bulky figure and thoughtful countenance gave such a forceful impression of authority that no one could possibly have guessed at his thoughts.

In actual fact, as he listened with half an ear to what the Examining Magistrate, with the goatee beard, was telling him, he was thinking about the green lampshade in front of him, about the one in his own office, how attractive the ribbed shade was, and how he would get one like it for himself.

"You can understand the situation. . . . A small, really a tiny, village . . . You will see for yourself. . . . It's miles from anywhere. . . . The jealousy, the envy, the unwarranted malice . . . My brother-in-law is a charming person, and sincere, too. As for my niece, she's just a child. . . . If you agree, I'll arrange for you to have a week's leave of absence. My entire family will be indebted to you, and . . . and . . ."

That was how he had become involved in a stupid venture. What exactly *had* the little man told him? He was still provincial in his outlook and, like all provincials, he let himself be carried away by local gossip about families whose names he pronounced as if they were of historical importance.

His sister, Louise Bréjon, had married Etienne Naud. The Examining Magistrate had added, as if the whole world had heard of him:

"The son of Sébastien Naud, you understand."

Now, Sébastien Naud was quite simply a stout cattle dealer from the village of Saint-Aubin, which was tucked away in the heart of the Vendée marshes.

"Etienne Naud is related, on his mother's side, to the best families in the district."

That was all very well. But what of it?

"They live about a mile outside the village, and their house almost touches the railway line—the one that runs between Niort and Fontenay-le-Comte. . . . About three weeks ago, a local boy—from quite a good family, too; at any rate, on his mother's side, because she's a Pelcau—was found dead on the tracks. At first, everybody thought it was an accident—and I still think it was. But since then, rumor has it . . . Anonymous letters have been sent around. . . . In a nutshell, my brother-in-law is now in a terrible state because people are accusing him almost openly of having killed the boy. . . . He wrote me a somewhat garbled letter about it. I then wrote to the Public Prosecutor in Fontenay-le-Comte for more detailed information, since Saint-Aubin comes under the jurisdiction of Fontenay. Contrary to what I expected, I discovered that the accusations were rather serious and that it will be difficult to avoid an official inquiry. . . . That is why, my dear Superintendent, I have taken it upon myself to ask you, purely as a friend . . . "

The train stopped. Maigret wiped the condensation from the window and saw a tiny station, with just one light, one platform, and one solitary railwayman, who was running along the side of the train blowing his whistle. A compartment door slammed shut, and the train set off again. But it was not the door of the next compartment that Maigret had heard closing. Inspector Cavre was still there.

Now and then, Maigret would glimpse a farm, nearby or in the distance but always beneath him as he peered through the window, and whenever he saw a light it would invariably be reflected in a pool of water, as if the train were skirting the edge of a lake.

"Saint-Aubin!"

He got out. Three people in all got off the train: a very old lady with a cumbersome black wicker basket, Cavre, and Maigret.

In the middle of the platform stood a very tall, very large man wearing leather gaiters and a leather jacket. It was obviously Naud, for he was looking hesitantly about him. His brother-in-law, the Examining Magistrate, had told him Maigret would be arriving that night. But which of the two men who had got out of the train was Maigret?

First, he walked toward the thinner one. His hand was already moving up to touch his hat; his mouth was slightly open, ready to ask the stranger's name in a faltering voice. But Cavre walked straight past, haughtily, as if to say, with a knowing look:

"It's not I. It's the other guy."

Bréjon's brother-in-law abruptly changed direction.

"Superintendent Maigret, I believe? I'm sorry I did not recognize you right away. Your photograph is so often in the papers. But in this little backwater, you know . . . "

He took it upon himself to carry Maigret's suitcase. As the Superintendent hunted in his pocket for his ticket, he said, steering him, not toward the station exit but toward the grade crossing:

"Don't worry about that."

Turning toward the stationmaster, he cried:

"Good evening, Pierre."

It was still raining. A horse harnessed to a pony cart was tied to a ring.

"Please climb up. The road is virtually impassable for cars in this weather."

Where was Cavre? Maigret had seen him disappear into the darkness. He had a strong desire to follow him, but it was too late. Moreover, would it not have looked extremely odd, so soon upon his arrival, to leave his host standing there and go off in hot pursuit of another passenger?

There was no sign of an actual village. Just a single lamppost about a hundred yards from the station, standing by some tall trees. At this point, a road seemed to open out.

"Put the coat over your legs. Yes, you must. Even with it, your knees will get wet, since we're going against the wind. . . . My brother-in-law wrote me a long letter all about you. . . . I feel embarrassed that he has involved someone like you in such an unimportant matter. . . . You have no idea what country folk are like. . . ."

He let the end of his whip dangle over the horse's rump. The wheels of the cart sank deep into the black mud as they drove along the road, which ran parallel to the railway line. On the other side, lamps threw a hazy light over some sort of canal.

A human figure appeared suddenly on the road, as if from nowhere. It was a man holding his jacket over his head. He moved out of the way as the cart came nearer.

"Good evening, Fabien!" Etienne Naud called, in the same way he had hailed the stationmaster, like a country squire who calls everyone by his first name, who knows everyone in the neighborhood.

But where the devil could Cavre be? Try as he might to put the matter out of his mind, Maigret could think of nothing else.

"Is there a hotel in Saint-Aubin?" he asked.

His companion roared with laughter.

"There's no question of your staying in a hotel! We have plenty of room at the house. A place is ready for you. We've arranged to have dinner an hour later than usual, since I thought you wouldn't have had anything to eat on your journey. I hope you were wise enough not to have dinner at the station restaurant in Niort? We live very simply, however."

Maigret could not have cared less how they lived or what sort of welcome he received. He had Cavre on the brain.

"I'd like to know if the man who got out of the train with me . . ."

"I don't know who he was," Etienne Naud hurriedly declared.

Why did he reply that way? It was not the answer to Maigret's question.

"I'd like to know if he will find somewhere to stay."

"Indeed! I don't know what my brother-in-law has been telling you about this part of the world. Now that he's living in Paris, he probably looks upon Saint-Aubin as an insignificant little hamlet. But, my dear fellow, it is almost a small town. You haven't seen any of it yet because the station is some way from the center. There are two excellent inns, the Lion d'Or, run by Monsieur Taponnier—Old François, as everyone calls him—and just opposite there's the Hôtel des Trois Mules. . . . Well! We're nearly home. That light you can see . . . Yes . . . That's our humble dwelling."

Needless to say, the tone of voice in which he spoke made it abundantly clear that it was a large house, and, sure enough, it was a big, low, solid-looking building with lights showing in four windows on the ground floor. On the center of the façade, an electric lamp shone like a star and gave light to any visitor.

Behind the house, there was probably a large courtyard surrounded by stables, so that one would occasionally catch the warm, sweet smell of the horses. A farm hand rushed up immediately to lead in the horse and cart. The door of the house opened, and a maid came forward to take the traveler's luggage.

"Here we are, then! It's not very far, you see. . . . At the time the house was built, unfortunately, no one foresaw that the railway line would one day pass virtually beneath our windows. You get used to it, it's true, and actually there are few trains, but . . . Do come in. . . . Give me your coat. . . . "

At that precise moment, Maigret was thinking:

"He has talked nonstop."

And then he could not think at all for a moment, because too many thoughts were assailing him and a totally new atmosphere was closing in on him.

The hallway was wide and paved with gray tiles; its walls were paneled with dark wood up to a height of about six feet. The electric light was enclosed in a lantern of colored glass. A large oak staircase with a red carpet and heavy, well-polished banisters led up to the second floor. A pleasing aroma of wax polish and casseroles simmering in the kitchen pervaded the whole house, and Maigret caught a whiff of something else, too, that bitter-sweet smell that for him was the very essence of the country.

But the most remarkable feature of the house was its stillness, a stillness that seemed to be immemorial. It was as if the furniture and every object in this house had remained in the same place for generations, as if the occupants themselves, as they moved about, were observing special rites, keeping at bay the unforeseen.

"Would you like to go up to your room for a moment before we eat? It's just the family. No fuss."

The master of the house pushed open a door, and two people rose to their feet simultaneously. Maigret was ushered into a warm, cozy living room.

"Superintendent Maigret, my wife . . ."

She had the same deferential air about her as her brother, the Examining Magistrate, the same courteousness, so characteristic of a sound bourgeois upbringing, but for a second Maigret thought he detected something harder, sharper in her countenance.

"I am appalled that my brother asked you to come all this way in weather like this."

As if the rain made any difference to the journey or was of any importance in the circumstances!

"May I introduce you to a friend of ours, Superintendent: Alban Groult-Cotelle. I suspect my brother-in-law mentioned his name to you."

Had the Examining Magistrate mentioned him? Perhaps he had. Maigret had been so preoccupied thinking about the green ribbed lampshade!

"How do you do, Superintendent. I'm a great admirer of yours."

Maigret was tempted to reply:

"Well, I'm not of yours."

He could not abide people like Groult-Cotelle.

"How about serving the port, Louise?"

The decanter was on a table in the living room. The light was soft, and there were few, if any, sharp lines. The chairs were old, most of them upholstered; the rugs were all in neutral or faded colors. A cat lay stretched out on the hearth in front of a log fire.

"Do sit down. . . .Our neighbor Groult-Cotelle is having dinner with us."

Whenever his name was mentioned, Groult-Cotelle would bow pretentiously, like a nobleman among commoners who takes it upon himself to behave as if he were in a salon.

"They insist on setting a place at their table for an old recluse like me."

A recluse, yes, and probably a bachelor, too. You could sense it, though you didn't know why. A pretentious, useless character, quite pleased with himself and his oddities.

The fact that he was neither a count nor a marquis, not even a simple nobleman, must cause him considerable annoyance. Yet he did have an affected first name, Alban, which he liked to hear, and an equally pretentious double-barreled surname to go with it.

He was a tall, lean man of about forty who obviously thought this leanness gave him an aristocratic distinction. The unbrushed look he had about him, in spite of the care with which he was dressed, his spiritless face and bald forehead gave the impression of someone without a wife. His clothes, elegant, their colors subtle, looked as though they had never been new, but also as though they would never become old or threadbare. They were part of his personality, and equally unchangeable. Whenever Maigret met him subsequently, he was always wearing the same greenish jacket, very much in the style of the country gentlemen, and the same horseshoe tie pin on a white ribbed-cotton tie.

"I hope the journey wasn't too tiring, Superintendent?" inquired Louise Bréjon Naud, handing him a glass of port.

And Maigret, firmly ensconced in an armchair that sagged beneath his weight, much to the distress of the mistress of the house, was prey to so many different emotions that his mind became rather blunted, and for part of the evening his hosts must have thought him somewhat slow-witted.

First of all, there was the house—the very prototype of the house he had dreamed of so often, with its protective walls enclosing air as thick as solid matter. The framed portraits reminded him of the Examining Magistrate's lengthy discourse about the Nauds, the Bréjons, the La Noues—for the Bréjons were connected with the La Noues through their mother. One would have liked to imagine that all these serious-looking and rather rigid faces belonged to one's own ancestors.

Judging by the smells coming from the kitchen, an elaborate meal was about to be served. Someone was carefully setting the table in the dining room next-door; the clinking of china and glass could be heard. In the stable, the farm hand was rubbing down the mare, and two long rows of reddish-brown cows were chewing the cud in their stalls.

Everything breathed peace, order, and virtue, and at the same time was the very expression of the petty habits and foibles of simple families living their self-contained lives.

Etienne Naud, broad-shouldered, with a ruddy complexion and protuberant eyes, looked cordially around him as if to say:

"Look at me! . . . Sincere . . . Kind . . ."

The good-natured giant. The perfect master of the house. The perfect father. The man who called out from his pony cart:

"Good evening, Pierre . . . Good evening, Fabien . . ."

His wife smiled shyly in the shadow of the huge fellow, as if to apologize for his taking up so much space.

"Will you excuse me for a moment, Superintendent."

Of course. He had been expecting it. The competent mistress of the house always goes into the kitchen to have a last look at the dinner preparations.

Even Alban Groult-Cotelle was predictable. Looking as if he had just stepped out of an engraving, he was the very picture of the superior friend—more refined, better bred, more intelligent, indeed, with his faintly condescending airs, the epitome of the old family friend.

"You see . . ." was written all over his face. "They're decent people, perfect neighbors. . . . You can't talk philosophy with them, but apart from that, they make you feel very much at home, and you'll see their burgundy is genuine enough and their brandy worthy of praise. . . ."

"Dinner is served, madame."

"Will you sit on my right, Superintendent."

But where was the note of anxiety in all this? For the Examining Magistrate had certainly been very concerned when he sent for Maigret.

"I know my brother-in-law," he insisted, "just as I know my sister and my niece. Anyway, you'll see them for yourself. . . . But all this doesn't alter the fact that this odious accusation takes on more substance day by day, to the point of forcing the Public Prosecutor to investigate the matter. My father was the notary in Saint-Aubin for forty years, having taken over the practice from *his* father. . . . They'll show you our family house in the center of town. . . . I am asking myself how such a blind hatred could have developed in so short a time. It is steadily gaining ground and is threatening to wreck the lives of innocent people. . . . My sister has never been very strong. She's high-strung and suffers from insomnia. The slightest problem upsets her."

One would never have guessed, from the looks of it, that the people present were involved in a tragedy. Everything would lead one to believe that Maigret had merely been asked to a good dinner and a game of bridge. While larks were being served, the Superintendent's hosts explained at great length how the peasants caught them at night by dragging nets over the meadows.

But why was their daughter not present?

"My niece, Geneviève," the Examining Magistrate had said, "is a perfect young lady, the like of which you only read about in novels now."

This was not, however, what the person or persons writing the anonymous letters thought, or, for that matter, what most of the local people thought. It was Geneviève they were accusing, after all.

Maigret was still puzzled by the story he had heard from Bréjon, because it was so out of keeping with the scene before him. Rumor had it that Albert Retailleau, the young man found dead on the railroad tracks, was Geneviève's lover. It was even said that he went to her house two or three times a week and spent the night in her room.

Albert had no money. He was barely twenty years old. His father had worked in the Saint-Aubin dairy and had died in a boiler explosion. His mother lived on an income the dairy had been obliged to give her as damages.

"Albert Retailleau would never have committed suicide," his friends declared. "He enjoyed life too much. And even if he had been drunk, as had been said, he would have known better than to cross the tracks when a train was coming."

The body had been found more than five hundred yards from the Nauds', about halfway between their house and the station.

There was nothing wrong in that, but it was now rumored that the young man's cap had been found in the reeds along the canal, much nearer the Nauds' house.

There was yet another, even more questionable, story in circulation. It seemed that someone had visited Madame Retailleau, the mother of the young man, a week after her son's death, and had seen her hurriedly hide a wad of thousand-franc notes. She had never been known to have such a large sum of money before.

"It is a pity, Superintendent, that you have made your first visit to our part of the world in wintertime. It is so pretty around here in the summer that the district is known as 'Green Venice.' . . . You'll have some more of the chicken, won't you?"

And Cavre? What was Inspector Cavre up to in Saint-Aubin?

Everyone ate and drank too much. It was too hot in the dining room. They all returned to the living room in a sluggish state and sat around the crackling log fire.

"I insist . . . I know you're particularly fond of your pipe, but you must have a cigar."

Were they trying to lull him to sleep? But that was a ridiculous thought. They were decent people. That was all there was to it. The Examining Magistrate in Paris must have exaggerated the situation. And Alban Groult-Cotelle was nothing but a stuck-up fool, one of those dandyish good-for-nothings to be found in any country district.

"You must be tired after your journey. Just say when you want to go to bed."

That meant nothing was going to be said that night. Perhaps because Groult-Cotelle was there? Or because Naud preferred not to speak in front of his wife?

"Do you take coffee at night? . . . No? . . . No tea either? . . . Please excuse me if I go up now, but our daughter hasn't been well for the past two or three days and I want to see whether she needs anything. . . . Young girls are always rather delicate, aren't they? Especially in a climate like ours."

The three men sat around the fire smoking and talking at random. They began discussing local politics; it appeared that there was a new mayor, who was acting counter to the wishes of all respectable members of the community and who . . .

"Well, gentlemen," Maigret grunted finally, half pleasantly, half crossly, "if you will excuse me, I think I'll go up to bed now."

"You must stay the night here, too, Alban. I'm not going to let you go home in this terrible weather."

They went upstairs. Maigret's room was at the end of the hallway. Its walls, covered with yellow cloth, brought back many childhood memories.

"Have you everything you need? . . . I forgot. . . . Let me show you the bathroom."

Maigret shook hands with the two men, then undressed and got into bed. As he lay there half-asleep, he thought he heard noises, the distant murmur of voices somewhere in the house, but soon, when all the lights were out, these sounds died away.

He fell asleep. Or he thought he did. The sinister face of Cavre, that luckless creature, kept creeping into his subconsciousness, and then he dreamed that the rosy-cheeked maid who had served the dinner was bringing him his breakfast.

He was sure he heard the door open gently. He sat up in bed and groped for the switch to the light bulb in the tulip-shaped opal glass covering attached to the wall above the headboard. The light went on, and Maigret saw standing in front of him a young girl with a brown wool coat over her nightgown.

"Ssh," she whispered. "I just had to speak to you. Don't make a noise."

And, like a sleepwalker, she sat down on a chair and stared into space.

2

THE GIRL IN
THE NIGHTGOWN

IT WAS A wearying night for Maigret, and yet not without charm. He slept without sleeping. He dreamed without dreaming, or, in other words, he was well aware he was dreaming and deliberately prolonged his dreams, being conscious all the time of noises from the real world.

For example, the sound of the mare kicking her hoofs against the stable wall was real enough, but the other images that flitted through Maigret's mind, as he lay in bed perspiring heavily, were tricks of the imagination. He conjured up a picture of the dim light in a stable, the horse's rump, the rack half full of hay; he imagined the rain still falling in the courtyard, with figures splashing their way through black puddles of water, and lastly he saw, from the outside, the house in which he was staying.

It was a kind of personality splitting. He was in his bed. He was keenly savoring its warmth and the delicious country smell of the mattress, which became even more pungent as it grew moist with his sweat. But at the same time he was in the whole house. Who knows if, at one moment in his dreams, he did not even become the house itself?

Throughout the night, he was conscious of the cows moving about in their stalls, and around four in the morning he heard the footsteps of a farm hand crossing the courtyard and the sound of the latch being lifted: what prevented him from actually seeing the man, by the light of a hurricane lamp, as he sat on a three-legged stool drawing the milk into tin buckets?

He must have fallen into a deep sleep again, for he woke up with a start at the sound of the toilet flushing. The sudden, violent noise gave him rather a fright. But immediately afterward he was back to his old tricks and imagined the master of the house coming out of the bathroom, with his suspenders around his thighs, and tiptoeing back to his room. Madame Naud was asleep, or pretending to be, with her face to the wall. Etienne Naud had left the room in darkness except for the small light above the dressing table. He started to shave, his fingers numbed by the icy water. His skin was pink, taut, and glossy.

Then he sat down in a chair to pull on his boots. Just as he was leaving the room, a sound came from beneath the blankets. What was his wife saying to him? He bent over her and murmured something in a low voice. He closed the door noiselessly behind him and tiptoed down the stairs. At this point, Maigret jumped out of bed and switched on the light. He had had enough of these spellbinding nocturnal activities.

He looked at his watch, which he had left on the bedside table. It was half past five. He listened carefully and decided that either it had stopped raining or the rain had turned into a fine, silent drizzle.

Admittedly, he had eaten and drunk well the previous evening, but he had not drunk too much. And yet this morning he felt as if he had drunk really heavily. As he took various things out of his suitcase he looked with heavy, swollen eyes at his unmade bed and in particular at that chair beside it.

He was convinced it had not been a dream: Geneviève Naud had come into his room. She had come in without knocking. She had positioned herself on that chair, sitting bolt upright without touching the back of it. At first, as he stared at her in sheer amazement, he had thought she was deranged. In reality, however, Maigret was infinitely more disturbed than she was. He had never been in such a delicate situation. Never before had a young girl who was ready to pour out her heart stationed herself at his bedside, with him in bed in his nightshirt, his hair ruffled by the pillow and his lips moist with spittle.

He had murmured something like:

"If you'll turn the other way for a moment, I'll get up and put some clothes on."

"It doesn't matter. . . . I have only a few words to say to you. . . . I am pregnant by Albert Retailleau. . . . If my father finds out, I'll kill myself; and no one will stop me."

He could not bring himself to look at her while he was laying in bed. She paused for a moment, as if expecting Maigret to react to her announcement, then rose to her feet, listened at the door, and said as she left the room:

"Do as you wish. I am in your hands."

Even now, he could scarcely believe all this had happened, and the thought that he had lain prostrate like a dummy throughout the proceedings humiliated him. He was not vain, in the way men can be, and yet he was ashamed that a young girl had caught him in bed with his face still bloated by sleep. And the girl's attitude was even more annoying; she had hardly glanced at him. She had not pleaded with him, as he might have expected, she had not thrown herself at his feet, she had not wept.

He recalled her face, its regular features making her look a little like her father. He could not have said if she was beautiful, but she had left him with an impression of maturity and poise, which even her insane overture had not dispelled.

"I am pregnant by Albert Retailleau. . . . If my father finds out, I'll kill myself; and no one will stop me."

Maigret finished dressing and mechanically lit his first pipe of the day. He then opened the door and, failing to find the light switch, groped his way along the hallway. He went down the stairs but could not see a light anywhere, even though he could hear someone stoking the stove. He made his way to where the noise was coming from and saw a shaft of yellow light beneath a door. He tapped gently, opened the door, and found himself in the kitchen.

Etienne Naud was sitting at one end of the table, his elbows resting on the light wood, and tucking into a bowl of soup. An elderly cook in a blue apron was sending showers of white-hot cinders into the ash bucket as she raked her stove.

Maigret saw the startled look on Naud's face as he came in and realized he was annoyed at having been caught unawares in the kitchen having his breakfast like a farm worker.

"Up already, Superintendent? I keep to the old country habits, you know. No matter what time I go to bed, I'm always up at five in the morning. I hope I didn't wake you?"

There was no point in telling him that it had been the sound of the toilet flushing that had awakened him.

"I won't offer you a bowl of soup, for I presume you . . ."

"But I'd love some."

"Léontine . . ."

"Yes, monsieur, I heard. . . . I'll have it ready in a moment."

"Did you sleep well?"

"Quite well. But at one point I thought I heard footsteps in the hallway. . . ."

Maigret had brought this up in order to find out whether Naud had pounced on his daughter after she had left his room, but the look of astonishment on his face seemed genuine enough.

"When? . . . I didn't hear anything. Though it's true it takes a lot to rouse me from my sleep early in the night. It was probably our friend Alban getting up to go to the bathroom. What do you think of him, incidentally? A likable fellow, isn't he? Far more cultured than he actually appears to be. He's read countless books, you know. . . . Pity he didn't have better luck with his wife."

"He was married, then?"

Having thought Groult-Cotelle to be the archetypal bachelor living in the provinces, Maigret viewed this snippet of information somewhat suspiciously. He felt as if they had hidden something from him, as if they had deliberately tried to mislead him.

"Indeed he was, and, what's more, he still is. He has two children, a girl and a boy. The elder of the two must be twelve or thirteen now."

"Does his wife live with him?"

"No. She lives on the Côte d'Azur. It's rather a sad story, and no one ever talks about it around here. She came from a very good family, though. She was a Deharme. . . . Yes, like the General . . . She's his niece. A rather eccentric woman who could never grasp the fact that she was living in Saint-Aubin and not in Paris. She scandalized the neighborhood on several occasions, and then, one winter, moved to Nice, ostensibly to escape the bitter cold here, but of course she never came back. She lives there with her children. . . . And she's not living alone, needless to say."

"Didn't her husband ask for a divorce?"

"That's not done in these parts."

"Which of them has the money?"

Etienne Naud looked at him disapprovingly, and it was obvious he did not want to go into details.

"She is undoubtedly a very rich woman. . . ."

The cook had sat down at the table to grind the coffee in an old-fashioned coffee mill with a large copper top.

"You are lucky. It has stopped raining. But my brother-in-law really ought to have told you to bring some boots. After all, he comes from this part of the world and knows it well. We are right in the middle of the marshes and even have to use a boat in winter to reach some of my farms. They're known as *cabanes* here, by the way. . . . But speaking of my brother-in-law, I feel rather embarrassed he had the nerve to ask a man of your standing to . . ."

The question Maigret kept asking himself, the question that had been constantly on his mind ever since his arrival the previous evening, was: Were the Nauds decent people who had nothing to hide and who were doing their utmost to make their guest from Paris feel at home, or was he in fact an unwelcome intruder whom Bréjon had most inconsiderately deposited in their midst and whose presence this disconcerted couple could well have done without?

He decided to try an experiment.

"Not many people get off the train at Saint-Aubin," he commented as he ate his soup. "I think only two of us did yesterday, apart from an old peasant woman wearing a bonnet."

"Yes, you're right."

"Does the man who got off the train with me live around here?"

Etienne Naud hesitated before replying. Why? Maigret was looking at him so intently that he was covered with confusion.

"I'd never seen him before," he answered hurriedly. "You must have noticed me dithering as to which one of you to approach."

Maigret tried another tactic:

"I wonder what he has come here for, or, rather, who asked him to come."

"Do you know him?"

"He's a private detective. I'll have to find out where he is and what he is up to this morning. He presumably checked in at one or another of the inns you mentioned yesterday."

"I'll take you into town shortly in the pony cart."

"Thanks, but I'd rather walk, if you don't mind, and then I'll be free to come and go as I like."

Something had just occurred to him. Supposing Naud had been counting on him to sleep soundly so that he could leave early for the village and meet Inspector Cavre?

Anything was possible here, and the Superintendent even began to wonder if the young girl's appearance in his room had not been part of a plot the whole family had planned.

A moment later, he dismissed such thoughts as foolish.

"I hope your daughter isn't seriously ill."

"No . . . Well, if you really want the truth, in spite of all we've done, she has got wind of what is being said around here. She's a proud young woman. All young women are. I'm sure that's the reason she has insisted on staying in her room for the past three days. And maybe your arrival has made her feel rather ashamed."

"Ashamed, is she!" thought Maigret, as he recalled her brief appearance in his room the night before.

"We can talk in front of Léontine," Naud went on. "She's known me from childhood. She's been with the family for . . . for how many years, Léontine?"

"Ever since I had my first communion, monsieur!"

"A little more soup? No? . . . To continue, I'm in a most awkward position, and I sometimes think my brother-in-law tackled the case in the wrong way. I'm sure you'll say he knows far more about such matters than I do; that's his job. . . . But maybe he has forgotten what it's like in our part of the world now that he lives in Paris."

It was hard to believe he was not speaking sincerely, since he seemed to want to talk over what was on his mind. He sat there with his legs apart, stuffing his pipe, while Maigret finished his breakfast. The kitchen smelled of the freshly made coffee, and the two men were enjoying the warm atmosphere of the room. Outside, in the darkness of the courtyard, the stable hand was whistling softly as he groomed one of the horses.

"To speak bluntly . . . From time to time, rumors about someone or other are spread around town. This time, it's a serious matter, I know. But I still wonder whether it would not be wiser to disregard the accusation. . . . You agreed to do what my brother-in-law asked. You have done us the honor of coming. . . . Everyone knows by now that you are here, that's for sure. Tongues are already wagging. No doubt you intend to question some people, and that is bound to stir their imaginations even more. . . . So that's why I really do wonder, quite sincerely, whether we are going about this whole business in the right way. . . . Are you sure you have had enough to eat? . . . If you don't mind the cold, I'll be glad to show you around. I go on a tour of inspection every morning."

Maigret was putting on his overcoat as the maid came downstairs; she got up an hour later than the old cook. The two men went out into the cold, damp courtyard and spent an hour going from one stable to another. Meanwhile, cans of milk were being loaded into a small truck.

Some cows were to be taken to market in a nearby town that very day and drovers in dark overalls were rounding them up. At the end of the yard was a small office with a little round stove, a table, ledgers, and a desk with an array of pigeonholes. Sitting at the table was a farm hand wearing the same sort of boots as his boss.

"Will you excuse me a moment?"

Madame Naud was getting up now, for there was a light on in her room on the second floor. The other rooms remained in darkness, which meant that Groult-Cotelle and the young girl were still fast asleep. The maid was cleaning the dining room.

Men and animals could be seen moving about in the dim light

of the courtyard and outbuildings, and Maigret could hear the motor of the milk truck running in the background.

"That's done. . . . I was just giving a few instructions. . . . I'll be leaving by car for the market shortly; I've got to meet some other farmers. . . . If I had time, and thought you would be interested, I would tell you how the farm is run. I have ordinary dairy cattle on my other farms, since we supply the local dairy with milk, but here we breed only the finest, most of which we sell abroad. I even send some to South America. But right now, I am entirely at your service. . . . It will be daylight in an hour. If you need the car or if you have any questions you would like to ask me . . . I want you to feel comfortable. You must treat this as your home."

His face was cheerfully beaming as he spoke, but his smile faded when Maigret merely answered:

"Well, if you don't mind, I'll be on my way."

The road surface was spongy, as if water from the canal on the left had soaked the ground beneath. The railroad embankment ran along the right-hand side of the road. After a little more than half a mile, a glaring light became visible, obviously the one at the station, since green and red signals flashed nearby.

Maigret looked back toward the house and saw that there were lights on in two more windows on the second floor. This brought Alban Groult-Cotelle into his mind, and he began to wonder why he had been so put out to discover that he was married.

The sky was brightening. One of the first houses Maigret caught sight of as he turned to the left of the station and approached the village had a signboard reading LE LION D'OR. The lights were on downstairs, and he went inside. He found himself in a long, low room where everything was brown—the walls, the beams of the ceiling, the long polished tables, and the backless benches. A kitchen range at the very end of the room had not yet been lit. A woman of indeterminate age was crouched over a log burning slowly on the hearth, waiting for the coffee to heat. She turned around to look at the stranger, but said nothing. Maigret sat down in the dim light of a very dusty lamp.

"I'd like to sample the local brandy!" he said, shaking his

overcoat, which the damp dawn had showered with grayish beads of moisture.

The woman did not reply, and he thought she had not heard. She went on stirring the saucepan of rather uninviting coffee with her spoon, and when it was to her liking she poured some into a cup, put it on a tray, and walked toward the staircase.

"I'll be down in a minute," she said.

Footsteps sounded above Maigret's head. He could hear voices but could not make out what was being said. Five minutes went by. Then another five. Every now and then Maigret rapped a coin on the wooden table, but nothing happened.

At last, a quarter of an hour later, the woman came downstairs again and spoke even less amicably than before.

"What did you say you wanted?"

"A glass of the local brandy."

"I haven't any."

"You've no brandy?"

"I've got cognac, but no local brandy."

"Then give me a cognac."

She gave him a glass so thick-bottomed that there was hardly any room for the drink.

"Tell me, madame . . . I believe a friend of mine arrived here last night."

"How am I to know if he's your friend?"

"Has he just got up?"

"I have one guest and I have just taken him his coffee."

"If he's the man I know, I bet he asked you lots of questions, didn't he?"

The glasses left by the previous evening's customers had made round wet marks on many of the tables, and the woman began to wipe them with a cloth.

"Albert Retailleau spent the evening here the day before he died, didn't he?"

"What's that got to do with you?"

"He was a good boy, I believe. Someone told me he played cards that evening. Is *belote* the favorite game in this part of the world?"

"No. We play *coinchée*."

"So he played *coinchée* with his friends. He lived with his mother, didn't he? A good woman, unless I'm mistaken."

"Hmm!"

"What's that?"

"Nothing. You're the one who's doing all the talking, and I don't know what you're getting at."

Upstairs, Inspector Cavre was getting dressed.

"Does she live far from here?"

"At the end of the street, in a small yard. It's the house with three stone steps."

"Do you happen to know if my friend Cavre—the man who's staying here with you—has been to see her yet?"

"And just how do you think he could have been to see her when he's only just getting up?"

"Will he be staying long?"

"I haven't asked him."

She opened the windows and pushed back the shutters. A milky-white light filtered into the room, for day had come.

"Do *you* think Retailleau was drunk that night?"

The woman suddenly became aggressive and snapped back:

"No more drunk than you are, drinking cognac at eight in the morning!"

"How much do I owe you?"

"Two francs."

The Trois Mules, a rather more modern-looking inn, was right opposite, but the Superintendent did not think he would gain anything by going inside. A blacksmith was lighting the fire in his forge. A woman standing on her doorstep was throwing a bucket of dirty water into the street. A bell, the sound of which reminded Maigret of his childhood, tinkled lightly, and a boy wearing clogs came out of the baker's with a loaf of bread under his arm.

Curtains parted as he made his way down the street. A hand wiped the condensation from a window, and a wrinkled old face with eyes that were ringed with red like Inspector Cavre's peered through the windowpane. On the right stood the church. It was built of gray stone and roofed with slate, which looked black and shiny after the heavy rain. A very thin woman of about fifty, in deep mourning and holding herself very erect, came out of the church holding a missal bound in black cloth.

Maigret stood idly for a while in a corner of the little square next to a board marked SCHOOL, which had doubtless been put up to caution drivers. He followed the woman with his eyes. The minute he saw her disappear into a kind of blind alley at the end of the street, he guessed at once that it was Madame Retailleau. Since Cavre had not yet visited her, he quickened his step.

He had guessed right. When he got to the corner of the alley, he saw the woman go up three steps to the door of a small house and take a key out of her bag. A few minutes later, he knocked at the glass door, which was faced by a lace curtain.

"Come in."

She had just had time to take off her coat and her black crepe veil. The missal was still on the oilcloth-covered table. The white enamel kitchen stove was already lit. The top was so clean that it must have been painstakingly rubbed with fine sandpaper.

"Please forgive me for disturbing you, madame. Madame Retailleau, I presume?"

He wasn't very sure of himself, for neither her voice nor her gestures gave him much encouragement. She stood quite still, with her hands over her stomach, her face almost the color of wax, and waited for Maigret to speak.

"I have been asked to investigate the rumors that are circulating with regard to the death of your son."

"Who are you?"

"Superintendent Maigret of the Police Judiciaire. Let me hasten to add that these inquiries are for the moment unofficial."

"What does that mean?"

"That the case has not yet been brought before the court."

"What case?"

"I am sorry to have to talk about such unpleasant matters, madame, but you are no doubt aware of the various rumors connected with your son's death."

"You can't keep people from talking."

Stalling for time, Maigret turned toward a photograph in an oval frame that was hanging on the wall to the left of the walnut kitchen sideboard. It was an enlarged photograph of a man of about thirty with a crew cut and a large mustache drooping over his lips.

"Is that your husband?"

"Yes."

"Unless I'm misinformed, you had the misfortune to lose him unexpectedly when your son was still a small boy. From what I have been told, you were forced to bring an action against the dairy that employed him in order to receive a pension."

"You have been told nonsense. There was never any court case. Monsieur Oscar Drouhet, the manager of the dairy, did what was necessary."

"And later, when your son was old enough to work, he gave him a job in the office. Your son was his bookkeeper, I believe."

"He did the work of an assistant manager. He would have been given the title if he hadn't been so young."

"You don't have a photograph of him, do you?"

Maigret could have kicked himself, for as he spoke he saw a tiny photograph on a small round table covered with red plush. He picked it up quickly, in case Madame Retailleau objected.

"How old was Albert when this photograph was taken?"

"Nineteen. It was last year."

A handsome boy, somewhat broad-faced, with sensuous lips and merry, sparkling eyes. He looked healthy and strong.

Madame Retailleau stood waiting, as before, heaving an occasional sigh.

"He wasn't engaged?"

"No."

"As far as you know, he had no relationships with women?"

"My son was too young to be chasing women. He was a serious boy and thought only about his career."

This was not the impression conveyed by the lively look, the thick glossy hair, and the well-developed physique.

"What was your reaction when . . . I do apologize . . . You must see what I am getting at. . . . Do you believe it was an accident?"

"One has to believe it was."

"You had no suspicions whatsoever, then?"

"What sort of suspicions?"

"He never mentioned Mademoiselle Naud? . . . He never used to come home late at night?"

"No."

"And Monsieur Naud hasn't been to see you since your son's death?"

"We have nothing to say to each other."

"I see. . . . But he might have. . . . Monsieur Groult-Cotelle hasn't called on you either, I take it?"

Was it Maigret's imagination, or had her eyes hardened momentarily? Maigret was sure they had.

"No," she murmured.

"So you consider the rumors concerning the circumstances of your son's death to be quite unfounded?"

"Yes, I do. I pay no attention to them. I don't want to know what people are saying. And if it's Monsieur Naud who sent you, you can go back and tell him what I've said."

For a few seconds, Maigret stood perfectly still, with his eyes half-shut, and repeated to himself what she had said, as if to lodge it in his mind:

"And if it's Monsieur Naud who sent you, you can go back and tell him what I've said."

Did she know that it was Etienne Naud who had met Maigret at the station the day before? Did she know that it was he, indirectly, who had caused him to make the journey from Paris? Or did she merely suspect this to be the case?

"Forgive me for having taken the liberty of calling on you, madame, especially at such an early hour."

"Time is of no importance to me."

"Good-bye, madame."

She remained where she was and said not a word as Maigret walked toward the door and closed it behind him. The Superintendent had not gone ten paces when he saw Inspector Cavre standing on the sidewalk as if he were on sentry duty.

Was Cavre waiting for Maigret to leave so that he, in turn, could talk to Albert's mother? Maigret wanted to make sure once and for all. His conversation with Madame Retailleau had put him in a bad temper, and he was in the mood to play a trick on his former colleague.

He relit his pipe, which he had put out with his thumb before entering Madame Retailleau's house, crossed the street, and took up a position on the other side, immediately opposite Cavre, standing resolutely on the pavement as if he meant to stay.

The town was awakening. Children were walking up to the school gate on one side of the little square in front of the church. Most of them had come from far away and were muffled up in scarves and thick blue or red woolen socks. Many were wearing clogs.

"Well, Old Cadaver, it's your turn now? Your move!" Maigret seemed to be saying, with a mischievous glint in his eyes.

Cavre did not budge, but looked haughtily in the other direction, as if he were above such frivolities.

Had he been summoned to Saint-Aubin by Madame Retailleau? It was quite possible. She was a strange woman, and it was very difficult to size her up. She had a peasant streak, the characteristic, almost innate mistrust of the peasant; but there was also, in her make-up, more than a touch of the bourgeois upper crust of the provinces. Beneath the glacial exterior, one sensed an arrogance that nothing could undermine. The way she had faced Maigret, with stony immobility, was impressive in itself. She had not moved a step, or made any gesture, as long as he was in her house, but had frozen, as some animals are said to do when, up against danger, they simulate death. Her lips barely moved when she spoke.

"Well, Cavre, you old misery! Make up your mind. . . . Do something."

Old Cadaver was stamping his feet to keep warm but seemed in no hurry to make any sort of move as long as Maigret was watching him.

It was a ridiculous situation. It was childish to stay rooted where he was, but Maigret did just that. Unfortunately, however, this tactic turned out to be a waste of time. At half past eight, a small, red-faced man came out of his house and made his way to the town hall. He opened the door with a key, and a moment afterward Cavre followed him inside.

This was the very move that Maigret had planned on making that morning. He had determined to find out what the local authorities had to say. His former colleague had beaten him to it, and he had no choice but to wait his turn.

3

AN UNDESIRABLE PERSON

MAIGRET WAS TO consider this undignified episode as unmentionable. He never spoke of what happened that day, and particularly that morning, and no doubt he would have preferred to forget all about it.

The most disconcerting experience was losing his sense of identity, of being Maigret. For what, in fact, did he represent in Saint-Aubin? Strictly speaking—nothing. Justin Cavre had gone into the town hall to talk to the local authorities while he, Maigret, had stood awkwardly outside in the street. The row of houses looked like a line of large, poisonous mushrooms, clustered as they were beneath a sky that reminded one of a blister ready to burst. Maigret knew he was being watched; faces were peering at him from behind every curtain.

True, he did not really mind what a few old ladies or the butcher's wife thought of him. People were free to take him for what they liked and laugh at him as he went by, as some of the children passing through the school gate had done.

No, the trouble was that he did not feel in his proper skin— perhaps an exaggerated way of putting it, but there it is.

What would happen, for example, if he were to go into the whitewashed lobby of the town hall and knock at the gray door with SECRETARY'S OFFICE displayed in black letters? He would be asked to wait his turn, just as if he had come to ask for a birth certificate or about a claim of some sort. And meanwhile, Old

Cadaver would continue questioning the secretary in his tiny overheated office for as long as he pleased.

Maigret was not here in an official capacity. He could not claim to be acting on behalf of the Police Judiciaire, and, anyway, who was to know whether anyone in this village surrounded by slimy marshes and stagnant water had even heard the name Maigret?

He was to find out soon enough. As he was waiting impatiently for Cavre to come out, he had one of the most extraordinary ideas of his entire career. He was all set to pursue his former colleague relentlessly, to follow him step by step and say, point-blank:

"Look here, Cavre, there's no point in trying to outwit each other. It is quite obvious you're not here for the fun of it. Someone asked you to come. Just tell me who it is and what you've been asked to do."

How comparatively simple a regular, official investigation seemed at this moment! Had he been on a case somewhere within his own jurisdiction he would only have had to go into the local post office and say:

"Superintendent Maigret. Get me the Police Judiciaire and make it snappy. . . . Hello! Is that you, Janvier? . . . Jump in your car and come down here. . . . When you see Old Cadaver come out . . . Yes, Justin Cavre . . . Right . . . Follow him and don't let him out of your sight."

Who knows? Maybe he would have had Etienne Naud tailed, too. He had just seen him drive past on the road to Fontenay.

Playing the role of Maigret was easy! An organization that ran like clockwork was at his disposal, and, what is more, he had only to say his name and people were so dazzled that they would go to any lengths to please him.

But here, he was so little known that despite the numerous articles and photographs that were always appearing in the newspapers, someone like Etienne Naud had walked straight up to Justin Cavre at the station.

Naud had welcomed Maigret effusively because his brother-in-law, the Examining Magistrate, had sent him all the way from Paris, but, on the other hand, had they not all behaved as if puzzled by his arrival? The gist of what their welcome meant was this:

"My brother-in-law, Bréjon, is a charming fellow, who wants to help, but he has been away from Saint-Aubin for too long and doesn't quite grasp the situation. It was kind of him to have thought of sending you here. It is kind of you to have come. We will look after you as best we can. Eat and drink your fill. Let me show you around the estate. But by no means feel constrained to stay in this damp, unattractive part of the world. And don't feel you have to look into this trivial matter, which concerns no one but ourselves."

On whose behalf was he working, anyway? For Etienne Naud. But it was palpably obvious that Etienne Naud did not want him to carry out a proper investigation.

And to cap it all, Geneviève had come into his room in the middle of the night and had admitted:

"I was Albert Retailleau's mistress and I am pregnant by him. But I'll kill myself if you breathe a word to my parents."

Now, if she really had been Albert's mistress, the accusations against Naud took on a terrible new meaning. Had she thought of that? Had she consciously charged her father with murder?

And even the victim's mother, who had said nothing, admitted nothing, denied nothing, in fact had made her meaning perfectly clear by her attitude:

"It's none of your business!"

Everyone, even the old ladies lying in wait behind their fluttering curtains, even the schoolchildren who had turned around to stare as they went by, considered him an intruder, an undesirable person. Worse still, no one knew where this steady plodder had come from or why he was in this village.

And so, in a setting just right, with hands deep in the pockets of his heavy overcoat, Maigret looked like one of those nasty characters tormented by some secret vice who prowl around the Porte Saint-Martin, or somewhere similar, with hunched shoulders and sidelong glances, and cautiously edge their way past the houses well out of sight of the police.

Was he turning into another Cavre? He felt like sending someone to Naud's house to get his suitcase and taking the first train back to Paris. He would tell Bréjon:

"They don't want me around there. . . . Leave your brother-in-law to his own devices."

And yet he had gone into the town hall as soon as the former inspector emerged, with a leather briefcase tucked under his arm. No doubt this would increase Cavre's standing in the village; now he would pass for a lawyer.

The secretary was a little man who smelled rather unpleasant. He did not get up when Maigret entered his office.

"Can I help you?"

"Superintendent Maigret of the Police Judiciaire. I am in Saint-Aubin on unofficial business and I would like to ask you one or two questions."

The little man hesitated and looked annoyed, but nonetheless bade Maigret sit down on a wicker chair.

"Did the private detective who has just left your office tell you whom he was working for?"

The secretary either did not understand or pretended he did not understand the question. And he reacted in similar fashion to all the other questions the Superintendent put to him.

"You knew Albert Retailleau. Tell me what you thought of him."

"He was a decent fellow. . . . Yes, that's how I'd describe him, a decent fellow. . . . Nothing to hold against him . . ."

"Was he a womanizer?"

"He was young, of course, and we don't always know what the young are up to, these days, but a womanizer . . . no, you couldn't call him that."

"Had he been Mademoiselle Naud's lover?"

"That's what people said. . . . Rumors were going around. . . . But it's all pure hearsay."

"Who discovered the body?"

"Ferchaud, the stationmaster. He telephoned the town hall, and the Deputy Mayor immediately contacted the Benet Police Headquarters. There's no police sergeant in Saint-Aubin."

"What did the doctor who examined the body say?"

"What did he say? Just that he was dead . . . There wasn't much of him left. . . . The train went right over him."

"But he was identified as Albert Retailleau?"

"What? . . . Of course . . . It was Retailleau, all right; there was no doubt about that."

"When did the last train pass through?"

"At 5:07 in the morning."

"Didn't people think it odd that Retailleau was on the tracks at five in the morning in the middle of winter?"

The secretary's reply was curious:

"It was dry at the time. There was hoarfrost on the ground."

"But people talked just the same."

"Rumors circulated, yes. . . . But you can never stop people from talking."

"Your opinion, then, is that Retailleau died a natural death?"

"It is very hard to say what happened."

And did Maigret bring up the subject of Madame Retailleau? He did, and the reply was as follows:

"She's an excellent woman. Nothing to be said against her."

And Naud, too, was described in similar terms:

"Such a pleasant man. His father was a splendid person, too, a county councillor."

And lastly, what did the secretary have to say about Geneviève?

"An attractive girl."

"Well behaved?"

"Of course she would be well behaved. . . . And her mother is one of the most respected members of the community."

All this was said politely enough, but without the ring of conviction, while the little man kept picking his nose and carefully examining what he had excavated.

"And what is your opinion of Monsieur Groult-Cotelle?"

"He's a decent fellow, too. Not stuck-up."

"Is he a close friend of the Nauds?"

"They see a good deal of one another, that's a fact. But that's only natural, since they move in the same circles."

"When exactly was Retailleau's cap discovered not far from the Nauds' house?"

"When? . . . Well . . . But was it just the cap that was found?"

"I was told that someone named Désiré who collects the milk

for the dairy found the cap in the reeds along the bank of the canal."

"So people said."

"It's not true, then?"

"It's difficult to say. Désiré is drunk half the time."

"And when he is drunk . . ."

"Sometimes he tells the truth and sometimes he doesn't."

"But a cap is something you can see and touch! Some people have seen it."

"Ah!"

"It must have been put into safekeeping by now. . . ."

"Maybe . . . I don't know. . . . May I remind you that this office is not a police station, and we believe in minding our own business."

This unpleasant-smelling, seemingly half-witted individual could not have spoken more plainly, and was obviously delighted he had given a Parisian such short shrift.

A few moments later, Maigret was back in the street, no further on with his investigation, but by now convinced that no one was going to help him find the truth.

And since no one wanted to establish the truth, what was the point of his being here? Would it not be more sensible to go back to Paris and say to Bréjon:

"Look, your brother-in-law has no wish for a proper investigation. No one down there likes the idea. I have come back. They had a wonderful dinner for me."

Maigret passed a large house built of gray stone and saw from the bright-yellow plaque on the wall that it belonged to the notary. This, then, was the house that Bréjon's father and sister had once lived in, and in the watery gray light it had the same air of timelessness and inscrutability as the rest of the town.

He walked a little farther on, until he came to the Lion d'Or. Inside, he could see someone talking to the woman who ran the inn, and he had the distinct impression that they were talking about him and standing by the window in order to get a better view.

A man on a bicycle came into sight. Maigret recognized the rider as he approached but did not have time to turn away. Alban

Groult-Cotelle was on his way home from the Nauds' and he jumped off his bicycle as soon as he saw Maigret.

"It's good to see you again. . . . We're only a stone's throw from my house. Will you do me the honor of coming in for a drink? . . . I insist. . . . My house is very modest but I've got a few bottles of vintage port."

Maigret followed him. He did not expect much to come of the visit but the prospect was vastly preferable to wandering alone through the hostile town.

It was a huge, solid house, which looked very appealing from a distance. Its squat shape, black iron-work, and high slate roof gave it the air of a bourgeois fortress.

Inside, everything was shabby and neglected. The surly-faced maid looked really slovenly, and yet it was obvious to Maigret, from certain looks they exchanged, that Groult-Cotelle was sleeping with her.

"I am sorry everything is so untidy. . . . I'm a bachelor and live alone. . . . I'm only interested in books, so . . ."

So . . . the wallpaper was peeling off the walls, which were covered with damp patches, the curtains were gray with dust, and one had to try three or four chairs before finding one that did not wobble. Only one room on the ground floor was heated, no doubt to save wood, and this served as a living room, dining room, and library. There was even a couch in one corner, which Maigret suspected his host slept on most of the time.

"Do sit down. . . . It really is a pity you didn't come in the summer, since it is rather more attractive around here then. . . . How do you like my friends the Nauds? . . . What a nice family they are! I know them well. You would not find a better man than Naud anywhere. He may not be a very deep thinker, he may be a tiny bit arrogant, but he is so unaffected and sincere. . . . He is very rich, you know."

"And Geneviève Naud?"

"A charming girl . . . without any . . . yes, charming is how I'd describe her."

"I presume I'll have the opportunity to meet her. . . . She'll soon be better, I hope?"

"Of course she will . . . of course. . . . You know what girls her age are like. . . . Cheers!"

"Did you know Retailleau?"

"By sight . . . His mother seems to be well thought of. . . . I would show you around if you were staying longer; there are some interesting people here and there in the villages. . . . My uncle the General used to say that it is in country districts, and especially here in our Vendée, that . . ."

Hot air! If Maigret gave Groult-Cotelle the chance, he would start retelling him the history of every family in the neighborhood.

"I am afraid I must go now."

"Oh, yes! Your investigation. . . . How are you getting on? Are you optimistic? . . . If you want my opinion, the answer is to get hold of whoever is responsible for all these false rumors."

"Have you any idea who it might be?"

"Me? Of course not. Don't start thinking I have any bright ideas on the subject, please. . . . I'll probably see you this evening. Etienne has asked me to dinner, and unless I'm too busy . . ."

Busy doing what, good God! Words in this particular part of the world took on a completely different meaning.

"Have you heard the rumor about the cap?"

"What cap? Oh, yes . . . I was lost for a moment. . . . I did hear some vague story. . . . But is it true? Has it really been found? That's the key to it all, isn't it?"

No, that was not the key to it all. The young girl's confession, for example, was just as important as the discovery of the cap. But would Maigret be able to keep what he knew to himself much longer?

Five minutes later, Maigret rang the doctor's bell. A maid of sorts answered the door and started to explain that the office was closed until one o'clock. He persisted, and was shown into the garage, where a tall, strapping man with a cheerful face was repairing a motorcycle.

It was the same story:

"Superintendent Maigret of the Police Judiciaire . . . I'm here in an unofficial capacity. . . ."

"I'll show you into my office, if I may, and then when I've washed my hands . . ."

Maigret waited near the hinged, oilcloth-covered table that was used for examining patients.

"So you're the famous Superintendent Maigret? I've heard quite a lot about you. . . . I've a friend who pores over the miscellaneous news items in the papers. He lives more than twenty miles away, but if he knew you were in Saint-Aubin, he'd be over here in a flash. . . . You solved the Landru case, didn't you?"

He had hit on one of the few cases Maigret had had nothing to do with.

"And to what do we owe the honor of your presence in Saint-Aubin? For it is, indeed, an honor. . . . I am sure you would like a drink. . . . I have a sick child in the living room at the moment—it's warmer there—so I had to bring you in here. . . . Will you have a brandy?"

And that was it. All Maigret garnered from his visit was brandy.

"Retailleau? A charming boy . . . I believe he was a good son to his mother. . . . Anyway, she never complained about him. She's one of my patients . . . a curious woman, whom life ought to have treated better. She came from a good family, too. Everyone was amazed when she married Joseph Retailleau, a workman at the dairy.

"Etienne Naud? He's a real character. . . . We go shooting together. He's a crack shot. . . . Groult-Cotelle? No, you could hardly call him a good shot, but that's because he is very near-sighted. . . .

"So, you have met everyone already. . . . Have you seen Clémentine, too? . . . You haven't seen Tine yet? . . . Note that I mention her name with great respect, like everyone else in Saint-Aubin. Tine is Madame Naud's mother . . . Madame Bréjon, if you prefer. . . . Her son is an examining magistrate in Paris. . . . Yes, that's right . . . he's the one you know, of course. His mother was a La Noue, one of the great families in the Vendée. She does not want to be a burden to her daughter and son-in-law and she lives by herself, near the church. . . . At the

age of eighty-two, she's still sound of wind and limb and she's one
of my worst patients.

"You're staying in Saint-Aubin for a few days, are you? . . .

"What? The cap? Oh, yes . . . No, I haven't heard anything
about that myself. . . . Well, I did hear one or two rumors. . . .

"All this was discovered rather late in the day, you see. . . . If
I had known at the time, I would have done an autopsy. But put
yourself in my position. I was told the poor boy had been run over
by a train. It was patently obvious to me he *had* been run over by
a train, and naturally I wrote my report along those lines."

Maigret scowled. He could have sworn that they were all in
league with one another, that whether peevish or merry like the
doctor, they had passed around the story as they might pass
around a ball, exchanging knowing looks as they did so.

The sky was almost bright now. Reflections shone in all the
puddles, and patches of mud glistened in places.

The Superintendent walked up the main street once more. He
had not looked to see what it was called but it was most probably
Rue de la République. He decided to go into the Trois Mules,
opposite the Lion d'Or, where he had received such a cold welcome that morning.

The bar was brighter than that of the Lion d'Or. There were
framed prints and a photograph of a president who had held office
some thirty or forty years earlier hanging on the whitewashed
walls. Behind the bar was another room, deserted and gloomy-
looking; this was evidently where the local people came to dance
on Sundays, for there was a platform at one end and the room was
festooned with paper chains.

Four men were seated at a table, enjoying a bottle of full-bodied
wine. One of them coughed affectedly when the Superintendent
came in, as if to say to the others:

"There he is."

Maigret sat down on one of the benches at the other end of the
room. He felt the atmosphere had changed. The men had stopped
talking, and he knew full well that, before he came in, they would
certainly not have been sitting there drinking and looking at each
other in dead silence.

They looked just like characters in a dumb show as they sat in

a huddle, elbows and shoulders touching. Eventually, the oldest
of the four, a plowman, by the look of the whip beside him, spat
on the floor, whereupon the others burst out laughing.

Was that long stream of spittle meant for Maigret?

"What will you have?" inquired a young woman, tilting her
hips in order to support her grubby-looking baby.

"I'd like some of your *vin rosé*."

"A carafe?"

"All right."

Maigret puffed furiously at his pipe. Up till now the townsfolk
had concealed, or at any rate disguised, their hostility toward
him, but now they were openly sneering at him—indeed, deliberately provoking him.

"Even the dirtiest jobs need to be done, if you ask me, sonny
boy," said the plowman after a long silence, although no one had
asked him for his opinion in the first place.

His cronies roared with laughter, as if that simple pronounce-
ment had some extraordinary significance for them. One man,
however, did not laugh, a youth of eighteen or nineteen with
pale-gray eyes and a spotty face. Leaning on one elbow, he looked
Maigret straight in the eye, as if he wanted him to feel the force of
his hatred or contempt.

"Some people have no pride!" growled another man.

"If you've got the cash, pride doesn't often come into it."

Perhaps their remarks did not amount to anything much, but
Maigret got the message, nonetheless. He had finally clashed
with the opposition party, to describe the situation in political
terms.

Who could know for sure? Undoubtedly, all the rumors flying
about had originated in the Trois Mules. And if the townspeople
laid the blame at Maigret's door, they obviously thought Etienne
Naud was paying him to hush up the truth.

"Tell me, gentlemen . . ."

Maigret rose to his feet and walked toward them. Although not
timid by nature, he felt the blood rushing to his ears.

He was greeted by total silence. Only the young man went on
glowering at the Superintendent, while the others, looking rather
awkward, turned their heads away.

"Those of you who live around here may be able to help me, in the interest of justice."

They were suspicious. Maigret's words had certainly stirred them up, but they still would not give in. The old man muttered crossly, looking at his spittle on the floor:

"Justice for who? For Naud?"

The Superintendent ignored the remark and went on talking. Meanwhile, the proprietress hovered in the kitchen doorway with the child in her arms.

"For justice to prevail, I need to discover two things in particular. First, I need to find one of Retailleau's friends, a real friend and, if possible, someone who was with him on that last evening. . . ."

Maigret realized that the person in question was the youngest of the four men, for the other three glanced in his direction.

"Secondly, I need to find the cap. You know what I'm talking about."

"Speak up, Louis!" growled the plowman, as he rolled a cigarette.

But the young man was not convinced.

"Who are you working for?"

It was certainly the first time Maigret's authority had been questioned by a country boy. And yet it was essential that he explain himself, since he was determined to gain the young man's confidence.

"Superintendent Maigret, Police Judiciaire."

Who knows? Perhaps luck would have it that the young man had heard of him. But alas, this was not the case.

"Why are you staying with the Nauds?"

"Because he was told I was coming and was at the station to meet me. And, since I didn't know the neighborhood . . ."

"There are inns."

"I didn't know that when I arrived."

"Who's the man in the inn across the road?"

It was Maigret who was being interrogated!

"A private detective."

"Who's he working for?"

"I don't know."

"Why has there still been no proper investigation into what happened? Albert died three weeks ago."

"That's the way, boy! Go on!" the three men seemed to be saying as the young man stood rigidly in front of them with a grim look on his face in an effort to combat his shyness.

"No one registered a complaint."

"So you can kill anyone, and so long as no one registers a complaint . . ."

"The doctor concluded that it was an accident."

"Was he there when it happened?"

"As soon as I have enough evidence, the investigation will be made official."

"What do you mean by evidence?"

"Well, if we could prove that the cap was discovered between Naud's house and the place where the body was found, for example . . ."

"We'll have to take him to Désiré," said the stoutest of the men, who was wearing a carpenter's coverall. "Another round, Mélie . . . and one more glass."

For Maigret, it was a victory.

"What time did Retailleau leave the café that night?"

"About half past eleven."

"Were there many people in the cafe?"

"Four . . . We played *coinchée*."

"Did you all leave together?"

"The two other men took the road to the left. . . . I went part of the way with Albert."

"In which direction?"

"Toward Naud's house."

"Did Albert confide in you?"

"No."

The young man's face darkened. He said no reluctantly, since he obviously wanted to be scrupulously honest.

"He didn't say why he was going to the Naud's?"

"No. He was very angry."

"With who?"

"With her."

"You mean Mademoiselle Naud? Had he told you about her before?"

"Yes."

"What did he tell you?"

"Everything and nothing . . . Not in words . . . He used to go there nearly every night."

"Did he brag about it?"

"No." He gave Maigret a reproachful look. "He was in love; everyone could see that. He couldn't hide it."

"And he was angry with her on that last day?"

"Yes. Something was on his mind the whole evening. He kept looking at his watch as we played cards. Just as we parted on the road . . ."

"Where exactly?"

"Five hundred yards from the Nauds' house."

"The place, then, where he was found dead?"

"More or less . . . I had gone halfway with him. . . ."

"And you are sure he went on along the road?"

"Yes . . . He squeezed my hands and said, with tears in his eyes:

" 'It's all over, Louis.' "

"What was all over?"

"It was all over between him and Geneviève. . . . That's what I assumed. . . . He meant he was going to see her for the last time."

"But did he go?"

"There was a moon that night. . . . It was freezing. . . . I could still see him when he was only about a hundred yards from the house."

"And the cap?"

Young Louis got up and looked at the others, his mind made up.

"Come with me. . . ."

"Can you trust him, Louis?" asked one of the older men. "Watch out, son."

But Louis was at the age when one is prepared to risk all to win all. He looked Maigret in the eye, as if to say:

"You're a real bastard if you let me down!"

"Come along . . . it's just a few steps."

"Your glass, Louis, and yours, Superintendent . . . And you can believe everything the boy says, I promise. . . . He's as honest as they come, that boy. . . ."

"Your good health, gentlemen."

Maigret had no choice but to drink a toast with the four men. The large glasses made a tinkling sound as they clinked them together. He then followed Louis out of the room, completely forgetting to pay for his carafe of wine.

As they came out, Maigret saw Old Cadaver on the opposite side of the street. He had his briefcase under his arm and was about to go into the Lion d'Or. Was Maigret mistaken? It seemed to him that his former colleague was smiling sardonically, although all he could see was the side of his face.

"Come with me. . . . This way."

They went along narrow lanes that Maigret hadn't even guessed existed and that linked the three or four streets in the village.

They came to a row of cottages, each with its own tiny fenced-in front garden. Louis pushed open a small gate with a bell attached to it and called out:

"It's me!"

He went into a kitchen, where four or five children were sitting around a table having their lunch.

"What is it, Louis?" asked his mother, looking uncomfortably at Maigret.

"Wait here. . . . I'll be back in a minute, monsieur."

Louis rushed up the stairs, which led straight out of the kitchen, and went into a room. Maigret heard the sounds of a drawer being pulled open, of quick steps and a chair knocked over. Meanwhile, Louis's mother did not quite know whether to make Maigret welcome or not, but at least she shut the kitchen door.

Louis came downstairs pale and worried-looking.

"Someone's stolen it!" he declared, stony-faced.

And then, turning to his mother, he said in a harsh voice:

"Someone's been here. . . . Who was it? Who came here this morning?"

"Look, Louis . . ."

"Who? Tell me who it was! Who stole the cap?"

"I don't even know what cap you're talking about."

"Someone went up to my room."

He was in such a state of excitement that he looked as if he would hit his mother.

"Will you please calm down! Can't you hear yourself speaking in that rude tone of voice?"

"Have you been in the house all morning?"

"I went out to the butcher's and the baker's. . . ."

"And what about the children?"

"I took the two boys next door, as usual." She meant the two who were not yet of school age.

"Forgive me, Superintendent. I just don't understand. The cap was in my drawer this morning. I am positive it was. I saw it."

"But what cap are you talking about? Will you answer me? You're behaving as though you've gone out of your mind! Why don't you sit down and have something to eat? And this gentleman you've left standing . . ."

Louis gave his mother a pointed look, full of suspicion, and pulled Maigret outside.

"Come . . . there's something else I have to tell you. I swear, on my father's dead body, that the cap . . ."

4

THE THEFT
OF THE CAP

THE IMPATIENT YOUNG man walked quickly up the lane, his neck taut and his body bent forward as he pulled the massive Maigret along with him. The Superintendent continued to be embarrassed by the awkwardness of his situation. What did they look like, the pair of them? The younger, talking volubly, dragging the older man along, not unlike the young hustlers in Montmartre trying to propel some intimidated provincial, almost against his will, toward dubious delights.

Louis's mother stood on the doorstep, and as they were turning the corner, she shouted:

"Aren't you going to have something to eat, Louis?"

Was he even listening? He was possessed by violent emotion. He had promised something to this gentleman from Paris and now was unable to keep his word because an unforeseen event had occurred. Would he not be taken for an impostor? Was he not endangering the cause he had all too hastily championed?

"I want Désiré to tell you himself. The cap was in my bedroom. I wonder if my mother was telling the truth."

Maigret was working the same thing and at the same time thought of Inspector Cavre, whom he could picture vividly wheedling information out of the woman surrounded by children.

"What time is it?"

"Ten after twelve."

"Désiré will still be at the dairy. Let's go this way. It's quicker."

308

Louis led Maigret through alleyways and past small, shabby houses which came as a surprise to the Superintendent. Once, a mud-covered sow rushed at their legs.

"One night—the night of the funeral, in fact—old Désiré came into the Lion d'Or and threw a cap on the table, asking whether anyone knew whose it was. I recognized it at once, because I was with Albert when he bought it in Niort. I remember our discussing which color he should choose.

"What is your job?" asked Maigret.

"I'm a carpenter. The largest of the men you saw just now in the Trois Mules is my boss. Well, Désiré was drunk that night. There were at least six people in the café. I asked him where he had found the cap. Désiré collects the milk from the small farms in the marshes, you see, and since you can't get to them by road in a truck, he does his rounds by boat. . . .

"'I found it in the reeds,' he said, 'close to the dead poplar.'

"There were at least six people who heard him say this. Everyone here knows that the dead poplar is between the Nauds' house and the spot where Albert's body was found. . . .

"This way . . . We're going to the dairy. You can see the chimney over there, on the left."

The village was now behind them. Dark hedges enclosed tiny gardens. A little farther on, the dairy came into view. The low buildings were painted white, and the tall chimney stood straight up against the sky.

"I don't know why I decided to shove the cap into my pocket. . . . I already had the feeling that too many people were eager to hush up the whole thing. . . .

"'It's young Retailleau's cap,' someone said.

"And Désiré, drunk as he was, frowned. He suddenly realized that he was not supposed to have found it where he did.

"Désiré, are you sure it was near the dead poplar?"

"'Why shouldn't I be sure?'

"Well, Superintendent, the very next day, he didn't want to admit to anything. When he was asked where exactly he had found the cap, he answered:

"'Over there . . . I don't really know exactly. Just leave me alone, will you! I'm sick of this cap business. . . .'"

Flat-bottomed boats filled with milk cans were tied up beside the dairy.

"Hello, Philippe. Has old Désiré gone home?"

"He can't have gone home, because he never left home. . . . He must have got plastered yesterday—he didn't do his round this morning."

An idea flashed into Maigret's mind.

"Would the manager be around at this time of day, do you think?" he asked his companion.

"He'll probably be in his office. . . . The little door at the side."

"Wait here a minute."

Oscar Drouhet, the manager of the dairy, was on the telephone when Maigret walked in. The Superintendent introduced himself. Drouhet had the gravity and poise of the local craftsman turned small businessman. Pulling on his pipe with short, sharp puffs, he watched Maigret and let him speak, trying to size him up.

"Albert Retailleau's father once worked for you, I believe? I've been told he was killed in an accident at the dairy."

"One of the boilers exploded."

"I understand his widow receives a sizable compensation from you?"

He was an intelligent man and he realized immediately that Maigret's question was loaded with innuendos.

"What do you mean?"

"Did his widow take you to court, or did you yourself . . ."

"Don't try to complicate the issue. It was my fault that the accident happened. Retailleau had been saying for at least two months that the boiler needed a complete overhaul, and even that it should be replaced. It was the busiest time of the year, and I kept putting it off."

"Were your workmen insured?"

"Nowhere near adequately . . ."

"Excuse me. Let me ask you whether you were the one who thought they were inadequately insured, or if . . ."

Once more, they both understood each other perfectly, and Maigret did not have to finish his sentence.

"His widow registered a complaint against us, as she was entitled to do," Oscar Drouhet admitted.

"I am sure," the Superintendent went on, smiling slightly, "that she did not simply come to ask you to consider the question of compensation pay. She sent lawyers to investigate. . . ."

"Is that so unusual? Women are ignorant in such matters, you'll agree. I acknowledged the validity of her claim, and in addition to the pension she received from the insurance company, I decided to give her a supplementary sum, which I pay out of my own pocket. On top of this, I paid for her son's education and gave him a job as soon as he was old enough to work. My kindness was rewarded, what's more, since he was a hard-working, honest fellow. Albert was clever and quite capable of running the dairy in my absence."

"Thank you . . . or, rather, just one more question: Albert's mother hasn't called on you since the death of her son, has she?"

Drouhet managed not to smile, but his brown eyes flickered briefly.

"No," he said, "she hasn't come to see me *yet*."

Maigret had been right, then, in this respect. Madame Retailleau was indeed a woman who knew how to defend herself, and to attack, if need be. She was undoubtedly the sort of person who would never lose sight of her interests.

"It seems that Désiré, your milk collector, did not come to work this morning?"

"That's not exceptional. . . . On the days when he is more drunk than usual . . ."

Maigret went back to the spotty youth, who was terrified he would no longer be taken seriously.

"What did he say? He's a decent man, but he's really on the other side."

"Whose side?"

"Monsieur Naud's, the doctor's, the Mayor's . . . He couldn't have said anything against me."

"Of course not . . ."

"We've got to find old Désiré. . . . We could go around to his house, if you like. . . . It's not very far."

They set off again, both forgetting it was lunchtime, and

eventually came to a house on the fringe of the little town. Louis knocked on a door with a window in it, pushed it open, and shouted into the semidarkness:

"Désiré! Hey! Désiré!"

But only a cat emerged, and rubbed itself against the young man's legs. Meanwhile, Maigret came upon a kind of den, which contained a bed without a cover or pillow, where Désiré obviously slept with all his clothes on, a small, cracked iron stove, a bundle of rags, empty bottles, and gnawed bones.

"He must have gone off drinking somewhere. Come on. . . ."

Still the same concern that he would not be taken seriously.

"He worked on Etienne Naud's farm, you see. . . . He's still on good terms with them, even though he was fired. He's the sort of person who wants to be on good terms with everyone, and that's why he put on an act when people started asking him questions about the cap the day after he found it.

"'What cap? Ah, yes! The tattered one I picked up someplace or other; I don't know where. . . . I've no idea what's happened to it.

"Well, monsieur, I, for one, can tell you that there were bloodstains on the cap. And I wrote and told the Public Prosecutor. . . ."

"So it was you who wrote the anonymous letters?"

"I wrote three. If there were more, someone else must have written them. I wrote about the cap and then about Albert's relationship with Geneviève Naud. . . . Wait, perhaps Désiré is in here."

Louis darted into a grocer's shop. Through the windows Maigret could see bottles at the end of the counter and two tables at the back of the shop for the use of customers. The young man looked crestfallen when he came out.

"He was here early this morning. He must have done the rounds."

Maigret had only been into two cafés: the Lion d'Or and the Trois Mules. In less than half an hour, he came to know a dozen or more, not cafés in the true sense of the word, but premises the average passer-by would not have suspected were licensed. The harness maker had a kind of bar next to his workshop, and the farrier had a similar arrangement. Old Désiré had been seen in almost every bar they visited.

"How was he?"

"He was all right enough."

And they knew what that meant.

"He was in a hurry when he left. He had to go to the post office."

"The post office is closed," Louis said. "But I know the postmistress, and she'll open up if I tap on her window."

"Especially when she learns I have a call to make," said Maigret.

And, sure enough, as soon as the boy tapped on the pane, the window opened.

"Is that you, Louis? What do you want?"

"The gentleman from Paris wants to make a call."

"I'll open up right away."

Maigret asked to be put through to the Nauds.

"Hello! Who is speaking?"

He did not recognize the voice, a man's voice.

"Hello! Who did you say? . . . Ah! Forgive me . . . Alban, yes . . . I hadn't realized. . . . This is Maigret. . . . Could you tell Madame Naud I won't be back for lunch? Give her my apologies. No, it's nothing important. . . . I don't know when I'll be back. . . ."

As he left the booth, he saw from the look on his young companion's face that he had something interesting to tell him.

"How much, mademoiselle? . . . Thank you . . . I'm sorry to have bothered you."

Back in the street once more, Louis informed Maigret excitedly:

"I *told* you something was up. Old Désiré came in on the dot of eleven. Do you know what he mailed? He sent a money order for five hundred francs to his son in Morocco. . . . His son's a good-for-nothing. He left home without any warning. He and his father used to quarrel and fight every day. . . . Désiré's never been known to be anything but drunk, you might say. . . . And now his son writes to him from time to time, either complaining or asking for money. . . . But all his money goes on drink, you see. . . . The old man never has a sou. . . . Sometimes he sends a money order for ten or twenty francs at the beginning of the month. . . . I wonder . . . Wait a minute. . . . If you still have time, we'll go and see his stepsister."

The streets, the houses they had been walking past all morning were now becoming familiar to the Superintendent. He was beginning to recognize people's faces and the names painted above the shops. Rather than brightening up, the sky had clouded over again and the air was heavy with moisture. Soon there would be fog.

"His stepsister knits for a living. She's an old spinster and used to work for our former priest. This is her house."

He went up the three steps to the blue-painted front door, knocked, and then opened it.

"Désiré's not here, is he?"

He then beckoned Maigret to come inside.

"Hello, Désiré . . . I'm sorry to barge in like this, Mademoiselle Jeanne. . . . There's a gentleman from Paris who'd like to have a few words with your step-brother."

The tiny room was spotless. The table stood near a mahogany bed covered with an enormous red eiderdown. Maigret glanced around and saw a crucifix with a sprig of boxwood behind it, a figure of the Virgin Mary in a glass case on the chest of drawers, and two cutlets on a plate with a decorated border.

Désiré tried to stand up but knew he was in danger of falling off his chair. He maintained a dignified pose and, muttering thickly, his tongue unable to articulate the words, brought out:

"What can I do for you?"

For he was polite. He was always anxious to make that clear.

"I may have been drinking too much. . . . Yes, maybe I've had more than one drink, but I *am* polite, monsieur. . . . Everyone'll tell you that Désiré is polite to one and all."

"Look, Désiré, the gentleman wants to know exactly where you found the cap. . . . You know, Albert's cap."

These few words were enough. The drunkard's face hardened and assumed a totally blank expression. His watery eyes became even more glaucous.

"Don't know what you mean."

"Don't be a fool, Désiré. . . . I've got the cap. . . . You remember when you threw it on the table at François's place, that evening, and said you'd found it by the dead poplar. . . ."

The old monkey was not satisfied with a simple denial. He smirked with delight and went on with more gusto than was necessary:

"Do you understand what he's saying, m'sieur? Why should I have thrown a cap on the table, I'd like to know? I've never worn a cap. . . . Jeanne! Where's my hat? Show this gentleman my hat. . . . These youngsters have no respect for their elders."

"Désiré . . ."

"Désiré, indeed! . . . Désiré may be drunk, but he's polite and would be obliged if you'd call him Monsieur Désiré. . . . Do you hear, you snotnose, you fatherless bastard!"

"Have you heard from your son recently?" Maigret interrupted suddenly.

"So, it's my son, now, eh? You want to know what my son's been up to? Well, just let me tell you. He's a soldier! He's a brave fellow, my son!"

"That's what I thought. He'll certainly be pleased with the money order."

"Soon I won't be allowed to send my son a money order, is that it? Hey, Jeanne! Do you hear? And maybe I won't be allowed to come and have a bite to eat with my stepsister either!"

At first, he had probably been frightened, but now he was really enjoying himself. He played the fool for his own entertainment, and when Maigret got up to go, he followed him out to the front doorstep, staggering all the way, and would have followed him into the street if Jeanne had not stopped him.

"Désiré's polite. . . . Do you hear, you rascal? And if anyone tells you, Monsieur le Parisien, that Désiré's son is not a fine, upstanding fellow . . ."

Doors opened. Maigret was glad to get away.

With tears in his eyes and clenched teeth, Louis stuttered:

"I swear to you, Superintendent . . ."

"It's all right, my boy. I believe you. . . ."

"It's that man staying at the Lion d'Or, isn't it?"

"I think so. I'd like to have proof, though. Do you know anyone who was at the Lion d'Or last night?"

"I'm sure Liboureau's son was there. He goes there every evening."

"I'll wait at the Trois Mules while you go and ask him if he saw Désiré. Find out if the old man got into conversation with our visitor from Paris. . . . Wait a minute. . . . We can eat at the Trois Mules, can't we? We'll have a bite of something together. . . . Off you go. Be quick!"

There was no tablecloth. The table was set with steel knives and forks. All that was offered at noon was a beet salad, a rabbit stew, and a piece of cheese, with some poor white wine. When Louis returned, however, he felt very uncomfortable sitting at the Superintendent's table.

"Well?"

"Désiré went to the Lion d'Or."

"Did he talk to Old Cadaver?"

"To who?"

"Never mind. It's a nickname we gave him. Did Désiré talk to him?"

"It didn't happen like that. The man you call Cadav . . . It sounds really odd to me. . . ."

"His name is Justin Cavre."

"Monsieur Cavre, according to Liboureau, spent a good part of the evening watching the cardplayers and saying nothing. Désiré was drinking in his usual corner. He left at about ten o'clock, and a few minutes later Liboureau noticed that the Parisian had disappeared, too. But he doesn't know if he left the inn or just went upstairs."

"He left."

"What are you going to do?"

He was so proud to be working with the Superintendent that he could not wait to get started.

"Who was it who reported seeing a considerable sum of money in Madame Retailleau's house?"

"The postman, Josaphat . . . Another alcoholic . . . He's called Josaphat because when his wife died he had more to drink than usual and kept on saying through his tears:

"'Good-by, Céline . . . We'll meet again in the valley of Josaphat. . . . Count on me. . . .'"

"What would you like for dessert?" asked the proprietress, who obviously had one of her children on her arm all day and worked with her one free hand. "I've cookies or apples."

"Make your choice," said Maigret.

And the young man replied, blushing:

"I don't care. . . . Some cookies, please . . . This is what happened. . . . About ten or twelve days after Albert's funeral, the postman went to collect for a delivery from Madame Retailleau. She was busy doing the housework. She looked in her purse but she needed fifty francs more. So she walked over to the sideboard, where the soup tureen is. . . . You must have noticed it. It's got the blue flowers on it. . . . She stood in front of it so that Josaphat couldn't see what she was doing, but that evening he swore he had seen some thousand-franc notes—at least ten, he said, maybe more. . . . Now, everybody knows that Madame Retailleau has never had that much money at one time. . . . Albert spent all he earned."

"What did he spend it for?"

"He was rather vain. . . . There's nothing wrong with that. He liked to be well dressed and he had his suits made in Niort. . . . He would often pay for a round of drinks, too. . . . He would tell his mother that as long as she had her pension . . ."

"They quarreled, then?"

"Sometimes . . . Albert was an independent fellow, you see. . . . His mother wanted to treat him like a little boy. If he had listened to her, he would have stayed home at night and he'd never have set foot in the café. . . . My mother's just the opposite. She can't get me out of the house quick enough."

"Where can we find Josaphat?"

"He'll probably be at home now, or else about to finish his first round. In half an hour he'll be at the station to collect the bags with the second mail. . . ."

"Will you bring us some liqueur, please, madame?"

Maigret stared through the curtains at the windows on the other side of the street, imagined Old Cadaver eating his lunch,

the same as he was, and watching him the same way. It was not
long before he realized his mistake. A car came noisily to a halt
opposite the Lion d'Or, and Cavre got out, his briefcase under his
arm. Maigret watched him lean over toward the driver to find out
how much he owed.

"Whose car is that?"

"It belongs to the man who owns the garage. We went past it a
little while ago. He acts as a taxi driver occasionally, if someone's
ill and needs to be taken to the hospital, or if there's some other
emergency."

The car made a half-turn and, judging from the noise, obviously
did not go far.

"You see. He's gone back to his garage."

"Are you on good terms with him?"

"He's a friend of my boss."

"Go and ask him where he took his client this morning."

Less than five minutes later, Louis came running back.

"He went to Fontenay-le Comte. It's exactly thirteen miles
from here."

"Didn't you ask him where they went in Fontenay?"

"He was told to stop at the Café du Commerce, on Rue de la
République. The man from Paris went in, came out with another
man, and told the driver to wait."

"You don't know who this man was?"

"The garage man didn't know him. . . . They were gone
about half an hour. Then the man you call Cavre was driven back.
He only gave a five-franc tip."

Hadn't Etienne Naud also gone to Fontenay?

"Let's go and see Josaphat."

He had already left his house. They met up with him at the
station, where he was waiting for the train. When he saw young
Louis with Maigret, from the other end of the platform, he looked
annoyed and went hurriedly into the stationmaster's office, as if
he had some business to attend to.

But Louis and Maigret waited for him to come out.

"Josaphat!" Louis called out.

"What do you want? I'm in a hurry."

"There's a gentleman here who'd like a word with you."

"Who? I'm on duty, and when I'm on duty . . ."

Maigret had the utmost difficulty steering him toward an empty spot between the storage room and the urinals.

"I just want an answer to a simple question."

The postman had his guard up, that was obvious. He pretended he heard the train, and was ready to rush off to the mail car. At the same time, he could not help glowering briefly at Louis for putting him in this position.

Maigret already knew he would get nothing out of him, that Cavre had been there before him.

"Hurry up. I can hear the train. . . ."

"About ten days ago, you called at Madame Retailleau's house to collect for a delivery."

"I'm not allowed to discuss my work."

"But you discussed it that very evening."

"In front of me!" interjected the young man. "Avrard was there, and so was Lhériteau and little Croman. . . ."

The postman shifted from one leg to the other, managing to look stupid and insolent at the same time.

"What right do you have to question me?"

"We can ask you a question, can't we? You're not the Pope, are you?"

"And what if I asked him to show me his credentials? He's been snooping around the neighborhood all morning!"

Maigret had already turned away, fully aware that it was pointless to persevere. Louis, however, lost his temper in the face of such blatant deviousness.

"Do you mean you have the nerve to say you didn't tell everyone about the thousand-franc notes you saw in the soup tureen?"

"I can say what I like, can't I? Or are you going to try to stop me?"

"You told everyone what you saw. I'll get the others to back me up; I'll get them to repeat what you said. You even said the notes were held together by a pin."

The postman shrugged his shoulders and walked away. This time the train really was coming into the station, and he walked down the platform to where the mail car usually stopped.

"The swine!" growled Louis under his breath. "You heard what he said, didn't you? But you can take my word for it. Why should I lie? I knew perfectly well this would happen. . . ."

"Why?"

"Because it's always the same with them. . . ."

"With who?"

"With the bunch of them . . . I can't really explain. . . . They stick together. . . . They're rich. . . . They're either related to magistrates or else friends of theirs. And of department heads and generals . . . I don't know whether you understand what I'm trying to say. . . . So the people are afraid. . . . They often gossip at night when they've had a bit too much to drink, and then regret it the next day.

"What are you going to do now? You're not going back to Paris, are you?"

"Of course not, son. Why do you ask?"

"I don't know. The other man looks . . ."

The young man stopped himself just in time. He was probably about to say something like:

"The other man looks so much stronger than you!"

And it was true. Through the mist that was beginning to settle, turning the light into a false dusk, Maigret thought he saw Cavre's face, his thin lips spreading into a sardonic smile.

"Isn't your boss going to be cross if you don't get back to work?"

"Oh, no! . . . He's not one of them. If he could help us prove poor Albert was murdered, he would, I promise you."

Maigret jumped when a voice behind him asked:

"How do I get to the Lion d'Or?"

The railway man on duty near the small gate pointed to the street about a hundred yards away.

"Straight ahead . . . You'll see it on your left."

A plump little man, faultlessly dressed and carrying a suitcase almost as large as himself, looked around for a nonexistent porter. The Superintendent examined him from head to foot. He had never seen him before.

5

THREE WOMEN IN
A LIVING ROOM

LOUIS DIVED INTO the fog with his head bowed, and before
he was enveloped completely, he said:

"If you want to get hold of me, I'll be at the Trois Mules all
evening."

It was five o'clock. A thick fog had descended, with the night,
over the town. Maigret had to walk the length of the main street
in Saint-Aubin to reach the station again, and then the road
leading to Etienne Naud's house. Louis had offered to go with
him, but there is a limit to everything, and Maigret had had
enough. He was beginning to get tired of being pulled along by
this overexcited, restless young man.

As they parted company, Louis, with a hint of reproach in his
voice, had said feelingly:

"They'll butter you up, and you'll start believing everything
they tell you." He was referring to the Nauds, of course.

With his hands in his pockets and the collar of his overcoat
turned up, Maigret walked cautiously toward the light in the
distance. Any lamp shining through the fog became a beacon.
Because of the intense brightness of its halo, which looked as if it
were still a long way off, you felt as though you were walking
toward an important goal. And then, all of a sudden, he almost
bumped into the cold window of the Vendée Co-operative, which
he had walked past twenty times that day. The narrow shop front
had been painted green fairly recently, and there were offers of
free glassware and earthenware displayed in the window.

Farther on, in total darkness, he came up against something hard and groped about in confusion for some time before realizing that he had landed in the middle of the carts standing outside the wheelwright's with their shafts in the air.

Bells sounded suddenly, immediately above his head. He was walking past the church. The post office was on the right, with its doll-size counter; opposite, on the other side of the street, stood the doctor's house.

The Lion d'Or was on one side of the street, the Trois Mules on the other. It was extraordinary to think that inside each lighted house people were living in a tiny circle of warmth, like incrustations in the icy infinity of the universe.

Saint-Aubin was on a small scale. The lights in the dairy made one think of a brightly lit factory at night. At the station a locomotive with huge wheels was sending out sparks.

Albert Retailleau had grown up in this miniature world. His mother had spent all of her life in Saint-Aubin. Apart from holidays in Les Sables-d'Olonne, somebody like Geneviève Naud might never leave the town.

As the train had slowed down somewhat before it reached Niort, Maigret had noticed empty streets in the rain, rows of lights and shuttered houses. He had thought to himself:

"There are people who spend an entire lifetime in that street."

Testing the ground with his feet, he made his way along the canal toward another beacon, which turned out to be the lantern outside the Naud's house. On cold nights or in driving rain, he had often noticed, from train windows, such isolated houses, a rectangle of yellow light, the only sign of their existence, arousing the imagination to picture all manner of things.

And now Maigret was coming into the orbit of one of these lights. He walked up the stone steps, groped for the bell, and then noticed that the door was ajar. He went into the hall, deliberately shuffling his feet to make his presence known, but this did not deter whoever was in the living room from continuing to hold forth in a monotonous tone. Maigret took off his wet overcoat, his hat, wiped his feet on the straw mat, and knocked on the door.

"Come in. . . . Geneviève, open the door."

He had already opened it. Only one of the lamps in the room

was lit. Madame Naud was sewing by the fireside, and a very old woman was sitting opposite her. The young girl was walking over to the door as Maigret came into the room.

"I'm sorry to disturb you."

The girl looked at him anxiously, unable to decide whether or not he would betray her. Maigret merely bowed.

"This is my daughter, Geneviève, Superintendent. She looked forward so much to meeting you. She is quite recovered now. . . . Allow me to introduce you to my mother. . . ."

So this was Clémentine Bréjon, a La Noue before she married, and commonly known as Tine. This small, sprightly old lady, with the grimacing look one sees on busts of Voltaire, rose to her feet and asked in a curious falsetto voice:

"Well, Superintendent, do you feel you have caused enough havoc in our poor Saint-Aubin? Upon my word, I've seen you walk up and down ten times or more this morning, and this afternoon I have it on good authority that you found yourself a young recruit. . . . Do you know, Louise, who acted as elephant driver to the Superintendent?"

Had she deliberately chosen the term "elephant driver" to emphasize the disproportion between the lanky youth and the elephantine Maigret?

Louise Naud, who had none of her mother's spirit and whose face was much longer and paler, did not look up from her work but just nodded her head and smiled faintly to show she was listening.

"Fillou's son . . . It was bound to happen. The boy must have lain in wait for him. . . . No doubt he has told you some pretty tall tales, Superintendent?"

"Not at all, madame . . . He merely directed me to the various persons I wanted to see. I'd have had difficulty finding their houses on my own, since the local people aren't exactly communicative."

Geneviéve had sat down and was staring at Maigret as if she were hypnotized by him. Madame Naud looked up occasionally from her work and glanced furtively at her daughter.

The living room looked exactly as it had the previous evening; everything was in its usual place. An oppressive stillness hung over the room. It was as if only the grandmother conveyed some sense of normality.

"I am an old woman, Superintendent. Let me tell you that some time ago, something much more serious happened, which nearly destroyed Saint-Aubin. There used to be a clog factory which employed fifty people, men and women. It was at a time when there were endless strikes in France and workers walked out on the slightest provocation."

Madame Naud had looked up from her work to listen, and Maigret saw that she found it difficult to conceal her anxiety. Her thin face bore a striking resemblance to that of Bréjon.

"One of the workmen in the clog factory was Fillou. He wasn't a bad man, but he was inclined to drink too much, and when he was tipsy he thought he was a real orator. What happened exactly? One day, he went into the manager's office to lodge a complaint of some sort. Shortly afterward the door opened. Fillou was catapulted out, staggered backward for several yards, and then fell into the canal."

"And he was the father of my young companion with the spotty face?" inquired Maigret.

"His father, yes. He is dead now. At the time, the town was divided into two factions. One side thought that the drunken Fillou had behaved like a madman and that the manager had been forced to take violent action to get rid of him. The other side felt that it was all the manager's fault, that he had provoked Fillou, taunting him by referring to the large families of his employees with remarks like:

"'I can't help it if they breed on Saturday nights when they're pissed. . . .'"

"Fillou is dead, you said?"

"He died two years ago of cancer of the stomach."

"Did many people support him at the time of the incident?"

"He didn't have the majority behind him, but the most fanatical people. Every morning someone else found threats written in chalk on his door."

"Are you implying, madame, that the case is similar to the one we are dealing with now?"

"I am not implying anything, Superintendent. Old people love rambling on, you know. There is always some scandal or other to discuss in small towns. Life would be very dull, otherwise. And there will always be a handful of people willing to fan the flames."

"What was the end of the Fillou affair?"

"Silence, of course."

"Yes, silence just about sums it up," thought Maigret. Despite the efforts of a small group of fanatics, silence always gets the upper hand. And he had been confronted with silence all day long.

Moreover, ever since he had come into the room, he had been in the grip of a strange feeling, a feeling that made him somewhat uneasy.

He had wandered through the streets from morning till night, sullenly and obstinately following Louis, who had passed on to him something of his own determination.

"She's one of them . . . " Louis would say.

And "them" in Louis's mind meant a number of people who had conspired not to talk, and who did not want any trouble, people who wanted to let sleeping dogs lie.

Basically, one might say, Maigret had thrown in his lot with the small group of rebels. He had had a drink with them at the Trois Mules. He had disowned the Nauds by declaring that he was not working for them, and when Louis doubted his word, he was sorely tempted to give him proof of his loyalty.

And yet Louis had been justified in looking with suspicion at the Superintendent when they parted, as if he had a premonition of what would happen once his companion was again the enemy's guest. That's why he had tried to escort Maigret all the way to the Naud's front door—to bolster him and caution him not to give in.

"If you want to get hold of me, I'll be at the Trois Mules all evening."

He would wait in vain. Now that he was back in this cozy, bourgeois living room, Maigret felt almost ashamed of himself for having wandered through the streets in the tow of a youngster and been snubbed by everyone he had persisted in questioning.

There was a portrait on the wall that Maigret had not noticed the night before, a portrait of Bréjon, the Examining Magistrate, who seemed to be staring down at the Superintendent as if to say:

"Don't forget the purpose of your visit."

He watched Louise Naud's fingers as she sewed and was hypnotized by their nervousness. Her face remained almost serene, but her fingers revealed a fear that bordered on panic.

"What do you think of our doctor?" asked the talkative old lady. "He's a real character, isn't he? You Parisians are wrong in thinking that no one of interest lives in the country. If you were to stay here for two months, no more . . . Louise, isn't your husband coming back?"

"He telephoned a moment ago to say he will be late. He's been called to La Roche-sur-Yon. He asked me to give you his apologies, Superintendent."

"I owe you an apology, too, for not having come back for lunch."

"Geneviève! Do give the Superintendent an apéritif."

"Well, children, I must be going."

"Stay to dinner, Maman. Etienne will take you home in the car when he gets back."

"I won't hear of it, my child. I don't need anyone to drive me home."

Her daughter helped her tie the ribbons of a small black bonnet that sat jauntily on her head, and gave her galoshes to wear over her shoes.

"You are sure you don't want me to have the carriage made ready?"

"Time enough for that the day of my funeral. Good-by, Superintendent. If you're passing my house again, come in and see me. Good night, Louise. Good night, Vièvre."

And suddenly, once the door closed again, there was a sense of emptiness. Maigret understood why they had tried to make old Tine stay. Now that she had gone, a heavy, anguished silence weighed on those left behind; the room seemed to rustle with fear. Louise Naud's fingers moved ever more rapidly over her work, while the young girl tried to find an excuse for leaving the room but did not dare.

And to think that although Albert Retailleau was dead, although his mutilated body had been discovered one morning on the railroad tracks, his son was alive in this room at this very moment, in the shape of a being that would be ready to be born in a few months' time.

When Maigret turned toward the girl, she did not avoid his eyes. On the contrary, she stood up straight and looked squarely at him, as if to say:

"No, you did not dream it. I came into your bedroom last night, and I wasn't sleepwalking. What I told you then is the truth. You can see I am not ashamed of it. I am not mad. Albert was my lover and I am expecting his child."

Albert, the son of Madame Retailleau, a woman who had stood up for her rights so bravely after her husband's death, Albert, Louis's young and fervent friend, used to creep into this house at night without anyone's knowing. And Geneviève would take him into the room, the one at the end of the right wing of the house.

"Will you excuse me, ladies? I would like to go for a short walk around the stable yards—if you have no objection, that is . . . ."

"May I come with you?"

"You'll catch cold, Geneviève."

"No, I won't, Maman. I'll wrap up warmly."

She went into the kitchen to fetch a hurricane lamp, which she brought back lit. In the hall, Maigret helped her on with the cape.

"What would you like to see?" she asked in a low voice.

"Let's go into the yard."

"We can go out this way. There's no point in going around the house. . . . Mind the steps."

Lights were on in the stables, whose doors were open, but the fog was so thick that nothing could be seen.

"Your room is the one directly above us, isn't it?"

"Yes . . . I know what you are getting at. . . . He didn't come in through the door, naturally. . . . Come with me. . . . You see this ladder. . . . It's always left here. He just had to push it a few yards. . . ."

"Which is your parents' room?"

"Three windows along."

"And the other two windows?"

"One is the spare bedroom, where Alban slept last night. The other is a room that hasn't been used since my little sister died, and Maman has the key."

She was cold; she tried not to show it so that it would not look as if she wanted to end the conversation.

"Your mother and father had no idea?"

"No."

"Had this affair been going on for some time?"

She answered at once.

"Three and a half months."

"Was Retailleau aware of the consequence of these meetings?"

"Yes."

"What did he intend to do?"

"He was going to confess everything to my parents and marry me."

"Why was he so angry, that last evening?"

Maigret looked at her closely, trying his best to glimpse the expression on her face through the fog. The ensuing silence betrayed the young girl's amazement.

"I asked you . . ."

"I heard what you said."

"Well!"

"I don't understand. Why do you say he was angry?"

And her hands trembled like her mother's, causing the lantern to shake.

"Nothing out of the ordinary happened between you that night?"

"No, nothing."

"Did Albert leave by the window, as usual?"

"Yes . . . There was a moon. . . . I saw him go over to the back of the yard, where he could jump over the little wall onto the road."

"What time was it?"

"About half past twelve."

"Did he always stay so briefly?"

"What do you mean?"

She was playing for time. Behind a window, not far from where they were standing, they could see the old cook moving about.

"He arrived at about midnight. I imagine he usually stayed longer. . . . You didn't quarrel?"

"Why should we have quarrelled?"

"I don't know. . . . I'm just asking. . . ."

"No."

"When was he to speak to your parents?"

"Soon . . . We were waiting for a propitious moment."

"Try to remember accurately. . . . Are you sure there were no lights on in the house that night? You heard no noise? There was no one skulking in the yard?"

"I didn't see anything. . . . I swear to you, Superintendent, I know nothing. . . . Maybe you don't believe me, but it's the truth. I'll never—do you hear?—never tell my father what I told you last night. . . . I shall leave. I don't yet know what I'll do. . . ."

"Why did you tell me?"

"I don't know. . . . I was frightened. . . . I thought you would find out everything and tell my parents."

"Shall we go back? You're shivering."

"You won't say anything?"

He did not know what to say. He did not want to be bound by a promise. He muttered:

"Trust me."

Was he, too, "one of them," to use Louis's phrase? Oh! Now he understood perfectly what the young man meant. Albert Retailleau was dead and buried. A certain number of people in Saint-Aubin—the majority, in fact—thought that since it was impossible to bring the young man back to life, the wisest course of action was to treat the subject as closed.

To be "one of them" was to belong to that tribe. Even Albert's mother was "one of them," since she had not seemed to understand why anyone would want to investigate her son's death.

And those who had not subscribed to this view at the outset had been brought to heel one after the other.

Désiré wished he had never found the cap. What cap? He now had money to drink his fill and could send a money order for five hundred francs to his good-for-nothing son.

Josaphat, the postman, could not remember having seen a wad of thousand-franc notes in the soup tureen.

Etienne Naud was embarrassed that his brother-in-law should have thought of sending someone like Maigret, a man bent on discovering the truth.

But what was the truth? And who stood to gain by discovering the truth? What good would it do?

The small group of men in the Trois Mules, a carpenter, a plowman, and a young man named Louis Fillou, whose father had already proved to be strong-willed, were the only ones to keep the affair alive.

"Aren't you hungry, Superintendent?" asked Madame Naud, when Maigret returned to the living room. "Where is my daughter?"

"She was in the hall just now. I suppose she has gone up to her room for a minute."

For the next quarter of an hour the atmosphere was gloomy indeed. Maigret and Louise Naud were now alone in the old-fashioned, stuffy room. From time to time a log toppled over and sent sparks flying in the grate. Only one lamp was lit, and its pink shade shed a soft glow over the furniture. Familiar sounds coming from the kitchen occasionally broke the silence. They could hear the stove being filled with coal, a saucepan being moved, an earthenware plate being put on the table.

Maigret sensed that Louise Naud would have liked to talk. She was possessed by a demon who was pushing her to say . . .

To say what? She was visibly tortured. Sometimes she would open her mouth, as if she had decided to speak, and Maigret was afraid of what she was going to say.

She said nothing. Her chest tightened in a nervous spasm and her shoulders shook for a second. She went on with her embroidery, making tiny stitches, weighed down by this cloak of immobility and stillness, which formed such a barrier between them.

Did she know that Retailleau and her daughter . . .

"Do you mind if I smoke, madame?"

She gave a start. Perhaps she had been afraid he was going to say something else. She stammered:

"Please do. . . . Make yourself at home."

Then she sat up straight and listened for a sound.

"Oh, good heavens . . ." Oh, good heavens, what? She was merely waiting for her husband to return, waiting for someone to come and end the torment of this tête-à-tête.

And then Maigret began to feel sorry for her. What was to stop him from getting up and saying:

"I think your brother made a mistake in asking me to come here. There is nothing I can do. This whole affair is none of my business, and, if you don't mind, I'll take the next train back to Paris. I am most grateful to you for your hospitality."

He recalled Louis's pale face, his fiery eyes, the sardonic smile.

But mostly he pictured Cavre, with his briefcase under his arm; Cavre, who after all these years had suddenly been given the chance to get the better of his hated former boss. For Cavre did hate him. Admittedly, he hated everyone, but he hated Maigret in particular, because Maigret was his alter ego, a successful version of his own self.

Cavre had doubtless been up to all sorts of shady tricks ever since he got off the train the night before and was nearly mistaken by Naud for Maigret himself.

Where was the clock that was going tick-tock? Maigret looked around for it. He felt really disturbed, and said to himself:

"Another five minutes and this poor woman's nerves will get the better of her. She'll make a clean breast of it. She can't stand it any longer. She's at the end of her tether."

All he had to do was ask her one specific question. Hardly that! He would go up to her and look at her searchingly. Would she be able to restrain herself then?

But instead, he remained silent and even timidly picked up a magazine that was lying on a small round table, to put her at her ease. It was a woman's magazine, full of embroidery patterns.

Just as in a dentist's waiting room one reads things one would never read anywhere else, Maigret turned the pages and looked carefully at the pink and blue pictures, but the invisible chain that bound him to his hostess remained as tight as ever.

They were saved by the entry of the maid. She was rather a rough-looking country girl, whose black dress and white apron merely accentuated her rugged, irregular features.

"Oh! Pardon . . . I didn't know there was someone . . ."

"What is it?"

"I wanted to know if I should set the table or wait for Monsieur."

"Set the table."

"Will Monsieur Alban be here for dinner?"

"I don't know. But set his place as usual. . . ."

What a relief to talk of everyday things! They were so simple and reassuring. She latched on to Alban as a topic of conversation.

"He came to lunch today. It was he who answered the telephone when you called. . . . He leads such a lonely life. We consider him one of the family now. . . ."

The maid's appearance had opened an avenue of escape, and she made the most of it.

"Will you excuse me for a moment? You know what it's like to run a house. There is always something to see to in the kitchen. . . . I'll ask the maid to tell my daughter to come down and keep you company."

"Please don't bother."

"Besides . . . " She listened carefully.

"Yes . . . That must be my husband. . . ."

A car drew up in front of the steps, but the engine kept running. They heard voices, and Maigret wondered whether his host had brought someone back with him, but he was only giving instructions to a servant who had rushed out on hearing the car.

Naud came into the living room, still wearing his leather coat. There was an anxious look in his eyes as he surveyed Maigret and his wife, astonished to find them alone together.

"Ah! You're . . ."

"I was just saying to the Superintendent, Etienne, that I would have to leave him for a minute and see to things in the kitchen."

"Forgive me, Superintendent. . . . I am on the board of the regional agricultural authority and I had forgotten to tell you we had an important meeting today."

He sneezed and poured himself a glass of port, still trying to gauge what might have happened in his absence.

"Well, have you had a good day? I was told on the telephone you were too busy to come back for lunch."

He, too, was afraid of being alone with the Superintendent. He looked around at the armchairs in the room, as if to reproach them for being empty.

"Alban's not here yet?" he said with a forced smile, turning toward the dining-room door, which was open.

And his wife answered from the kitchen:

"He came to lunch. He didn't say whether he'd be back for dinner."

"Where's Geneviève?"

"She went up to her room."

He did not dare sit down, settle in a chair. Maigret understood how he felt and almost came to share his anxiety. In order to feel strong, or simply to control their trembling, the three of them needed to be together, side by side, in an unbroken family circle.

Only then would the Superintendent be able to sense the spirit of the house in normal times. The atmosphere of mutual support, the small talk that provided a continuous reassuring background.

"Will you have a glass of port?"

"I just had one."

"Well, have another. . . . Now, tell me what you've been doing. Or, rather . . . for perhaps I am being indiscreet . . ."

"The cap has disappeared," declared Maigret, his eyes on the carpet.

"Has it really? This famous cap was to be proof. . . . And where had it been? Mind you, I have always had my doubts as to whether it really existed. . . ."

"A young fellow by the name of Louis Fillou claims it was in one of the drawers in his bedroom."

"In Louis's house? And you mean it was stolen? This morning? Don't you think that is rather odd?"

He stood there laughing, a tall, strong, sturdy figure of a man, with a ruddy complexion. He was the owner of this house, the head of the family, and he had just taken part in administrative duties in La Roche-sur-Yon. He was Etienne Naud—Squire Naud, as the local people would have said—the son of Sébastien Naud, a man known and respected by everyone in the district.

But his laughter sounded shaky as he took a glass of port and looked around in vain for the habitual support his family would give him—he would have liked them to be present, his wife, his daughter, and even Alban, who had decided to stay away today of all days.

"Will you have a cigar? . . . No, you are sure?"

He paced back and forth restlessly, as though to sit down would have been to fall into a trap, to play right into the hands of the formidable Superintendent, whom that half-wit of a brother-in-law had foisted on him. Etienne Naud felt doomed.

6

ALBAN
GROULT-COTELLE'S
ALIBI

BEFORE DINNER THAT evening, an incident occurred which, although insignificant in itself, nonetheless gave Maigret food for thought. Etienne Naud had still not sat down, as though afraid of being even more at the mercy of the Superintendent if he did not move. They could hear voices in the dining room. Madame Naud was reprimanding the maid for not cleaning the silver properly. Geneviève had just come downstairs.

Maigret saw the look her father gave her as she came into the room. It held a trace of anxiety. Naud had not seen his daughter since she had retired to her room the day before, saying she did not feel well. It was perfectly natural, too, that Geneviève should reassure him with a smile.

Just at that moment the telephone rang, and Naud went into the hall to answer it. He left the door open.

"What?" he said, in an astonished tone of voice. "Of course he's here, damn it. What did you say? . . . Yes, hurry up. We're expecting you."

When he came back into the living room, he was still shrugging his shoulders.

"I wonder what has got into our friend Alban. There's been a place for him at our table for years. Now he calls this evening to find out if you're here, and when I say you are, he asks if he can come to dinner and says he must talk to you. . . ."

By chance, Maigret happened to be looking, not at Naud, but at his daughter, and he was surprised to see a fierce expression on her face.

"He did the same thing earlier today," she said crossly. "He came here for lunch and looked very peeved when he realized the Superintendent hadn't come back. I thought he was going to leave. He muttered:

"'What a pity. I had something to show him.'

"He took his leave as soon as he had gulped down his dessert. You must have met him in the town, Superintendent."

Whatever it was, was so subtle that Maigret could not pinpoint it. A hint of something in the girl's voice. And yet it was not really the voice. What is it, for example, that makes an experienced man suddenly realize that a young girl has become a woman?

Maigret noticed something of this sort. It seemed to him that Geneviève's peevish words conveyed something more than plain ill temper, and he decided to watch young Mademoiselle Naud more closely.

Madame Naud came in, apologizing for her absence. Her daughter took the opportunity to repeat:

"Alban has just called to say he's coming to dinner. But first of all he asked whether the Superintendent was here. He's not coming to see *us*. . . ."

"He'll be here in a minute," said her father, who had finally sat down now that his family was around him. "It will take him three minutes by bicycle."

Maigret dutifully remained seated, looking somewhat dispirited. His large eyes were expressionless, as was usual with him when he found himself in an awkward situation. He watched them in turn, responding with a half-smile when spoken to and thinking to himself:

"They must be cursing their idiot of a brother-in-law and me, too. They all know what happened, including their friend Alban. That's why they are jittery the minute they are on their own. They feel reassured when they are together and gang up. . . ."

What had happened, in fact? Had Etienne Naud discovered the young Retailleau in his daughter's bedroom? Had they quarreled?

Had they had a fight? Or had Naud quite simply shot him down as he would a rabbit?

What a night to have lived through! Geneviève's mother must have been in a terrible state, and the servants, who probably heard the noise, must have been petrified.

Someone was scraping his feet at the front door. Geneviève made a move, as if to go to open the door, but then decided to remain seated, and Naud himself, somewhat taken aback, as if his daughter's behavior was a serious breach of habit, got up and went into the hall. Maigret heard him talking about the fog, and then the two men came into the room.

This was actually the first time that Maigret was seeing Geneviève and Alban together. She held out her hand rather stiffly. Alban bowed, kissed the back of her hand, and then turned toward Maigret, obviously anxious to tell him or show him something.

"Would you believe it, Superintendent? After you left this morning I came across this quite by chance. . . ."

And he held out a small sheet of paper, which had been attached to some others with a pin, for there were two tiny prick marks in it.

"What is it?" asked Naud, quite naturally, while his daughter looked distrustfully at Alban.

"You have all made fun of my mania for hoarding the smallest scrap of paper. I could produce the tiniest laundry bill dated three or eight years back!"

The piece of paper that Maigret was twirling between his thick fingers was a bill from the Hôtel de l'Europe in La Roche-sur-Yon. Room: 30 francs. Breakfast: 6 francs. Service . . . The date: January 7.

"Of course," said Alban, as though he were apologizing, "it's not important. However, I remembered the police like alibis. Look at the date. Quite by chance, I was in La Roche, do you see, on the night the person you're interested in met his death. . . ."

Naud and his wife reacted as well-bred people do when confronted with a breach of manners. Unable to believe her ears, Madame Naud looked first at Alban, as though she would not have expected such behavior from him, and then looked down with a sigh at the logs in the grate. Her husband frowned. He was slower on the uptake. Perhaps he was hunting for some deeper meaning to his friend's ploy.

As for Geneviève, she had turned pale with anger. She had obviously had a real shock, and her eyes were throwing sparks. Maigret had been so intrigued by her behavior a few moments before that he tried not to look at anyone else.

The thin, lanky Alban, with his balding forehead, stood sheepishly in the middle of the room.

"Well, you're making quite sure you are in the clear without waiting to be accused," said Naud when he finally spoke, having had time to weigh his words.

"What do you mean by that, Etienne? I think you're all misreading me. I came across this hotel bill quite by chance when I was sorting out some papers. I was eager to show it to the Superintendent because it was such a strange coincidence—the same date as the day . . ."

Madame Naud even chipped in, something that rarely happened.

"So you've already said," she retorted. "I think dinner is ready now. . . ."

The atmosphere was strained. Although the meal was as elaborate and well cooked as it had been on the previous evening, their efforts to create a friendly ambience, or, at any rate, an outward show of relaxation, failed dismally. Geneviève was the most agitated. For a long time afterward Maigret could picture her, her chest heaving with emotion: a woman's anger—but also a mistress's rage, Maigret was sure. She pecked at her food disdainfully. Not once did she look at Alban, who, for his part, made sure he caught no one's eye.

Alban was just the sort of man to keep the smallest scraps of paper and file them away, pinning them together in bundles as if they were bank notes. It was also just like him to extricate himself from a difficulty if he had the chance, and with a clear conscience leave his friends in hot water.

All this made itself felt. Something nasty had entered the atmosphere. Madame Naud's anxiety increased. Naud, on the other hand, endeavored to reassure his family, although quite probably with another objective in mind.

"By the way, I happened to meet the Public Prosecutor in Fontenay this morning. In fact, Alban, he is almost a relative of yours, on the distaff side, since he married a Deharme, from Cholet."

"The Cholet Deharmes aren't related to the General's family. They originally came from Nantes, and their . . ."

Naud went on:

"He was most reassuring, you know, Superintendent. Although he has told my brother-in-law, Bréjon, that there is bound to be an official investigation, it will be just a formality, at any rate as far as we are concerned. I told him you were here. . . ."

He immediately regretted this slip of the tongue. Blushing slightly, he hurriedly put a large piece of lobster *à la crème* into his mouth.

"What did he have to say to that?"

"He admires you greatly and has followed most of your cases in the papers. It is precisely because he admires you . . ."

The poor man did not know how to extricate himself.

"He is amazed that my brother-in-law thought it necessary to involve a man like you in such a trivial matter. . . ."

"I see."

"You're not annoyed, I hope? He said this only because of his admiration for . . ."

"Are you sure he didn't also say that my appearance here may well make the case seem more important than it actually is?"

"How did you know? Have you seen him?"

Maigret smiled. What else could he do? Was he not a guest in their house? The Nauds had entertained him as well as they could. And again, that night, the dinner they served was a consummate example of traditional provincial cooking.

In a pleasant, very polite way, his hosts now began to make him feel that his presence in their midst was a threat, a potentially harmful factor.

There was a silence, as there had been a short while before, after the Alban episode. It was Madame Naud who tried to straighten things out, and she made a bigger blunder than her husband had.

"Anyway, I hope you'll stay a few more days with us. I expect there will be a frost after the fog has gone, and you will be able to have some walks with my husband. . . . Don't you think so Etienne?"

How relieved they all would have been if Maigret had replied, as they assumed he would, as any well-bred man would:

"I would be delighted to stay, and greatly appreciate your hospitality, but alas, I must return to my duties in Paris. I may pass this way during the holidays. . . . But I have enjoyed myself enormously. . . ."

He said nothing of the kind. He went on eating and did not reply. Inwardly, he felt like a brute. These people had behaved well toward him from the outset. Perhaps Albert Retailleau's death weighed heavily on their consciences. But had not the young man robbed their daughter of her honor, as they put it in their circles? And had Albert's mother, Madame Retailleau, made a fuss? Or had she been the first to realize that it was far better to let sleeping dogs lie?

Three or four people, perhaps more, were trying to keep their secret, desperately trying to prevent anyone from discovering the truth, and for someone like Madame Naud, just Maigret's presence must have been an intolerable strain. Had she not been on the point of crying out in anguish a short while ago, at the end of a quarter of an hour alone with the Superintendent?

It would be so simple! He would leave the following morning, with the whole family's blessing, and back in Paris, Bréjon, the Examining Magistrate, would thank him with tears in his eyes.

And if Maigret did not leave, was it his passion for justice only that prompted him to do otherwise? He would not have dared to assert this, in an eyeball-to-eyeball confrontation. For there was Cavre. There were the successive defeats Cavre had inflicted on him ever since their arrival the night before, without so much as a glance in the direction of his former boss. He came and went as if Maigret did not exist, or as if he were a totally innocuous opponent.

In Cavre's wake, as though by magic, evidence melted away,

witnesses could remember nothing or refused to speak, and items of unmistakable proof, like the cap, vanished into thin air.

At last, after so many years, the hapless, envy-stricken, wretched Cavre was having his moment of triumph!

"What are you thinking about, Superintendent?"

He gave a start.

"Nothing . . . I'm so sorry. My mind wanders sometimes. . . ."

He had helped himself to a huge plateful of food without realizing what he was doing and was now ashamed of himself. To put him at his ease, Madame Naud said quietly:

"Nothing gives the hostess more pleasure than to see her cooking appreciated. Alban eats like a wolf, so he doesn't count; he'd eat anything put in front of him. Everything tastes good to him. He's not a gourmet. He's a glutton."

She was joking, of course, but nonetheless there was a trace of spite in her voice and expression.

A few glasses of wine had heightened the color of Etienne Naud's complexion. Playing with his knife, he ventured:

"So what do you make of it all, Superintendent, now that you've seen something of the neighborhood and have asked a few questions?"

"He has met young Fillou," his wife informed him, as though in warning.

And Maigret, who was being watched by all of them as by so many hawks, said slowly and clearly:

"I think Albert Retailleau had very bad luck."

This remark was quite meaningless, and Geneviève grew pale, indeed seemed so taken aback by these few insignificant words that for a moment it appeared that she might get up and leave the room. Her father looked puzzled. Alban sneered:

"That's a statement quite worthy of the ancient oracles! I'd certainly be very uneasy if I hadn't miraculously found proof that I was sleeping peacefully in a room in the Hôtel de l'Europe five miles from here, on that very night. . . ."

"Don't you know," retorted Maigret, "that we in the police force consider the person with the best alibi a prime suspect?"

Alban was annoyed. Taking Maigret's little joke seriously, he answered:

"If that's so, you will have to include the Prefect's private secretary among your suspects, since he spent the evening with me. He is a childhood friend of mine, and whenever we meet and spend an evening together we don't usually get to bed until two or three in the morning."

What made Maigret decide to carry on with the game? Was it the blatant cowardice of this trumped-up aristocrat that stimulated him? He took a large notebook with an elastic band around it out of his pocket and asked, in all seriousness:

"What is his name?"

"Do you really want it? As you wish . . . Musellier, Pierre Musellier . . . He's single. He has an apartment on Place Napoléon, above the Murs garages, about fifty yards from the Hôtel de l'Europe."

"Shall we have coffee in the living room?" suggested Madame Naud. "Will you serve it, Geneviève? You're not too tired? You look pale to me. Do you think you had better go upstairs to bed?"

"No."

She was not tired. She was tense. It was as if she had various accounts to settle with Alban. She did not take her eyes off him.

"Did you return to Saint-Aubin the following morning?" asked Maigret, with a pencil in his hand.

"The very next morning, yes. A friend gave me a lift in his car to Fontenay-le-Comte, where I had lunch with some other friends, and just as I was leaving I bumped into Etienne, who brought me back."

"You make your way from friend to friend, as it were. . . ."

He could not have made it clearer that he thought Alban a sponger, which was the truth. Everyone understood perfectly the implication of Maigret's words. Geneviève blushed and looked away.

"Are you sure you won't change your mind and have one of my cigars, Superintendent?"

"Would you be so kind as to tell me if you have finished questioning me? If you have, I would like to take my leave. I want to get home early tonight."

"That's absolutely fine. In fact, I'd like to walk as far as the town, so if it's all right with you, we can go together."

"I came by bicycle."

"That doesn't matter. A bicycle can be pushed by hand, can't it? And anyway, you might bicycle into the canal in this fog."

What *was* going on? For one thing, when Maigret had talked of leaving with Alban Groult-Cotelle, Etienne Naud had frowned and had looked to be on the point of accompanying them.

Was he afraid that Alban, who was far too nervous that night, might be tempted to say too much? He had given him a long look, as if to say:

"For heaven's sake, watch out! Look at the state you are in. He is tougher than you are."

Geneviève gave Alban an even sterner, more contemptuous look, which said:

"At least try to control yourself!"

Madame Naud did not look at anyone. She was worn out. She no longer understood what was going on. It would not be long before she cracked under such nervous tension.

But the person to behave most strangely was Alban himself. He made no move to leave, but wandered aimlessly around the living room, the ulterior motive in all probability being to have a private talk with Naud.

"Shouldn't we have a word in your study about that insurance matter?"

"What insurance matter?" Naud asked stupidly.

"Never mind. We'll talk about it tomorrow."

What did he want to tell Naud that was so important?

"Are you coming, my dear fellow?" persisted the Superintendent.

"Are you sure you don't want me to take you in the car? If you would like to have the car and drive yourself . . ."

"No, thank you. We'll have a good chat on the way."

The fog swirled around them. Alban pushed his bicycle with one hand and walked quickly along, constantly having to stop because Maigret would not walk more briskly.

"They are such nice people! Such a close-knit family . . . But it must be rather a dull life for a young girl, don't you think? Has she many friends?"

"Not that I know of, at least not around here . . . Every once in a while she goes off to spend a week or so with her cousins, and they come down here in the summer, but apart from that . . ."

"I imagine she also visits with the Bréjons in Paris?"

"Yes, indeed. She stayed with them this winter."

Maigret changed the subject, playing the innocent. The two men could scarcely see each other in the icy white mist that enveloped them. The electric light in the station acted as a beacon and, farther on, two more lights, which could have been boats out at sea, shone through the haze.

"So apart from staying in La Roche-sur-Yon from time to time, you hardly ever leave Saint-Aubin?"

"I sometimes go to Nantes, since I have friends there, and also to Bordeaux, where my cousin from Chièvre lives. Her husband is a ship owner."

"Do you ever go to Paris?"

"I was there a month ago."

"At the same time as Mademoiselle Naud?"

"Maybe. I'm not sure. . . ."

They walked past the two inns that faced each other. Maigret stopped and suggested:

"What about having a drink in the Lion d'Or? It would be most interesting to see my old colleague Cavre. I saw a man at the station just recently and I suspect him to have been called in as reinforcement."

"I'll take my leave, then," said Alban quickly.

"No, no . . . If you don't want to stop, I'll keep you company on your way home. You can't object to that, now, can you?"

"I am in a hurry to get back and to bed. I'll be frank with you. . . . I am prone to the most dreadful migraines, and I am in the throes of one now."

"All the more reason to escort you home. Does your maid sleep in the house?"

"Of course."

"Some people don't like their servants to be under the same roof at night. . . . Look! There's a light."

"It's the maid."

"Is she in the living room? Of course, the room is heated. . . . Does she do odd sewing jobs for you at night?"

They stopped outside the front door, and Alban, instead of knocking, hunted in his pocket for the key.

"See you tomorrow, Superintendent! No doubt we will meet at my friends the Nauds'."

"Tell me . . ."

Alban took care not to open the door, lest Maigret think he was inviting him inside.

"It's embarrassing. . . . Please forgive me. . . . But the call of nature, you know—and since we're here . . . Among men, I needn't be shy."

"Come in. . . . I'll show you the way."

Although the light was not on in the hallway, the living-room door on the left was half open and revealed a rectangle of light. Alban tried to lead Maigret down the hallway, but the Superintendent, with an almost instinctive gesture, pushed the door wide open. Then he stopped in his tracks and cried out:

"Well, I never! It's my old friend Cavre! What are you doing here, my dear fellow?"

The former inspector had risen to his feet, looking as pale and sullen as ever. He glowered at Groult-Cotelle, whom he deemed responsible for this disastrous meeting.

Alban was completely out of his depth. He tried hard to think of an explanation but, unable to do so, merely asked:

"Where is the maid?"

Old Cadaverous was the first to regain his composure and, bowing, said:

"Monsieur Groult-Cotelle, I presume?"

Alban was slow to join in the inspector's game.

"I am sorry to disturb you at such an hour, but I just wanted a few words with you. Since your maid told me you would not be back late . . ."

"All right!" growled Maigret.

"What?" said Alban with a start.

"I said: All right!"

"What do you mean?"

"I don't mean anything. Cavre, where is this maid who showed you in? There is no other light on in the house. So she was in bed."

"She told me . . ."

"All right! I'll give it another try, and this time I don't want any claptrap. You can sit down, Cavre. . . . You made yourself comfortable; you took off your overcoat and left your hat on the coatrack. What have you been reading?"

Maigret's eyes opened wide when he inspected the book lying on a table near Cavre's chair.

"*Sexual Perversions!* Well, now! And you found this charming book in the library of our friend Groult-Cotelle. . . . Tell me, gentlemen, why don't you sit down? Does my presence disturb you? Don't forget your migraine, Monsieur Groult-Cotelle. You should take an aspirin."

In spite of everything, Alban still had enough presence of mind to retort:

"I thought you needed to relieve yourself?"

"Well, I don't any more. . . . Now, my dear Cavre, what is this investigation of yours all about? You must have been really put out when you realized I was involved in this, too, eh?"

"Ah! You're involved? How do you mean, involved?"

"So Groult-Cotelle availed himself of your expertise, did he? Far be it from me to underrate it, by the way."

"I had never even heard of Monsieur Groult-Cotelle until this morning."

"It was Etienne Naud who told you about him when you met in Fontenay-le-Comte, wasn't it?"

"Superintendent, if you wish to submit me to a formal interrogation, I would like my lawyer to be present when I answer your questions."

"In the event of your being accused of stealing a cap, for instance?"

"In that event, yes."

The light bulb cast a gray light over the room because, apart from the fact that it was of insufficient voltage for the size of the room, it was also coated with dust.

"May I perhaps be permitted to offer you something to drink?"

"Why not?" answered Maigret. "Since fate has thrown us together . . . By the way, Cavre, was it one of your men I saw just now at the station?"

"He works for me, yes."

"Reinforcement?"

"Call it what you like."

"Were you planning to settle important matters with Monsieur Groult-Cotelle tonight?"

"I wanted to ask him one or two questions."

"If you wanted to see him about his alibi, you can rest assured. He thought of everything. He even kept his bill from the Hôtel de l'Europe."

Cavre kept his nerve. He had sat down in the chair he had occupied before and, with his legs crossed and his morocco-leather briefcase on his lap, appeared to be biding his time, determined, so it seemed, to have the last word yet.

Groult-Cotelle, who had filled three glasses with Armagnac, offered him one, which he refused.

"No, thank you. I only drink water."

He had been teased a great deal about this at Police Headquarters, an unintentionally cruel thing to do, since Cavre was not abstemious by choice but because of a liver ailment.

"And what about you, Superintendent?"

"Gladly!"

They fell silent. All three men appeared to be playing a strange kind of game, such as trying to see who would be the first to break the silence. Alban had emptied his glass with one swallow and had poured himself another. He remained standing, and from time to time pushed one of the books in his library back into place if it was out of line.

"Are you aware, monsieur," Cavre said to him at last in a quiet voice, icy calm, "that you are in your own house?"

"What do you mean?"

"That as master of the house you are at liberty to entertain whomever you think fit. I would have liked to talk to you alone, not in front of the Superintendent. If you prefer his company to mine, I will be glad to take my leave and arrange a meeting for some other time."

"In short, the Inspector is politely asking you to show one of us to the door forthwith."

"Gentlemen, I don't understand what this discussion is all about. Indeed, this whole affair has nothing to do with me. I was in La Roche, as you know, when the boy died. Granted, I am a friend of the Nauds. I have been a frequent visitor to their house. In a small town like ours, one's choice of friends is limited."

"Remember Saint Peter!"

"What do you mean?"

"That if you go on like this, you will have thrice denied your friends the Nauds before sunrise—assuming, of course, the fog allows the sun to rise."

"It is all very well for you to joke. My position is a delicate one, just the same. The Nauds often invite me to their house. Etienne is my friend; I don't deny the fact. But if you ask me what happened at the Nauds' that night, I don't know. And what is more, I don't want to know. So I am the wrong person to question. That's all."

"Perhaps Mademoiselle Naud would be the best person to question, then? Incidentally, I wonder if you were aware that she was looking at you far from lovingly this evening. I got the distinct impression that she had a bone to pick with you."

"With me?"

"Especially when you handed me your hotel bill and tried with such style to save your own skin. She didn't think that was very nice, not nice at all. I would be on my guard, so that she doesn't get her own back, if I were you. . . ."

Alban forced a laugh.

"You are joking. Geneviève is a charming child who . . ."

What made Maigret suddenly decide to play his last card?

". . . who is three months pregnant," he let drop, moving closer to Alban.

"What? . . . What did you say?"

As for Cavre, he was stunned. For the first time that day, he no longer looked his confident self, and he stared at his former boss in spontaneous admiration.

"Were you unaware of the fact, Monsieur Groult-Cotelle?"

"Just what are you getting at?"

"Nothing . . . I am looking for . . . You want to know the truth, too, don't you? . . . Then we will try to find it together. . . . Cavre has already laid his hands on the blood-stained cap, which is proof enough of the crime. . . . Where is that cap, Cavre?"

The Inspector slipped deeper into his armchair and did not reply.

"I had better warn you that you will pay dearly for it if you've destroyed it. . . . And now, I have the feeling that my presence is disturbing you. . . . I will therefore take leave of you both. . . . I presume I will see you for lunch tomorrow at your friends the Nauds', Monsieur Groult-Cotelle?"

He went out of the room. As soon as he had banged the front door shut, he saw a thin figure standing close by.

"Is that you, Superintendent?"

It was young Louis. Lying in wait behind the windows of the Trois Mules, he had doubtless seen the shadowy figures of Maigret and Alban as they went past. He had followed them.

"Do you know what they are saying, what everyone is saying in the town?"

His voice was trembling with anxiety and indignation.

"People are saying that *they* have got the better of you and that you are leaving on the three o'clock train tomorrow. . . ."

And this had very nearly been the truth.

7

THE OLD
POSTMISTRESS

ONE IMPORTANT CONTRIBUTING factor must have
made Maigret more sensitive than usual at that particular moment. Scarcely had he walked out of Groult-Cotelle's front door
and taken a few steps in the darkness, the fog clinging to his skin
like a cold compress, when he suddenly stopped. Young Louis,
who was walking beside him, asked:

"What's the matter, Superintendent?"

Something had just occurred to Maigret and he was trying to
follow the thought through. He was still mindful of the sound of
voices, blurred but noisy, coming to him from behind the shutters of the house. At the same time, he understood why the young
man was alarmed: Maigret had stopped dead for no apparent
reason in the middle of the sidewalk, like a heart patient immo-
bilized by a sudden attack.

This had nothing to do with Maigret's current preoccupations.
He did, however, make a mental note:

"Ah! So there's a cardiac in Saint-Aubin. . . ."

He was later to learn, in fact, that the old doctor had died of
angina pectoris. For years the townspeople had seen him suddenly stop in the middle of the street, rooted to the spot, with his
hand on his heart.

There was a violent argument going on inside the house, or at
least the sound of angry voices gave that impression, but Maigret
paid no attention. The spotty Louis, who thought he had discovered the cause of the Superintendent's sudden halt, listened

conscientiously. The louder the voices, the harder it was to make out the words. The noise sounded exactly like a record turning off-center, because a second hole had been bored in it, and blaring out unintelligible sounds.

But it was not the argument between Inspector Cavre and Alban Groult-Cotelle that made Maigret stop in his tracks and look about him somewhat distractedly.

The minute he left the house, an idea had come to his mind; it wasn't even an idea, but something less precise, so vague, in fact, that he was now striving to recapture the memory of it. Every now and then, an insignificant happening, usually a whiff of some scent, brings back in a split second a particular moment in life. The sensation is so vivid, so gripping, that we want to hold on to this living fragment of our past, but it vanishes almost at once and we are unable to say what had stirred our thought. And since no answer to our questions is forthcoming, we end up wondering if it was not an unconscious evocation of a dream, or—who knows?—of some previous life.

Something struck Maigret the moment the front door banged shut. He knew he was leaving behind two embarrassed and angry men. Brought together by fate that night, the two of them had one thing in common, for which there was no rational explanation, however. Cavre made one think not of a bachelor, but of a husband who has been subjected to ridicule and looks woeful and abashed. Envy oozed from every pore, and envy can make one behave as deviously as certain hidden vices.

In his heart of hearts, Maigret did not bear him a grudge. Actually, he felt sorry for him. All through his relentless pursuit, his determination to get the better of his rival, Maigret could not help feeling pity for him, a man who, in the last analysis, was fated to be a failure.

What was the connection between Cavre and Alban? The connection that exists between two completely dissimilar yet equally sordid things. It was almost a question of color. Both men were somehow gray, greenish, bedecked with moral and material dust.

Cavre exuded hatred. Alban Groult-Cotelle exuded panic and cowardice. His whole life had been run on the principle of cowardice. His wife had left him and taken the children with her. He had made no effort to either join them or bring them back. He probably had not suffered. He had selfishly reorganized his existence. A man of humble means, he lived in other people's homes, like the cuckoo. And if some misfortune befell his friends, he was the first to let them down.

And now Maigret suddenly recalled the trifling matter that had triggered this train of thought: it was the book he had caught Cavre holding when they came into the room, one of those disgustingly salacious books that are sold under the counter in seedy shops on Faubourg Saint-Martin.

Groult-Cotelle kept such books in his country library; and Cavre had zeroed in on them instinctively!

But there had been something else, and it was this something else that the Superintendent was struggling to put his finger on. For a split second, perhaps, his mind had been lit up, as by a glaring truth, but no sooner had he realized this than the thought vanished and all that remained was a vague impression. This was why he stood motionless, like a sufferer from heart disease trying to outwit his heart.

Maigret was trying to outwit his memory. He was hoping . . .

"What is that light?" he asked.

They were standing still in the fog. A little way off, Maigret could see a large halo of white, diffuse light. He concentrated his thoughts on this material thing in order to give his intuition time to revive. He now knew the town. So where, then, was this light almost opposite Groult-Cotelle's house coming from?

"It isn't the post office, is it?"

"It's the window next door," Louis replied. "The postmistress's window. She sleeps badly and reads novels late in the night. Hers is always the last light to be switched off in Saint-Aubin."

He was still aware of the sound of angry voices. Groult-Cotelle was shouting the loudest, like a man who obstinately refuses to listen to reason. Cavre's voice was more controlled, more commanding.

Why was Maigret strongly tempted to cross the street and press his face against the postmistress's window? She was doubtless sitting reading in her kitchen. Was it intuition? A moment afterward, the thought had gone from his mind. He knew that Louis was looking at him anxiously and impatiently as he wondered what on earth was going on in his hero's head.

What was it he had sensed as the front door closed behind him? Well . . . First of all, Paris had come to mind. . . . The books, the shops on Faubourg Saint-Martin that sell that type of book had made him think of Paris. . . . Groult-Cotelle had gone to Paris . . . and Geneviève Naud must have been there at the same time. . . .

Maigret saw again, with his mind's eye, the look on Geneviève's face when Alban had produced his alibi in such an unsavory manner. He had read there more than mere scorn. A naked woman, not a young girl, had appeared to him. . . . A mistress, suddenly aware of the baseness of . . .

He had just got to this point in his thoughts when an inkling of something else had flashed through his mind, only to vanish again, leaving a vague memory of something rather nasty.

Yes, the whole affair was decidedly different from what Maigret had initially envisaged. Up until now, he had perceived only the bourgeois view of things, had witnessed a thoroughly bourgeois family's indignation upon discovering that a penniless youth with no prospects was making love to their daughter.

Had Naud shot him in a fit of fury? It was possible. Maigret almost pitied Naud, and especially his wife, who knew what had happened. She was desperately trying to control herself and overcome her terror. For her, every minute spent alone with the Superintendent was a terrible ordeal.

But now, Etienne Naud and his wife ceased to be foremost in his mind.

What was the missing link between these thoughts? The dull, balding Alban had an alibi. Was this really just a fluke? Was it also just a fluke that he had suddenly come across that bill from the Hôtel de l'Europe?

No doubt he really had spent the night there. The Superintendent was convinced of this, although he decided to check the fact just the same.

But why had he gone to La Roche-sur-Yon on that particular night? Had the Prefect's private secretary been expecting him?

"I must find out!" grumbled Maigret to himself.

He went on looking at the dim light in the room next to the post office; he still had his tobacco pouch in one hand and his pipe, which he was too preoccupied to fill, in the other.

Albert Retailleau was angry. . . .

Who had said that? None other than his young companion, Louis, Albert's friend.

"Was he really angry?" the Superintendent suddenly asked.

"Who?"

"Your friend Albert . . . You said that when he left you that last evening . . ."

"He was extremely excited. He had several brandies before going off to meet Geneviève. . . ."

"He didn't tell you anything?"

"Wait . . . He said he probably wouldn't stay forever in this godforsaken place."

"How long had he been Mademoiselle Naud's lover?"

"I don't know. . . . Wait, though . . . They weren't lovers in midsummer. They must have started sleeping together around October."

"He wasn't in love with her before that?"

"Well, if he was, he didn't talk to her."

"Ssh . . ."

Maigret stood quite still and listened carefully. The sound of voices had died away, and now, to his astonishment, the Superintendent heard a different sound.

"It's the telephone!" he exclaimed.

He had recognized the familiar sound of country telephones. Someone was turning a handle to call the woman in the post office.

"Run and have a look through the postmistress's window. . . . You'll get there quicker than I will."

He was right. A second light went on, in the window next to the first. The postmistress had gone through the door, which was slightly ajar, into the post office.

Maigret took his time. He loathed running anywhere. In particular, it was Louis's presence that bothered him. He wanted to maintain a certain dignity in front of the young man. He at last filled his pipe, lit it, and walked slowly across the street.

"Well?"

"I knew she would listen in to the call," whispered Louis. "The old shrew always listens. The doctor even complained to La Roche about it once, but she still goes on doing it."

They could see her through the window, a small woman dressed in black, with dark hair and an ageless face. She had one hand on an earphone and held a plug in the other. The call must have come to an end at that very moment, because she moved the plugs into different holes and walked across the room to switch off the light.

"Do you think she would let us in?"

"If you knock on the little door at the back . . . This way . . . We'll go through the yard."

They groped about in pitch darkness, edging their way past various tubs filled with washing. A cat jumped out of a garbage can.

"Mademoiselle Rinquet!" the young man called out. "Please open up for a minute."

"What is it?"

"It's me, Louis. . . . Will you open up for a minute, please?"

As soon as she had unbolted the door, Maigret stepped quickly inside, afraid she might shut it again.

"There is nothing to be afraid of, mademoiselle."

He was too tall and too bulky for the tiny postmistress's tiny kitchen, which was cluttered with embroidered tray cloths and knickknacks made of cheap china or spun glass she had bought at fairs.

"Groult-Cotelle has just made a call."

"How do you know?"

"He called his friend Naud. . . . You listened in to their conversation."

Caught in the act, she defended herself awkwardly.

"But the post office is closed, monsieur. I'm not supposed to give anyone a line after nine o'clock. I sometimes do, though, since I'm up and like to be helpful."

"What did he say?"

"Who?"

"Look, if you're not going to answer my questions, I will have to come back tomorrow, officially, and draw up a written report, which will go through proper channels. . . . Now, what did he say?"

"There were two of them on the line."

"At the same time?"

"Pretty much. Sometimes they spoke at the same time. It turned into a shouting match between the two of them, and in the end I couldn't catch what they were saying. . . . They must both have had a receiver and were obviously pushing each other out of the way in front of the telephone."

"What did they say?"

"Monsieur Groult was first:

"'Listen, Etienne, this can't go on. The Superintendent has just left. He came face to face with your man. I'm sure he knows everything, and if you continue . . .'"

"Well?" said Maigret.

"Wait . . . The other man butted in.

"'Hello . . . Monsieur Naud? . . . Cavre speaking . . . Of course it's a great pity you didn't manage to detain him and keep him from finding me here, but . . .'

"'But I'm the one who is compromised,' yelled Monsieur Groult. 'I've had enough; do you hear, Etienne? Put an end to all this! Telephone your lunatic brother-in-law and tell him never to meddle in our affairs again. He's this wretched Superintendent's superior, and since he's the one who sent him down here, he must call him back to Paris. . . . So I'm warning you . . . if he is at your house the next time I come around, I'll . . .'

"'Hello! Hello!' shouted Monsieur Etienne, in a real state at the other end of the line. 'Are you still there, Monsieur Cavre? . . . Alban's got me very upset. . . . Are you sure . . .'

"'Hello! . . . This is Cavre. . . . Will you be quiet, Monsieur Groult. . . . Let me get a word in. . . . Stop pushing me. . . . Is that you, Monsieur Naud? . . . Yes . . . Well! There is nothing to worry about provided your friend Groult-Cotelle doesn't panic and . . . What? . . . Should you call your brother-in-law? . . . I'd have advised against it a moment ago. . . . No, I'm not afraid of him.' "

The postmistress, thoroughly enjoying reporting the telephone conversation, pointed a finger at Maigret and declared:

"He meant you, didn't he? . . . So he said he wasn't afraid of you, but that, because of Groult-Cotelle, who was thoroughly unreliable . . . Ssh . . ."

The bell rang in the post office. The little old lady rushed next door and switched on the light.

"Hello! . . . What? . . . Galvani 17.98? I don't know. . . . No, there shouldn't be any delay at this time of night. . . . I'll call you back."

Galvani 17.98 was Bréjon's home telephone number, and Maigret recognized it at once.

He looked at his watch to see what time it was. Ten minutes to eleven. Unless he had gone to the movies or the theater with his family, the Examining Magistrate was bound to be in bed. Everyone at the Palais de Justice knew that he got up at six in the morning and studied his briefs as day broke.

The plugs went into different holes.

"Is that Noirt? Can you get me Galvani 17.98? Line 3 is free? Will you connect me, please? Line 2 was awful just now. . . . How are you? . . . You're on duty all night? . . . What? . . . No, you know perfectly well I never go to bed before one in the morning. . . . Yes, there's fog here, too. . . . You can't see more than a couple of yards in front of you. . . . It'll be icy on the roads tomorrow morning. . . . Hello! Paris? . . . Paris? . . . Hello! Paris? . . . Galvani 17.98? . . . Come on, dear. . . . Speak more clearly. . . . I want Galvani 17.98. . . . What? . . . It's ringing? . . . I can't hear anything. . . . Let it go on ringing. . . . It's urgent. . . . Yes, now there's someone. . . ."

She turned around, terrified, for Maigret's bulky frame towered behind her as he stretched out a hand, ready to take the phone at the appropriate moment.

"Monsieur Naud? . . . Hello! . . . Monsieur Naud? . . . Yes, I'm putting you through. . . . One moment; it's ringing. . . . Hold on. . . . Galvani 17.98? Saint-Aubin, here . . . Here's line 3. . . . Go ahead, 3. . . ."

She did not dare protest when the Superintendent took the headset authoritatively from her and placed it on his head. She put the plug firmly in the hole.

"Hello! Is that you, Victor? . . . What? . . ."

There was interference on the line, and Maigret had the feeling that the Examining Magistrate was taking the call in bed. A moment later, in response to his brother-in-law's name:

"It's Etienne. . . ."

He was probably speaking to his wife, who was lying in bed beside him.

"What? . . . There has been a new development? . . . No? . . . Yes? . . . Don't shout. . . . It's making the line vibrate. . . ."

Etienne Naud was one of those men who yell on the telephone as if they are afraid of not being heard.

"Hello! . . . Listen, Victor. . . . There's nothing new to report really, no. . . . Believe me. . . . I'll write to you, anyhow. . . . Maybe I'll come and see you in Paris in two or three days. . . ."

"Please talk more slowly. . . . Move over a bit, Marthe."

"What did you say?"

"I was telling Marthe to move over. . . . Well? . . . What's going on? The Superintendent arrived safely, didn't he? . . . What do you think of him?"

"Yes . . . Never mind. . . . In fact, it's because of him that I am calling. . . ."

"Doesn't he want to investigate the case?"

"Yes . . . But he's investigating it too thoroughly. . . . Listen, Victor, you've simply got to find a way of getting him back to Paris. . . . No, I can't talk now. . . . I know the postmistress and . . ."

Maigret smiled as he watched the tiny postmistress. She was bubbling over with curiosity.

"You'll find a way, I'm sure. . . . What? It will be difficult? . . . There must be a way, somehow. . . . It's absolutely vital, I assure you. . . ."

It was not hard to picture the Examining Magistrate frowning anxiously as waves of suspicion with regard to his brother-in-law began to creep into his mind.

"It is not what you are thinking. . . . But he's poking his nose here and there, talking to everyone, and doing far more harm than good. . . . Do you see? . . . If he goes on much longer, the whole town will be in an uproar, and my position will become untenable. . . ."

"I don't know what to do."

"Aren't you on good terms with his boss?"

"Yes, I am. . . . Of course, I could ask the head of the Police Judiciaire. . . . It's a delicate matter. . . . The Superintendent will find out sooner or later. It was as a pure favor to me that he agreed to go. . . . Do you understand?"

"Do you or don't you want to cause trouble for your niece? And she's your goddaughter, may I remind you."

"It really is a serious matter, then?"

"I have already told you. . . ."

Etienne Naud's impatience was almost palpable. Alban's panic had rubbed off on him, and the fact that Cavre had not been against calling Bréjon to get him to summon Maigret back to Paris had not exactly reassured him.

"Can't I have a word with my sister?"

"Your sister has gone to bed. . . . I'm the only one downstairs. . . ."

"What does Geneviève say?"

The Examining Magistrate was obviously beginning to falter, and so fell back on commonplace remarks.

"Is it raining in your part of the world, too?"

"I don't know!" Naud yelled back. "I don't give a damn! Do you hear! Just get that confounded Superintendent of yours out of here."

"What on earth has got into you?"

"What has got into me? If this goes on, we won't be able to stay in this place, that's all. He is poking his nose into everything. He says nothing. He . . . he . . ."

"Now calm down. I'll do my best."

"When?"

"Tomorrow morning . . . I'll go and see the head of the Police Judiciaire as soon as the offices are open. But it goes against the grain, let me tell you. It's the first time in my career that . . ."

"But you will do it, won't you?"

"I've told you I will."

"A telegram would probably arrive at about noon. . . . He'll be able to take the three o'clock train. . . . Make sure the telegram arrives in time."

"Is Louise all right?"

"Yes, she's all right. . . . Good night . . . Don't forget. . . . I'll explain later. . . . And don't start imagining things, please. . . . Say good night to your wife for me."

The postmistress realized from the look on Maigret's face that the conversation was over, and she took the headset from him and moved the plugs once more.

"Hello! . . . Are you through? . . . Hello, Paris . . . How many calls? . . . Two? . . . Thank you . . . Good night, my dear."

And then she turned to the Superintendent, who was putting his hat on again and relighting his pipe:

"I could be fired for this. . . . Do you think it is true, then?"

"What?"

"What people are saying . . . I can't think that a man like Monsieur Etienne, who has everything he could possibly want to make him happy . . ."

"Good night, mademoiselle. Don't worry. I'll be very discreet."

"What did they say?"

"Nothing much. Just family news . . ."

"Are you going back to Paris?"

"Maybe . . . Yes . . . It is quite possible I'll take the train tomorrow afternoon."

Maigret was calm now. He felt like himself again. He was almost surprised to find Louis waiting for him in the kitchen, and the young man was equally surprised when he sensed the change in his hero's mood. The Superintendent paid virtually no attention to him. He treated him superciliously, perhaps even with contempt, or so thought young Louis, who was cut to the quick.

Once more, they began to make their way through the fog,

which seemed to reduce the world to absurdly small proportions. As before, an occasional light shone through the gloom.

"He did it, didn't he?"

"Who? . . . Did what?"

"Naud . . . He's the one who killed Albert."

"I honestly don't know, my boy. . . . It . . ."

Maigret stopped himself in time. He was going to say:

"It doesn't matter."

Because that was what he thought, or, rather, what he felt. But he realized that a statement such as this would only shock the young man.

"What did he say?"

"Nothing much . . . Incidentally, speaking of Groult-Cotelle . . ."

They were approaching the two inns. The lights were still on, and on one side of the street faces could be seen through the window like silhouettes in a Chinese shadow play.

"Yes?"

"Has he always been a close friend of the Nauds?"

"Let me think. . . . Not always, no . . . I was a small boy at the time, you see. . . . The house has been in his family for a long time, but when I was a kid we used to go there to play. It was empty then. I remember because we got into the cellar quite a few times. One of the basement windows didn't shut properly. Monsieur Groult-Cotelle was staying with some relatives of his at the time. They have a castle in Brittany, I think. . . . When he came back here, he was married. . . . You should ask some of the older people. . . . I was six or seven then. I remember his wife had a lovely little yellow car, which she drove herself, and she often used to go off in it alone."

"Were the two on visiting terms with the Nauds?"

"No . . . I am sure they weren't. Because I remember Monsieur Groult was constantly in and out at the old doctor's, who was a widower. . . . I used to see them sitting by the window playing chess. I think it was because of his wife that he didn't see the Nauds. He was friendly with them before his marriage. He and Naud went to the same school. They used to say hello to each other in the street. I used to see them chatting on the sidewalk, but that's all."

"So it was after Madame Groult-Cotelle left . . ."

"Yes . . . About three years ago . . . Mademoiselle Naud was sixteen or seventeen years old. She was back from school. She had been at a boarding school in Niort for some years and came back home only one Sunday each month. . . . I remember that, too, because whenever you saw her during the school year, you knew it was the third Sunday in the month. . . . They became friends. . . . Monsieur Groult used to spend half his time at the Nauds'."

"Do they go on holidays together?"

"Yes. To Les Sables-d'Olonne . . . The Nauds built a house there. . . . Are you going back? . . . Don't you want to know if the detective . . ."

The young man looked back at Groult-Cotelle's house and could still see a glimmer of light filtering through the shutters. Although he dared not show it, he was somewhat disillusioned with the unorthodox way Maigret seemed to be conducting this investigation.

"What did he say when you went in?"

"Cavre? Nothing . . . No, he had nothing to say. . . . Anyway, nothing of importance."

The fact of the matter was that at that particular moment Maigret was living in a world of his own and not in the present at all. He answered his young companion abstractedly, not aware what his questions amounted to.

His colleagues at the Police Judiciaire frequently joked about his going off into one of his trances, and he also knew that this habit was gossiped about behind his back.

At such moments, Maigret seemed to puff himself up out of all proportion, to become dense and weighty, inaccessible, like someone blind and dumb, a Maigret whom an uninitiated outsider would take for a half-wit or a sloth.

"So, you're concentrating your thoughts?" said someone who prided himself on his psychological acuity.

And Maigret had replied with comic sincerity:

"I never think."

And it was almost true. For Maigret was not thinking now, as he stood in the damp, cold street. He was not following any train of thought. He made himself into a sponge, as it were.

It was Sergeant Lucas who had hit on this description; he had worked with Maigret over a long period of time and knew him better than anyone.

"There comes a moment in the course of an investigation," Lucas had said, "when the boss suddenly swells up like a sponge. You'd think he was filling up."

But filling up with what? At present, for instance, he was absorbing the fog and the darkness. The village around him was not just any old village. And he was not merely someone who had been cast into these surroundings by chance.

He was, rather, like God the Father. He knew this village like the back of his hand. It was as if he had always lived here, or, better still, as if he had created the little town. He knew what went on inside all those small, low houses nestling in the darkness. He could see men and women turning in the moist warmth of their beds and he followed the thread of their dreams. A dim light in a window enabled him to see a mother, half-asleep, giving a bottle of warm milk to her infant. He felt the shooting pain of the sick woman on the corner and imagined the drowsy grocer's wife waking up with a start.

He was in the café. Men holding grubby cards and totting up red and yellow counters were seated at the polished brown tables.

He was in Geneviève's bedroom. He was suffering with her, feeling for her pride as a woman. Doubtless, she had just lived through the most painful day of her life and might even be anxiously awaiting Maigret's return so that she could slip into his room once more.

Madame Naud was wide awake. She had gone to bed, but could not get to sleep, and in the darkness of her room she lay listening for the slightest sound in the house. She wondered why Maigret had not come back, pictured her husband cooling his heels in the living room, torn between hope after his telephone call to Bréjon and anxiety at the Superintendent's absence.

Maigret felt the warmth of the cattle in the stables, heard the mare kicking, visualized the old cook in her camisole. . . . And in Groult-Cotelle's house . . . What's that? A door was opening. Alban was leading his visitor out. How he hated him! What had he and Cavre said to each other in the dusty, stale-smelling living room after the telephone call to Naud?

The door closed again. Cavre walked quickly along, his brief-case under his arm. He was pleased, yet displeased. After all, he had almost won the game. He had beaten Maigret. Tomorrow the Superintendent would be summoned back to Paris. But nonethe-less he felt a little humiliated that he had not brought this about single-handed. Furthermore, he felt thoroughly ruffled by the Superintendent's menacing tone with regard to the whereabouts of Albert Retailleau's cap. . . .

Cavre's employee would be waiting for him at the Lion d'Or, drinking brandy to while away the time.

"Are you going back right away?" asked Louis.

"Yes, my boy . . . What else can I do?"

"You're not going to give up?"

"Give up what?"

Maigret knew them all so well! He had come across so many young men like Louis in his life, boys who were just as enthusi-astic, just as naïve and at the same time crafty, attacking every difficulty head on, resolved to attain their ends no matter what.

"You'll get over it, my dear fellow," he thought. "A few years from now you will bow respectfully to a Naud or a Groult-Cotelle because you'll have understood that it's the wisest thing for the son of Fillou."

And what about Madame Retailleau, all alone in her house? She was sure carefully to have removed all the franc notes from the soup tureen. She had understood long ago. She had doubtless been as good a wife and as good a mother as they come. It was probably not that she lacked feelings, but that she had realized that feelings get you nowhere. She had resigned herself to this truth.

But she was determined to defend herself with other arms. She was determined to turn all life's misfortunes into cash. Her husband's death had secured her her house and an income that allowed her to bring up and educate her son.

The death of Albert . . .

"I bet," he muttered to himself in a low voice, "she wants a little house in Niort, not in Saint-Aubin. . . . A brand-new little house, spotlessly clean, with pictures of her husband and son on the wall . . . somewhere she can live comfortably and securely in her old age."

As for Groult-Cotelle and his *Sexual Perversions* . . .

"You're walking awfully quickly, Superintendent."

"Are you coming back with me?"

"Do you mind?"

"Won't your mother be worried?"

"Oh, she pays no attention to me."

He said these words with a mixture of pride and regret in his voice.

Off they went, past the station, along the water-logged path bordering the canal. Old Désiré would be sleeping off his wine on his dirty straw mattress. Josaphat, the postman, was proud of himself and was no doubt reckoning what he had gained from his cleverness and cunning. . . .

Ahead of them, at the end of the path, there was a circle of light, like the moon seen through the veil of a cloud, and a large, warm, and peaceful-looking house, one of those houses that passers-by look at enviously, thinking how nice it must be to live there.

"Off you go, son. . . . We're here now."

"When will I see you again? Promise me you won't leave without . . ."

"I promise."

"You're sure you're not giving up?"

"Sure."

Alas! Maigret was not exactly thrilled at the thought of what remained to be done, and he walked up to the steps of the house with his shoulders hunched. The front door was ajar. They had left it like that so that he could get in. There was a light on in the living room.

He sighed as he took off his heavy overcoat, which the fog had made even heavier, then stood for a moment on the doormat to light his pipe.

"In we go!"

Poor Etienne had sat up waiting for him, torn between hope

and a deadly anxiety. That very afternoon, Madame Naud had tormented herself in similar fashion, in the same armchair as her husband was sitting in now.

A bottle of Armagnac on a small round table looked as if it had served its purpose well.

8

MAIGRET
PLAYS MAIGRET

THERE WAS NOTHING affected about Maigret's stance. If his shoulders were hunched and his head somewhat off-center, as if he were frozen to the marrow and bent on warming himself by the stove, it was because he was cold. He had been out in the fog for some time and had paid no attention to the temperature. With his overcoat off, he shivered and suddenly seemed aware of the icy dampness, which chilled his bones.

He felt irritable, as one does when about to come down with flu. He also felt uneasy, since he disliked the task that faced him. And he was hesitant. As he was about to enter the living room, he had suddenly thought of two diametrically opposed methods of tackling the situation, just when he had to make up his mind to come to a final decision.

It was this, rather than an attempt to live up to his reputation, that made him walk into the room looking grim, with large eyes that appeared unfocused, and the swaying gait of a bear.

He looked at nothing, yet saw everything: the glass and the bottle of Armagnac, the overly smooth hair on Etienne Naud, who said with false cheerfulness:

"Did you have a good evening, Superintendent?"

He had obviously just run a comb through his hair. He always kept one in his pocket, since he was always conscious of his appearance. Earlier, however, while he was gloomily waiting for Maigret's return, he had probably run his shaking fingers through his hair.

Instead of replying, Maigret went over to the wall on the left and adjusted a picture that was not hanging straight. This was not affectation. He could not abide seeing a picture askew on a wall. It quite simply irritated him, and he had no wish to be irritated for such a stupid reason just when he was all set to play the detective.

It was stuffy. The smell of food still lingered in the room and mingled with the scent of the Armagnac, to which the Superintendent finally helped himself.

"There!" he sighed.

Naud jumped in surprise and anxiety at that resounding "There!" It was as if Maigret, having debated the situation in his mind, had reached a conclusion.

If the Superintendent had been at Police Headquarters or had even been officially investigating the case, he would have felt obliged, in order to put the odds on his side, to use traditional methods. But traditional methods, in this particular case, would tend to weaken Naud's resistance, to scare him and shatter his nerve by making him oscillate between hope and fear.

It was easy. Just let him get entangled in his own lies first. Then vaguely bring up the subject of the two telephone calls. And then—why not, after all?—say point-blank:

"Your friend Alban will be arrested tomorrow morning."

Not that way, however! Maigret quite simply stood leaning against the mantelpiece. The flames in the fireplace scorched his legs. Naud was sitting near him, presumably going on hoping.

"I shall leave tomorrow at three o'clock, as you wish," sighed the Superintendent at last, having puffed at his pipe two or three times in quick succession.

He pitied Naud. He felt uncomfortable facing a man approximately his own age who up to now had lived a sheltered, peaceful, upright life, and who, threatened as he was by the possibility of being shut behind prison walls for the rest of his days, was playing his last cards.

Was he going to fight, to go on lying? Maigret hoped not, just as, out of compassion, one hopes that a wounded animal, clumsily shot, will die quickly. He avoided looking at him and fixed his eyes on the carpet.

"Why do you say that, Superintendent? You know you are welcome here and that my family not only likes but respects you, as I do. . . ."

"I overheard your telephone conversation with your brother-in-law, Monsieur Naud."

He put himself in the other man's shoes. Afterward, he preferred to forget such moments as these. He hurried on:

"Furthermore, you are mistaken about me. Your brother-in-law, Bréjon, asked me as a favor to come and help you in a delicate matter. I realized at once, believe me, that he had wrongly interpreted your wishes, and that it was not help of this kind that you wanted from him. You wrote to him in a moment of panic to ask his advice. You told him about the rumors circulating but you did not admit, of course, that they were true. And he, poor man, being an honest, conscientious magistrate who works by the rules, sent you a detective to sort out the mess."

Naud struggled slowly to his feet, walked over to the small round table, and poured himself a generous glass of Armagnac. His hands were shaking. There were probably beads of sweat on his forehead, although Maigret could not see it. Even if he had not pitied the man, he would have looked the other way at this crucial moment, out of human consideration.

"If you had not called in Justin Cavre, I would have left the district immediately after our initial meeting, but his presence somehow goaded me into staying."

Naud said not a word in protest, but fiddled with his watch chain and stared at the portrait of his mother-in-law.

"Of course, since I am not here on official business, I am not accountable to anyone. So you have nothing to fear from me, Monsieur Naud, and I am in a position to talk to you all the more freely. You have just been through a hellish few weeks, haven't you? And so has your wife, for I am sure she knows all about it. . . ."

The other man still did not surrender. It had got to the point where a nod of the head, a whisper, or a flutter of the eyelids was all that was required to put an end to the suspense. After that, peace would come. He could relax. He would have nothing more to hide, no game to play.

Upstairs, his wife was probably awake, straining to hear and fretting because there was no sign of the two men's coming up to bed. And what of his daughter? Had she managed to get to sleep?

"Now, Monsieur Naud, I am going to tell you what I really think, and you will understand why I have not left without coming out with it, which, strange, though it may seem, I was on the point of doing. Listen carefully, and don't be too ready to misconstrue what I say. I have the distinct impression, the near certitude, that however guilty you may be in the death of Albert Retailleau, you are also a victim of his death. I will go further. If you have been the instrument of death, you are not primarily responsible for it."

And Maigret helped himself to a drink, in order to give the other man time to weigh his words. Because Naud remained silent, he finally looked him in the eye and forced him to look back. He asked:

"Don't you trust me?"

The result was as distressing as it was unexpected, for Naud, a man in the prime of his life, capitulated by bursting into tears. His swollen eyes brimmed with tears and his lips pouted like a child's. For a few minutes he tried to control himself, standing awkwardly in the middle of the room. Then he rushed over and leaned against the wall. Covering his face with his arms, he started to sob violently, his shoulders shaking spasmodically.

Maigret now needed only to wait. Twice, Naud tried to speak, but it was too soon; he had not regained sufficient control of himself. As if out of discretion, Maigret had sat down in front of the fire and, since he did not feel free to stir it up, as he would do at home, he rearranged the logs with a pair of tongs.

"If you like, you can tell me in your own good time what really happened, although it won't serve much purpose, because it is a simple matter to reconstruct the events of the night in question. But what followed is another matter altogether."

"What do you mean?"

Naud looked just as tall and strong, but he seemed to have lost all substance. He had the air of a child who had shot up too fast and at the age of twelve is as tall and well filled out as a fully grown man.

"Did you not suspect that something was going on between your daughter and that young man?"

"But I didn't even know him, Superintendent! I mean, I knew of his existence, because I know more or less everyone in the village, but I could not have put a name to his face. I still wonder how on earth Geneviève managed to meet him, since she virtually never left the house."

"On the night in question, you and your wife were in bed, were you not?"

"Yes . . . And another thing . . . It's ridiculous, but we'd had goose for dinner. . . ."

He clung to facts of this kind, as though by investing the truth with such intimate details he somehow made it less tragic.

"I love goose, but I find it difficult to digest. . . . At about one in the morning, I got up to take some bicarbonate of soda. . . . You know the layout of the rooms upstairs, more or less. Our bathroom is next to our bedroom, then there's a spare room, and next to that a room we never go into because . . ."

"I know. . . . The memory of a child."

"My daughter's room is at the far end of the hallway, and so it is rather isolated from the rest of the house. The two maids sleep on the floor above. . . . While I was in our bathroom, groping about in the dark—I didn't want to wake up my wife; she'd have scolded me for being greedy—I heard the sound of voices. There was an argument going on. It did not cross my mind that the noise could be coming from my daughter's room.

"However, when I went into the hallway to find out for myself, I realized this was so. There was a light under her door, too. . . . I heard a man's voice.

"I don't know what you would have done in my place, Superintendent. . . . I don't know if you have a daughter. . . . We're still rather behind the times here in Saint-Aubin. . . . Perhaps I am particularly naïve. Geneviève is twenty. But it had never occurred to me she might hide something like this from her mother and me. . . . To think that a man . . . No! You know, even now . . ."

He wiped his eyes and mechanically took his pack of cigarettes out of his pocket.

"I almost rushed into the room in my nightshirt. . . . I'm rather old-fashioned in that respect, too, and still wear night-shirts, and not pajamas. . . . But at the last moment I realized how ridiculous I looked and went back into the bathroom. I got dressed in the dark, and just as I was putting on my socks, I heard another noise, this time outside. Since the bathroom shutters had not been closed, I drew back the curtain. There was a moon, and I could see a man climbing down a ladder into the courtyard. . . .

"I got my shoes on somehow and rushed downstairs. . . . I am not sure, but I think I heard my wife calling:

"'Etienne . . .'

"Have you already thought of looking at the keys to the door that opens into the courtyard? . . . It's an old key, a huge one, a real hammer. . . . I would not be prepared to swear that I took it off its hook without thinking, but it wasn't a premeditated action either. It had not occurred to me to kill, and if anyone had said then . . ."

He spoke softly but in a shaky voice. To calm himself, he lit his cigarette and puffed slowly at it several times, in the manner of the condemned.

"The man went around the house and jumped over the low wall by the road. I jumped over it behind him, not thinking to stifle the sound of my footsteps. He must have heard me, but he went on walking at the same pace. When I had almost caught up with him, he turned around, and, although I could not see his face, for some reason or other I got the impression he was jeering at me.

"'What do you want of me?' he asked in an aggressive, scornful tone of voice.

"I swear to you, Superintendent, those are moments I wish with all my heart I had never lived through. I recognized him. He was only a youngster to me, but he had just left my daughter's bedroom and now he was sneering at me. I didn't know what to do. This kind of thing doesn't happen the way you imagine. I shook him by the shoulders but couldn't find the words to express what I wanted to say.

"'So you're angry because I'm jilting your daughter, are you!

The whore! . . . You were hand in glove, weren't you?' He flung these words at me."

Naud passed his hand over his face.

"I am not sure of anything any more, Superintendent. With the best will in the world, I could not give you an exact account of what happened. He was every bit as angry as I was but more in control of himself. He was insulting me, insulting my daughter. . . . Instead of falling on his knees at my feet, as I had stupidly half imagined he would do, he was making fun of me, my wife, my whole family. He said things like:

"'A fine family, indeed!'

"He used the most obscene language when referring to my daughter, words I cannot bring myself to repeat, and then I began to hit him. I don't know how it happened. I had the key in my hand. The youth suddenly punched me hard in the stomach, and the pain was such that I began to hit him as hard as I could. . . .

"He fell. . . .

"And then I ran away. All I wanted to do was to get back to the house. . . .

"I swear to you this is the truth. . . . My first thought was to telephone the police in Benet. . . . When I got closer to the house, I saw a light on in my daughter's room. I suddenly thought that if I told the truth . . . But you must understand. . . . I went back to where I had left him. He was dead."

"You carried him to the railroad tracks," Maigret continued, to help him bring this sorry story more quickly to an end.

"That's right."

"All by yourself?"

"Yes."

"And you returned home?"

"My wife was standing behind the door that opens onto the road. She asked in a whisper:

"'What have you done?'

"I tried to deny it all, but she knew. There was terror and pity in the look she gave me. I went to bed feeling somewhat feverish, and she went through all my clothes in the bathroom to make sure that . . ."

"I understand."

"You may or may not believe it, but neither my wife nor I has had the courage to broach the subject with our daughter. We've never talked about it, or even once referred to it together. That's probably the hardest thing of all. It is sometimes unnerving. Our household routine is exactly the same as it was in the past, and yet all three of us know. . . ."

"And Alban?"

"I don't know how to tell you. . . . At first, I did not give him a thought. . . . Then the next day I was surprised when he didn't turn up as usual as we were about to eat. I started to talk about him, for the sake of something to say. I said:

"'I must call Alban.'

"When I did, his maid told me he wasn't in. Yet I was certain I heard his voice when the maid answered the phone. . . .

"It became an obsession with me. . . . Why doesn't Alban come? Does Alban suspect something? . . . Stupid as it may seem, I convinced myself that he constituted the only real threat, and four days later, when he still hadn't come near us, I went over to his house.

"I wanted to know the reason for his silence. I had no intention of confiding in him, but somehow I ended up telling him everything. . . .

"I needed him. . . . You would understand why if you had been in my position. . . . He used to tell me the local gossip. He also described the funeral. . . .

"I was well aware of what people were thinking from the beginning, and another idea took root in my mind. I felt I had to atone for what I had done, and this thought never left me. . . . Don't laugh at me, I beg of you."

"I have seen a great many men like you, Monsieur Naud!"

"And did they behave as stupidly as I did? Did they, one fine day, go and see the victim's mother, like I did? In melodramatic fashion, I waited until it was dark one evening, and then paid her a visit after Groult had made sure there was no one on the road. . . . I did not tell her the brutal truth. I said what a terrible misfortune it was that she, a widow, had lost her only support. . . .

"I am not sure whether it was a devil or an angel that prompted me, Superintendent. I can still see her, white-faced and motionless, standing by the hearth with a shawl around her shoulders. I had twenty thousand-franc notes in two bundles in my pocket. I didn't know how to go about putting them on the table. I was ashamed of myself. I was . . . yes, I was ashamed of her, too. . . .

"And yet the notes passed from my pocket to the table.

"'Each year, madame, I will make it my duty to . . .'

"And when she frowned, I hurriedly added:

"'Unless you would rather I give you a lump sum in your name which . . .'"

He could not go on, and had such difficulty breathing that he had to pour himself another glass of Armagnac.

"There it is. . . . I was wrong not to confess to everything at the beginning. . . . It was too late afterward. . . . Nothing has changed at home, at least on the surface. . . . I don't know how Geneviève has had the courage to go on living as if nothing had happened. There have been times when I have wondered if my imagination hasn't been playing tricks on me. . . .

"When I realized that people in the village suspected me, when I began receiving anonymous letters and found out that more had been sent to the Public Prosecutor, I wrote to my brother-in-law. It was stupid of me, because what could he do—since I had not told him the truth? One so often hears it said that magistrates have the power to cover up a scandal that I vaguely imagined Bréjon would use his authority in the same way. . . .

"Instead, he sent you down here just when I had written to a private detective agency in Paris. . . . Yes! I did that, too! I picked an address at random from newspaper advertisements! Unable to bring myself to confide in my brother-in-law, I told a total stranger everything that had happened. I simply had to be reassured. . . .

"He knew you were on your way, because when my brother-in-law told me you were arriving, I immediately sent a telegram to Cavre's agency. We arranged to meet in Fontenay the following day. . . .

"What else do you want to know, Superintendent? . . . How you must despise me! . . . Yes, you do! . . . And I despise myself, too, I assure you. . . . Of all the criminals you have known, I bet you haven't come across one as stupid, as . . ."

Maigret smiled for the first time. Etienne Naud was sincere. There was nothing artificial about his despair. And yet, as with all criminals, to use the word he himself had just used, his attitude revealed a certain pride.

It was annoying and humiliating to have bungled being a criminal!

For a few moments, or even several minutes, Maigret sat quite still and stared down at the flames curling around the blackened logs. Etienne Naud was so disconcerted by this unexpected reaction that he was at a loss what to do and stood hesitantly in the middle of the room, unsure of his next move.

Since he had confessed to everything, since he had chosen to abase himself, he had naturally supposed that the Superintendent would show him more consideration and come morally to his aid.

Had he not sunk lower than the low? Had he not painted a pathetic picture of his own and his family's plight?

Earlier, before confessing, Naud had sensed that Maigret was already sympathetic to his case and prepared to be more so. He had counted on this.

And now, all trace of sympathy had vanished. The game was over, and the Superintendent was calmly smoking his pipe, his expression one of deep thought devoid of any sentimentality.

"What would you do in my position?" Naud ventured once more.

One look made him wonder if he had gone too far. Perhaps he had overstepped the mark, like a child who is forgiven for misbehaving and as a result of such lenient treatment becomes more demanding and tiresome than ever.

What was Maigret thinking? Naud began to suspect that his manner had merely been part of a trap. He expected him to rise to his feet, take a pair of handcuffs out of his pocket, and say the sacred words:

"In the name of the law . . ."

"I am wondering . . ."

It was Maigret who hesitated, still puffing at his pipe as he crossed and uncrossed his legs.

"I am wondering . . . yes . . . I am wondering if we couldn't telephone your friend Alban. . . . What time is it? . . . Ten minutes past midnight . . . The postmistress will probably still be up and will put us through. . . . Yes, indeed . . . If you're not too tired, Monsieur Naud, I think it would be best if we got everything over with tonight, so that I can catch my train tomorrow."

"But . . ."

He could not find the right words, or, rather, dared not say what was on the tip of his tongue:

"But isn't it all over?"

"Will you excuse me?"

Maigret walked across the room, into the hall, and turned the handle of the telephone.

"Hello . . .I am sorry to bother you, dear mademoiselle. . . . Yes, it's I. . . . Did you recognize my voice? . . . Of course not . . . No problem at all . . . Could you very kindly put me through to Monsieur Groult-Cotelle, please? . . . Let it ring loud and clear, in case he's a heavy sleeper."

Through the half-open door he saw a bewildered Etienne Naud take a large gulp of Armagnac, as though resigned to his fate. The poor man was in a terrible state and seemed to have lost all his strength and nerve.

"Monsieur Groult-Cotelle? . . . How are you? . . . You were in bed? . . . What's that? . . . You were reading in bed? . . . Yes, this is Superintendent Maigret. . . . Yes, I'm with your friend. We've been having a chat. . . . What? . . . You've got a cold? . . . That's most unfortunate. . . . Anyone would think you have guessed what I was going to say. . . . We would like you to pop over here. . . . Yes, I know it is foggy. . . . You aren't dressed? . . . Well, in that case we'll come to you. . . . We'll be around in a jiffy if we take the car. . . . What? . . . You'd rather come over here? . . . No . . . Nothing in particular . . . I am leaving tomorrow. . . . I have important business to see to in Paris. . . ."

Poor Naud understood less and less what was in Maigret's

mind, and stared up at the ceiling, thinking, no doubt, that his wife could hear everything and must be thoroughly alarmed. Should he go upstairs to reassure her? But was he really in a position to do so? Maigret's behavior now made him uneasy, and he was beginning to regret having admitted to the crime.

"What did you say? . . . A quarter of an hour? . . . That's too long. Be as quick as you can. . . . See you in a few minutes. . . . Thank you."

Perhaps the Superintendent was playacting to a certain extent. Perhaps he was not really angry. Perhaps he did not want to be alone with Etienne Naud and have to wait ten minutes or a quarter of an hour in the living room with him.

"He is coming over," he announced. "He's very worried. You cannot imagine what a state my telephone call has put him in."

"But he's got no reason to . . ."

"Is that what you think?" asked Maigret simply.

Naud was more and more perplexed.

"Do you mind if I go and get a bite to eat in the kitchen? . . . Stay where you are. . . . I'll find the switch. I know where the icebox is."

He switched on the light in the kitchen. The stove had gone out. He found a chicken leg glazed with sauce. He cut and buttered a thick slice of bread.

"Tell me . . ."

He came back into the living room smiling.

"Have you got any beer?"

"Wouldn't you rather have a glass of burgundy?"

"I'd prefer beer, but if you haven't got any . . ."

"There must be some in the cellar. I always have one or two crates brought in. But since we don't drink beer very often, I don't know if . . ."

Just as, during the saddest of deathbed scenes, the family will cease weeping for a short time in the middle of the night and have a little something to eat, so the two men, after an hour of high drama, went matter-of-factly down to the cellar.

"No . . . This is lemonade. . . . Wait a minute. . . . The beer must be under the stairs."

He was right. They went back upstairs with bottles of beer

under their arms and then set about finding two large glasses. Maigret resumed munching the chicken leg, which he held between his fingers; the sauce got all over his chin.

"I wonder," he said casually, "if your friend Alban will come alone."

"What do you mean?"

"Nothing. I'm willing to bet that . . ."

There was no time to finish the wager. Someone was tapping on the front door. Etienne Naud rushed to open it. Maigret meanwhile stood calmly waiting in the middle of the room with his glass of beer in one hand and chicken and bread in the other.

He heard low voices:

"I have taken the liberty of bringing this gentleman with me. I met him on the way over here, and he . . ."

For a second, Maigret's eyes hardened, and then, with no warning, they suddenly flickered mischievously as he called to the man outside:

"Come in, Cavre! I was expecting you. . . ."

9

NOISE BEHIND
THE DOOR

AN IMPRESSION OF a dream can remain within us for a long time, sometimes all our lives, whereas the dream itself, so we are told, only lasts a few seconds. Thus, for a moment the three men entering the room seemed to Maigret to bear no resemblance to the kind of men they actually were, or, at any rate, considered themselves to be, and it was this new image of them that was to remain so vividly in his mind in later years.

They were all more or less the same age, Maigret included. And as he observed them, each in turn, he felt rather as if he was looking at a gathering of schoolboys in their senior year.

Etienne Naud was probably just as pudgy when he took his last exam as he was now. He would have had the same sturdy physique, the same soft look about him, and would undoubtedly have been very well mannered and rather shy.

The Superintendent had met Cavre not long after he had left school, and even then he had been a loner, and an ill-tempered one at that. However hard he tried—because he took pride in his appearance then—clothes simply did not sit as well on him as on other people. He always looked shabby and badly dressed. He cut a sad figure. When he was a little boy, his mother must have been forever saying to him:

"Run along and play with the others, Justin."

And no doubt she would confide to her neighbors:

"My son never plays. It worries me a bit, from the point of view of his health. He's too clever. He never stops thinking."

As for Alban, his looks had probably changed remarkably little since he was a young man: the long, thin legs, the elongated, rather aristocratic-looking face, the long, pale hands covered with reddish hairs, the upper-class elegance. . . . He would have copied his friends' compositions, borrowed cigarettes from them, and told them dirty jokes in corners.

And now they were struggling with utmost seriousness with a matter that could send one of them to jail for life. They were mature men. Two children somewhere bore the name of Groult-Cotelle, children who perhaps harbored some of their father's vices. In the house were a wife and daughter who would probably not sleep that night. As for Cavre, he was doubtless fuming at the thought that his wife might be making the most of his absence.

Something rather curious was happening. Whereas, shortly before, Etienne had confessed his crime to Maigret without a trace of shame and had laid bare, man to man, his innermost fears, now he blushed to the very roots of his hair as he ushered the visitors into the living room, trying in vain to look unconcerned.

Was it not, actually, rather a childish fancy that caused him to blush so violently? For a few seconds, Maigret became the headmaster or teacher. Naud had been kept behind to be questioned about some misdeed and been given a reprimand. His friends were now returning to the classroom and looking at him searchingly, as if to say:

"How did you make out?"

Well, he had not made out at all well. He had not defended himself. He had wept. He now wondered if there were still traces of tears on his cheeks and eyelids.

He would have liked to boast and make them think that everything had gone smoothly. Instead, he bustled about, went into the dining room to get some glasses out of the sideboard, and then poured out the Armagnac.

Did these glimpses of a time of life when our actions and conduct are as yet unimportant inspire the Superintendent? He waited until everyone was seated, then positioned himself in the middle of the room and, looking at Cavre and Alban in turn, said firmly:

"Well, gentlemen, the game's up!"

Only at this point, and for the first time since he had become involved in this case, did he play Maigret, as was said of inspectors at the Police Judiciaire who tried to imitate the great man. With his pipe between his teeth, his hands in his pockets, and his back to the fire, he talked and growled, poked at the logs with the end of the tongs, and moved with bearlike gait from one suspect to the other, either firing questions at them or suddenly breaking off so that a disturbing silence fell over the room.

"Monsieur Naud and I have just had a long and friendly chat. I announced my intention of returning to Paris tomorrow. It was far better, was it not, before taking leave of each other, to come out with the truth, and this is what we did. Why do you jump, Monsieur Groult-Cotelle? In fact, Cavre, I must apologize for having made you come out just when you were going to bed. Yes indeed! I am the guilty one. I knew perfectly well when I called our friend Alban that he wouldn't have the guts to come here alone. I wonder why he considered my invitation to come for a chat a threat. . . . He had a detective at hand and, since there was no lawyer around, he brought along the detective. . . . Isn't that right, Groult?"

"It wasn't me who sent to Paris for him!" replied the bogus country gentleman, now stripped of his air of importance.

"I know. It wasn't you who beat the unfortunate Retailleau to death, because you just happened to be in La Roche on that night. It wasn't you who left your wife; she was the one who left you. It wasn't you who . . . In fact, you're a somewhat negative character altogether, aren't you? . . . You have never done a good deed in your life. . . ."

Alarmed at being reprimanded like this, Groult-Cotelle called Cavre to his aid, but the detective, his leather briefcase on his lap, was looking at Maigret in a somewhat anxious fashion.

He was sufficiently well acquainted with the police, and with the boss in particular, to know that this little scene was being staged for a definite purpose and that when the meeting was over, the case would be closed.

Etienne Naud had not protested when the Superintendent had declared:

"The game's up!"

What more did Maigret want? He walked up and down, stood in front of one of the portraits, went from one door to the other, all the time keeping up a steady flow of words. It was almost as if he was improvising, and now and again Cavre began to wonder if he might not be playing for time and waiting for something to happen that he knew would happen but was taking a long time to do so.

"I am leaving tomorrow, then, as you all wish me to do, and while I am about it, I could reproach you all, and especially you, Cavre, since you know me, for not having trusted me more. You knew quite well, damn it, that I was just a guest and treated as well as any guest could be.

"What happened in this house before I arrived is none of my business. At most, one might have asked my advice. What, actually, is Naud's position? He did something most unfortunate—very unfortunate even. But did anyone come forward and complain?

"No! The young man's mother declared herself satisfied. If I may say so . . ."

And Maigret deliberately made light of his next, ominous, statement, a move that misled all three men.

"The drama in question was enacted by gentlemen, all well-bred people. There were rumors abroad, admittedly. Two or three unpleasant pieces of evidence gave cause for concern, but the diplomacy of our friend Cavre and Naud's money, combined with the liking of certain individuals for liquor, averted any possible danger. And as for the cap, which in any case would not have constituted sufficient proof, I presume Cavre took the precaution of destroying it. Isn't that right, Justin?"

Cavre jumped on hearing himself addressed by his Christian name. Everybody turned to look at him, but he said nothing.

"That, in a nutshell, is the position at present, or, rather, our host's position. Anonymous letters are in circulation. The Public Prosecutor and the police have received some of them. There may be an official inquiry into the case. What have you advised your client, Cavre?"

"I am not a lawyer."

"How modest you are! If you want to know what I think, and this is my own personal view and not a professional opinion, for I am not a lawyer either, in a few days' time, Naud will feel the need to depart with his family. He is rich enough to sell his property and retire elsewhere, possibly abroad. . . ."

Naud let out a sigh in the form of a sob at the thought of leaving what had been his whole life until now.

"That leaves our friend Alban. . . . What do you propose to do, Monsieur Alban Groult-Cotelle?"

"You don't have to answer," Cavre hurriedly interjected on seeing him open his mouth. "I would also like to say that we are under no obligation to put up with this interrogation, which, in any case, is phony. If you knew the Superintendent as well as I do, you would realize he is taking us for a real ride, as they would say at the Quai des Orfèvres. I don't know whether you have confessed, Monsieur Naud, or how the Superintendent got the truth out of you, but of one thing I am sure, and that is that my former colleague has a purpose in mind. I do not know what that purpose is, but I am telling you to be on your guard."

"Well said, Justin!"

"I did not ask for your opinion."

"Well, I am giving it anyway."

And suddenly his tone changed. For the past quarter of an hour he had been waiting for something and had been forced into all this playacting as a result, but now that something had finally happened. It was not without good reason that he had continued pacing up and down, going from the hall door to the door opening into the dining room.

Nor was it hunger or greed earlier that had caused him to go into the kitchen for some bread and a hunk of chicken. He needed to know if there was another staircase besides the one leading down into the hall. And indeed there was a second staircase, for the staff, near the kitchen.

When he telephoned Groult-Cotelle, he had talked in a very loud voice, as though unaware of the fact that two women were supposed to be asleep.

Now, there was someone behind the half-open dining-room door.

"You are right, Cavre. You are no fool, even though you are rather a sorry character. . . . I have one purpose in mind and that is—let me declare it forthwith—to prove that Naud is not the real culprit."

This statement by the Superintendent stupefied Etienne Naud more than anyone else. He had to restrain himself from crying out. As for Alban, he had turned deathly pale, and small red blotches, which Maigret had not noticed before, appeared on his forehead, as if he were prey to a sudden attack of hives—a clear proof of his inner collapse.

When he saw the rash, the Superintendent remembered how a certain rather celebrated murderer, after a twenty-eight-hour interrogation, during which he had defended himself inch by inch, had suddenly wet his pants like a frightened child. Maigret and Lucas had been conducting the interrogation, and they had sniffed, looked at each other, and realized they had the upper hand.

Alban Groult-Cotelle's hives were a similar symptom of guilt, and the Superintendent had difficulty in suppressing a smile.

"Tell me, Monsieur Groult, would you rather tell us the truth yourself, or would you like me to do it for you? Take your time before answering. Naturally, you have my permission to consult your lawyer. . . . I mean Justin Cavre. Go off into a corner, if you like, and work something out between you."

"I have nothing to say."

"So it is my job to tell Monsieur Naud, who still does not know, why Albert Retailleau was killed, is it? Because strange as it might seem, even though Etienne Naud knows the young man was killed, he has absolutely no idea *why*. . . . What were you going to say, Alban?"

"You're a liar!"

"How can you say I am a liar when I haven't said anything yet? Come now! I will put the question a different way, and it will still come to the same thing. Will you tell us why, on a certain, carefully chosen day, you suddenly felt the need to go to La Roche-sur-Yon and bring back your hotel bill with meticulous care?"

Etienne Naud still did not understand, and looked anxiously at

Maigret, convinced that this line of attack would prove the Superintendent's undoing. At first he had been impressed by Maigret's manner, but now the Superintendent was rapidly going down in Naud's estimation. His animosity toward Groult-Cotelle was pointless and beginning to be thoroughly obnoxious.

It had reached the point where Naud felt he had to intervene. He was an honest fellow who disliked seeing an innocent man accused, and, as host, he would not allow one of his guests to be raked over the coals.

"I assure you, Superintendent, you are barking up the wrong tree."

"My dear fellow, I am sorry to have to disillusion you, and even sorrier that what you are about to learn is extremely unpleasant. Isn't that so, Groult?"

Groult-Cotelle had shot to his feet, and it looked as if he was going to rush at his tormentor. He had the greatest possible difficulty in restraining himself. He clenched his fists, and his whole body shook. Finally, he started toward the door, but Maigret stopped him in his tracks by simply asking, in the most natural tone:

"Are you going upstairs?"

Who would have thought, on seeing the stubborn and stolid Maigret, that he was as warm as his victim? His shirt was sticking to his back. He was listening carefully. And the truth of the matter was, he was frightened.

A few minutes before, he was convinced that Geneviève was behind the door, as he hoped. He had been thinking of her when he had telephoned Groult-Cotelle earlier, and had consequently talked in a loud voice in the hall.

"If I am right," he was thinking then, "she'll come down. . . ."

And she had come down. At all events, he had heard a faint rustling sound behind the door into the dining room, and one side of the door had moved.

It was on Geneviève's account, too, that he had addressed Groult-Cotelle in such a way a moment ago. Now he was wondering if she was still there, since he could not hear a sound. It had crossed his mind that she might have fainted, but presumably he would have heard her fall.

He was longing to look behind the half-open door, and began thinking of how he could do so.

"Are you going upstairs?" he had flung at Alban.

And Alban, who seemed no longer to care, retraced his steps and positioned himself a few inches away from his enemy.

"Just what are you insinuating? Out with it! What other slanders have you got up your sleeve? There's not a word of truth in what you are going to say, do you hear?"

"Take a look at your lawyer."

Cavre looked pitiful, indeed, for he realized that Maigret was on the right track and that his client was caught in his own web of lies.

"I don't need anyone to advise me. I don't know what you might have been told or who could have fabricated such stories, but before you say anything, I would like to state that they are untrue. If some superexcited brains have succeeded in . . ."

"You are vile, Groult."

"What?"

"I say that you are a repulsive character. I say, and I repeat, that you are the real cause of Albert Retailleau's death, and that if the laws created by men were perfect, life imprisonment would not be a harsh-enough punishment for you. In fact, it would give me great personal pleasure, though I don't often feel like this, to accompany you to the foot of the guillotine."

"Gentlemen, I call you to witness . . ."

"It was not only Retailleau you killed, but others, too."

"I killed Retailleau? . . . I? . . . You're mad, Superintendent! He's mad! He's raving mad, I swear to you! . . . Where are these people I've killed? . . . Show them to me, then, if you please. . . . Well, we're waiting, Monsieur Sherlock Holmes."

He was sneering. His agitation had reached its peak.

"There is one of them," Maigret calmly replied, pointing to Etienne Naud, who was looking increasingly bewildered.

"It seems to me he's a dead man in very good health, as the saying goes, and if all my victims . . ."

Alban had walked over to where Maigret was standing in such an arrogant manner that the Superintendent's hand automatically jerked up and came down on Alban's pale cheek with a thud.

Perhaps they were going to come to blows, grab each other by the waist and roll around on the carpet, as befitted the schoolboys the Superintendent had visualized a short while before. But the sound of a hysterical voice shrieking from the top of the stairs stopped them in their tracks.

"Etienne!   Etienne! . . . Superintendent! . . . Quick! . . . Geneviève . . ."

Madame Naud came down a few more steps, amazed that no one appeared to have heard her. She had already been shouting for some minutes.

"Hurry," Maigret said to Naud. "Go up to your daughter. . . ."

And he turned to face Cavre and said in a tone that invited no reply:

"Just make sure he doesn't escape. . . . Do you hear?"

He followed Etienne Naud up the stairs and went with him into the young girl's bedroom.

"Look . . ." moaned Madame Naud, distraught.

Geneviève was lying across her bed with her clothes on. Her eyes were half-open but had the glazed look of a sleepwalker. A vial of Veronal lay broken on the carpet where she had dropped it.

"Help me, madame. . . ."

The opiate was only just beginning to take effect, and the girl was still half-conscious. She drew back, terrified, as the Superintendent bent down and, gripping her hard, forced open her mouth.

"Bring me some water, a lot of water, warm if possible. . . ."

"You go, Etienne. . . . In the kitchen . . ."

Poor Etienne bumped his way down the hallway and back stairs like a giddy goose.

"Don't be afraid, madame. . . . We are still in time. . . . It's my fault. I didn't think she would react like this. . . . Get me a handkerchief, a towel, anything will do."

Less than two minutes later, the girl had vomited violently. Then she sat dejectedly on the edge of her bed obediently drinking down all the water the Superintendent gave her, which made her sick all over again.

"You can telephone the doctor. He won't do much more, but to be on the safe side . . ."

Geneviève suddenly broke down and began to cry, softly but with such weariness that the tears seemed to lull her to sleep.

"I'll leave you to look after her, madame. . . . I think it is best if she rests before the doctor comes. . . . In my opinion—and unfortunately I've seen rather a lot of cases like this, believe me—the danger is over."

They could hear Naud on the telephone downstairs:

"Immediately, yes . . . It's my daughter. . . . I'll explain when you get here. . . . No . . . Come as you are—in your dressing gown, if you like. It doesn't matter."

As he passed Naud in the hall, Maigret took the letter he was holding in his hand. He had noticed it lying on Geneviève's bedside table but had not had a moment to pick it up.

Naud tried to get the letter back as soon as he had put down the receiver.

"What are you doing?" he exclaimed. "It's for her mother and me."

"I will give it back to you in a moment. . . . Go upstairs and sit with her."

"But . . ."

"It's the best place for you to be, I assure you."

And Maigret went back into the living room, carefully closing the door behind him. He held the letter in his hand and was obviously reluctant to open it.

"Well! Groult?"

"You have no right to arrest me."

"I know . . ."

"I have done nothing illegal."

This momentous word almost made Maigret think he deserved to be slapped again, but he would have had to cross the room to do so and he did not have the energy.

He toyed with the letter and hesitated before finally slitting open the mauve envelope.

"Is that letter addressed to you?" protested Groult-Cotelle.

"No, and it's not addressed to you either. . . . Geneviève

wrote it before taking the overdose. . . . Would you like me to return it to her parents?"

Dear Mummy, dear Daddy,
  I love you dearly. I beg you to believe me. But I must put an end to my life. I cannot go on living any longer. Do not try to find out why, and, above all, don't ask Alban to the house any more. He . . .

"Tell me, Cavre, did he tell you the whole story while we were upstairs?"

Maigret was convinced that in his agitated state, Alban had confessed because of a desperate need to cling to someone, a man who could defend him, whose job it was to do so, provided he was paid for his services.

As Cavre lowered his head, Maigret added:

"Well, what have you got to say?"

And Groult-Cotelle, whose cowardice knew no limits, chipped in:

"She was the one who started it!"

"And she, no doubt, gave you nasty little pornographic books to read?"

"I never gave her any . . ."

"And you never showed her certain pictures I saw in your library?"

"She came across them when my back was turned."

"And no doubt you felt the need to explain them to her?"

"I am not the first man of my age to take a young girl for a mistress. . . . I didn't force her. . . . She was very much in love. . . ."

Maigret laughed derisively as he looked Alban up and down.

"And it was her idea, too, to call in Retailleau?"

"If she took another lover, that is certainly no affair of mine, you must admit. I think you have colossal nerve to blame me! Me! In front of my friend Naud, just now . . ."

"What was that?"

"In front of Naud, then, I didn't dare answer, and you had the upper hand. . . ."

A car pulled up in front of the steps. Maigret went out of the room to open the front door and said, just as if he were master of the house:

"Go straight up to Geneviève's room. Hurry . . ."

Then he went back into the living room, still holding Geneviève's letter in his hand.

"It was you, Groult, who panicked when she told you she was pregnant. You're a coward and always have been. You are so afraid of life that you don't trust your own efforts and so you clutch at other people's lives. . . .

"You were going to foist that child on some poor idiot, who would then become its father. . . .

"It was such a practical solution! . . . Geneviève was to snare a young man, who would think he was sincerely loved. . . . He would be told one fine day that his ardor had resulted in a pregnancy. . . . He had only to go to her father, ask to be forgiven on bended knees, and declare himself willing to make amends. . . .

"And you would have gone on being her lover, wouldn't you?

"You bastard!"

It was young Louis who had put him on the trail, when he had said:

"*Albert was angry. . . . He had several brandies before going off to meet her.*"

And Albert's behavior toward Geneviève's father? He had been insolent. He had used the foulest language in speaking of Geneviève.

"How did he find out?" demanded Maigret.

"I don't know."

"Would you rather I go and ask Geneviève?"

Groult-Cotelle shrugged his shoulders. What difference did it make, after all? Maigret could not pin a charge on him.

"Every morning Retailleau used to go to the post office to collect his employers' mail as it was being sorted. . . . He would go behind the counter and sometimes help to sort the letters. . . . He recognized Geneviève's handwriting on an envelope addressed to me. She had not been able to see me alone for several days, and so . . ."

"I see."

"If that hadn't happened, everything would have gone according to plan. . . . And if you hadn't meddled . . ."

Of course Albert had been angry that night, when, with the incriminating letter in his pocket, he went to see the girl who had used him so shamefully for the last time. Moreover, everyone had conspired to make a fool of him, her parents included. How could he think otherwise?

They had led him up a fine garden path, and they were still trying to deceive him. The father was even pretending to have caught him, in order to make him marry his daughter.

"How did you know he had intercepted the letter?"

"I went to the post office shortly afterward. . . . The postmistress said:

"'Wait a minute! I thought there was a letter for you.'

"She looked everywhere. . . . I called Geneviève. . . . Then I asked the postmistress who had been there when the mail was being sorted, and I realized, I . . .'"

"You realized that things had taken a turn for the worse and you decided to go and see your friend the Prefect's private secretary, in La Roche."

"That's my business."

"What do you think, Justin?"

But Cavre did not reply.

Heavy footsteps were heard on the stairs. The door opened. Etienne Naud came in, looking spent and dejected, his large eyes full of questions he sought in vain to answer. At that very moment, Maigret dropped the letter he was holding in so clumsy a fashion that it fell on top of the logs and flared up immediately.

"What have you done?"

"I'm so sorry. . . . It doesn't really matter, since your daughter is saved and she will be able to tell you herself what she put in her letter."

Was Naud fooled? Or was he like a certain type of patient, who suspects he is not being told the truth, who believes the doctor's optimistic words only partially, or not at all, but who nonetheless longs for those words, who needs to be reassured beyond all things?

"She is much better now, isn't she?"

"She is asleep. . . . It looks as though the danger is over, thanks to your swift action. . . . I don't know how to thank you, Superintendent. . . ."

The poor fellow seemed to be swimming around in the room, as if it had suddenly become too large for him, like an article of clothing that has stretched and engulfs the wearer. He looked at the bottle of Armagnac, almost poured himself a glass, but a sense of decorum held him back, and finally Maigret had to do it for him. He helped himself to a glass at the same time.

"Here's to your daughter and the end of all these misunderstandings."

Naud looked at him in wide-eyed astonishment. "Misunderstanding" was the very last word he had expected to hear.

"We have been chatting while you were upstairs. . . . I think your friend Groult has something very important to say to you. . . . Believe it or not, he is in the process of getting a divorce, though he hasn't told a soul. . . ."

Naud looked more and more at sea.

"Yes . . . And he has other plans. . . . All this probably won't make you jump for joy. . . . A cracked pot will never be the same as a perfect one, but it's still a pot. . . . Didn't someone mention that there is a morning train?"

"It leaves at 6:11," said Cavre. "And I think I'll take it."

"We'll travel together, then. . . . In the meantime, I am going to try to snatch a few hours' sleep."

He could not help saying to Alban as he went out:

"What a dirty trick!"

It was still foggy. Maigret refused point-blank to let anyone take him to the station, and Etienne Naud bowed before his wish.

"I don't know how to thank you, Superintendent. I didn't behave toward you as I should have. . . ."

"You have treated me extremely well, and I've shared some excellent meals with you."

"Will you tell my brother-in-law . . ."

"Of course I will! Oh! One piece of advice, if I may be so bold . . . Don't be too hard on your daughter."

A pathetic smile made Maigret realize that Naud had understood, perhaps better than might have been supposed.

"You're a first-rate person, Superintendent. . . . You really are! . . . I am so grateful."

"You'll be grateful for the rest of your days, as a friend of mine used to say. . . . Good-by! . . . Send me a postcard from time to time."

He left the lights of the house, which now seemed stilled, behind him. Smoke rose from two or three chimneys in the village, only to disappear into the fog. The dairy was working at full capacity and, from a distance, looked like a factory. Meanwhile, old Désiré was steering his boat, laden with pitchers of milk, along the canal.

Madame Retailleau would probably be asleep by now, and the tiny postmistress, too. . . . Josaphat would be sleeping off his wine, and . . .

Right up to the last minute, Maigret was afraid he would bump into Louis. The young man had put so much faith in him and, on discovering that the Superintendent had left, would doubtless think bitterly:

"He was one of them, too!"

Or else:

"They got the better of him!"

If they *had* got the better of him, they hadn't done so with money or fine words, at any rate.

And as he stood at the end of the platform waiting for the train, and keeping an eye on his suitcase, he mumbled to himself:

"Look here, son, I, too, wish everything could be clean and beautiful, just as you do. I, too, get upset and angry when . . ."

Surprise, surprise! Cavre walked onto the platform, stopping some fifty yards away from the Superintendent.

"That fellow, there, for instance . . . He's a crook. He is capable of all sorts of dirty tricks. I know this for a fact. And yet I feel rather sorry for him. I've worked with him. I know what he amounts to and what he suffers. . . . What would have been the point of having Etienne Naud condemned? And would they have found him guilty, anyway? . . . There is no real evidence. . . . The whole case would have stirred up a lot of dirt. Geneviève would have been called to the witness box. And Alban would have gone scot-free, probably delighted to be rid of his responsibilities."

There was no sign of Louis, which was just as well, for in spite of everything, Maigret was not proud of himself. This early-morning departure smacked too much of an escape.

"Later on you will understand. . . . They *are* strong, as you say. They stick together."

Having noticed Maigret, Justin Cavre came over but did not dare open a conversation.

"Do you hear, Cavre? I've been talking to myself, like a lonely old man."

"Have you any news?"

"What sort of news? The girl is all right now. The father and mother . . . I don't like you, Cavre. I am sorry for you, but I don't like you. . . . It can't be helped. Some people you warm up to and others you don't. . . . But I am going to tell you something. There is one phrase of popular wisdom that I thoroughly detest. It makes me wince and grind my teeth whenever I hear it. . . . Do you know what it is?"

"No."

"Everything will turn out all right."

The train came into the station, and in the growing din Maigret shouted:

"And you will see; everything *will* come out all right!"

Two years later, in fact, Maigret learned by chance that Alban Groult-Cotelle had married Mademoiselle Geneviève Naud in Argentina, where her father had built up a huge cattle ranch.

"Tough luck for our friend Albert, don't you think, Louis? But some poor devil always has to be the scapegoat!"

Saint-Mesmin-le-Vieux
March 3, 1943

MAIGRET
IN VICHY

1

"Do YOU KNOW them?" Madame Maigret asked in an undertone, observing that her husband was looking back over his shoulder at the couple who had just gone past.

The man, too, had turned his head and was smiling. He seemed hesitant, as though considering retracing his steps to shake the Chief Superintendent by the hand.

"No, I don't think so. . . . I don't know. . . ."

He was a squat little man. His wife, too, was small and plump, though perhaps an inch or so taller. Why was it Maigret had the impression that she was a Belgian? Because of her fair skin, her hair that was almost buttercup yellow, her protuberant blue eyes?

This was their fifth or sixth encounter. The first time, the man had stopped dead, beaming in delighted surprise. He had stood there uncertainly, as if about to speak, while the Chief Superintendent, frowning, searched his memory in vain.

There was certainly something familiar about that face and figure, but what the devil was it? Where had he last seen this cheerful little man, with the wife who looked as though she were made of brightly colored marzipan?

"I really can't think. . . ."

It did not much matter. Besides, everybody here was different from the people one met in everyday life. Any minute, now, there would be a burst of music. On the bandstand, with its slender columns and ornate canopy, the uniformed bandsmen, their eyes fixed on the conductor, sat waiting to raise the brass instruments to their lips. This presumably was the Municipal Band, made up of firemen and other Council workers. Their uniform was splendid, with scarlet tabs, white sashes, and enough gold braid and embroidery to satisfy a South American General.

Hundreds—thousands, it seemed to him—of iron chairs done up with yellow paint were set out in concentric circles around the bandstand, and nearly all were occupied by silent, waiting men and women with solemn faces.

In a minute or two, at nine o'clock, amid the great trees of the park, the concert would begin. After an oppressively hot day, the evening air seemed almost cool, and a light breeze rustled the leaves. Here and there, lamp standards surmounted by milky globes lightened the dark foliage with patches of paler green.

"Do you want to sit?"

There were still a few empty chairs, but they did not avail themselves of them. This evening, as always, they preferred to walk about in a leisurely way. Other couples, like themselves, came and went, half listening to the music, but there was also a number of solitary men and women, almost all elderly.

Nothing seemed quite real somehow. The white casino, plastered with the ornate moldings so much in vogue at the turn of the century, was floodlit. Except for the occasional blare of a motor horn in Rue Georges-Clemenceau, one could almost believe that here time stood still.

"There she is . . ." whispered Madame Maigret, pointing with her chin.

It had become a sort of game. She had got into the habit of following her husband's glance, watching for any glimmer of surprise or interest.

What else was there for them to do with their time? They walked, or rather strolled, about the streets. From time to time they paused, not because they were out of breath, but to look more closely at the play of light on a tree, a house, or a face.

They felt as though they had been in Vichy since the dawn of time, although, in fact, this was only their fifth day. Already they had established a routine, to which they adhered rigorously, as though it really mattered, and their days were given up to a succession of rituals, which they performed with the utmost solemnity.

How seriously, in fact, did Maigret take it all? His wife sometimes wondered, stealing a covert glance at him, trying to read his mind. He was not the man he was in Paris. His walk was less brisk, his features were less drawn. He went about most of the time smiling but abstracted. His expression suggested a degree of satisfaction, certainly, but also, perhaps, a touch of sardonic self-mockery.

"She's wearing her white shawl."

Each new day found them in the same place at the same hour, in one of the shaded park walks, beside the Allier, on a boulevard lined with plane trees, or in a crowded or a deserted side street, and, because of this, they had come to recognize, here and there, a face or a figure, and these were already getting to be part of their world.

Was it not the case that everyone here was going through the same motions at the same time every hour of the day, and not just at the mineral springs, where they all forgathered for the hallowed glass of water?

Maigret's eyes rested on a figure in the crowd, and sharpened. His wife followed his glance.

"Is she a widow, do you think?"

They might well have christened her "the lady in mauve," or rather "the lady in lilac," because that was the color she always wore. Tonight she must have arrived late, because she was sitting in one of the back rows.

The previous evening, at about eight o'clock, the Maigrets had come upon her unexpectedly as they were walking past the bandstand. There was still an hour to go before the concert. The little yellow chairs were so neatly arranged in concentric rings that they might have been circles drawn with a compass. All the chairs were vacant except one, in the front row, where the lady in lilac was sitting. There was something pathetic about her. She did not attempt to read by the light of the nearby lamp. She was not knitting. She was not doing anything. She did not seem in the least restless. She sat motionless, very upright, with her hands lying flat in her lap, looking straight in front of her, like a public figure avoiding the stares of the crowd.

She could have come straight out of a picture book. Unlike most of the women here, who went about bareheaded, she wore a white hat. The filmy shawl draped over her shoulders was white too. Her dress was of that distinctive lilac color that she seemed so much attached to.

She had an unusually long, narrow face and thin lips.

"She must be an old maid, don't you think?"

Maigret was unwilling to commit himself. He was not conducting an inquiry or following a trail. Here he was under no obligation to study people's faces, hoping that they would reveal the truth about themselves.

All the same, every now and then he caught himself doing it. He could not help it. It had become second nature. For no reason at all, he would find himself taking an interest in someone in the crowd, trying to guess his occupation, his domestic circumstances, the kind of life he led when he was not taking the waters.

It was by no means easy. After the first few days, sometimes after the first few hours, everyone seemed to become assimilated. Almost all wore the same expression of slightly vacant serenity, except those who were seriously ill, and who stood out from the rest by virtue of their deformities, their painful movements, and, still more, the unmistakable look in their eyes of pain tempered with hope.

The lady in lilac was one of what might be described as Maigret's circle of intimates, one of those who had attracted his attention and intrigued him from the first.

It was hard to guess her age. She might be forty-five or fifty-five. Time had not imprinted any telltale lines on her face.

She gave the impression of a woman accustomed to silence, like a nun, used to solitude, even perhaps enjoying it. Whether walking or, as at present, sitting, she totally ignored the people around her. No doubt it would have surprised her to know that Chief Superintendent Maigret, not as a matter of professional duty but simply for his own satisfaction, was studying her, in the hope of finding out what she was really like.

"She's never lived with a man, I'd say," he replied, as the opening burst of music came from the bandstand.

"Nor with children. Perhaps with someone very old, though. She might, perhaps, have had an aged mother to look after."

If so, she was unlikely to have been a good nurse, since she appeared unbending and unsociable. If she failed to see the people around her, it was because she did not look at them. She looked inward. She looked within herself, seeing no one but herself, deriving, no doubt, some secret satisfaction from this self-absorption.

"Shall we go?"

They had not come to listen to the music. They had simply got into the habit of walking past the bandstand at this time of the evening. Besides, it was not every night that there was a concert. Some evenings, it was virtually deserted on this side of the park. They strolled across the park, turning right into the colonnade which ran beside a street brilliant with neon signs. They could see hotels, restaurants, shops, a cinema. They had not yet been to the cinema. It did not fit in with their timetable.

There were other people taking a walk like themselves, at more or less the same leisurely pace, some coming, some going. A few had cut short their walk to go to the casino theater. They were late, and could be seen hurrying in, one or two here and there in evening dress.

Every one of these people lived quite a different life somewhere else, in a district of Paris, in some little provincial town, in Brussels, Amsterdam, Rome, or Philadelphia.

Each was a part of some predetermined social order, with its own rules, taboos, and passwords. Some were rich, others poor. Some were so ill that the treatment could do no more than give them a little extra time; others felt that, after taking the cure, they could forget about their health for the rest of the year.

This place was a kind of melting pot. Maigret's own case was typical. It had all started one evening when they were dining with the Pardons. Madame Pardon had served *canard au sang*, a dish that she made to perfection, and which the Chief Superintendent particularly relished.

"Is there anything wrong with it?" she had asked anxiously, seeing that Maigret had barely tasted it.

Surprised, Pardon had turned to his guest and subjected him to a searching look. Then, sounding really worried, he had asked:

"Aren't you feeling well?"

"Just a twinge . . . It's nothing. . . ."

The doctor, however, had not failed to notice his friend's unwonted pallor, and the beads of perspiration on his forehead.

The subject was not mentioned again during dinner. The Chief Superintendent had scarcely touched his wine, and when, over coffee, he was offered a glass of old Armagnac, he had waved it away:

"Not tonight, if you don't mind."

It was not until some time later that Doctor Pardon had said quietly:

"Let's go into my consulting room, shall we?"

Maigret had agreed reluctantly. He had known for some time that this was bound to happen, but he had kept putting it off from one day to the next. Doctor Pardon's consulting room was small and by no means luxurious. His stethoscope lay on the desk amid a litter of bottles, jars, and papers, and the couch on which he examined his patients sagged in the middle, as though the last one had left the imprint of his body on it.

"What seems to be the trouble, Maigret?"

"I don't know. It's my age, I daresay."

"How old are you? Fifty-two?"

"Fifty-three. . . . I've had a lot on my hands lately. Work . . . Worry . . . No sensational cases . . . Nothing exciting . . . Just the opposite . . . On the one hand, a flood of paperwork arising out of the reorganization at the Law Courts. . . . On the other, an epidemic of assaults on young girls and women living alone, in some cases including rape, in some not. . . . The press is howling for blood, and I haven't the staff to put on full-scale patrols without disrupting my whole department. . . ."

"Do you suffer from indigestion?"

"I do occasionally have stomach cramps . . . pains . . . as I did tonight . . . or rather a kind of constriction in the chest and abdomen. . . . I feel leaden . . . tired."

"Would you mind if I had a look at you?"

His wife, in the next room, must have guessed, Madame Pardon too, and this bothered Maigret. He had a horror of anything to do with illness.

As he stripped off his tie, jacket, shirt, and undershirt, he recalled something he had said when he was still in his teens: "I'd rather die young than live the life of an invalid, all pills and potions and diets, and being made to do this and not being allowed to do that."

In his vocabulary, being an invalid meant listening to one's heart, worrying about one's stomach, liver, and kidneys, and, at more or less regular intervals, exposing one's naked body to a doctor.

He no longer talked glibly of dying young, but he still did not feel ready to enter the invalid state.

"My trousers too?"

"Just pull them down a little."

Pardon took his blood pressure, listened to his chest, felt his diaphragm and stomach, pressing here and there with a finger.

"Am I hurting you?"

"No. . . . A little tenderness there, I think. . . . No . . . lower down. . . ."

Well, here he was, behaving just like anyone else, apprehensive, ashamed of his own cowardice, afraid to look his old friend in the face. Awkwardly, he began putting on his clothes again. When Pardon spoke, there was no change in his voice:

"When did you last take a holiday?"

"Last year I managed to get away for a week, then I was recalled because . . ."

"What about the year before last?"

"I couldn't leave Paris."

"Considering the life you lead, you ought to be in very much worse shape than you are."

"What about my liver?"

"It has stood up valiantly, considering the way you've treated it. . . . Admittedly, it's slightly enlarged, but it's in excellent working order."

"What's wrong then?"

"There's nothing precisely wrong. . . . A little of every-thing. . . . You're overtired, there's no doubt about that, and it will take more than a week's holiday to put that right. . . . How do you feel when you wake up in the morning?"

"Like a bear with a sore head."

Pardon laughed.

"Do you sleep well?"

"According to my wife, I thrash about in bed, and occasionally talk in my sleep."

"I see you're not smoking."

"I'm trying to cut down on it."

"Why?"

"I don't know. . . . I'm trying to cut down on drink, too."

"Sit down, won't you?"

Pardon sat in the chair behind his desk. Here, in his consulting room, he was very much the medical man, quite different from the host entertaining in his drawing room or dining room.

"Just you listen to me. You're not ill. As a matter of fact, considering your age and the life you lead, you're quite remark-ably fit. I'll thank you to get that into your head once and for all. Stop fretting about every little twinge and odd pain here and there, and don't start worrying every time you go up a flight of stairs. . . ."

"How did you know?"

"Tell me, when you're questioning a suspect, how do *you* know?"

They were both smiling.

"Here we are in June. Paris is sweltering. You'll oblige me by taking a holiday at once, if possible leaving no forwarding address. . . . At any rate, I'm sure you'll have the good sense not to call up the Quai des Orfèvres every day. . . ."

"I daresay it could be managed," Maigret said, not very gra-ciously. "There's our cottage at Meung-sur-Loire. . . ."

"You'll have plenty of time to enjoy that when you retire. . . . This year, I have other plans for you. . . . Do you know Vichy at all?"

"I've never set foot in the place, in spite of the fact that I was born within forty miles of it, near Moulins. . . . But in those days, of course, not everyone owned a car. . . ."

"That reminds me, has your wife passed her test?"

"We've actually got as far as buying a small car."

"I don't think you could do better than take the waters at Vichy. It will do you a world of good. . . . A thorough clean-out of the system. . . ."

When he saw the look on Chief Superintendent's face, he almost burst out laughing.

"You want me to take the cure?"

"It will only mean drinking a few pints of water every day. . . . I don't suppose the specialist will insist on your having all the trimmings: mud baths, mineral baths, vibro-massage, and all that nonsense. There's nothing seriously wrong with you. Three weeks of rest and regular exercise, no worry . . ."

"No beer, no wine, nothing to eat but rabbit's food . . ."

"You've had a good many years of eating and drinking whatever you fancied, haven't you?"

"That's true," he had to admit.

"And you have many more ahead, even if you do have to be a little more moderate in the future. . . . Are we agreed, then?"

Maigret got to his feet and, much to his own astonishment, heard himself saying, just as though he were any other patient of Pardon's:

"Agreed."

"When will you go?"

"In a day or two, a week at the outside. Just long enough to catch up with my paper work."

"I'll have to hand you over to a man on the spot who will be able to tell you more than I can. . . . I could name half a dozen. Let me think. . . . There's Rian, a decent young fellow, not too full of himself. . . . I'll give you his address and telephone number. And I'll drop him a line tomorrow, to put him in the picture. . . ."

"I'm much obliged, Pardon."

"I wasn't too rough with you, I hope?"

"You couldn't have been more gentle."

Returning to the drawing room, he smiled at his wife, a reassuring smile. But nothing was said, illness not being considered a suitable topic for after-dinner conversation at the Pardons'.

It was not until they reached Rue Popincourt, walking arm in arm, that Maigret remarked casually, as though it were a matter of no importance:

"We're going to Vichy for our holiday."

"Will you be taking the cure?"

"I suppose I might as well while I'm there!" he said wryly. "There's nothing wrong with me. In fact, I gather I'm exceptionally healthy, which is why I'm being packed off to take the waters, I daresay!"

That evening at the Pardons' had not really been the start of it. He had for some time been obsessed by the strange notion that everybody was younger than he was, from the Chief Commissioner and the examining magistrates to the prisoners brought in for questioning. And now there was Doctor Rian, fair-haired and affable, and well on the right side of forty.

A kid, in other words, at any rate a young man, but none the less sober and self-assured for all that. And this was the man who was to be the arbiter of his, Chief Superintendent Maigret's fate. Well, more or less. . . .

Maigret was irritated and at the same time apprehensive, for he certainly did not feel old, nor even middle-aged.

For all his youth, Doctor Rian lived in an elegant red-brick house in Boulevard des Etats-Unis. Maybe it was rather too Edwardian in style, but it had a certain grandeur, with its marble staircase, its handsome carpets, its highly polished furniture. There was even a maid in a lace-trimmed cap.

"I presume your parents are dead? What did your father die of?"

The doctor carefully wrote down his answers on a memo pad, in a neat, clerical hand.

"And your mother? . . . Any brothers? . . . Sisters . . . Childhood ailments? . . . Measles? . . . Chicken pox? . . ."

Chicken pox, no, measles yes, when he was very small and his mother was still living. It was, in fact, his warmest and most vivid memory of his mother, who died very shortly afterward.

"How about games and sports? . . . Have you ever had an

accident? . . . Are you subject to sore-throats? . . . You're a heavy smoker, I take it? . . ."

The young doctor smiled, with a touch of mischief, by way of showing Maigret that he knew him by repute.

"No one could say that you lead a sedentary life, exactly."

"It varies. Sometimes I don't set foot outside my office for two or three weeks at a time, and then, all of a sudden, I'm running around all over the place for days on end."

"Regular meals?"

"No."

"Do you watch your diet?"

He was forced to admit that he liked rich food, especially highly seasoned stews and sauces.

"Not just a gourmet, in fact, but a hearty eater?"

"You could say so, yes."

"What about wine? A half-bottle, a bottle a day?"

"Yes . . . No . . . More . . . As a rule I don't have more than two or three glasses with my dinner. . . . Occasionally I have a beer sent up to the office from the brasserie nearby."

"Spirits?"

"I quite often have an apéritif with a colleague."

In the Brasserie Dauphine. It wasn't the drink itself but the clubbable atmosphere, the cooking smells, the aroma of aniseed and Calvados, with which, by this time, the very walls were impregnated. Why should he feel ashamed, all of a sudden, in the presence of this neat, well-set-up young man in his luxurious consulting room?

"In other words, you don't drink to excess?"

He had no wish to conceal anything.

"It depends on what you mean by excess. I'm not averse to a glass or two of sloe gin after dinner. My sister-in-law sends it from Alsace. . . . And then often, when I'm working on a case, I'm in and out of cafés and bars a great deal. . . . How shall I put it? If, at the start of a case, I happen to be in a bistro where Vouvray is a speciality, as likely as not I'll go drinking Vouvray right through to the end."

"How much in a day?"

It reminded him of his boyhood, the confessional in the village church, smelling of mildew and the curé's snuff.

"A lot?"

"It would seem a lot to you, I daresay."

"For how long at a stretch?"

"Anything from three to ten days, sometimes even longer. It's a matter of chance. . . ."

There were no reproaches, no penances, but he had a pretty shrewd idea what the doctor thought of him, as he sat, elbows on his handsome mahogany desk, with the sun shining on his fair hair.

"No severe indigestion? No heartburn or giddiness?"

Giddiness, yes. Nothing serious. From time to time, especially of late, the ground seems to tilt slightly, and everything about him appeared a little unreal. He felt off balance, unsteady on his feet.

It was not bad enough to cause him any serious anxiety, but it was an unpleasant sensation. Fortunately, it never lasted more than a couple of minutes. On one occasion, he had just left the Law Courts and was about to cross the road. He had waited until it was over, before venturing to step off the pavement.

"I see . . . I see."

What did he see? That he was a sick man? That he smoked heavily and drank too much? That it was high time, at his age, that he learned to watch his diet?

Maigret was not letting it get him down. He smiled in the way his wife had grown used to, since they had come to Vichy. It was a self-mocking smile, if a little morose.

"Come with me, please."

This time he was given the full treatment. He was made to climb up and down a ladder repeatedly for three full minutes. He had his blood pressure taken lying down, sitting up, and standing. Then he was X-rayed.

"Breathe in . . . Deeper . . . Hold it . . . Breathe out . . . In . . . Hold it . . . Out . . ."

It was comical yet somehow distressing, dramatic and all at the same time slightly dotty. He had, perhaps, thirty years of life to look forward to, and yet any minute now he might be tactfully informed that his life as a healthy, active man was over, and that henceforth he would be reduced to the status of an invalid.

They had all been through this experience, all the people one saw in the park, under the spreading trees, at the mineral springs, on the lake shore. Even the members of the Sporting Club across the river, whom one could watch sunbathing, or playing tennis or bowls in the shade, had been through it.

"Mademoiselle Jeanne."

"Yes, sir."

The receptionist knew what was wanted. It was all part of a familiar routine. Soon the Maigrets would be following a routine of their own.

First, the little needle or the prick on the finger tip, then the glass slides and phials for the blood smears.

"Relax. . . . Clench your fist."

He felt the prick of a needle in the crook of his elbow.

"Right, that will do."

He had had blood samples taken before, but this time, it seemed to him, there was something portentous about it.

"Thank you. You can get dressed now."

A few minutes later they were back in the consulting room, with its walls lined with books and bound volumes of medical journals.

"I don't think any very drastic treatment is needed in your case. Come and see me again at this time the day after tomorrow. By then I shall have the results of the tests. Meanwhile, I'm going to put you on a diet. I presume you're staying in a hotel? Here is a diet sheet. All you have to do is hand it to the headwaiter. He'll attend to it."

It was a card with forbidden foods printed in one column and permitted ones in the other. It even went so far as to list sample menus on the back.

"I don't know if you are aware of the different chemical properties of the various springs. There is an excellent little handbook on the subject, written by one of my colleagues, but it may be out of print. For a start, I want you to alternate between two springs, Chomel and Grande Grille. You'll find them both in the park."

Both men looked equally solemn. Maigret felt not the least inclination, as he watched the doctor scribbling notes on his pad, to shrug the whole thing off, or indulge in a little secret smile.

"Do you usually have an early breakfast? I see. . . . Is your wife here with you? . . . In that case, I don't want to send you halfway across town on an empty stomach. Let's see. You'd better start at about ten thirty in the morning at the Grande Grille. There are plenty of chairs, so you won't have to stand about, and if it rains there's a huge glass enclosure for shelter. . . . I want you to have three half-pints of water at half-hourly intervals, and it should be drunk as hot as you can take it.

"I want you to repeat the process in the afternoons at about five, at the Chomel spring.

"Don't worry if you feel a bit languid the first day. It's a purely temporary side effect of the treatment. . . . Anyway, I shall be seeing you. . . ."

Those early days, before his initiation into the mysteries of each individual spring, seemed very far away now. Now, as for thousands of others, as for tens of thousands of others, with whom he rubbed shoulders every hour of the day, the cure had become a part of his life.

Just as in the evening, when there was a concert, every one of the little yellow chairs around the bandstand was occupied, so, at certain times of day, there was not a chair to be had, so great was the crowd gathered around the springs, all waiting for a second, third, or fourth glass of the waters.

Like everyone else, they had brought measuring glasses, Madame Maigret having insisted on getting one for herself.

"But *you're* not taking the waters!"

"Why shouldn't I? Where's the harm? It says in one of the pamphlets that the waters are slimming. . . ."

Each glass had its own case of plaited straw, and Madame Maigret carried both of theirs slung over one shoulder like binoculars at a race meeting.

They had never walked so much in their lives. Their hotel was in the France district, a quiet part of the town near the Célestins spring. They were out and about by nine every morning, when, apart from the delivery man, they had the streets almost to themselves.

A few minutes' walk from their hotel there was a children's playground with a wading pool, swings, play apparatus of all sorts, even a puppet theater, more elaborate than the one in the Champs-Elysées.

"Your tickets, sir?"

They had bought two one-franc tickets, and strolled among the trees, watching the half-naked children at play. Next day they had come again.

"We sell books of twenty tickets at a reduced rate."

They were reluctant to commit themselves so far ahead. They had come upon the playground by chance and, for want of anything better to do, had fallen into the habit of returning there every day at the same hour.

Regularly, they went on from there to the bowling club, where they would watch two or three games being played, with Maigret attentively following every throw, especially those of the tall, thin, one-armed man, always to be found under the same tree, who was, in spite of his disability, the finest player of all. Another regular player was a dignified old gentleman with pink cheeks, snow-white hair, and a southern accent, always addressed by his companions as "Senator."

It was not far from there to the lifeguards' station and the beach, with buoys bobbing in the water to mark the limits of the bathing area. Here, too, they would find the same familiar faces under the same familiar beach umbrellas.

"You're not bored, are you?" she had asked him on their second day.

"Why on earth should I be?" he had retorted in surprise.

For indeed he was not bored. Little by little his habits, his tempo of living, were changing. For instance, he caught himself filling his pipe on the Pont de Bellerive and realized, to his amazement, that he always smoked a pipe just at this time and place. There was also the Yacht Club pipe, which he smoked while watching the young people skimming over the water on skis.

"It's a dangerous sport, wouldn't you say?"

"In what way?"

Finally the park, the attendant filling their glasses from the spring, the two of them drinking the water in little sips. It was hot and salty. The water from the Chomel spring tasted strongly of sulphur, and after drinking it Maigret could hardly wait to light his pipe.

It amazed Madame Maigret that he should take it all so calmly. It was most unlike him to be so docile. It quite worried her at times, until it dawned on her that he was amusing himself by playing at detection. Almost in spite of himself he watched people, classifying them, taking note of everything about them, down to the smallest detail. He had, for instance, already discovered which of their fellow guests in the Hôtel de la Bérézina—more a family pension than a hotel—had liver trouble and which diabetes, simply by observing what they had to eat.

What was this one's life history? What did that one do for a living? These were his preoccupations, in which he sometimes invited his wife to share.

Especially intriguing to them were the couple whom they called "the happy pair," the dumpy little man who seemed always on the verge of coming up to shake his hand, and his diminutive wife who looked like something out of a confectioner's shop. What was their station in life? They seemed to recognize the Chief Superintendent, but was this not perhaps merely because they had seen his picture in the papers?

Not many people here did, in fact, recognize him, many fewer than in Paris. Admittedly, his wife had insisted on buying him a light mohair jacket, almost white in fact, of the kind that elderly men used to wear when he was a boy. But even allowing for this, it would probably not have occurred to most people that the head of the Paris C.I.D. could be here, in Vichy. When anyone peered at him with a puzzled frown, or turned back to look at him, he felt sure that they were thinking:

"Good heavens! That might almost be Maigret!"

But they did not think that it *was* Maigret. And no wonder. He scarcely recognized himself!

Another person who intrigued them was the lady in lilac. She too was taking the waters, but only at the Grande Grille, where she could be seen every morning. She always sat a little removed from the crowd, near the newspaper stand. She never drank more than a mouthful of the water. Afterward, with her usual air of remote dignity, she would rinse out her glass, and put it away carefully in its straw case.

There were usually one or two people in the crowd who seemed to know her well enough to greet her. The Maigrets never saw her in the afternoon. Was she perhaps undergoing hydrotherapy? Or had she been ordered by her doctor to take an afternoon rest?

Doctor Rian had said:

"E.R.S., perfect. Average sed rate: 6 mm. per hour. . . . Cholesterol, a little on the high side, but well within the normal range. . . . Urea normal. . . . You're a bit low on iron, but there's no cause for anxiety. . . . No need to worry about uric acid, either . . . just keep off game, shellfish, and variety meats. As to your blood count, it could scarcely be better, with 98 per cent hemoglobin.

"There's nothing wrong with you that a thorough clean-out won't cure. . . . Any headaches or unusual fatigue? . . . Right, then, we'll keep you on the same treatment and diet for the next few days. . . . Come and see me again on Saturday."

There was an open-air band concert that night. They did not see the lady in lilac leave, because, as usual, they themselves left early, well before the end. The Hôtel de la Bérézina, in the France district of the town, gleamed with fresh paint, and its double doors were flanked on either side by flowering shrubs in urns. The Maigrets enjoyed walking back to it through the deserted streets.

They slept in a brass bed, and all the furniture in their room was in the style of the early 1900s—like the bath, which was raised on legs, and had old-fashioned goose-neck taps.

The hotel was well kept and very quiet, except when the Gagnaire boys, who had rooms on the first floor, were let loose in the garden to play at cowboys and Indians.

Everyone was asleep.

Was it the fifth day? Or the sixth? Of the two, it was Madame Maigret who was the more confused, waking up as she did every morning to the realization that she need not get up to make coffee. Their breakfast was brought in on a tray at seven o'clock, coffee and fresh croissants, and the *Journal de Clermont-Ferrand*, which devoted two pages to news and features about life in Vichy.

Maigret had got into the habit of reading the paper from cover to cover, so that by now there was precious little he did not know about local affairs. He even read the obituaries and the small ads.

"Desirable residence, in excellent repair. Three rooms, bathroom, all mod. cons. Uninterrupted view . . ."

"Are you thinking of buying a house?"

"No, but this is interesting. I can't help wondering who will buy it. A family coming regularly for the cure, who won't live in it for more than a month each year? An elderly couple from Paris who want to retire here? Or . . ."

They got dressed, taking turns in the bathroom, and went down the staircase, with its red carpet held in place by triangular brass clips. The proprietor was there in the hall, always ready with a friendly greeting. He was not a local man, as was obvious from his accent, but came from Montélimar.

They nibbled the hours away. The children's playground . . . The bowling greens . . .

"I see, by the way, that Wednesdays and Saturdays are market days. It's a big market. We might go and have a look around. . . ."

They had always been attracted to markets, their stalls laden with sides of beef, fish, and live lobsters, and their all-pervading smell of fresh fruit and vegetables.

"Well, Rian did advise me to walk four miles a day," he remarked with heavy irony, adding:

"Little does he know that, on the average, we cover the best part of twelve!"

"Do you really think so?"

"Work it out. We spend at least five hours a day walking. . . . We may not be striding out like a couple of athletes, but all the same we can't be doing much less than three miles an hour."

"I'd never have thought it!"

The glass of water. Sitting on one of the yellow chairs, reading the papers that had just come from Paris. Lunch in the white dining room, where the only touch of color was an opened bottle of wine on a table here and there, labeled with the name of the resident who had ordered it. There was no wine on the Maigrets' table.

"Did he say no wine?"

"Not in so many words. But while I'm about it . . ."

She could not get over the fact that, while scrupulously keeping to his diet, he was, at the same time, perfectly good-tempered about it.

They permitted themselves a short rest after lunch, before setting off again, this time for the opposite end of the town. Here, where most of the shops were, the pavements were so crowded that they were seldom able to walk abreast.

"Was there ever a town with so many osteopaths and chiropodists!"

"It's no wonder, if everyone walks as much as we do!"

That evening the bandstand in the park was deserted. Instead, there was a concert in the gardens of the Grand Casino. Here, in place of the brass band, a string orchestra played. The music was of a more serious kind, matched by the expressions on the faces of the audience.

They did not see the lady in lilac. They had not seen her in the park either, though they had caught a glimpse of "the happy pair," who tonight were more formally dressed than usual, and seemed to be going to the casino theater, where a light comedy was playing.

The brass bedstead. It was astonishing how quickly the days went by, even when one was doing absolutely nothing. Croissants, coffee, cubes of sugar in greaseproof wrappings, the *Journal de Clermont-Ferrand.*

Maigret, in pajamas, was sitting in an armchair next to the window, smoking his first pipe of the day. His coffee cup was still half full. He enjoyed lingering over it as long as possible.

His sudden exclamation brought Madame Maigret from the bathroom, in a blue flower-printed dressing gown, with her toothbrush still in her hand.

"What's the matter?"

"Look at this."

There, on the first page devoted to Vichy, was a photograph, a photograph of the lady in lilac. It was not a very recent one. She looked several years younger in it and, for the occasion, had managed to produce a tight-lipped semblance of a smile.

"What's happened to her?"

"She's been murdered."

"Last night?"

"If it had happened last night, it wouldn't be in this morning's paper. No, it was the night before."

"But we saw her at the band concert."

"Yes, at nine o'clock. . . . She lived only a couple of streets from here, Rue du Bourbonnais. . . . I have a feeling that we were almost neighbors. . . . She went home. . . . She had to take off her shawl and hat and go into the sitting room, which leads off to the left from the hall. . . ."

"How was she killed?"

"She was strangled. Yesterday morning, the lodgers were surprised not to hear her moving about downstairs as usual."

"She wasn't just here for the cure, then?"

"No, she lived in Vichy. . . . She owned the house, and let furnished rooms on the upper floor. . . ."

Maigret was still in his armchair, and his wife well knew just how much self-control was needed to keep him there.

"Was it a sex maniac?"

"The place was ransacked from top to bottom, but nothing seems to have been taken. . . . In one of the drawers that had been broken into, they found jewelry and quite a lot of money. . . ."

"She wasn't . . . ?"

"Raped? No."

He stared out of the window in silence.

"Who's in charge of the case, do you know?"

"Of course I don't! How could I?

"The Chief C.I.D. Officer at Clermont-Ferrand is Lecoeur, who used to work under me. . . . He's here. . . . Naturally, he has no idea that I'm here too. . . ."

"Will you be going to see him?"

To this he made no immediate answer.

2

IT WAS FIVE minutes to nine, and Maigret had not yet answered his wife's question. It seemed as though he had put himself on his honor to behave exactly as he would have done any other morning, to adhere, without the smallest deviation, to their established Vichy routine.

He had read the paper from beginning to end, while finishing his coffee. He had shaved and bathed, as usual, listening meanwhile to the news on the radio. At five minutes to nine he was ready, and together they went down the staircase, with its red carpet held in place by the triangular brass clips.

The proprietor, in white coat and chef's hat, was waiting for them below.

"Well, Monsieur Maigret, you can't say we don't look after you in Vichy, even to the extent of handing you a splendid murder on a platter. . . ."

He managed to force a noncommittal smile.

"You will be attending to it, I trust?"

"This is not Paris. I have no authority here. . . ."

Madame Maigret was watching him. She thought he was unaware of this, but she was wrong. When they came to Rue d'Auvergne, he composed his features in an expression of guileless innocence and, instead of going down it toward the Allier and the children's playground, turned right.

Admittedly, they did occasionally take a different route, but, up to now, only on the way back. Her husband's unerring sense of direction never failed to astonish Madame Maigret. He never looked at a map, and would wander off, apparently at random, into a maze of little side streets. Often, just when it seemed to Madame Maigret that they must be lost, she would suddenly realize, with a start, that there in front of them was the door of their hotel, flanked on either side by the flowering shrubs in their green-painted urns.

On this occasion, he turned right again, and then again, until they came to a house where a small crowd was gathering, hoping to catch a glimpse inside.

There was a twinkle in Madame Maigret's eye. The Chief Superintendent, after a moment's hesitation, crossed the road, stopped, gave his pipe a sharp tap against his heel to knock out the ash, and then slowly filled it with fresh tobacco. At times like these, he seemed to her just a great baby, and a wave of tenderness swept over her.

He was having a struggle with himself. At last, trying to look as though he had no idea where he was, he joined the group of spectators, and stood gaping like the rest at the house across the street, where a policeman was standing guard and, nearby, a car was parked.

It was an attractive house, like most of the others in the street. It had recently had a fresh coat of warm-white paint, and the shutters and balcony were almond green.

On a marble plaque, in Gothic lettering, was inscribed the name: *Les Iris.*

Madame Maigret had been following every move in this little private drama, from his decision not to call at the Police Station to his present determination *not* to cross the road, make himself known to the policeman on duty, and gain admission to the house.

There was no cloud in the sky. The air was fresh, clear, invigorating, here in this clean little street. A few doors along, a woman, standing at her window shaking the dust out of her rugs, looked with disapproval at the people down below. But had she not herself been among the first, yesterday, when the murder was discovered and the police arrived in force, to join with her neighbors in gaping at a house that she had seen every day of her life for years?

Someone in the crowd remarked:

"They say it was a *crime passionel.*"

This suggestion was received with derision:

"Oh, come! She can't have been a day under fifty."

A face could be dimly seen at one of the upstairs windows, a pointed nose, dark hair, and from time to time, behind it, the shadowy figure of a youngish man.

The door was painted white. A milk cart was moving slowly along the street, leaving bottles on doorsteps behind it. The milkman, with a bottle of milk in his hand, went up to the white door. The policeman spoke to him, no doubt telling him that there was no point in leaving it, but the milkman shrugged and left the bottle just the same.

Wasn't anyone going to notice that Maigret . . . ? He couldn't hang about here indefinitely. . . .

He was just about to move off when there appeared in the doorway a tall young man with an unruly mop of hair. He crossed the road, making straight for the Chief Superintendent.

"The Divisional Superintendent would very much like to see you, sir."

His wife, repressing a smile, asked:

"Where shall I wait for you?"

"At the usual place, the spring. . . ."

Had they seen and recognized him from the window? With dignity, he crossed the road, assuming a grumpy expression to hide his gratification. It was cool in the entrance. There was a hatrack on the right, with two hats hanging from its branches. He added his own, a straw hat which his wife had made him buy at the same time as the mohair jacket, and in which he felt slightly foolish.

"Come on in, Chief."

A voice full of warm pleasure, a face and figure Maigret instantly recognized.

"Lecoeur!"

They had not met for fifteen years, not since the days when

Désiré Lecoeur had been an inspector on Maigret's staff at the Quai des Orfèvres.

"Oh, yes, Chief, here I am, longer in the tooth, wider in girth, and higher up the ladder. Here I am, as I say, Divisional Superintendent at Clermont-Ferrand, which is why I'm stuck with this ghastly business. . . . Come on in."

He led him into a little parlor painted a bluish-gray, and sat at a table covered with papers, which he was using as an improvised desk.

Maigret lowered himself cautiously into a fragile, reproduction Louis XVI chair. Lecoeur must have noticed his puzzled expression, because he said at once:

"I daresay you're wondering how I knew you were here. In the first place, Moinet—you haven't met him, he's the head of the Vichy police—noticed the name on your registration form. . . . Naturally, he didn't want to intrude, but his men have seen you out and about every day. It seems, in fact, that the fellows doing duty on the beach have been laying bets as to when you would make up your mind to try your hand at bowls. Your interest in the game, according to them, was visibly growing, day by day. So much so that . . ."

"Have you been here since yesterday?"

"Yes, of course, with two of my men from Clermont-Ferrand. One of them is the young fellow, Dicelle, whom I sent out to fetch you when I saw you out there in the street. I was reluctant to send you a message at your hotel. I reckoned you were here for the cure, not for the purpose of giving us a helping hand. Besides, I knew that, in the end, if you were interested, you would . . ."

By now, Maigret really was looking grumpy.

"A sex maniac?" he mumbled.

"No, that's one thing we can say for sure."

"A jealous lover?"

"Unlikely. Mind you, I could be wrong. I've been at it for twenty-four hours, but I'm not much wiser than when I got here yesterday morning."

Referring from time to time to the papers on his desk, he went on:

"The murdered woman's name was Hélène Lange. She was

forty-eight years old, born at Marsilly, about ten miles from La Rochelle. I telephoned the town hall at Marsilly and was told that her mother, who was widowed very young, had for many years kept a small dry goods store in Place de l'Eglise.

"There were two daughters. Hélène, the elder, took a course in shorthand and typing at La Rochelle. After that she worked for a time in a shipping office, and later went to Paris, after which nothing more was heard of her.

"No request for a copy of her birth certificate was ever received, from which one must infer that she never married, besides which her identity card is made out in her maiden name.

"There was a sister, six or seven years younger, who also began her working life in La Rochelle, as a manicurist.

"Like her elder sister, she subsequently migrated to Paris, but returned home about ten years ago.

"She must have had substantial savings, because she bought a hairdressing establishment in the Place des Armes, which she still owns. I tried to get her on the phone but was told by the assistant in charge that she was on holiday in Majorca. I cabled to her hotel, asking her to return immediately, and she should be here sometime today.

"This sister—her name is Francine—is also unmarried. . . . The mother has been dead eight years. . . . There's no other family, as far as anyone knows."

Quite unwittingly, Maigret had slipped back into his familiar professional role. To all appearances, he was in charge of the case, and Lecoeur was a subordinate reporting to him in his office.

But there was no pipe rack for him to fidget with as he listened, no sturdy armchair for him to lean back in, and no view of the Seine from the window.

As Lecoeur talked, Maigret was struck by one or two unusual features of this little parlor, which had obviously been used as a living room, in particular the fact that there were no photographs of anyone but Hélène Lange herself. There she was on a little bow-fronted chest, aged about six, in a dress that was too long for her, with tight braids hanging down on either side of her face.

A larger photograph, obviously taken by a skilled photographer, hung on the wall. In this she was older, about twenty, and her pose was romantic, her expression ethereal.

A third photograph showed her on a beach, wearing not a bathing suit but a white dress, the wide skirt of which, blown to one side by the breeze, streamed out like a flag, and holding in both hands a light, wide-brimmed hat.

"Do you know how and when the murder was committed?"

"We're having difficulty in finding out what exactly did happen that evening. . . . We've been working on it since yesterday morning, but we haven't made much headway.

"The night before last—Monday night, that is—Hélène Lange had supper alone in her kitchen. She washed up—or at any rate we didn't find any dirty dishes in the sink—got dressed, switched off all the lights, and went out. If you want to know, she ate two boiled eggs. She wore a mauve dress, a white woolen shawl, and a hat, also white. . . ."

Maigret, after an internal struggle, couldn't in the end resist saying:

"I know."

"Have you been making inquiries, then?"

"No, but I saw her on Monday evening, sitting near the bandstand, listening to the concert."

"Do you know what time she left?"

"She was still there just before half past nine, when my wife and I went for our walk as we do every evening."

"Was she alone?"

"She was always alone."

Lecoeur made no attempt to hide his astonishment.

"So you'd noticed her on other occasions?"

Maigret, now looking much more good-humored, nodded.

"What was it about her?"

"Nothing in particular. One spends one's time here just walking about, and, almost unconsciously, one registers a face here and there in the crowd. You know how it is . . . one is always running into the same people in the same places at certain times of day. . . ."

"Have you any ideas?"

"What about?"

"What sort of woman she was."

"She was no ordinary woman, I'm sure of that, but that's all I can say."

"Well, to proceed . . . Two of the three bedrooms on the upper floor are let, the largest to the Maleskis, a couple from Grenoble. He's an engineer. They were out at the cinema. They left the house a few minutes after Mademoiselle Lange and didn't get back till half past eleven. All the shutters were closed as usual, but they could see through the slats that the lights were still on downstairs. When they got inside, they noticed strips of light under the doors of Mademoiselle Lange's living room and bedroom. That's the room on the right. . . ."

"Did they hear anything?"

"Maleski heard nothing, but his wife said, with some hesitation, that she thought she had heard a murmur of voices. . . . They went straight up to bed, and slept undisturbed until morning. . . .

"The other lodger is a Madame Vireveau, a widow from Paris, Rue Lamarck. She's rather an overbearing woman, aged about sixty. She comes to Vichy every year to lose weight. . . . This is the first time she's taken a room in Mademoiselle Lange's house. In former years she always stayed at a hotel.

"She's seen better days, apparently. Her husband was a rich man, but extravagant, and when he died she found herself in financial difficulties. . . . To put it briefly, she's loaded with imitation jewelry, and she booms like a dowager in a bad play. . . . She left the house at nine. She saw no one, and claims that, when she went out, the house was in total darkness."

"Do the lodgers have their own keys?"

"Yes. Madame Vireveau spent the evening at the Carlton Bridge Club, and left just before midnight. She hasn't a car. The Maleskis have a mini, but they seldom use it in Vichy. Most of the time it's left in a garage nearby. . . ."

"Were the lights still on?"

"I'm coming to that, Chief. Naturally, I saw the old girl only after the crime had been discovered, and by then the whole street was in a turmoil. . . . Maybe all that fancy jewelry goes with a vivid imagination . . . I really can't say. . . . Anyway, according to her story, she almost bumped into a man as she turned the corner, the corner of Boulevard de LaSalle and Rue du Bourbonnais, that is. He couldn't possibly have seen her coming, and she swears that he was visibly startled, and shielded his face with his hand to avoid being recognized."

"Did she, in fact, recognize him?"

"No, but she swears nevertheless that she would recognize him if she saw him again face to face. He was very tall and heavily built—with a great bulging chest like a gorilla, she says. He was hunched up and walking fast. He gave her a real fright, she says, but all the same she turned back to watch him striding away toward the center of town."

"Had she any idea of his age?"

"Not young . . . Not old, either . . . Very heavily built . . . Frightening. . . . She almost ran the rest of the way. She didn't feel safe until her key was in the lock. . . ."

"Were the lights still showing on the ground floor?"

"That's just it, they weren't, that is, if one can take her word for it. She didn't hear a thing. She went up to bed, so shaken that she had to take a teaspoonful of peppermint essence on a lump of sugar."

"Who discovered the body?"

"All in good time, Chief. Mademoiselle Lange, while quite willing to let her rooms to respectable people, was not prepared to serve meals. No cooking was allowed. She wouldn't even let them have an alcohol stove for a cup of morning coffee.

"Yesterday morning, at about eight, Madame Maleski came downstairs with her thermos flask, as she always did, to get it filled and buy some croissants at a nearby coffee bar. She didn't notice anything amiss, then or when she got back. What did surprise her, though, was the absolute quiet downstairs, especially the second time, because Mademoiselle Lange was an early riser and could usually be heard moving about from one room to another.

"'Perhaps she's not well,' she remarked to her husband over breakfast.

"Because it seems that the landlady often complained of poor health. At nine o'clock—Madame Vireveau was still in her room—the Maleskis went downstairs, where they found Charlotte looking worried. . . ."

"Charlotte?"

"The girl who comes in every morning from nine to twelve to clean the rooms. She bicycles in from a village about ten miles away. She's a bit simple.

"'All the doors are locked,' she said to the Maleskis.

"Usually she arrived to find all the doors and windows on the ground floor wide open; Mademoiselle Lange was a great one for fresh air."

"'Haven't you got a key?'

"'No, if she's not in, I might as well go home.'

"Maleski tried to open the door with the key of his room, but it didn't fit, so in the end he went to the coffee bar where his wife gets their breakfast, and called the police from there.

"And that's about all. An inspector from Vichy Police Headquarters arrived within minutes with a locksmith. The key to the living-room door was missing, and the kitchen and bedroom doors were locked from inside, with the keys in the locks.

"They found Hélène Lange here, in this room. She was lying stretched out, or rather doubled up, on the edge of the carpet, here in this exact spot. She had been strangled. . . . It wasn't a pretty sight. . . .

"She was still wearing her mauve dress, but she had taken off her hat and shawl, which were both found hanging on the hatrack in the hall. All the drawers were open, and there were papers and cardboard boxes scattered all over the floor."

"Had she been raped?"

"No, nothing of that sort was even attempted. And as far as we know, nothing was stolen. The report in this morning's *Journal* is reasonably accurate. . . . In one of the drawers we found five hundred-franc notes. . . . The assailant had been through the dead woman's handbag, and the contents were scattered about the room. These included four hundred francs in small notes, some silver, and a season ticket for the Grand Casino theater. . . ."

"Has she lived here long?"

"Nine years. Before that she lived for some years in Nice. . . ."

"Did she work there?"

"No. She lived in rather a shabby lodginghouse in Boulevard Albert I. Presumably she had a small private income."

"Did she travel at all?"

"She was in the habit of going away about once a month, for a day or two at a time."

"Do you know where she went?"

"She was very secretive about her comings and goings."

"And after she came here?"

"For the first two years she had the whole house to herself. Then she advertised three rooms to let during the season, but the house was not always full. Just now, for instance, the blue room isn't let. . . . I should perhaps mention that each bedroom has a different color scheme. Besides the blue room, there are a white room and a pink room."

At this point, Maigret suddenly noticed another odd thing. Nowhere in the living room was there the smallest touch of green, not a single ornament or cushion, not even a trimming.

"Was she superstitious?"

"How did you guess? One day she got into quite a state because Madame Maleski had brought home a bunch of carnations. She said they were flowers of ill-omen, and she wouldn't have them in the house.

"On another occasion she warned Madame Vireveau against wearing a green dress, prophesying that she would pay dearly for it. . . ."

"Did she ever have visitors?"

"According to the neighbors, never."

"Any mail?"

"We've spoken to the postman. There was an occasional letter from La Rochelle, but apart from that, nothing but circulars and bills from local shops."

"Did she have a bank account?"

"With the Crédit Lyonnais, on the corner of Rue Georges-Clemenceau."

"You've made inquiries there, of course?"

"She deposited regularly, about five thousand francs a month, but not always on the same day of the month."

"In cash?"

"Yes. During the season she deposited more, because of the money coming in from the lodgers."

"Did she ever sign checks?"

"There were a number of checks made out to shops in Vichy and Moulins, where she sometimes went to do her shopping. Occasionally she would order something from Paris—something she had seen in a mail-order catalogue: look, there's a pile of them over there—and for these things, too, she would pay by check."

Lecoeur was watching the Chief Superintendent and thinking how different he looked, in his off-white jacket, from the man he had worked for in the Quai des Orfèvres.

"What do you make of it, Chief?"

"I'll have to be going. My wife is waiting for me."

"Not to mention your first glass of water!"

"So the Vichy police know about that too, do they?" grumbled Maigret.

"But you'll be back, won't you? The C.I.D. hasn't a branch in Vichy. I drive back to Clermont-Ferrand every night. It's only fifty miles. The Vichy Chief of Police has offered me the use of an office with a telephone, but I'd sooner have my headquarters here on the spot. My men are trying to trace any neighbors or passers-by who may have seen Mademoiselle Lange returning home on Monday night, because we still don't know whether the murderer came with her or was waiting for her in the house."

"Forgive me, my dear fellow. . . . My wife . . ."

"Of course, Chief."

Maigret was still determined to stick to his routine, though curiosity very nearly got the better of him. He felt he really ought not to have turned right instead of left when setting out from the Hôtel de la Bérézina. Had he not done so, he would have lingered, as always up till now, in the children's playground, and then, farther on, stopped to watch a game or two of bowls.

He wondered whether Madame Maigret, all on her own, had followed the familiar route, stopping at all the places where they usually stopped together.

"Would you care for a lift? My car is at the door, and I'm sure there's nothing young Dicelle would like better than to . . ."

"No, thank you, I shall walk. That's what I'm here for."

And walk he did, alone, striding along at a brisk pace to make up for lost time.

He had drunk his first glass of water and returned to his seat, midway between the great glass hall built around the spring and the nearest tree. Although his wife asked no questions, he could feel her watching his every movement, trying to interpret his expression.

With the newspapers spread out on his lap, he sat gazing at the sky through the trees. There was scarcely any movement among the leaves, and the sky was still the same clear blue, with one small solitary cloud, dazzlingly white, drifting across it.

Sometimes in Paris he would feel a twinge of nostalgia for half-forgotten sensory experiences: a puff of wind, warmed by the sun, against his cheek, the play of light among leaves or on a gravel path, the crunch of gravel under running feet, even the taste of dust.

And here, miraculously, they all were. While reflecting on his meeting with Lecoeur, he was at the same time basking in his surroundings, savoring every little thing.

Was he really deep in thought, or just daydreaming? There were small family groups to be seen here and there, as there are everywhere, but in this place the proportion of elderly couples was greater.

And what about the solitary figures in the crowd? Were there more men than women? Women, especially old women, tend to be gregarious. They could be seen arranging their chairs in little groups of six or eight, leaning forward as though to exchange confidences, although they had probably known one another not more than a few days.

Were they really exchanging confidences? Who could say? No doubt they discussed their illnesses, their doctors, their treatment, and went on to talk about their married sons and daughters, and to display the photographs of their grandchildren, which they carried about in their handbags.

It was uncommon to see one of them remaining aloof, keeping

herself to herself, like the lady in lilac, to whom he could now attach a name.

Solitary men were more numerous. Often these showed signs of exhaustion and pain, and it was an obvious effort for them to move with dignity among the crowd. Their drawn features and sad eyes bespoke a vague, distressed apprehension that they might crumple to the ground, and lie there in a patch of sunlight or shade, in among the legs of the people passing by.

Hélène Lange was one of the solitary ones, and everything about her, her expression, her bearing, told that she was a proud woman. She would not allow herself to be treated as an old maid, she would not accept pity. She went her way, very erect, chin held high, walking with a firm tread.

She consorted with no one, having no need of the relief of facile confidences.

Was it by choice that she had lived alone?

This was the question uppermost in his mind, as he tried to conjure up an image of her as he had seen her, sitting, standing, in motion, still.

"Have they any clue?"

Madame Maigret was beginning to feel a little aggrieved at his daydreaming. In Paris she would never have dared question her husband while he was working on a case. But here it was different. Here, walking side by side for hours on end, they had got into the habit of thinking aloud.

They did not converse exactly, exchanging question and answer, but rather one or the other would occasionally let fall the odd, disjointed phrase to indicate what he or she was thinking.

"No. They can't do much until the sister gets here."

"Has she no other family?"

"Apparently not."

"It's time for your second glass."

They went into the hall. The heads of the girl attendants showed above the sides of the well in which they stood. Hélène Lange came here every day to take the waters. Was this on medical advice, or was it just to give some point to her morning walk?

"What's bothering you?"

"I'm wondering why Vichy."

It was almost ten years since she had come to settle in the town, and had bought her house. She was therefore thirty-seven at the time, and must have had independent means, since it was not until she had had the house to herself for two years that she starting letting rooms.

"Why not Vichy?" retorted Madame Maigret.

"There are hundreds of towns in France, small towns, larger towns, where she might have gone to settle, not to mention La Rochelle, where she grew up. . . . Her sister, having spent some time in Paris, went back to La Rochelle and stayed there. . . ."

"Perhaps the two sisters didn't get on."

It wasn't as simple as that. Maigret was still watching the people strolling about. The tempo of the moving crowds reminded him of something, of a constant stream of people, ebbing and flowing in hot sunshine. In Nice, on the Promenade des Anglais.

For Hélène Lange, before coming to Vichy, had lived five years in Nice.

"She lived five years in Nice," he said, speaking his thoughts aloud.

"Like a lot of other people on small fixed incomes."

"Exactly. . . . People on small fixed incomes, but also people from all walks of life, the same as here. . . . Only the day before yesterday I was trying to remember what I was reminded of by the crowds strolling in the park and sitting on the chairs. . . . They're just like the crowds on the sea-front at Nice . . . an agglomeration of elements so diverse that they cancel each other out. Vichy, like Nice, must surely have its share of superannuated sirens, former stars of stage and screen. . . . You've seen for yourself the streets of opulent private villas, where there are actually footmen in striped waistcoats still.

"And up in the hills, well away from the public gaze, there are villas even more opulent."

"As in Nice. . . . And what do you deduce from that?"

"Nothing. She was thirty-two when she went to live in Nice,

and she was as much on her own there as she was here. Solitude doesn't, as a rule, come so early in life."

"There are such things as unhappy love affairs."

"Yes, but the sufferers don't look as she did."

"Broken marriages are not unknown."

"Ninety-five per cent of those women remarry."

"What about the men?"

With a broad grin, he retorted:

"A hundred per cent!"

She could not be sure whether he was teasing her or not.

Nice has a floating population, several casinos, and branches of nearly all the main Paris shops. Vichy virtually changes its population every three weeks, as the hundreds of thousands taking the cure come and go. It has branches of the same shops, three casinos, and a dozen cinemas.

Anywhere else, she would have been known. People would have taken an interest in her, they would have pried into her mode of life, her comings and goings.

Not in Nice. Not in Vichy. Was it that she had something to hide?

"Are you going back to see Lecoeur?"

"He said to come whenever I felt like it. He calls me 'Chief,' just as though he were still working under me."

"They all do."

"That's true. It's just habit, I daresay."

"You don't think it could be affection?"

He shrugged, and suggested that it was time they were on their way. This time, they went through the old town, stopping to look in the windows of the antique shops, where so many old and some touchingly pathetic objects were displayed.

In the dining room they were conscious of being stared at by their fellow guests. Oh, well, they would just have to get used to it.

Maigret had conscientiously modified his eating habits in accordance with the doctor's instructions: chew everything thoroughly before swallowing, even mashed potatoes; never replenish your fork until you have swallowed the previous mouthful;

do not drink more than a couple of sips of water with your meals, flavored with a drop of wine, if you must.

He preferred to do without wine altogether.

On the way upstairs he permitted himself a couple of puffs at his pipe, before stretching out, fully dressed, for his afternoon rest. His wife sat in the armchair by the window. There was just enough light coming in through the slats in the blinds to enable her to read the paper, as he had done earlier. From time to time, as he lay dozing, he could hear the rustle of a page being turned.

He had been resting for barely twenty minutes when there was a knock at the door. Madame Maigret got up hastily and went out, shutting the door behind her. After a whispered consultation, she went downstairs. She was back within minutes.

"It was Lecoeur."

"Any fresh news?"

"The sister has just arrived in Vichy. She went straight to the Police Station. She's about to be taken to the mortuary, to make a formal identification. Lecoeur will be waiting to see her in Rue du Bourbonnais. He thought you might like to be present when he questioned her."

Maigret, grumbling to himself, was already on his feet. For a start, he would have the shutters open, to let a little light and life into the place.

"Shall we meet at the spring?"

Five o'clock in the afternoon: the spring, the first glass of water, the iron chair.

"It won't take that long. You'd better wait for me on one of the benches near the bowling greens."

He was looking dubiously at his straw hat.

"What's the matter? Are you afraid of being laughed at?"

Well, let them laugh. He was on holiday, wasn't he? Defiantly, he put it on.

The same policeman was on guard outside the house. There were still a good many people about, drawn there by curiosity, but when they found that there was nothing to be seen through the closed windows, most of them moved off, shaking their heads.

"Take a seat, Chief. If you move your chair into that corner over there by the window, you'll be able to see her with the light full on her."

"Have you seen her yet?"

"I was in a restaurant having lunch—and a very good lunch it was, I must say—when I got a message that she was at the Police Station. They said they'd see to it that she was taken to the mortuary, and brought on here afterward."

And at that moment they saw, through the net curtains, a black car with a policeman in uniform at the wheel and, following behind, a long, red, open sports car. It was plain from their disheveled hair and tanned faces that the man and woman in the front seats had just got back from holiday.

The couple talked for a minute or two, their heads close together. They exchanged a hurried kiss, and she got out of the car and slammed the door. Her companion, still sitting behind the wheel, lit a cigarette.

He was dark, with strong features and athletic shoulders, which were clearly outlined under his close-fitting, yellow, polo-neck sweater. He was surveying the house with a bored expression, when the policeman ushered the young woman into the living room.

"I am Superintendent Lecoeur. . . . You are Francine Lange, I presume?"

"That's right."

She glanced briefly at Maigret, whose face was in shadow, and to whom she had not been introduced.

"Madame or Mademoiselle?"

"I'm not married, if that's what you mean. I have a friend with me; he's in the car. But I know too much about men to marry one of them. It's the devil's own job to get rid of them afterward. . . ."

She was a fine-looking woman, who appeared much younger than her forty years, and her provocative curves seemed out of place in this conventional little room. She was wearing a flame-colored dress of material so thin that her bare flesh showed through it, and the salt tang of the sea seemed still to cling to her.

"I got your telegram last night. Lucien managed to get seats on

the first plane to Paris. . . . We had left our car at Orly, so we
drove the rest of the way from there. . . ."

"I take it she was, indeed, your sister?"

Showing no sign of emotion, she nodded.

"Won't you sit down?"

"Thank you. Do you mind if I smoke?"

She looked meaningfully at the smoke rising up from Maigret's
pipe, as if to say:

"If he can smoke, what's to stop me?"

"Please do. . . . I take it you were no more prepared for this
murder than we were?"

"Well, naturally, I wasn't expecting it!"

"Do you know of anyone who might have had a grudge against
your sister?"

"Why should anyone have had a grudge against Hélène?"

"When did you see her last?"

"Six or seven years ago, I can't say exactly. . . . It was winter,
I remember, and there was a storm raging. . . . She hadn't let me
know she was coming, so I was taken by surprise when she coolly
walked into my hairdressing salon."

"Did you get on well together?"

"As well as most sisters. . . . We never saw much of one
another, because of the difference in our ages. . . . When I was
starting school, she had just left. . . . Then she went to the
Secretarial School in La Rochelle. . . . I didn't train as a manicurist till years after. . . . Later, she left the town."

"How old was she then?"

"Let me think. . . . I was in the second year of my
training . . . so I must have been sixteen. . . . She was seven
years older. . . . That would make her twenty-three. . . ."

"Did you correspond?"

"Very rarely. . . . We don't go in much for letter-writing in
our family."

"Was your mother still alive then?"

"Yes . . . she died two years later, and Hélène came to Marsilly for the division of her property. . . . Not that there was
much to divide. . . . The shop was almost worthless. . . ."

"What was your sister doing in Paris?"

Maigret never took his eyes off her, making a mental comparison, line by line, between her face and figure and those of the dead woman. There was very little resemblance between the two women, the dark-eyed, long-jawed Hélène and the blue-eyed Francine, who was almost certainly not a natural blonde, with that bizarre streak of firey red dangling over her forehead.

At first sight she seemed a good sort, hail-fellow-well-met with her clientele, no doubt, exuberantly cheerful if a little coarse. She made no pretense of refinement, indeed she seemed bent on accentuating her natural vulgarity, almost as if she relished it.

It was not half an hour since she had viewed her sister's body in the mortuary, yet here she was answering Lecoeur's questions good-humoredly, almost gaily, and—probably just from habit—attempting to make a conquest of him.

"What was she doing in Paris? Working as a stenographer in an office presumably, though I never went there to find out. . . . We had very little in common. I was just fifteen when I had my first boy friend—a taxi driver, he was—and I've had a good many since. . . . I don't think that was Hélène's style at all, unless she was a very dark horse. . . ."

"What address did you write to?"

"At the beginning, as far as I remember, it was a hotel in Avenue de Clichy. . . . I forget the name. . . . She moved several times. . . . Later she took an apartment in Rue Notre-Dame-de-Lorette. . . . I can't remember the number."

"You yourself went to live in Paris after a time. . . . Did you never go and see her?"

"Yes, I did. She was living in Rue Notre-Dame-de-Lorette by then. A very nice little apartment it was. I was amazed. . . . I remember remarking on it. . . . She had a large bedroom looking out on the street, a living room, a kitchenette, and a real bathroom. . . ."

"Was there a man in her life?"

"I never found out. I wanted to stay a few days with her, while I looked for a suitable room. She said she knew of a very clean, modestly priced hotel where I could stay, but she couldn't bear to have anyone living with her."

"Not even for three or four days?"

"Apparently not."

"Did it surprise you?"

"Not all that much. . . . I may say, it takes a lot to surprise me. . . . I don't like other people to meddle in my affairs, and I don't interfere in theirs."

"How long were you in Paris?"

"Eleven years."

"Working as a manicurist?"

"To begin with. I worked in several salons in the neighborhood, and then I moved to a beauty parlor in Champs-Elysées. That was where I trained as a beauty specialist."

"Were you living alone?"

"Sometimes alone, sometimes not."

"Did you see anything of your sister?"

"To all intents and purposes, nothing."

"So that you can't really tell us anything about her life in Paris?"

"All I know is that she had a job. . . ."

"When you returned to La Rochelle to open your own salon, did you have much in the way of savings?"

"A fair amount."

He did not ask how she had earned this money, nor did she volunteer the information, but she probably took it for granted that he understood.

"You never married?"

"I've answered that already. I'm not such a fool as to . . ."

And, turning to the window, from which they could see her companion lounging at the wheel of the red sports car:

"He looks like a real lout, don't you think?"

"And yet you're living with him. . . ."

"He works for me, and what's more, he's a first-class hairdresser. We don't live together in La Rochelle; I wouldn't want him around all night as well as all day. . . . On holiday, it's different. . . ."

"Is the car yours?"

"Of course."

"But he chose it?"

"How did you guess?"

"Did your sister ever have a child?"

"Why do you ask?"

"I don't know . . . she was a woman. . . ."

"Not to my knowledge, she didn't. . . . I shouldn't have thought it was the kind of thing you could hide. . . ."

"What about you?"

"I had a child while I was living in Paris. Fifteen years ago . . . My first thought was to get rid of it. . . . It would have been better if I had. . . . It was my sister who urged me not to. . . ."

"So you were in touch with her then?"

"It was because of it that I went to see her. . . . I needed someone to talk to—a member of my own family. . . . You may think it silly, but there are times when one instinctively turns to one's family. . . . Anyway, I had a son, Philippe. . . . I put him out to foster parents in the Vosges. . . ."

"Why the Vosges? Did you have any ties there?"

"None whatever. Hélène saw an advertisement somewhere or other. . . . I used to go and see him. . . . I suppose I went about ten times in two years. . . . He was well cared for. . . . The foster parents were very kind. . . . They had a small farm, beautifully kept. . . . Then one day I heard from them that the child was dead, drowned in a pond. . . ."

She was silent and thoughtful for a moment or two, then she shrugged:

"All things considered, it was probably for the best. . . ."

"Did you know of no one who was close to your sister, man or woman?"

"I doubt if she had many friends. Even in the old days in Marsilly she looked down her nose at the other girls. They used to call her the Princess. . . . It was no different, I imagine, at the Secretarial School in La Rochelle. . . ."

"Was it pride?"

She thought this over, then said uncertainly:

"I don't know. . . . That's not the word I would choose. . . . She didn't like people. . . . She didn't like the company of other people. . . . That's it! She was happiest on her own."

"Did she ever attempt suicide?"

"Why should she? You don't think . . ."

Lecoeur smiled.

"No, no one commits suicide by strangulation. . . . I just wondered whether, at any time in the past, she had been tempted to put an end to her life."

"I'm sure it never entered her head. . . . She had a good opinion of herself. Basically, she was very self-satisfied."

Yes, thought Maigret, that was it, self-satisfied. In his mind's eye he saw once again the lady in lilac sitting facing the bandstand. At the time, he had tried to interpret her expression, and failed.

Francine had put her finger on it: self-satisfaction.

She was so self-absorbed that she kept no less than three photographs of herself in her living room, and no doubt there were others in the dining room and bedroom, which he had not yet seen. She had no photograph of anyone else. None of her mother, none of her sister, none of any friend, man or woman. Even on the beach she had been photographed alone, against a background of waves.

"I take it that, as far as you know, you are her sole heir? . . . We found no will among her papers. Admittedly, the murderer scattered them all over the place, but I can't imagine any reason why he should have made off with her will. . . . So far, we have heard nothing from any lawyer. . . ."

"When is the funeral to be?"

"That's up to you. The forensic laboratory have completed their work, so you can claim your sister's body whenever you wish."

"Where do you think she should be buried?"

"I haven't the least idea."

"I don't know a soul here. . . . If I took her back to Marsilly the whole village would turn out for the funeral—to gape. . . . I wonder if it really would have been her wish to end up in Marsilly. . . . Look, if you don't need me any more, I'd like to go and book into a hotel. I'm longing for a good hot bath. . . . Let me think it over, and tomorrow morning . . ."

"Very well. I shall expect to see you tomorrow morning."

Just as she was leaving, having shaken hands with Lecoeur, she turned to glance briefly at Maigret. She was frowning, as though puzzled by the presence of this silent man sitting in shadow.

Did she recognize him?"

"Till tomorrow, then. You have been most kind."

They saw her get into the car and lean over to say something to her companion at the wheel, and then the car drove off.

In the living room the two men looked at one another. Lecoeur was the first to speak:

"Well?" he said. I was almost comical.

And Maigret, puffing at his pipe, retorted:

"Well, what?"

He didn't feel like discussing the case. Besides, he hadn't forgotten that he had promised to meet his wife near the bowling greens.

"I must be going, my dear fellow. I'll see you tomorrow."

"Till tomorrow, then."

The policeman's military salute was no more than was due to him. All the same, he felt a glow of pride.

3

HE WAS BACK in his old place, sitting in the green armchair near the open window. The weather had not changed since the day they arrived, warm sunshine in abundance, yet with a cool breeze at the start of the day, when the municipal sprinkler-carts made their rounds of the streets. And later on it would be pleasantly cool in the shade of the thickly wooded park, the many tree-lined boulevards, and the Allier promenade.

He had eaten his three croissants. His coffee cup was still half full. His wife was having her bath next door, and on the floor below he could hear the sounds of people moving about their rooms, getting ready to go downstairs.

It was not without a touch of wry amusement that he noted how quickly he had formed new habits. That was always his way. Wherever he was, he would almost instinctively establish a routine, and then adhere to it, as though subject to some immutable law.

It would be true to say that, when he was in Paris, each separate investigation had a tempo of its own, which included periods of rest in one particular bistro or brasserie, with its own characteristic smells and quality of light.

Here, in Vichy, he felt much more like a man on holiday than a man taking the cure, and even the death of the lady in lilac had failed to shatter his indolent mood.

The night before, they had gone for their customary walk in the park, where several hundred others like themselves appeared as dark shadows, except when they moved through a pool of light cast by one of the frosted globes of the lamp standards. At this hour, most people were at the theater, the cinema, or the casino. Everywhere, after a light meal of cold ham, people were coming out of their hotels, pensions, and lodgings, in search of their own chosen form of entertainment.

Many were quite happy just to sit and relax on the florid little yellow chairs, and Maigret, without thinking, had caught himself searching in the crowd for an erect and dignified figure, a face with a long jaw line, a chin held high, and an expression that was at once wistful and hard.

Hélène Lange was dead, and Francine, no doubt, was consulting with her gigolo as to where she should have her sister buried.

Somewhere in this town there was a man who could solve the mystery of the lonely woman who owned a house called *Les Iris*, the man who had strangled her.

Was he taking his customary walk in the park, or was he, at this minute, on his way to the theater or the cinema?

Maigret and his wife had undressed and gone to bed in silence, but each had known what the other was thinking.

He lit his pipe and opened his paper at the section devoted to local news.

A photograph of himself spread over two columns caused him to draw in his breath sharply. It was a recent photograph, showing him drinking one of his daily glasses of water. He could not imagine when it had been taken. His wife had been sitting beside him at this time—they had left in about a third of her—and in the background were several blurred, anonymous faces.

MAIGRET TO THE RESCUE?

Out of consideration for his privacy, we have not hitherto informed our readers of the presence among us of Chief Superintendent Maigret. He is in Vichy in a private capacity, having come, like so many other distinguished public figures, to take advantage of the beneficial properties of our mineral springs.

The question now arises, will the Chief Superintendent be able to resist the temptation to try his hand at solving the mystery of Rue du Bourbonnais?

He has been seen in the neighborhood of the house where the murder was committed, and rumor has it that he is in touch with Superintendent Lecoeur, the popular head of C.I.D., Clermont-Ferrand, who is in charge of the case.

With loyalties divided between the cure and the case, which will he choose?

He dropped the paper with a shrug. He was used to personal gossip of this sort, and it no longer angered him. He turned, and stared absent-mindedly out of the window.

Up to now—it was nine o'clock—he had behaved exactly as he did every morning, and when Madame Maigret reappeared, wearing her pink suit, they went downstairs as usual.

"Monsieur, madame, good morning. . . . " As usual, the proprietor was there to greet them. Maigret had already seen the two men outside, and the glint of their camera lens.

"They've been waiting for you for the past hour. They're from the Saint-Etienne *Tribune*, not from the local paper."

The photographer was tall, with red hair. The man with him, small and dark, had one shoulder higher than the other. They ran up to the door.

"May we take a picture? Just one?"

What was the use of saying no? He stood quite still for a moment on the doorstep, between the two flowering shrubs, Madame Maigret having retreated into the shadows.

"Look up, please, sir. Your hat . . ."

He could not remember when he had last been photographed wearing a straw hat. The only other he now possessed was the one he kept at Meung-sur-Loire for gardening.

"One more. . . . It won't take a second. Thank you. . . ."

"Just one question, Monsieur Maigret, is it true that you are taking part in the Investigation?"

"As Chief of the Criminal Investigation Department at the Quai des Orfèvres, I have no authority here."

"All the same, you must be taking an interest?"

"No more than all your other readers."

"It has one or two peculiar features, don't you think?"

"What do you mean?"

"The victim was a recluse. . . . She had no friends. . . . There is no obvious motive. . . ."

"When we know more about her, the motive, no doubt, will become apparent."

It was not a particularly profound remark, and it committed him to nothing, but, all the same, it contained a germ of essential truth. For a long time now, others besides Maigret have seen the importance of studying the character of the victim. Increasingly, the attention of criminologists has centered upon the dead person, even to the extent of laying a large share of the blame at the victim's door.

Might there not have been something in Hélène Lange's manner and way of life which had, in a sense, doomed her to death by violence? From the very first, when he had seen her under the trees in the park, the Chief Superintendent had fixed upon her as an object of interest.

True, she was not the only one. The two whom he and his wife always referred to as "the happy pair" had also aroused his interest.

"Isn't it a fact that Superintendent Lecoeur used to be on your staff?"

"He did work for a time in the Law Courts in Paris."

"Have you seen him?"

"I paid him a friendly call."

"Will you be seeing him again?"

"Very likely."

"Will you be discussing the murder with him?"

"Very likely. Unless we confine ourselves to the weather, and the strange quality of the light in your charming town."

"What's so strange about it?"

"It's soft and shimmering at one and the same time."

"Do you intend to come back to Vichy next year?"

"That depends on my doctor."

"Many thanks. . . ."

As the two men leapt into their battered motorcar, Maigret and his wife walked slowly away from the hotel.

"Where shall I wait for you?"

She took it for granted that her husband was going to Rue du Bourbonnais.

"At the spring?"

"At the bowling greens."

In other words, he didn't intend to stay long with Lecoeur. He found him in the tiny parlor, talking on the telephone.

"Take a seat, Chief. . . . Hello! . . . Yes. . . . It's a bit of luck finding the same concierge there after all these years. . . . Yes. . . . She doesn't know where? . . . She went by métro? . . . From Saint-Georges? . . . Don't cut us off, miss. . . . Carry on, chum. . . ."

The call lasted for another two or three minutes.

"Thanks. . . . I'll see you get a formal authorization, just for the record. You can send us your report then. . . . How's the wife? . . . Of course. There's always something to worry about with kids. . . . I should know, with four boys of my own. . . ."

He hung up and turned to Maigret.

"That was Julien. He's an inspector in the IXth *Arrondissement* now. . . . You must have known him. . . . I called him up yesterday, and he agreed to look through his departmental files. . . . He's located the place in Rue Notre-Dame-de-Lorette where Hélène Lange lived for four years."

"From the age of twenty-eight to thirty-two, in fact. . . ."

"Roughly. . . . The concierge is still there. . . . Mademoiselle Lange, it seems, was a nice, quiet young woman. . . . She went out and came back at regular hours, as one would expect of a working girl. . . . It seems that she seldom went out in the evenings, except occasionally to the theater or cinema.

"Her place of work must have been some distance away, as she used the métro. . . . She always went out early to do her shopping, and she had no domestic help. . . . She usually got home for lunch at about twenty past twelve, and left again at half past one. After that she wasn't seen again until she got back from work at half past six."

"Did she have any visitors?"

"Only one, a man. Always the same man."

"Did you get his name from the concierge?"

"She knew nothing about him, except that he used to call once or twice a week at about half past eight at night, and always left before ten."

"What sort of man?"

"Very respectable, according to her. He drove his own car. It never occurred to the concierge to make a note of the number. It was a large black car, American, I imagine."

"What age?"

"In his forties. . . . On the heavy side. . . . Very well groomed. . . . Expensive clothes. . . ."

"Was he paying the rent?"

"He never set foot in the concierge's lodge."

"Did they go away together for weekends?"

"Only once."

"What about holidays?"

"No. . . . At that time, Hélène Lange only got two weeks' holiday, and she nearly always went to Etretat, staying in a family pension, to which her mail was forwarded."

"Did she get many letters?"

"Very few. . . . One from her sister occasionally. . . . She subscribed to a lending library nearby. She was a great reader."

"Do you mind if I take a look around the apartment?"

"Of course not. Make yourself at home, Chief."

He noted that the television set was not in the little parlor, but in the dining room, which was furnished in provincial style, with the inevitable brass hardware much in evidence. On the sideboard was a photograph of Hélène Lange bowling a hoop, and another of her in a bathing suit, with a cliff in the background, probably taken at Etretat. She had a well-proportioned figure, the long slender lines of the face being carried through to the body, though she was by no means thin or sharp. She was one of those women to whom clothes are unflattering.

In the kitchen, which was modern and bright, there was a dishwasher, not to mention every other labor-saving appliance.

Across the hall was a bathroom, also modern and well equipped, and the dead woman's bedroom.

Maigret was amused to find that it was almost a replica of his own hotel bedroom, with the same style of brass bedstead and the same elaborately carved furniture. The wallpaper was striped, lavender blue and pale pink, and here too hung a photograph of Hélène Lange, taken when she was about thirty.

But he scarcely recognized, behind that wide, spontaneous, joyous smile, the secretive face he had come to know.

It was an enlarged snapshot, probably taken in a wood, if the foliage in the background was anything to go by. She was looking straight into the lens, her features softened in an expression almost of tenderness.

"It would be interesting to know who it was holding the camera," mumbled Maigret to Lecoeur, who had just come into the room.

"A bit of a mystery, isn't she?"

"I take it you've checked up on the lodgers?"

"It was my first idea, too, that it might be an inside job. The widow is in the clear, and anyway, in spite of her bulk, she wouldn't have the strength to strangle anyone who put up a fight like Mademoiselle Lange. . . . The Carlton staff confirm that she was there playing bridge until twenty past eleven. . . . And, according to the police surgeon, the murder was committed between ten and eleven. . . ."

"In other words, by the time Madame Vireveau got home, Hélène Lange was dead."

"Almost certainly.

"The Maleskis saw a light under the living-room door. . . . It follows, since the lights were later turned off, that the murderer was still in the apartment. . . .

"That's what I keep telling myself. . . . Either he came in with his victim and strangled her before searching the apartment, or she found him at it, and had to be silenced. . . ."

"What about the man Madame Vireveau claims to have seen on the corner?"

"We're working on that. Just about that time, as the proprietor of a nearby bar was pulling down his iron shutter, he saw a heavily built man walking rapidly past. He seemed out of breath, he says. . . ."

"Which way was he going?"

"Toward the Célestins."

"Did he describe him?"

"He wasn't paying much attention. . . . All he could say was that he was wearing a dark suit and no hat. . . . He thinks he remembers noticing that he had receding hair."

"Any anonymous letters?"

"Not so far."

There would be. There had never been a crime with a bit of mystery to it that did not produce its crop of anonymous letters and cryptic telephone calls.

"Have you seen the sister again?"

"I'm still waiting to hear from her what she wants done with the body."

And, after a brief pause, he added:

"You could scarcely find two sisters more unlike, could you? The one so reserved, so introverted, so superior, and the other a thoroughgoing extrovert, overflowing with health and vitality. . . . And yet. . . . "

Maigret looked at Lecoeur with an indulgent smile, noting that he had put on weight around the middle, and that there were one or two white hairs among the bristles of his red mustache. His blue eyes were innocent, almost childlike, and yet, Maigret remembered, he had been one of his ablest assistants.

"What are you smiling at?"

"Because I saw her alive, and yet you, who know her only from photographs and hearsay, have reached the same conclusions as I have."

"You mean that Hélène Lange was a prey to sentimental and romantic delusions?"

"I believe she was playing a part, deceiving even herself perhaps, but she couldn't hide the look in her eyes, which was hard and shrewd."

"Like her sister . . ."

"Francine Lange has cast herself in the role of the emancipated woman, who doesn't give a damn for anyone or anything. . . . If you were to ask in La Rochelle, I'm sure you'd find that she had a wide circle of friends, all of whom would regale you with colorful details of the conversations and escapades. . . ."

"Which is not to say . . ."

There was no need for either of them to spell things out.

"That, underneath it all, she doesn't know that two and two makes four!"

"And what's more, gigolos or no gigolos, she knows what she wants. . . . Starting with a miserable little shop in Marsilly, she now owns, at the age of forty, one of the smartest hairdressing salons in La Rochelle. I know the town. Place des Armes . . ."

He took out his pocket watch.

"My wife will be waiting. . . ."

"At the spring?"

"No, I'm going to watch a game or two of bowls first. It will give me something else to think about. . . . I used to play a bit years ago, at Porquerolles. If only some of those fellows would twist my arm . . ."

He went on his way, filling a fresh pipe. It was warmer than it had been. By the time he got there, he was glad of the shade of the great trees.

"Anything new?"

"Nothing of any interest."

"Haven't they found out about her life in Paris yet?"

His wife was eyeing him warily, not wishing to overstep the mark, but he answered with perfect good humor:

"Nothing definite. . . . Only that she had at least one lover."

Madame Maigret grew bolder.

"Anyone would think you were pleased!"

"In a way, perhaps. It shows that, for a time at least, she got a bit of fun out of life, that she wasn't always shut up inside herself, chewing over God knows what obsessions and fantasies. . . ."

"What do you know about him?"

"Practically nothing, except that he drove a big black car, and went to see her once or twice a week in the evening, and always left before ten. They never went away together for a holiday, or even a weekend. . . ."

"A married man . . ."

"Probably. . . . Aged about forty, ten years older than she was. . . ."

"What about the neighbors in Rue du Bourbonnais? Did none of them ever see him?"

"Well, for one thing, he's not a man of forty now. More like sixty. . . ."

"Do you think . . ."

"I don't think anything. I'd like to know what sort of life she lived in Nice. Was it a period of transition, or had she already acquired the habits of an old maid? . . . Watch out, he's going to bowl. . . ."

The one-armed player, bowling with great deliberation, sent the jack spinning.

Involuntarily, he exclaimed:

"I envy them."

"Why?"

Her skin, dappled with sunlight and shade, was smooth. She's looking younger, he thought. His holiday mood was coming back. With a twinkle, he said:

"Haven't you noticed how completely engrossed they are? To them, bowling a good ball is the supreme fulfillment. It really is important to them. But when we come to the end of an inquiry . . ."

He left the sentence in the air, but his wry little grimace was eloquent. In this job, when they had finished with a man, he was abandoned, left to stand alone at the bar of Justice. . . . The end was prison, sometimes death. . . .

Shaking himself out of it, he emptied his pipe, and then said:

"What about our walk?"

Well, that was what they were here for, wasn't it?

Lecoeur's assistants had questioned all the neighbors.

Not only had no one heard or seen anything on the night of the murder, but all were agreed that Hélène Lange had no friends of either sex, and that she had never been known to have a visitor.

From time to time she was seen to leave the house carrying a small overnight bag, and on these occasions the shutters would remain closed for two or three days.

She never took any heavy luggage. She never ordered a taxi, and she had no car.

Nor had she ever been seen in the street with a companion, man or woman.

Every morning of the week, she went out to do her shopping in the local shops. Although she was not exactly mean, she knew the value of money, and on Saturdays always did her weekend shopping in the market. Invariably, she wore a hat, white in summer, dark in winter.

As to her present lodgers, they were completely in the clear. Madame Vireveau had come on the recommendation of a friend in Montmartre, who had stayed at Mademoiselle Lange's during the season, for several years in succession. A bit showy she might be, with her ample figure and flamboyant paste jewels, but she was not the woman to commit a murder, especially without motive. Her husband had been a florist in Paris, and up to the time of his death she had worked in the shop in Boulevard des Batignolles. Afterward she had moved to a little apartment in Rue Lamarck.

"I had nothing against her," she said of Hélène Lange, "except that she had very little to say for herself."

The Maleskis had been coming to Vichy for the cure for the past four years. The first year, they had gone to a hotel, and had discovered Mademoiselle Lange quite by chance, through a card in a shop window advertising rooms to let, which they had noticed one day when they were out for a walk. They had inquired about her charges, and had at once booked a room for the following season. This was their third summer at *Les Iris*.

Maleski suffered from a disease of the liver, which meant that he had to take care of himself and keep to a very strict diet. Although only forty-two, he was already burned out, a shadow of a man with a sad smile. Inquiries made over the telephone to Grenoble, however, revealed that he was at the top of his profession, and highly regarded as a man of scrupulous honesty.

It had been made clear to him and his wife from the first that Mademoiselle Lange preferred to keep her distance with the lodgers. The only room they had ever been into on the ground floor was the little parlor, and then not more than two or three times. They had never been asked in for a drink, or even a cup of coffee.

Occasionally, when they stayed in on wet evenings, they could hear the television, but it was always turned off quite early.

All this information was buzzing in Maigret's head as he lay on the bed dozing, as he did every afternoon, while Madame Maigret sat at the window reading. Through half-closed eyes, he could see the lines of light thrown on the wall opposite the window by the slats of the Venetian blind, and was conscious of a golden afternoon outside.

Ideas swirled around in his head, broke up and reassembled, and suddenly he was asking himself, as though it were the key question:

"Why that night in particular?"

Why had she not been murdered the night before, or the night after, or last month, or two months ago?

On the face of it, it was a pointless question, and yet, half asleep as he was, he felt it to be of the utmost significance.

For ten years, ten long years, she had lived alone in that quiet Vichy street. No one had ever visited her. She, as far as anyone could tell, had never visited anyone, except perhaps when she was away on one of her brief monthly trips.

The neighbors had seen her as she came and went. She was also to be seen, sitting on one of the yellow chairs in the park, sipping her glass of water, or, in the evening near the bandstand, listening to the music.

Had Maigret personally questioned the shopkeepers, they would probably have been amazed at the things he wanted to know.

"Did she ever indulge in small talk? . . . Did you ever see her bend down and stroke your dog? Did she talk to the other housewives in the queue, or exchange greetings with those whom she regularly met at the same time, more or less every day?"

And finally:

"Have you ever known her to laugh? . . . Only smile?

It was necessary to go back fifteen years to find evidence of any kind of personal relationship with another human being, the man who used to visit her once or twice a week in her apartment in Rue Notre-Dame-de-Lorette.

Was it possible that she could have lived all those years with-

out ever feeling the need to unburden herself to anyone, to speak
her thoughts aloud?

Someone had strangled her.

"But why that night in particular?"

To Maigret, half asleep as he was, this question was assuming
obsessional proportions. He was still seeking an answer when his
wife's voice broke in with the announcement that it was three
o'clock.

"Were you asleep?"

"Dozing."

"Are we going out?"

"Of course we're going out! Don't we always go out? Why do
you ask?"

"I thought you might be meeting Lecoeur."

"I'm not meeting anyone."

And, to prove it, he took her on a grand tour of the town,
starting with the children's playground, and going on via the
bowling greens and the beach, across the Pont de Bellerive, to
walk the length of the boulevard leading to the Yacht Club,
where they stopped for a while to watch the antics of the water
skiers.

Then on much farther, as far as the new buildings, twelve
stories high, towering white blocks that were, in themselves, a
town on the outskirts of the town.

Across the Allier they could see the horses cantering alongside
the white fence posts of the racecourse, and the heads and
shoulders of the people in the stands, and, on the lawns, groups of
figures in sunlight and in shadow.

"The proprietor of the hotel says that every year more and
more retired people are coming to live in Vichy."

Teasingly, he asked:

"Is that what you're softening me up for?"

"We've got our house at Meung. . . ."

They came upon a street of older houses. Each district had its
own style, representing its own period. The houses had their own
individuality, and one could envisage the kind of people who had
built them.

It amused Maigret to stop outside every one of the innumerable little restaurants they passed, and read the menu.

"Room to let. Room with kitchen. Luxurious furnished rooms."

That explained the restaurants, and also the tens of thousands of people streaming through the streets and along the promenades.

At five o'clock, at the spring, they were both glad to take the weight off their aching feet. They smiled understandingly at one another. Maybe they had overdone it a bit. What were they trying to prove? That they were both young still?

In the crowd, they recognized two faces, those of "the happy pair," but there was something different about the way the man was looking at Maigret. What was more, instead of walking past, he was coming straight up to the Chief Superintendent, with his hand held out.

What could Maigret do, but take it?

"Don't you remember me?"

"I know I've seen you before, but I can't for the life of me recall . . ."

"Does the name Bébert mean anything to you?"

Nicknames like Bébert, P'tit Louis, and Grand Jules were common enough in his experience.

"The métro."

Smiling more broadly than ever, he turned to his wife, as if seeking confirmation.

"The first time you arrested me, it was during a procession in Boulevard des Capucines. . . . And, would you believe it, I can't even remember which Head of State it was in honor of, only the horse guards on either side of his carriage. . . . The second time was outside the entrance to the métro at the Bastille. You'd been following me for some time. . . . All this didn't happen yesterday. . . . I was a young man then. So, if I may say so, were you. . . ."

All Maigret could remember about the métro affair was that he had lost his hat while chasing the culprit across the Place de la Bastille, and good Lord, now he came to think of it, it had been a straw boater of the kind fashionable at the time—so this wasn't the first time he had worn a straw hat.

"How long were you sent down for?"

"Two years. . . . It taught me a lesson. . . . Made me pull myself together. To begin with, I worked for a junk dealer, mending vast quantities of old glass—I always was good with my hands."

He gave a knowing wink, intended, no doubt, to convey that this had been very useful to him in the days when he was a pickpocket.

"Then I met Madame."

He laid great emphasis on the "Madame," and quite glowed with pride as he spoke.

"No police record. She's always been straight. She was fresh from Brittany, working in a dairy. . . . It was never anything but serious with her, so we were married. . . . She even insisted on our going back home to her village for a real white wedding in church."

He exuded *joie de vivre* at every pore.

"I was almost sure it was you. . . . Every time I saw you . . . But I couldn't be quite certain . . . until this morning, when I opened my paper, and there was your photograph. . . ."

He pointed to the glasses in their little straw cases.

"Nothing serious, I hope?"

"I'm in excellent health."

"Me too, or so all the doctors say, but here I am all the same, on account of pains in the knee joints. . . . Hydro-therapy, massage under water, ultra-violet rays, the lot. . . . And you?"

"A few glasses of water."

"Oh, well, there can't be much wrong then. . . . But I mustn't keep you and your good lady. . . . You played very fair with me in the old days. . . . Lovely weather, isn't it? . . . Good day to you, sir. . . . Say good-by, Bobonne. . . ."

As he watched them disappear into the distance, Maigret was still smiling at the resolute little ex-pickpocket's success story. Then his wife saw the smile fade, and a worried frown take its place. At length, with a sigh of relief, he said:

"I think I now know why . . ."

"Why the woman was murdered?"

"No, why she was murdered on that particular day. . . . Why she wasn't murdered last month or last year. . . ."

"What do you mean?"

"Ever since we got here we've been meeting the same people two or three times a day, and have come to know them quite well by sight. . . . Take that nut case. . . . He's never spoken to me until today, because he couldn't be sure about me until he saw my picture in the paper. . . .

"But then, this is the first time we've come for the cure, and it will probably be the last. But if we were to come back next year, we'd very likely see quite a few familiar faces about the place.

"What I'm trying to say is this: there is someone else in Vichy who, like ourselves, is here for the first time . . . going through the same routine: medical examination, tests, prescribed course of treatment, visits to the springs, measured doses of the waters to be taken at fixed hours. . . .

"He must have seen Hélène Lange somewhere, and thought he recognized her.

"Then he saw her again, and again. . . . Maybe he was not far from where she was sitting the other night, when she was listening to the music."

It all sounded so simple: Madame Maigret was surprised he should be making such a song and dance about it.

The Chief Superintendent, sensing this, hastened to add, not without a touch of self-mockery:

"According to the brochures, some two hundred thousand people come to Vichy every year for the cure. The season lasts six months, so presumably they pour in at the rate of more than thirty thousand a month. Assuming a third of them are newcomers like ourselves, that leaves us with about two thousand suspects. . . . No! Wait a bit . . . we can exclude the women and children. . . . What's the proportion of women and children, would you say?"

"There are more women than men. As to children . . ."

"No, wait! What about the people in wheel chairs, and those on crutches or walking with a stick? None of them, not to mention the very old, would be capable of strangling a healthy woman still in her prime. . . ."

Was he teasing her, or did he really mean it, she wondered.

"Let's say we're left with a thousand men capable of committing this murder. But, according to the evidence of Madame Vireveau and the proprietor of the bar, the murderer was unusually tall and thickset, so we can ignore the skinny and undersized . . . which leaves us with about five hundred."

It was a relief to hear him laugh.

"What's the joke?"

"The policeman's lot. Our job. I shall shortly inform the good Lecoeur that I have narrowed the field down to five hundred suspects, unless we are able to eliminate a few more, those who were at the theater that night, for instance, or who can prove that they spent the whole evening at the bridge tables, or what have you. . . . And to think that, more often than not, that's how criminals are caught! In one case, Scotland Yard questioned every single inhabitant of a town with a population of two hundred thousand. . . . It took months. . . ."

"Did they find their man?"

Wryly, Maigret had to admit:

"Quite by chance, in some other town. The fellow was drunk, and opened his mouth too wide."

It was probably too late to see Lecoeur today. There were still two glasses of water to be drunk, with a half-hour interval between. He tried to concentrate on the evening paper, which was full of gossip about visiting celebrities. It was an odd thing, but even those well known for the dissolute lives they led liked to be photographed surrounded by their children or grandchildren, asserting that they wanted nothing better than to spend all their time with them.

By the time they reached the corner of Rue d'Auvergne, there was a fresh breeze blowing. A truck was parked outside Mademoiselle Lange's house.

As they drew near, they could hear the sound of hammering.

"Shall I go back to the hotel?" murmured Madame Maigret.

"Yes. This won't take long."

The living-room door was open, and men in buff overalls were hanging black draperies on the walls.

Lecoeur came forward to meet him.

"I thought you might be coming. . . . We'll go in here. . . ."

Lecoeur led the way into the bedroom, where it was quieter.

"Is she to be buried in Vichy?" Maigret asked. "Is that what her sister has decided?"

"Yes, she was here just before lunch."

"With the gigolo?"

"No, she came alone in a taxi."

"When is the funeral?"

"The day after tomorrow, to give time for the neighbors to pay their last respects."

"Will there be prayers?"

"Apparently not."

"Are the Langes not Catholics?"

"The old people were. The children were baptized, and took their First Communion. After that . . ."

"I was wondering if she was divorced."

"To find the answer to that we should need to know whether she was ever married."

Lecoeur, twiddling the ends of his red mustache, looked inquiringly at Maigret.

"You yourself had never set eyes on either of them before, I take it?"

"Never."

"But you did spend some time in La Rochelle?"

"I've been there twice. . . . Each time, for about ten days. Why do you ask?"

"Because I noticed a change in Francine Lange this morning. She was a good deal less lively . . . less forthright. I had the feeling that she had something on her mind . . . that there was something she wanted to tell me, but she was of two minds about it. . . .

"At one point she said:

"'Wasn't that Chief Superintendent Maigret who was here yesterday?'

"I asked her if she had ever seen you before, and she said no, but she had recognized your picture in the morning paper."

"She's not the only one. I suppose there must be about fifty others among the thousands I meet in the street every day. . . . Only today, an old customer of mine bore down on me with his hand outstretched. I was lucky to escape a hearty slap on the back."

"I think there's more to it than that," said Lecoeur, still following his own train of thought.

"You mean you think I may have had dealings with her when she was living in Paris?"

"Considering her mode of life, it's not all that far-fetched. . . . No! It's something less obvious, more subtle. . . . As far as she's concerned, I'm just a country cop, doing his best, asking the standard questions, noting the answers, and moving on to the next. . . . Do you see what I'm getting at? It would explain why, when she came here the first time, she was very much at her ease, as she was yesterday afternoon. . . . I caught her looking at you once or twice sitting there in the corner, but I could see she hadn't recognized you. . . .

"Then she booked in at the Hôtel de la Gare. There, as in most other hotels here, the local newspaper is sent up on the breakfast trays. . . . And when she saw your photograph, no doubt, she began to wonder what you were doing sitting in on our interview."

"And what are your conclusions?"

"Aren't you forgetting your reputation, your public image?"

He flushed suddenly, fearful that he might have given offense.

"Besides, it's not only the public. . . . We in the force are the first to . . ."

"Skip it. . . ."

"No, it's important. . . . It would never have crossed her mind that your presence—sitting in that armchair—might be fortuitous. . . . And even if it was, the very fact that you were interested in the case . . ."

"Did she seem at all frightened?"

"I wouldn't go as far as that. Her manner was different, more guarded. I only asked a few harmless questions, but even so, she weighed every word before answering. . . ."

"Has she traced the notary?"

"I wondered about that too. I did ask her. Apparently, the boy friend got a list of all the notaries in town, and rang every single one. . . . Hélène Lange, it seems, had never consulted any of them, though there was one who remembered that, ten years ago, when he was still an articled clerk, his firm had drawn up the deed of conveyance for her house."

"Do you know his name?"

"Maître Rambaud."

"What about giving him a ring?"

"At this hour?"

"Surely most lawyers outside Paris practice from their homes. . . ."

"What do you want me to ask him?"

"Whether she paid by check or bank draft."

"I'll have to stop those fellows' hammering first."

In the meantime, Maigret prowled back and forth from the bathroom to the kitchen, though not with anything particular in mind.

"Well?"

"You guessed, didn't you?"

"What?"

"That she paid in cash. It's the only time Rambaud had ever known it to happen, which is why he still remembers it. There were enough notes to fill a small suitcase."

"Have you taken statements from the ticket clerks at the railway station?"

"Good Lord! I never thought of that!"

"It would be interesting to find out whether she always went to the same place on her monthly trips, or to a different place each time. . . ."

"I'll let you know tomorrow. . . . It's time you were off to your dinner. . . . Enjoy yourself! . . ."

There was a band concert in the park that night, and the Maigrets permitted themselves the luxury of sitting down to listen to it. They had walked far enough for one day.

4

FOR SOME MYSTERIOUS reason, he was ten minutes ahead of schedule. Maybe there was less news than usual in this morning's *Journal de Clermont-Ferrand*? Madame Maigret, who always waited until he had finished before going into the bathroom, was still in there. He called to her through the half-open door:

"I'm going out. . . . Wait for me downstairs."

There was a green wooden seat on the sidewalk outside the hotel, for the convenience of residents. The sky was as cloudless as ever. During the whole of their stay in Vichy, it had not rained once.

Needless to say, the proprietor was waiting for him at the foot of the stairs.

"Well, what news of the murder?"

"It's no concern of mine," he answered with a smile.

"Do you think that these Clermont-Ferrand people are really up to the job? It's very bad, in a place like this, to have a strangler on the loose. Quite a number of old ladies have left already, I hear. . . ."

With a noncommittal smile, he set off for Rue du Bourbonnais. He saw, from the far end of the street, that the front door of *Les Iris* was draped in black, with a large letter "L" embroidered in silver on the pelmet. There was no longer a policeman on guard outside. Had there been one last night? He had not noticed. After all, it was none of his business. He was here to take the waters,

462

and his only interest in the case was as a bystander, an amateur.

He was about to ring the bell when he noticed that the white door was ajar. He pushed it open and went in. A very young girl, barely sixteen, he judged, was mopping the floor of the entrance with a damp cloth. Her dress was so short that, when she bent forward, he could see her pink bloomers. She had plump, shapeless legs, as girls so often do at the awkward age. They reminded him of the crudely painted legs of a cheap doll.

She turned to look at him, a pair of expressionless eyes staring at him out of a round face. She did not ask his name, nor what he was doing there.

"In there," was all she said, pointing to the living room.

The room, all draped in black, was dark, with the coffin resting on what must have been the dining-room table. There were unlit candles, holy water in a glass bowl, and a sprig of rosemary.

The kitchen and dining-room doors were open. The living-room furniture and ornaments had been stacked in the dining room. The young policeman, Dicelle, was sitting in the kitchen reading a comic, with a cup of coffee on the table in front of him.

"Will you join me in a cup of coffee? I've made a full pot."

On Hélène Lange's gas cooker, which would scarcely have met with her approval!

"Hasn't Superintendent Lecoeur arrived yet?"

"He was called back urgently to Clermont-Ferrand late last night. . . . A holdup at the Savings Bank. . . . One man killed . . . a passer-by, who noticed the door ajar and went in to investigate, just as the thieves were coming out. . . . One of them shot him at point-blank range. . . ."

"Nothing new here?"

"Not that I know of."

"Have you questioned the station staff?"

"Trigaud—one of my colleagues—is looking into it. He's not back yet."

"I presume the little servant-girl out there has been questioned? What has she to say?"

"That half-wit! It's a wonder she can talk at all! She doesn't know a thing. She was only taken on for the season, to see to the lodgers' rooms. She didn't do the ground floor; Mademoiselle Lange saw to her own housework."

"Did she ever see any visitors?"

"Only the man who reads the gas meter, and the delivery boys. She came to work at nine and left at twelve. . . . The Maleskis upstairs are a bit worried. . . . They've paid in advance to the end of the month, and they want to know whether they'll be able to stay on. . . . It isn't easy to find rooms in the middle of the season, and they don't want to move to a hotel."

"What does the Superintendent say?"

"I think, as far as he's concerned, they can stay. . . . They're up there now, at any rate. . . . The other one, the fat one, has gone to the masseur for her daily pummeling."

"Have you seen Francine Lange?"

"I'm expecting her any time. . . . No one seems to know what's happening. . . . She insisted on the lying-in-state, but it wouldn't surprise me if no one turned up. . . . My instructions are to stay here and keep a discreet eye on the callers, if any."

"I wish you joy of it," mumbled Maigret, going out of the kitchen.

The books, like everything else from the living room, had been moved into the dining room. Mechanically, he picked one up off the top of a pile stacked on a small occasional table. It was *Lucien Leuwen*. The yellowing pages had the distinctive smell of well-thumbed books from lending libraries, public or private.

The name and address of the library was stamped in violet ink on the flyleaf.

He put the book back on top of the pile and slipped quietly out into the street. A ground-floor window opened, and a woman in a dressing gown and hair-rollers looked out.

"Excuse me, Superintendent, can you tell me if one can call and pay one's respects?"

It seemed to him rather an odd way of putting it, and for a moment he was nonplused.

"I imagine so. The door is open, and they've turned the living room into a little chapel."

"Can one see her?"

"As far as I know, the coffin is closed."

She sighed:

"I prefer it that way. . . . It's less distressing."

He found Madame Maigret waiting for him on the green seat. She seemed surprised to see him back so soon.

They set off on their usual morning walk. They were only a couple of minutes behind schedule, a schedule that they had never planned, but now adhered to as though their lives depended on it.

"Were there many people?"

"Not a soul. They're waiting. . . ."

This time they went straight to the children's playground, where they strolled for a time in the shade of the trees, some of which—like those along the banks of the Allier—were very rare specimens, from America, India, and Japan. These were distinguished by little metal plates, bearing their botanical names in Latin and French. Many were tokens of gratitude from long-forgotten Heads of State, who had benefited from the cure at Vichy, obscure maharajahs and other Eastern princelings.

They did not stop more than a minute or two at the bowling greens. Madame Maigret never asked her husband where they were making for. He always walked purposefully, as though he knew exactly where he was going, but more often than not he would turn down this street rather than that, just for a change of scene, because he enjoyed savoring new sights and sounds.

They still had a little time in hand before the first glass of water, when he turned into Rue Georges-Clemenceau. Was there something he wanted from the shops, she wondered? But he turned left into one of the little side alleys, the one leading to the theater, and stopped at a bookshop, where there were some second-hand books in trays on the sidewalk, and more books inside on revolving shelves.

"Come on," he said to his wife, who was looking at him inquiringly.

The proprietor, in a long gray overall, was tidying the shelves. He obviously recognized Maigret, but waited for him to speak.

"Can you spare me a few minutes?"

"With pleasure, Monsieur Maigret. It's about Mademoiselle Lange, I daresay."

"She was one of your subscribers, wasn't she?"

"She came in at least once a week, twice more often than not, to change her books. Her subscription allowed her to have two books out at a time."

"How long have you known her?"

"I took over here six years ago. I'm not a local man. I came here from Paris, Montparnasse. She was already a subscriber in my predecessor's time."

"Did she ever stop for a chat?"

"Well, you know, she wasn't very outgoing. . . ."

"Didn't she ever ask your advice, when she was choosing new books?"

"She had very decided views of her own. Come with me. . . ."

He led the way to a room at the back of the shop, lined from floor to ceiling with books in black cloth bindings.

"She would often spend half an hour to an hour browsing in here, reading a paragraph here and a page there."

"Her last book was Stendhal's *Lucien Leuwen*."

"Stendhal was her latest discovery. Before that, she had read all Chateaubriand, Alfred de Vigny, Jules Sandeau, Benjamin Constant, Musset, and George Sand. It was always the romantics. On one occasion she took one of Balzac's novels—I can't remember which—but she brought it back the next day. Apparently it didn't appeal to her. I asked her why. She said: 'It's too coarse . . .' or words to that effect. . . . Balzac coarse, I ask you!"

"No contemporary writers?"

"She never gave them a chance. On the other hand, she read the letters of George Sand and Musset over and over again."

"I'm much obliged to you. . . ."

He was almost at the door when the bookseller called him back.

"Just one more thing that might interest you. I discovered, to my astonishment, that someone had been marking passages in pencil, underling words and phrases and, here and there, putting a cross in the margin. I wondered who on earth it could be. It turned out in the end to be Mademoiselle Lange."

"Did you mention it to her?"

"I had to. . . . My assistant was having to spend all his time rubbing out the marks. . . ."

"How did she react?"

"She looked very prim and said 'I'm sorry. . . . When I'm reading I forget that the books don't belong to me.'"

Everything looked just the same, the people taking the waters, the pale trunks of the plane trees, the patches of sun and shade, the thousands of yellow chairs.

She had not been able to stomach Balzac. . . . His realism had been too much for her, no doubt. She had restricted herself to the first half of the nineteenth century, grandly dismissing Flaubert, Hugo, Zola, Maupassant. . . . At the same time Maigret had noticed, that very first day, a pile of glossy magazines in a corner of the living room. . . .

It was as though he could not help himself, he must forever be adding fresh touches to the picture of her that he was building up. Her reading was confined to the romantic, the sentimental, and yet he had more than once seen her eyes narrow in a hard, shrewd look.

"Did you see Lecoeur?"

"No. He's been called back to Clermont-Ferrand because of a bank holdup."

"Do you think he'll find the murderer?"

Maigret started. He was the one who needed bringing down to earth! The truth was that he had not been thinking about the case in terms of murder. He had almost forgotten that the woman who owned the house with the green shutters had been strangled, and that the first priority was to find the killer.

True, he was looking for someone, more intensely, indeed, than he himself would have wished, almost to the point where it was becoming an obsession.

The really intriguing figure, as far as he was concerned, was the man who, at a given moment, had broken into the life of this solitary woman.

There was no trace of him in Rue du Bourbonnais, no photograph, not a single letter, not even a note.

Nothing! Nothing from anyone else either, apart from bills and receipts.

One had to go back twelve years, to Paris, to Rue Notre-Dame-de-Lorette, to find anyone who remembered a shadowy figure who called once or twice a week, and spent an hour in the apartment of Mademoiselle Lange, then still a comparatively young woman.

Even Francine, her own sister, who was living in the same city at the time, claimed to know nothing about him.

She read voraciously, watched television, did her shopping and her housework, walked under the trees in the park like the summer visitors, sat and listened to the band, staring straight in front of her, and never addressing a word to anyone.

This was what puzzled him. Often, in the course of his career, he had met individuals, both men and women, who clung fiercely to their independence. He had also met eccentrics who, having renounced the world, had taken refuge in the most unlikely, sometimes the most sordid, surroundings.

But even men and women such as these, in his experience, kept some link with the outside world. The old ones, for instance, often had a favorite bench in a square, where they would meet some other old crone to talk to, or they were members of a church, going to confession, exchanging greetings with the priest. Some had a favorite bistro, where they were known, and welcomed as old friends.

But here was a case, Maigret realized—the first he had ever known—of stark, unrelieved isolation.

There was not even an element of aggression. Mademoiselle Lange had been civil enough to the neighbors and shopkeepers. She had not been high-handed with them nor, in spite of her somewhat formal style of dress and her preference for certain colors, had she put on superior airs.

It was rather that she did not concern herself with other people. She had no need of them. She took in lodgers because the spare bedrooms were there, and they provided a small income. Between the apartment on the ground floor and the bedrooms upstairs, she had erected an invisible barrier, and to clean the guest rooms she had engaged a servant-girl, who was little better than a moron.

"Can you spare a moment, sir?"

A shadow fell across Maigret. He looked up to see a tall man holding a chair by its back. The Chief Superintendent recognized him as one of the men he had seen with Dicelle in Rue du Bourbonnais, Trigaud presumably.

"How did you find me?" Maigret asked.

"Dicelle said you would be here."

"And how did Dicelle . . . ?"

"There isn't a man in the local force, sir, who doesn't know you by sight, so that wherever you go . . ."

"Any fresh news?"

"I was at the station for an hour last night, interviewing the night staff, and this morning I went back to question the day staff. . . . Then I called Superintendent Lecoeur, who is still at Clermont-Ferrand. . . ."

"Won't he be back today?"

"He's not sure yet. But whatever happens, he'll be coming early tomorrow for the funeral. I presume you'll be there, too. . . ."

"Have you seen Francine?"

"She called in at the undertaker's. The hearse will be leaving the house at nine o'clock. . . . Some flowers were delivered at the house. . . . They must have come from her, I imagine. . . ."

"How many wreaths?"

"Just the one."

"Check whether it did come from her. . . . I beg your pardon. . . . I was forgetting . . . it's really none of my business."

"I don't think the Super would agree with you there. He told me to be sure and let you know what I'd found out. He made a special point of it. I expect that there are a good many in the force, including your humble servant, who would go along with that. . . ."

"On these monthly trips of hers, did she go far?"

Trigaud pulled a bundle of papers out of his pocket and, after some searching, found what he was looking for.

"They couldn't remember all the details, of course, but one or two places stuck in their minds, because they are by no means easy to get to from here: Strasbourg, for instance, and the following month, Brest. Some of her trips involved changing trains two or three times: Carcassonne . . . Dieppe . . . Lyons . . . not quite so far . . . Lyons was, in fact, exceptional. . . . Mostly, she went much farther afield: Nancy, Montélimar."

"Never to a small town or a village?"

"No, she always seemed to choose a fairly large town, though, of course, she may have gone on somewhere by bus."

"Did she never take a ticket to Paris?"

"Never."

"How long has this been going on?"

"The last man I spoke to has been working at the same window for nine years."

" 'I ought to know my regular customers by now,' he said.

"She was well known to the station staff. They looked forward to her coming, and even laid bets as to where she would choose to go next."

"Did she always go on the same day of the month?"

"No, that's the odd thing. Sometimes there would be an interval of six weeks, usually in the summer. I daresay it was on account of the lodgers. It wasn't always the end of the month, or any fixed date."

"Did Lecoeur tell you what he intends to do next?"

"He's having copies made of her photographs. . . . For a start, he'll send a couple of men to the nearest towns, and copies of the photographs to the various local police stations. . . ."

"You don't happen to know why Lecoeur wanted me put in the picture?"

"He didn't say. . . . No doubt he thought you had formed your own view. . . . That's what I think, too. . . ."

Everyone always credited him with knowing more than he let on. It was no good protesting. They would only think it was the old fox up to his usual tricks.

"Has anyone turned up at the house?"

"According to Dicelle, things started livening up around ten o'clock. . . . A woman in an apron put her head around the door, and then, rather hesitantly, went in to see the coffin. She took a rosary out of her pocket and muttered a prayer. Then she crossed herself with holy water and left. . . .

"She must have told the neighbors, because they all came after that, in ones and twos. . . ."

"Any men?"

"A few . . . the butcher, and a carpenter who lives at the end of the street . . . all local people. . . ."

Why assume that the murderer wasn't a local man? They were searching up and down the country, in all the widely separated towns visited by the lady in lilac, in Nice, in Paris, trying to unravel the mystery of her life. But no one had given a thought to the thousands of people who lived in the France district of Vichy.

Maigret himself had not.

"Can you suggest anything further I should do?"

Trigaud wasn't saying this on his own. That cunning devil Lecoeur must have put him up to it. After all, here was Maigret on the spot. Why not make use of him?

"I was wondering whether the ticket clerks could remember any precise dates. We wouldn't need very many. Two or three would do."

"I have one already. . . . June 11th. . . . The fellow remembered it because she took a ticket for Rheims, and his wife comes from there, and, as it happened, June 11th was her birthday."

"If I were you, I'd find out from her bank manager whether she deposited any money on the 13th or 14th. . . ."

"I think I see what you're driving at . . . blackmail."

"Or an allowance . . ."

"Why should anyone pay out an allowance at irregular intervals?"

"Just what I was wondering myself."

Trigaud stole a sideways glance at Maigret, convinced that he was either keeping something from him or making fun of him.

"I'd much rather they'd put me on the holdup," he grumbled. "At least you know where you stand with pros. . . . I'm sorry to have bothered you. . . . My best respects, madame."

He got up awkwardly, not quite knowing how to make his escape, blinking, with the sun full in his eyes.

"It's too late now for the bank. I'll call in there after lunch. Then, if necessary, I'll go back to the railway station."

Maigret had been through it all in his time. Pounding the beat for hours at a stretch, on pavements scorching hot or slippery with rain, questioning wary witnesses, whose words had to be coaxed out of them, one by one.

"We'd better go and have our glass of water."

While Trigaud, no doubt, would be regaling himself with a long, cool glass of beer.

"You'd better be at the spring at about eleven. . . . I hope I'll be able to get there."

He sounded a little out of temper. Madame Maigret had been afraid that he would get bored in Vichy, with nothing to do, and no one but herself for company, from morning to night.

The good-humored contentment that he had shown in the first few days had not wholly reassured her. She could not help wondering how long it would last.

However, in the past two or three days, he had been thoroughly put out every time they had had to miss one of their regular walks.

Today there was the funeral. He had promised Lecoeur to be there. The sun was still shining, and, as usual in the morning, the streets were damp, and a fresh breeze was blowing.

Rue du Bourbonnais was unusually crowded. Apart from the neighbors who could be seen leaning out of their windows, like spectators at a public procession, there were people all along the sidewalk several deep outside the house itself.

The hearse was already there. Behind it was a black car, supplied, no doubt, by the undertaker, and behind that another, which Maigret had not seen before.

Lecoeur came out to meet him.

"I've had to drop the bank robbery for the time being," he explained. "There's a holdup practically every day of the week. The public are used to them, and they don't get het up about them any more. But a woman strangled in her own house, in a law-abiding town like Vichy, and for no apparent reason . . ."

Maigret recognized the scruffy mop of red hair belonging to the *Tribune* photographers. There were two or three other photographers there as well. One of them took a shot of the two police officers crossing the road.

The fact was that there was nothing to see, and, from the expressions on their faces, some of the bystanders were wondering whether it had really been worth their while to come.

"Have you got men on watch in the street?"

"Three. . . . I can't see Dicelle, but he's somewhere around. . . . He thought it would be a good idea to have the butcher's boy with him. . . . He knows everyone hereabouts, and will be able to point out any strangers."

There was no feeling of sadness, no sense of horror. Everyone, Maigret included, was waiting.

"Will you be going to the cemetery?" he asked Lecoeur.

"I'd be glad if you'd come with me, Chief. I've brought my own car. I felt a police car wouldn't be quite the thing. . . ."

"What about Francine?"

"She got here a few minutes ago, with the boy friend. . . . They're in the house."

"I don't see their car."

"I daresay the undertakers, who know what's what, dropped a hint that an open red sports job would look just as much out of place in a funeral procession as a police car. . . . Those two will go in the black car."

"Have you spoken to her?"

"She gave me a nod when she arrived. I thought she looked nervous . . . anxious. . . . She stood for a moment, before coming into the house, scanning the crowd as though she was looking for someone. . . ."

"I still can't see young Dicelle."

"That's because he's wangled a seat in someone's window, for himself and the butcher's boy."

Several people came out of the house, two more went in and reappeared almost at once. Then the driver of the hearse took his seat at the wheel.

As though in response to a signal, four men, not without difficulty, maneuvered the coffin through the door and slid it into the hearse. One of them went back into the house and returned carrying a wreath and a small spray of flowers.

"The spray is from the lodgers."

Francine Lange stood at the door, in a black dress that did not suite her. She must have bought it for the occasion in Rue Georges-Clemenceau. Her companion was behind her, a shadowy figure in the darkness of the entrance hall.

The hearse moved forward a few feet. Francine and her lover got into the black car.

"Let's go, Chief."

All along the street there were people, standing very still. Only the photographers were darting hither and thither.

"Is that all?" Maigret asked, looking over his shoulder.

"She had no other relatives . . . no friends. . . ."

"What about the lodgers?"

"Maleski is seeing his doctor at ten, and the fat woman, Madame Vireveau, has her massage. . . ."

They drove through streets that Maigret recognized from his exploration of the town. He filled his pipe, and watched the houses go by. Soon, to his surprise, they were at the railway station.

The cemetery was nearby, just on the other side of the track. It was deserted. The hearse stopped at the end of the drive.

So here they were, just the four of them, except for the undertaker's men, standing on the gravel path. Lecoeur and Maigret went up to the other two. The gigolo was wearing sunglasses.

"Will you be staying long?" Maigret asked the young woman.

Maigret had spoken idly, just for something to say, but it did not escape him that she was looking penetratingly at him, as though searching for some hidden meaning in his words.

"Probably another two or three days, just to get things sorted out."

"What about the lodgers?"

"They can stay till the end of the month. There's no reason why not. I'll just have to lock up the ground-floor apartment."

"Will you be selling the house?"

Before she could answer, one of the men in black came up to her. They wheeled the coffin, on a handcart, down a narrow side turning to the edge of an open grave.

A photographer—not the tall, redheaded man, but another whom Maigret had not seen before—appeared, apparently from nowhere, and took a few shots while the coffin was being lowered into the grave, then another as Francine, at a sign from the master of ceremonies, threw a handful of earth onto the coffin.

The grave was at the far end of the cemetery, a few yards from the low surrounding wall which divided it from a patch of waste ground, where derelict cars lay rotting. Beyond, in the background, were one or two white villas.

The hearse drove away, then the photographer. Lecoeur looked inquiringly at Maigret, who, however, did not respond, and seemed to be lost in thought. What precisely was he thinking of? Of La Rochelle, a town he had always liked, of Rue Notre-Dame-de-Lorette, as it was in the very early days when he was personal assistant to the Superintendent of Police in the IXth *Arrondissement*, of the bowling greens, and the men he had seen there. . . .

Francine, clutching a crumpled handkerchief, was coming toward them. She had not used the handkerchief to dry her tears. She had not shed a tear. She had been no more moved than the undertaker's men or the gravedigger. Indeed, there had been nothing in the least moving about the ceremony. It could not have been more matter-of-fact.

The crumpled handkerchief was just for the sake of appearances.

"I don't know the form. . . . It's usual, isn't it, to provide refreshments of some sort after a funeral? But I'm sure you wouldn't want to have lunch with us. . . ."

"There's so much to be done," murmured Lecoeur.

"At least allow me to buy you a drink."

Maigret was astonished at the change in her. Even here, in this desert of a cemetery, from which even the photographer had fled, she was still looking about her anxiously, as though she felt some danger threatening her.

"I'm sure there will be other opportunities," replied Lecoeur diplomatically.

"Haven't you got a lead yet?"

It was not at Lecoeur that she looked as she spoke, but at Chief Superintendent Maigret, as though he were the one she was afraid of.

"We're still making inquiries."

Maigret filled his pipe, and pressed down the tobacco with his forefinger. He was puzzled. This was a woman who had certainly had a few knocks in her time, and was quite capable of taking things in her stride. It was not her sister's death that had changed her. She had been cheerful and ebullient enough when she had first heard of it.

"In that case, gentlemen . . . I don't know how to put it. . . . Oh, well, I daresay I'll be seeing you. . . . Thanks for coming."

If she had waited a minute or two longer, Maigret might have asked her point-blank whether she had received any threats. But she went, teetering on her high heels, impatient to get back to her hotel room, where she could shut the door and change out of the black dress, bought especially for the occasion.

Maigret turned to his colleague from Clermont-Ferrand.

"What do you make of her?" he asked.

"So you noticed it, too? I'd very much like a private chat with her in my office. But I'd have to find a plausible excuse. It wouldn't be decent today, somehow. . . . She looked scared, to me."

"That was what I thought."

"Do you think she's been threatened? What would you do, if you were I?"

"What do you mean?"

"We don't know why her sister was strangled. . . . It might, after all, turn out to be a family affair. . . . We know precious little about these people. . . . Maybe it was some business in which both women were concerned. . . . Didn't I hear her tell you she'd be staying on in Vichy for another two or three days? I'm short-handed, of course, but the holdup can wait. . . . The pros always get caught in the end. . . ."

They had returned to their car and were driving toward the cemetery gates.

"I shall have her followed, discreetly, though in a hotel that's almost impossible. . . . Where would you like me to drop you?"

"Anywhere near the park."

"Ah, yes, I'd almost forgotten you were here for the cure. . . . I don't know why I've never got around to taking it myself. . . ."

* * *

At first he thought his wife had not yet arrived. She wasn't sitting in her usual place. He was so used to seeing her there that it gave him quite a start when he found her sitting in the shade, under a different tree.

For a moment he watched her, unseen. Sitting there placidly, with her hands folded in the lap of her light dress, she was looking at the people passing by, with a contented little smile, as though she were quite prepared to wait for him forever.

"Oh, there you are!" she exclaimed, then, without pausing, "Our chairs were taken. . . . I heard them talking. . . . They're Dutch, I think. . . . I hope they're not staying . . . otherwise we've probably lost our seats for good. . . . I didn't think it would be over so soon. . . ."

"It's not far to the cemetery."

"Were there many people?"

"In the street outside the house. . . . There were only the four of us at the funeral."

"So the boy friend went too, did he? Come on, it's time for our glass of water. . . ."

They had to wait in a queue for a time. Afterward, Maigret bought the Paris newspapers, but there was scarcely a mention of the Vichy strangler. One paper only, the evening paper of the previous day, had a photograph of Maigret under a headline in those very words: "The Vichy Strangler."

He was anxious to hear what, if anything, had been discovered as a result of the inquiries made in several of the many towns visited at various times by the lady in lilac.

Nevertheless, he allowed his mind to wander. With half an eye on the news, he could see the people walking past, over the top of his paper. After a time, they had to push their chairs back into the receding shade.

That was why they had chosen the place now occupied by the Dutch couple. The sun never reached it at the times they were in the park.

"Don't you want a paper?"

"No. . . . Those two comics have just gone by, and he swept you a tremendous bow."

They were already lost in the crowd.

"Did the sister cry?"

"No."

He was still puzzled by her. If he had been in charge of the case, he too would have wanted to have her in his office for a private chat.

Several times, in the course of the morning, his thoughts returned to her. They walked back to the Hôtel de la Bérézina and, after going upstairs to wash, sat down at their table in the dining room. As usual, at every table except theirs, there were opened wine bottles beside the little trumpet-shaped vases, each holding one or two fresh flowers."There's cutlet Milanaise and calves' liver *à la bourgeoise. . . .*"

"I'll have the cutlet," he said with a sigh. "It will be grilled as usual, of course. I'll be gone by the end of the season, but Rian will still be here next year and the year after. What he says goes. . . ."

"Don't you feel the better for it?"

"Only because I'm away from Paris. Besides, I never felt really ill. A bit weighed down . . . giddiness from time to time. . . . These things happen to most people at some time or other, I imagine."

"Still, you do have faith in Pardon. . . . "

"I haven't much choice."

They had had noodles as a first course and were just starting on their cutlets when Maigret was called to the telephone.

The telephone booth was in one of the smaller reception rooms, with a window overlooking the street.

"Hello! I'm not disturbing you, I hope? Had you started your lunch?"

Recognizing Lecoeur's voice, he replied crossly:

"For all they give me to eat!"

"I have news for you. . . . I sent one of my men to keep watch on the Hôtel de la Gare. . . . But first he thought he'd better find out the number of Francine Lange's room. The receptionist looked surprised, and told him she'd checked out. . . ."

"When?"

"Barely half an hour after they left us. It seems that, when they got back to the hotel, the man stopped at the desk before going up to their room, and asked them to get their bill ready. They must have packed in a great hurry, because ten minutes later they rang for a porter. They flung everything into the back of the red car, and off they went."

Maigret said nothing, and Lecoeur did not prompt him. After an appreciable pause, Lecoeur said:

"What do you make of it, Chief?"

"She's a frightened woman. . . ."

"Agreed, but she was this morning, too, anyone could see that. . . . But that didn't prevent her from saying she intended staying another two or three days in Vichy."

"That might have been just to prevent you from detaining her."

"How could I detain her, not having anything against her?"

"You know the law, but she may not."

"Anyway, we shall know tomorrow morning, if not tonight, whether she's gone back to La Rochelle."

"It's the most likely thing."

"I agree. I'm furious, all the same. I'd made up my mind that we were going to have a long chat. . . . Admittedly, I may find out more, as a result of this. . . . Could you be here at two?"

It would mean missing his afternoon rest. He said, rather grudgingly:

"I'm not doing anything in particular, as you very well know."

"This morning, while I was out, someone phoned the local Police Station asking to speak to me. . . . That's where I am now. . . . I decided, after all, to take them up on their offer of a room here. . . . The caller was a young woman, apparently by the name of Madeleine Dubois, and guess what she does for a living. . . ."

Maigret said nothing.

"She's a switchboard operator on the night shift at the Hôtel de la Gare. My colleague here told her that I would probably be here at the station—it's in Avenue Victoria—at two o'clock. . . . He suggested that she should leave a message, but she said she'd prefer to see me personally. . . . So I'm here, waiting for her. . . ."

"I'll be there."

He missed his rest but, by way of compensation, had the pleasure of seeing for the first time the exquisite, white turreted villa set in extensive grounds which did duty as a police station in Vichy. He was taken to the upper floor by a policeman and, at the end of a corridor, found Lecoeur ensconced in an office almost entirely devoid of furniture.

"It's just five to two," remarked Lecoeur. "I hope she hasn't changed her mind. Which reminds me, I'd better try and find another chair."

Maigret could hear him in the hall opening and shutting doors. Eventually he found what he wanted, and came back carrying it.

On the dot of two, the police officer on duty knocked at the door and announced:

"Madame Dubois."

She was a lively little woman, with dark hair and very expressive eyes. She stood there, looking from one to the other.

"Which of you is the officer I have come to see?"

Lecoeur introduced himself but not Maigret, who was sitting unobtrusively in a corner of the room.

"I don't know whether what I have to tell you is important. . . . It didn't seem so at the time. . . . The hotel is full, and I was kept very busy until one in the morning. . . . After that I dozed off, as I usually do. . . . It's about one of the hotel guests, Madame Lange. . . ."

"I presume you mean Mademoiselle Francine Lange?"

"I thought she was married. I know her sister is dead, and that her funeral was this morning. . . . Last evening, at about half past eight, someone asked to speak to her. . . ."

"A man?"

"Yes, a man. He had an odd sort of voice. . . . Asthmatic, I think . . . I'm almost sure. . . . I had an uncle who suffered from asthma, and he sounded just like that. . . ."

"Did he give his name?"

"No."

"Did he ask for her room number?"

"No. I rang, and there was no reply . . . so I told him that the person he wanted to speak to was out. . . . He called again at about nine, but there was still no reply from Room 406. . . ."

"Did Mademoiselle Lange and her companion share a double room?"

"Yes. . . . The man phoned the third time at eleven, and this time Mademoiselle Lange answered. . . . I put him through. . . ."

She seemed embarrassed, and glanced quickly at Maigret, as though trying to gauge his reactions. Presumably she, like everyone else, had recognized him.

"Did you listen?" murmured Lecoeur, with an encouraging smile.

"I'm afraid I did. . . . I don't make a habit of it. . . . I know everyone imagines switchboard girls are always listening to people's conversations. If they only knew how boring they were, they'd think differently. . . . Perhaps it was because of the murder of her sister . . . Or because the man had such a peculiar voice . . .

"'Who's speaking?' she said.

"'Is that Mademoiselle Francine Lange?'

"'Yes. . . .'

"'Are you alone?'

"She hesitated. . . . I'm almost sure the man was in there with her.

"'Yes,' she said, 'but what business is it of yours?'

"'I have something very private to tell you. . . . Listen carefully. . . . If I'm interrupted, I shall call back in half an hour. . . .'

"He had difficulty with his breathing, and every now and again he wheezed, just like my uncle.

"'I'm listening . . . you still haven't told me who you are. . . .'

"'It's of no importance. . . . What is of the utmost importance—what is essential—is that you should stay on in Vichy for a few days. . . . It's in your own interests. . . . I'll be in touch with you again. . . . I can't say when exactly. . . . There may be a great deal in it for you . . . a large sum of money. . . . Do you understand?'

"Then suddenly he stopped speaking, and hung up. A few minutes later a call came through from Room 406.

"'Mademoiselle Lange here. . . . I've just had a phone call. . . . Could you tell me whether it was a local or a long-distance call?'

"'Local.'

"'Thank you!'

"Well, that's it! At first I thought it wasn't any business of mine. But when I came off duty this morning, I just couldn't go to sleep, so I phoned here and asked to speak to the officer in charge of the case."

She was fidgeting nervously with her handbag, her glance shifting from one man to the other.

"Do you think it's important?"

"You haven't been back to the hotel?"

"I don't go on duty until eight o'clock in the evening."

"Mademoiselle Lange has left."

"Wasn't she at her sister's funeral?"

"She left almost immediately after the funeral."

"Oh!"

Then, after a pause for thought:

"You think the man was setting a trap for her, don't you? Could it, by any chance, have been the strangler?"

The color drained from her face at the thought that she had actually heard the voice of the lady in lilac's murderer.

Maigret was no longer regretting having missed his afternoon rest.

5

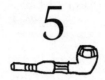

THE TWO MEN stayed where they were after the telephone girl had left, Maigret puffing reflectively at his pipe, and Lecoeur smoking a cigarette that looked as if it were going to set fire to his mustache at any minute. The smoke rose, spread out, and hung above their heads. Down below in the yard, they could hear a squad of policemen drilling.

For a time, neither spoke. They were both old hands, and there was little anyone could teach them about their trade. They had had dealings with every sort of criminal, every sort of witness.

"There's no doubt that it was he calling her," Lecoeur said at last, with a sigh.

Maigret did not reply at once. His reaction was different. It wasn't so much a question of method—a term they both disliked—as of approach to a problem.

Thus, since the strangling of the lady in lilac, Maigret had given very little thought to the murderer. It was not deliberate, but simply because he was haunted by the recollection of this woman, sitting on her yellow chair near the bandstand, haunted by the memory of her long jaw line, and by her gentle smile, which belied the hard expression of her eyes.

Little details had been added to his picture of her as a result of his visits to her house in Rue du Bourbonnais. He had learned something, though not much, of her stay in Nice, her life in Paris, and a great deal about her taste in literature.

The strangler was still a very shadowy figure, a tall, heavily built man, whom Madame Vireveau claimed to have seen, walking very rapidly, at the corner of the street, and who had been glimpsed by the proprietor of a bar, who could not describe his features.

Almost without realizing it, he began thinking about him.

"I wonder how he found out that Francine Lange was staying at the Hôtel de la Gare."

The newspapers, which had announced the arrival in Vichy of the victim's sister, had given no address.

Maigret was feeling his way forward cautiously, one step at a time.

"Come to think of it, there was nothing to prevent him from ringing one hotel after another, and asking for Mademoiselle Lange."

He could picture him poring over a classified directory. The list of hotels in a place like this would be a long one. Had he gone through it in alphabetical order?

"You might try one of the hotels beginning with the letter 'A' or 'B.'"

With a twinkle in his eye, Lecoeur picked up the receiver.

"Get me the Hôtel d'Angleterre, will you? No, not the manager or the desk—I want the switchboard operator. Hello! Is that the switchboard of the Hôtel d'Angleterre? I'm a police officer. . . . Can you tell me if anyone has been asking to speak to Mademoiselle Lange? . . . No, not the murdered woman. . . . Her sister, Francine Lange. . . . That's right. . . . Perhaps your colleague would know. . . ."

He turned to Maigret:

"There are two girls on the switchboard. . . . It's a huge place. . . . Five or six hundred rooms. . . . Hello, yes. . . . Hello! You say you took the call yourself? . . . Anything strike you as odd? . . . A hoarse voice, did you say? . . . As though the man . . . Yes, I see. . . . Thank you. . . ."

And to Maigret:

"Yesterday morning at about ten. A man with a hoarse voice, or rather one who seemed to have trouble with his breathing. . . ."

Someone who was here for the cure, as Maigret had suspected

from the very first, and who, quite by chance, had run into Hélène Lange. No doubt he had discovered where she lived by the simple expedient of following her home. . . .

The telephone rang. It was the inspector whom Lecoeur had dispatched to Lyons. There was no record of the dead woman having stayed in any of the hotels in the town, but he had found a post office clerk who remembered her. She had been in the post office twice, on each occasion to collect a large manilla envelope. The first time, the envelope had lain there a week. On the last occasion, it had just arrived when she called.

"Have you got the dates?"

Thoughtfully, still puffing lingeringly at his pipe, Maigret watched his colleague at work.

"Hello! . . . Is that the Crédit Lyonnais? . . . Have you got out that list of deposits I asked for? . . . No. . . . I'll send for it later today. . . . Can you tell me if she made deposits on January 14th or 15th, and February 23rd or 24th? . . . Yes, I'll hang on."

It didn't take long.

"Eight thousand francs on January 15th, and five thousand on February 23rd of this year. . . ."

"Usually about five thousand francs, you say?"

"Almost always, with a few exceptions. . . . I have the figures here. . . . I see that, five years ago, the sum of twenty-five thousand francs was credited to her account. . . . That's the only time such a large sum was ever paid in."

"In notes, as usual?"

"Yes."

"How does the account stand at the moment?"

"In credit to the tune of four hundred and fifty-two thousand, six hundred and fifty. . . ."

Lecoeur repeated the figure to Maigret.

"She was a rich woman," he murmured, "and still she let furnished rooms during the season. . . ."

The Chief Superintendent's reply surprised him:

"He's a very rich man."

"You're right. . . . It does look as though she was getting all the money from a single source. A man who can lay out five thousand francs a month, sometimes more . . ."

Yet this man had been kept in ignorance of the fact that Hélène Lange was the owner of a little white villa with pale green shutters in the France district of Vichy. Each payment had been made to a different address.

The money had been paid every month, but not on any fixed date. Presumably, it was no accident that Mademoiselle Lange had generally allowed a few days to elapse before collecting it, no doubt as a precaution against being seen going into the post office by anyone who might be looking out for her.

A rich man, or at any rate comfortably well off. When he had finally tracked down the sister, he had not attempted to arrange a meeting, but had merely asked her to stay on in Vichy for a day or two, until she heard from him again. . . . Why?

"He must be a married man. . . . Here with his wife, and possibly his children too. . . . Obviously, he's not master of his own time. . . ."

Lecoeur, in his turn, was obviously enjoying seeing Maigret's mind at work. But was it really his mind at work? He was making every effort to get inside the mind of the murderer. . . .

"He couldn't find what he was looking for in Rue du Bourbonnais. . . . And he could get nothing out of Hélène Lange. . . . If he had, she would probably still be alive today. . . . He tried to frighten her into telling him whatever it was he wanted to know. . . ."

"Whether his wife is with him or not, we know that he was able to get away that night."

Maigret was silent, pondering this objection.

"What was on at the theater on Monday night?"

Lecoeur took up the receiver to find out.

"*Tosca*. . . . It was sold out."

Moving toward a conclusion, Maigret was not exactly reasoning it out, but rather progressing by leaps of the imagination. Here was this man, a person of some social standing, staying, no doubt, at one of the best hotels in Vichy, with his wife and, very probably, a party of friends.

The night before the performance, or possibly the night before that, he had seen Hélène Lange, and followed her, to find out where she lived.

On the night of the murder, *Tosca* was being performed in the theater of the Grand Casino. Is it not a well-known fact that women are generally more partial than men to Italian grand opera?

"Why don't you go without me? . . . I feel rather tired at the end of the day . . . the treatment . . . I'd be glad of the chance of an early night. . . ."

What was it he wanted to find out from Hélène Lange, which she had so stubbornly refused to tell him?

Had he reached the house before her, forcing the flimsy lock, and searching through drawers and cupboards, while she was still at the concert?

Or had he followed her home, strangled her, and searched the apartment afterward, throwing everything in confusion on the floor?

"What are you smiling at, Chief?"

"Something quite absurd that has just occurred to me. . . . Before he had that bit of luck with the Hôtel de la Gare, the murderer, if he really did telephone all the hotels in alphabetical order, must have made about thirty telephone calls. . . . What does that suggest to you?"

He refilled his pipe, thoughtfully.

"The entire police force is searching for him. . . . Almost certainly he shares a double room in the hotel with his wife. . . . But he's faced with the necessity of repeating the name of his victim aloud, over and over again.

"In a hotel, all phone calls go through the switchboard. . . . Besides, there's his wife. . . . It's reasonable, therefore, to suppose . . .

"Too chancy to make the calls from a café or bar, with the risk of being overheard. . . .

"If I were you, Lecoeur, I should detail as many men as I could spare to watch the public telephone booths."

"But, since he did get through to Francine Lange in the end. . . ."

"He'd said he'd call her back. . . ."

"But she's left Vichy. . . ."

"He doesn't know that."

In Paris, Maigret, in common with most married men, saw his wife three times a day, on waking in the morning, at midday, and at night. And often, when he wasn't able to get home for lunch, only twice.

For the rest of the day, for all she knew, he might have been up to anything.

But in Vichy? They, like most other married couples there for the cure, were in each other's company almost twenty-four hours a day.

"He wouldn't have been able to risk a long absence, even to use a public telephone booth," he said with a sigh.

More than likely he had made some excuse—he was out of cigarettes or wanted a breath of air—while his wife was dressing. . . . One or two quick calls . . . If she too was taking the cure, perhaps having hydrotherapy, that would give him a little more time to himself. . . .

He could imagine him, taking advantage of every opportunity, making opportunities whenever he could, lying to his wife like a naughty child to its mother.

A heavily built man, elderly, rich, of some standing, having come to Vichy in the hope of finding relief from chronic asthma.

"Doesn't it surprise you that the sister has decamped?"

Francine Lange liked money. Heaven knows what depths she had sunk to when she was living in Paris, in order to get it. And now she was the owner of a flourishing business, and her sister's sole heir.

Surely she was not the sort of woman to turn up her nose at the offer of a further substantial sum?

Was it the police she was afraid of? Unlikely, unless she intended to make a clean break, and leave the country.

No! She had gone back to La Rochelle, where she was just as accessible to police questioning as in Vichy. For the moment, she was still on the road with her gigolo at the wheel, in the open, red sports car, which must surely be the envy of every young person who saw it.

For a car like that would eat up the miles. She would probably reach La Rochelle sometime in the middle of the afternoon.

"Did any of the papers mention that she lived in La Rochelle?"

"No, they just announced her arrival."

"She was a frightened woman already, this morning in the house, and at the cemetery. . . ."

"I wonder why it was you she kept peering at, when she thought we weren't looking. . . ."

"I think I know why. . . ."

Maigret, smiling, went on, though not without some embarrassment:

"I've been built up in the newspapers as a sort of father confessor. . . . She must have been tempted to confide in me, to ask my advice. . . . But then, on reflection, she decided the stakes were too high."

Lecoeur frowned.

"I don't quite see . . ."

"The man tried to get some information out of Hélène Lange. It must have been important, because her refusal to give it drove him berserk. A man doesn't strangle a woman in cold blood. . . . He came unarmed to Rue du Bourbonnais. He never meant to kill her. . . . And then he went away empty-handed. . . ."

Brooding over the manner of her death, Maigret went on:

"If I may venture to say so . . ."

"You mean, he thinks the sister knows what she knew?"

"No doubt about it. . . . Otherwise, he'd never have taken so much trouble and run so many risks to find out where she was staying. . . . He would never have phoned her, and dropped that hint of a large bribe. . . ."

"And what about her? Does she know what he wants from her?"

"It's possible," murmured Maigret, looking at his watch.

"She must, surely? Unless she was scared out of her wits, why should she have run off without a word to us?"

"I must be off to meet my wife. . . ."

He might have added:

"Just like that other fellow!"

Just like that broad-shouldered, corpulent man, who had been forced to resort to every kind of childish trick in order to slip out to a public telephone booth to make his calls.

In the course of their daily walks, the Maigrets might well have passed that particular couple more than once. Who could tell? It was possible that they had sat side by side, drinking their glasses of water, that their chairs . . .

"Don't forget the telephone booths. . . ."

"It would take as many men as you have in Paris. . . ."

"There are never enough. . . . When will you be calling La Rochelle?"

"About six o'clock, before I leave for Clermont-Ferrand, where I have an appointment with the examining magistrate. I'm seeing him at his house. . . . This business is worrying him. He's in very well with the Compagnie Fermière, and they don't much care for publicity of this sort. . . . If you want to be present . . ."

He found Madame Maigret waiting for him on a bench. Never in all their lives had the Maigrets spent so much time sitting on park benches and garden chairs. He was late, but, quick to note that his mood had changed since the morning, she made no mention of it.

How well she knew that preoccupied frown.

"Where are we going?"

"For a walk."

Just as on any other day. Just like the other couple. The wife, surely, could have suspected nothing. How could she guess, as she walked at his side, that he blenched inwardly at the sight of every policeman in uniform?

He was a murderer. He could not cut short his cure and leave, without arousing suspicion. He would have to carry on with the daily round like the Maigrets.

Was he staying at one of the two or three luxury hotels in the town? It wasn't Maigret's business, but if he were in Lecoeur's place . . .

"Lecoeur is a first-class man," he murmured, by which he really meant: "He's sure to think of it. There aren't so many people staying in that class of hotel that . . ."

All the same, he would have liked to ferret about a bit for himself.

"We mustn't forget your appointment with Rian."

"Is it today?"

"No, tomorrow at four. . . ."

He would have to go through it all again, undressing, allowing himself to be prodded and then weighed, listening to the fair-haired young doctor solemnly laying down the law about how many glasses of water he should drink from then on. Perhaps he would prescribe water from one or more of the other springs this time.

He thought of Janvier, who had taken over his office, as Lucas was also away on holiday. He had gone to the mountains, somewhere around Chamonix.

Little boats in single file sailed gently into the wind and, one by one, tacked. Occasionally they saw a couple in a pedal boat. There was a wall all along the Allier, and beyond it, every fifty yards or so, was a miniature golf course.

Maigret caught himself looking back over his shoulder every time they passed a heavily built, elderly man.

To him, Hélène Lange's murderer was no longer a shadowy figure. He was beginning to take shape and assume a personality.

He was somewhere in this town, possibly on one of the promenades where the Maigrets so often walked. He was going through more or less the same motions as themselves, seeing the same sights, the sailing boats, the pedal boats, the yellow chairs in the park, and the constant ebb and flow of the crowds in the streets and gardens.

Rightly or wrongly, Maigret saw him with a woman at his side, perhaps, like himself, rather overweight, complaining of sore feet.

What did they talk about as they walked? What, for that matter, did all the other couples like them talk about?

He had killed Hélène Lange. . . . He was a wanted man. It needed only a careless word or an unguarded action to bring the police about his ears.

A ruined life. His name on the front page of every newspaper. His friends shocked and incredulous. The security of his home and family threatened.

From a luxurious hotel suite to a police cell.

It could all happen in a matter of minutes, or even seconds. At any time, he might feel a strange hand on his shoulder and, turning, see the glint of a police badge.

"You are Monsieur . . . , if I am not mistaken?"

Monsieur what? It was immaterial. His wife's astonished indignation . . .

"It's all a mistake, officer! . . . I know him so well. . . . I should. I'm his wife. . . . Anyone will tell you . . . Say something, Jean!"

Jean or Pierre or Gaston. . . .

Maigret was looking about him blankly, as though he had no idea where he was.

"And even so, he persists . . ."

"What does he persist in?"

"In trying to get at the truth."

"What are you talking about?"

"You know very well whom I'm talking about. . . . He telephoned Francine Lange. . . . He wants to meet her. . . ."

"Surely he won't run the risk of being caught?"

"If only she'd warned Lecoeur in time, he could have set a trap. . . . It's still not too late. . . . He's only heard her voice that once. . . . Lecoeur must have thought of it. . . . One would only need to plant a woman of about her age in Room 406. . . . Then when he rang . . ."

Maigret stopped short where he stood, clenched his fists, and uttered a grunt of fury.

"What the devil can he be at, taking that sort of risk?"

A man's voice answered:

"Hello! Whom do you wish to speak to?"

"Mademoiselle Francine Lange."

"Who is that?"

"Divisional Superintendent Lecoeur."

"Hold on, please."

Maigret was sitting opposite Lecoeur in the bare little office, listening on an extension.

"Hello! Can't it wait till morning?"

"No."

"Can you call back in half an hour?"

"I shall have left by then."

"We've only just got here. . . . Francine, Mademoiselle Lange, that is to say, is in the bath."

"Be good enough to ask her, from me, to get out of it. . . ."

Lecoeur winked at his colleague from Paris. Once again, they heard the voice of Lucien Romanel:

"She won't keep you a moment. She's just rubbing down with a towel. . . ."

"You don't seem to have made very good time. . . ."

"We had a blowout. . . . We wasted an hour trying to get a spare tire. . . . Here she is!"

"Hello!"

Her voice came across more faintly than the gigolo's.

"Mademoiselle Lange? . . . I understood from you this morning that you were planning to spend two or three more days in Vichy. . . ."

"I had intended to, but I changed my mind."

"May I ask why?"

"I could say: 'I just did, that's all.' There's no law against it, is there?"

"No, and there's no law against my taking out a summons to compel you to answer my questions. . . ."

"What difference does it make whether I'm in Vichy or La Rochelle?"

"It makes a great deal of difference to me. . . . I will repeat my question: What made you change your mind?"

"I was frightened. . . ."

"What of?"

"You know the answer to that. . . . I was frightened this morning, but I kept saying to myself that he wouldn't dare . . ."

"Could you be more explicit, please. Whom were you afraid of?"

"Of my sister's murderer. . . . I said to myself, if he attacked her, he's quite capable of attacking me. . . ."

"For what reason?"

"I don't know. . . ."

"Is it someone you know?"

"No. . . ."

"Haven't you the least idea who it could be?"

"No. . . ."

"And yet, having told me that you were staying on in Vichy, you suddenly decided, early this afternoon, that you couldn't get away fast enough. . . ."

"I was frightened. . . ."

"You're lying, or rather prevaricating. . . . You had a very particular reason for being frightened. . . ."

"I told you. . . . He killed my sister. . . . He might equally well . . ."

"For what reason?"

"I don't know. . . ."

"Are you telling me that you don't know why your sister was killed?"

"If I had known, I should have told you. . . ."

"In that case, why didn't you tell me about the phone call?"

He could imagine her wrapped in a bathrobe, with her hair still damp, surrounded by suitcases which she had not yet had time to unpack. Was there an extension in the apartment, he wondered? If not, Romanel must be straining his ears, trying to hear what he was saying.

"What telephone call?"

"The one you received last night at your hotel."

"I don't see what you . . ."

"Do you wish me to repeat what he said? Did he not, in fact, advise you to stay on in Vichy for a day or two longer? Did he not say that he would be getting in touch with you again, and that there could be big money in it for you?"

"I was scarcely listening. . . ."

"Why not?"

"Because I thought it was some sort of spoofing. . . . Isn't that how it struck you?"

"No."

A very emphatic "no," followed by a menacing silence. She was badly shaken, standing there, all those miles away, holding the receiver, and trying to think of something to say.

"I'm not a policeman. . . . I tell you I thought it was a spoof. . . ."

"Have you ever known it to happen before?"

"Not quite like that. . . ."

"Is it not a fact that you were so badly shaken by this telephone call that you felt you must get away from Vichy as soon as you possibly could?"

"Well, since you obviously don't believe me . . ."

"If you tell me the truth, I'll believe you. . . ."

"It was frightening. . . ."

"What?"

"The realization that the man was still at large in Vichy. . . . It's enough to frighten any woman, the thought of a strangler roaming the streets."

"Nevertheless, I haven't noticed any mass exodus from the hotels. . . . Had you ever heard that voice before?"

"I don't think so. . . ."

"A very distinctive voice. . . ."

"I didn't notice. . . . I was taken by surprise. . . ."

"Just now you were talking in terms of a spoof. . . ."

"I'm tired. . . . The day before yesterday I was still on holiday in Majorca. I've scarcely had an hour's sleep since then."

"That's no reason for lying to me."

"I'm not used to being harried in this way. And now you have me out of my bath, and subject me to an inquisition over the telephone. . . ."

"If you wish, I can arrange for my colleague in La Rochelle to call on you officially in an hour's time, and take down your statement in writing."

"I'm doing my best to answer your questions."

Maigret's eyes sparkled with pleasure. Lecoeur was doing splendidly. He himself would not have set about it in precisely that way, but it would come to the same thing in the end.

"You knew yesterday that the police were looking for your sister's murderer. . . . You must also have known that the smallest clue might prove invaluable. . . ."

"I suppose so, yes."

"Now, there was every reason to believe that your anonymous caller was the murderer. . . . You thought so yourself. . . . In fact, you were sure of it. . . . That's why you were so frightened . . . though I wouldn't have thought you were the type to be easily scared. . . ."

"Maybe I did think it might be the murderer, but I couldn't be sure."

"Anyone else in your place would have informed the police immediately. . . . Why didn't you?"

"Aren't you forgetting that I had just lost my sister—my only relative? . . . She was not even buried. . . ."

"I was at the funeral, remember? You didn't turn a hair."

"What do you know about my feelings?"

"Answer my questions. . . ."

"You might have prevented me from leaving."

"There can't be anything very urgent for you to attend to in La Rochelle, since you were supposed to be still on holiday in Majorca."

"I found the atmosphere oppressive. . . . The thought that that man . . ."

"Or the thought that, if you mentioned the telephone call, you might have to answer some awkward questions?"

"You might have wanted to use me as a decoy. . . . When he called back to suggest a meeting, you might have insisted on my going, and . . ."

"And?"

"Nothing. . . . I was frightened, that's all. . . ."

"Why was your sister murdered?"

"How should I know?"

"Someone whom she hadn't seen for years recognized her, followed her, and forced his way into her house. . . ."

"I thought perhaps she had come upon a burglar unexpectedly. . . ."

"You're not as naïve as all that. . . . There was something he wanted from her, the answer to a question, a vital question. . . ."

"What question?"

"That is precisely what I'm trying to find out. . . . Your sister came into some money, Mademoiselle Lange. . . ."

"From whom?"

"You tell me."

"She and I jointly inherited my mother's estate. . . . She wasn't a rich woman. . . . There was just a little dry goods shop in Marsilly, and a few thousand francs in a savings bank. . . ."

"Was her lover a rich man?"

"What lover?"

"The one who used to call at her apartment in Rue Notre-Dame-de-Lorette once or twice a week, when she was living in Paris."

"I know nothing about that."

"Did you never meet him?"

"No."

"Don't hang up, mademoiselle, I haven't nearly finished with you yet. . . . Hello!"

"I'm still here. . . ."

"Your sister was a stenographer. . . . You were a manicurist."

"Later I trained as a beautician."

"Quite so. . . . Two young girls from a humble home in Marsilly. . . . You both went to Paris. . . . You didn't go together, but for several years you were both living there at the same time. . . ."

"So what?"

"You claim to know nothing about your sister's life at that time. . . . You can't even tell me where she worked. . . ."

"In the first place, there was a very big difference in our ages. . . . And besides, we never got on, even as children. . . ."

"Let me finish. . . . Not so very long after, you turn up again in La Rochelle—a young woman still—as proprietress of a hairdressing salon, and that must have cost you a pretty penny. . . ."

"I paid a lump sum down, and the rest in yearly installments. . . ."

"We may have to go further into that later. . . . As for your sister, she—if I may put it that way—went out of circulation. . . . To begin with, she moved to Nice, where she spent five years. . . . Did you ever visit her there?"

"No."

"Did you know her address?"

"I got three or four postcards from her. . . ."

"In five years?"

"We had nothing to say to one another."

"And when she came to live in Vichy?"

"She said nothing to me about it."

"You never heard from her that she had moved here permanently, and bought a house?"

"I heard about it from friends."

"Who were these friends?"

"I don't remember. . . . Just some people who had run into her in Vichy. . . ."

"Did they speak to her?"

"They may have. . . . You're confusing me. . . ."

Lecoeur, very pleased with himself, once more winked at Maigret, who was struggling to relight his pipe, which had gone out, without putting down the receiver.

"Did you go to the Crédit Lyonnais?"

"Where?"

"In Vichy."

"No."

"Didn't it occur to you to wonder how much your sister had left you?"

"I shall leave all that to my lawyer here in La Rochelle. I don't understand those things. . . ."

"Indeed? You're a businesswoman, aren't you? Haven't you any idea how much money your sister had in the bank?"

Another long silence.

"I'm waiting. . . ."

"I can't answer that. . . ."

"Why not?"

"Because I don't know. . . ."

"Would it surprise you to learn that it was something approaching five hundred thousand francs?"

"That's a great deal of money."

She sounded rather matter-of-fact about it.

"A lot, I mean, for a girl coming from a little village like Marsilly, who worked as a stenographer in Paris for barely ten years."

"I wasn't in her confidence. . . ."

"Is it not a fact that when you took over the hairdressing

business in La Rochelle, it was your sister who provided the money in the first place? Think carefully before you answer, and remember that we have ways and means of getting at the truth."

Another long silence. Between two people who are face to face, silence is less alarming than in the course of a telephone conversation, when all contact is temporarily broken.

"It's surely not a thing you could forget!"

"She did lend me a little money. . . ."

"How much?"

"I'd have to ask my lawyer."

"At that time your sister was still living in Nice, was she not?"

"Possibly. . . . Yes. . . ."

"So you were in touch with her, not just through the exchange of postcards. . . . It seems more than likely that you went to see her, to explain the details of your project. . . ."

"I must have. . . ."

"A moment ago, you denied it."

"All these questions . . . I'm confused. . . . I don't know what I'm saying."

"It's not my questions that are confusing. . . . It's your answers."

"Have you finished with me?"

"Not quite. . . . And I must impress upon you once again that you would be well advised to stay on the line, otherwise I should be forced into taking more drastic measures. . . . This time I want a straight answer, yes or no. . . . In whose name was the deed of sale drawn up, yours or your sister's? In other words, was your sister, in fact, the owner?"

"No."

"Then you were?"

"No."

"Who, then?"

"We owned it jointly."

"In other words, you and she were partners, and yet you've been trying to make me believe that there was no contact between you. . . ."

"It's a family matter, and nobody's business but our own. . . ."

"May I remind you that this is a case of murder?"

"That has nothing to do with it."

"Are you so sure?"

"I hardly think . . ."

"You hardly think . . . In that case why did you rush away from Vichy like a madwoman?"

"Have you any more questions to ask me?"

Maigret nodded, took a pencil from the desk, and scribbled a few words on the pad.

"One moment. . . . Don't hang up. . . ."

"Will you be long?"

"Here it is. . . . You had a child, did you not?"

"I told you so."

"Was it born in Paris?"

"No."

"Why not?"

All Maigret's note said was: "Where was the child born? Where was the birth registered?"

Lecoeur was spinning it out, possibly in order to impress his famous colleague from Paris.

"I didn't want it generally known. . . ."

"Where did you go?"

"Burgundy."

"Where exactly?"

"Mesnil-le-Mont."

"Is that a village?"

"Scarcely more than a hamlet, really."

"Is there a resident doctor?"

"There wasn't then."

"And you chose to have your child in this remote hamlet, out of reach of a doctor?"

"How do you suppose our mothers managed?"

"Was it you who chose the place? Had you been there before?"

"No, I found it on the map."

"Did you go alone?"

"I can't help wondering how you treat criminals, if you can torture innocent people in this way. . . . I haven't done anything. . . . In fact . . ."

"I asked you whether you were alone."

"No."

"That's better. It's much simpler, you know, to tell the truth than to lie. Who went with you?"

"My sister."

"Do you mean your sister Hélène?"

"I have no other."

"This was when you were both living in Paris, and never met except by chance. . . . You had no idea where she worked. . . . For all you knew, she might have been a kept woman. . . ."

"It was no business of mine. . . ."

"You didn't get on. . . . You saw as little as possible of one another, and yet, all of a sudden, she dropped everything, gave up her job, and went with you to some god-forsaken hamlet in Burgundy. . . ."

There was nothing she could say.

"How long were you there?"

"A month."

"In the local hotel?"

"It was just an inn, really."

"Did you have a midwife?"

"I don't know whether she was qualified, but she acted as midwife to all the women in the district."

"What was her name?"

"She was about sixty-five at the time. She must be dead by now."

"Don't you remember her name?"

"Madame Radèche."

"Did you register the birth?"

"Of course."

"You, personally?"

"I was still in bed. . . . My sister went with the innkeeper. He witnessed her signature."

"Did you go yourself later to look at the entry?"

"Why on earth should I?"

"Have you a copy of the birth certificate?"

"It was so long ago . . ."

"Where did you go next?"

"Look here, I can't take any more of this. . . . If you must put me through hours of questioning, come and see me here. . . ."

Unmoved, Lecoeur asked:

"Where did you take the child?"

"To Saint-André. Saint-André-du-Lavion, in the Vosges."

"By car?"

"I didn't have a car then. . . ."

"And your sister?"

"She never learned to drive."

"Did she go with you?"

"Yes! Yes! Yes! I'm sick of all this, do you hear me? Sick of it! Sick of it! Sick of it!"

Whereupon she hung up.

6

"**W**HAT'S ON YOUR mind?"

In every marriage where husband and wife have been together for years, each observing the actions and emotions of the other, there are times when one partner, baffled by the expression on the other's face, asks diffidently:

"What's on your mind?"

Madame Maigret, it must be said, needed to be very sure that her husband was not under strain before she would ask this question, for there were certain boundaries in their relationship which she felt she had no right to overstep.

Following the long telephone call to La Rochelle, they had dined quietly in the relaxing atmosphere of the white dining room of their hotel, with its potted palms in the alcoves, and wine bottles and flowers on the tables.

Ostensibly, no one paid any attention to the Maigrets, though they were in fact the focus of discreet interest, admiration, and affection.

They were now taking their evening walk. From time to time there was a rumble of thunder in the sky, and the still evening air was churned up every few minutes by little flurries of wind.

They had come, almost as if by accident, to Rue du Bourbonnais. There was a light showing in one of the upper windows, in the room occupied by the stout widow, Madame Vireveau. The Maleskis were out, walking, possibly, or at the cinema.

On the ground floor, all was darkness and silence. The furniture had been put back in place. Hélène Lange had been blotted out.

Sooner or later, no doubt, the contents of the house would be carted into the street, and the props and chattels which had once been part of a human life would fall under the hammer of some wise-cracking auctioneer.

Had Francine taken away the photographs? It seemed unlikely. Probably she would not even bother to send for them. They, too, would be sold.

They had reached the park where, inevitably it seemed, they always ended up, when Madame Maigret ventured to put her question.

"I'm thinking about Lecoeur. He really is first-class at his job," replied her husband.

The manner in which the Superintendent from Clermont-Ferrand had hammered away at Francine, giving her no time to collect herself, was a good example. He had made the fullest use of the facts at his disposal, to get the fuller information he needed to carry the inquiry a stage further.

Why, then, was Maigret not entirely satisfied? No doubt he would have set about it differently. But then what two men, even when working to the same end, go about it in precisely the same way?

It was not a question of method. Maigret was, if anything, a little envious of his ebullient colleague's assurance and self-confidence.

No, it was something else. To Maigret, the lady in lilac was not just a murder victim. He was not primarily concerned with the kind of life she had led, nor with what had happened to her. He was beginning to know her as an individual and, almost without realizing it, to penetrate the mystery of her personality.

And while he was walking back to his hotel, pondering, to the exclusion of all else, the relationship between the two sisters, Lecoeur was bounding off, without a care in the world, to keep his appointment with the examining magistrate.

What could the examining magistrate really know about a case like this one, closeted in his office, and seeing nothing of life but what was laid before him, encapsulated in the official reports?

Two sisters in a village on the Atlantic coast, a little shop next door to the church. Maigret knew the village, whose people reaped a harvest from both land and sea. A village dominated by four or five big landowners, who were also the owners of oyster beds and mussel farms.

He recalled the women, old women, young women, and little girls, setting out at daybreak, sometimes even at night, depending on the tides, dressed in rubber boots, thick fishermen's jerseys, and shabby men's jackets.

Down on the shore, they gathered the oysters which lay exposed at low tide, while the men scraped the mussels off the wickerwork, which was pegged down by stakes.

Few of these girls were ever educated beyond the most elementary stage, and even the boys fared little better, at least at the time when the Lange girls were growing up.

Hélène was the exception. She had gone to school in the town, and had reached a sufficiently high standard to go to work in an office.

Cycling to work in the morning and returning at night, she was quite the young lady.

And later, her sister too had somehow contrived to better herself.

They are both living in Paris. . . . They are never to be seen in the village now . . . they think themselves too good for us. . . .

The girls who had once been their playmates were still going out every morning to gather oysters and mussels. They had married and borne children, who, in their turn, had romped in the square outside the church.

It was cold-blooded determination that had got Hélène Lange what she wanted. Even as a child, she had turned her back on the life that should have been hers. She had mapped out for herself a different life, and retreated into a world of her own, peopled only by the characters in her favorite romantic novels.

She had been unable to stomach Balzac. His world had reminded her too much of Marsilly, her mother's shop, the freezing oyster beds, and the roughened hands of the women.

Francine, too, had managed to escape, in her own fashion. At fifteen, she had had her eyes opened by a taxi driver. She was plump and seductive. Men were attracted by her saucy smile. And why not, she thought, why not turn her charms to good account?

And had she not, in the end, succeeded?

The elder sister had acquired a house in Vichy and amassed a small fortune. The younger had chosen to return home, and flaunt her wealth in the most elegant beauty salon in town.

Lecoeur did not feel the need to enter into their lives, to understand them. He uncovered facts, from which he drew conclusions, and, in consequence, was spared the discomforts of an uneasy conscience.

Intimately concerned with the lives of these two women there was a man. Unidentified, he was nevertheless here in Vichy, in a hotel bedroom, in the park, in one of the gaming rooms of the Grand Casino, somewhere, anywhere.

This man was a killer. And he was caught in a trap. He must know that the police, with their formidable resources, were closing in on him, that the invisible cordon was tightening about him, and that, very soon, the impartial hand of the law would be laid on his shoulder.

He too had a whole life behind him. He had been a child, a youth, he had fallen in love, almost certainly married, or else why should he, the nameless man who had called once or twice a week at Rue Notre-Dame-de-Lorette, not have been able to stay more than an hour at a time?

Hélène had disappeared from Paris. When next heard of, she was living a solitary life in Nice, deliberately shunning attention, it seemed, in that town crowded with people who were all strangers to one another.

Now they knew that, before settling in Nice, she had gone to a tiny village in Burgundy, lived in the local inn for a month, to be with her sister when she gave birth to a child.

Maigret was beginning to understand the two women, but he needed to know more about the man. He was tall and heavily built. He had a distinctive voice, because he suffered from asthma, which was no doubt what had brought him to Vichy in the first place.

He had committed a murder, and gained nothing by it. He had

gone to Rue du Bourbonnais, not to take a life, but to ask a question.

Hélène Lange had brought about her own death. She had refused to answer. Even when he had seized her by the throat— probably just to frighten her—she had not spoken, and her silence had cost her her life.

He could have abandoned his quest. It would have been the sensible thing to do. Any further step he took was bound to entail grave risks. The machinery of the law had already been set in motion.

Had he known previously of the existence of the sister, Francine Lange? She claimed that he had not, and she could be telling the truth.

He could have learned from the newspapers that Hélène Lange had a sister, and that she had just arrived in Vichy. He had got it into his head that he must speak to her, and, with astonishing thoroughness and guile, had managed to track her down to her hotel.

Héléne had refused to speak, but would the younger sister prove equally stubborn, if faced with the added inducement of a substantial bribe?

The man was rich, a person of some standing. It must be so, or he could not have afforded to part with more than five hundred thousand francs over a period of a few years.

Five hundred thousand francs in return for what? In return for nothing. He did not even know the address of the woman to whom he sent the money, poste restante, at the various towns designated by her up and down the country.

Had he been able to find her, would Hélène Lange have died sooner?

"Stay on in Vichy for another two or three days. . . ."

It was his last chance. He had to take it, even if it meant getting caught. He would phone her again. It wouldn't be easy, but he would find a way. He would do it as soon as he could escape from his wife without arousing suspicion.

But by now there was scarcely a public telephone booth in the town which was not being watched by one of Lecoeur's men.

Had Maigret been right in believing that he would not risk telephoning from a bar, a café, or his hotel bedroom?

He and his wife walked past one of these public telephone booths. Through the glass panes they could see a teen-age girl chattering away with cheerful animation.

"Do you think he'll be caught?"

"Any time now, yes."

Because here was a man with an overriding obsession. Very likely he had lived with it for years. Probably ever since the very first monthly payment, he had been waiting and hoping for the chance meeting which had occurred at last, after fifteen years.

It might well be that he was a sound businessman, very level-headed as far as his everyday life was concerned.

Fifteen years of brooding . . .

He had squeezed too hard. He never meant to kill her. Or else . . .

Maigret stopped dead in his tracks, right in the middle of a busy boulevard. His wife, with a quick, sidelong glance at his face, stopped too.

"Or else, he came face to face with something so monstrous, so unforeseen, so shocking . . .

"I wonder how Lecoeur will set about it," he murmured.

"Set about what?"

"Getting him to make a clean breast of it. . . ."

"He'll have to find him and arrest him first. . . ."

"He'll give himself up. . . ."

It would be a relief to him to surrender . . . an end to lying and contriving. . . .

"I hope he's not armed."

Because there was a wife in the case, Maigret could envisage an alternative outcome. Instead of giving himself up, the man might decide to end it, once for all. . . .

Had Lecoeur warned his subordinates to proceed with caution? It wasn't for Maigret to interfere. In this instance he was merely a passive spectator, keeping well in the background, as far as was possible.

Even if he did not resist arrest, was there any reason why he should talk? It would not mitigate his crime, nor carry any weight with a jury. To them, he would be just another strangler, and, whatever the provocation, in such a case leniency, still less pity, was not to be hoped for.

"What you really mean is, you wish you were handling it yourself!"

She found that in Vichy she could say things to him that, in Paris, she would never have dared to utter. Was it because they were on holiday?

Because, as a result of being together all day and every day, a new intimacy had grown up between them?

She could almost hear his thoughts.

"I wonder . . . No . . . I don't think so. . . ."

Why should he worry? He was here for a rest, for a thorough clean-out of the system, to use Doctor Rian's phrase. In fact, he had an appointment with the doctor for tomorrow, and then, for half an hour at least, he would be just another patient, preoccupied with his digestion, his liver, his pulse rate, his blood pressure, and his fits of giddiness.

How old was Lecoeur? Barely five years younger than himself. In five years' time, Lecoeur too would be thinking about retirement, and wondering what on earth he would find to do with himself when the time came.

They were behind the casino now, walking past the town's two most luxurious hotels. Long, sleek cars slumbered along the curb. In the garden, to one side of the revolving door, a man in a dinner jacket was leaning back in a deck chair, enjoying the cool of the evening.

A crystal chandelier filled the entrance hall with a blaze of light. They could see oriental carpets, marble pillars, and the liveried hall porter bending forward to answer an inquiry from an old lady in evening dress.

This hotel, or the one next to it, was perhaps where the man was staying. If not, then he was probably at the Pavillon Sévigné, near the Pont Bellerive. Beside the elevator stood a very young page-boy, but not too young to be looking about him with a very supercilious air.

Lecoeur had concentrated his attention on the weakest link, in other words, Francine Lange, and she, taken by surprise, had revealed a good deal.

Presumably he would take the first opportunity of questioning her further. Was there anything more to be got out of her, or had she told all she knew?

"I won't be a minute. . . . I must get some tobacco. . . ."

He went into a noisy bar, where a great many people were looking at a television screen set up on a pedestal above eye level. There was a strong smell of wine and beer. The bald barman was filling glasses without a moment's pause, and a waitress in black dress and white apron was going to and from the tables with laden trays of drinks.

Without thinking, he glanced at the telephone booth, at the far end near the washrooms. It had a glass door. There was no one in it.

"Three ounces of shag."

They were not far from the Hôtel de la Bérézina, and, as they approached, they saw young Dicelle waiting on the steps.

"Could I have a word with you, sir?"

Madame Maigret, leaving them to it, went in to collect her key from the desk.

"Let's walk, shall we?"

Their footsteps echoed in the deserted street.

"Did Lecoeur send you?"

"Yes, he's been on the phone with me. He'd gone home to Clermont, to his wife and kids. . . ."

"How many children has he?"

"Four. The eldest is eighteen. He's shaping up to be a swimming champion. . . ."

"What's been happening?"

"There are ten of us watching the telephone booths. The Super can't spare enough men for all of them, so we're concentrating on those in the center, especially the ones closest to the big hotels."

"Have you made an arrest?"

"Not yet. . . . I'm waiting for the Super. . . . He should be on his way by now. . . . There's been a slip-up, I'm afraid. . . . My fault, entirely. . . . I was on watch near the phone booth in Boulevard Kennedy. . . . It wasn't too difficult to keep out of sight, with all those trees. . . ."

"And you saw a man go in to use the telephone?"

"Yes. . . . A big, heavily built man, answering to the description. He was behaving suspiciously. . . . He kept peering through the door . . . but he didn't see me. . . .

"He began dialing a number, and then, all of a sudden, changed his mind. Maybe I poked my head out too far. I don't know. At any rate, he dialed the first three figures, then thought better of it and came out. . . ."

"And you made no attempt to stop him?"

"My instructions were not to interfere with him in any way, but to follow him. To my surprise, there was a woman waiting for him in the shadows, not twenty yards away. . . ."

"What was she like?"

"Distinguished-looking, well-dressed, fiftyish. . . ."

"Did you get the impression that there was any collusion between them?"

"No. She just took his arm, and they walked back to the Hôtel des Ambassadeurs."

The hotel with the sumptuous entrance hall and the crystal chandelier, which Maigret had stood and gazed at barely an hour earlier.

"What next?"

"Nothing. The man went up to the desk and got his key from the hall porter, who wished him good night."

"Did you get a good look at him?"

"Enough to know him again. . . . I got the impression that he was older than his wife. . . . Nearer sixty, I'd say. They got into the elevator, and I didn't see them again. . . ."

"Was he wearing a dinner jacket?"

"No, a very well-cut dark suit. . . . He has graying hair brushed back, a healthy complexion, and, I think, a small white mustache. . . ."

"Did you make inquiries at the desk?"

"Of course. He and his wife have a suite—a large bedroom with an adjoining sitting room—on the first floor, number 105. This is their first visit to Vichy, but they are friends of the proprietor of the hotel, who also owns a hotel in La Baule. The man's name is Louis Pélardeau. He's an industrialist, and lives in Paris, Boulevard Suchet."

"Is he here for the cure?"

"Yes. . . . I asked the hall porter whether he had an unusually distinctive voice. He said yes, he suffered from asthma. . . . They're both being treated by Doctor Rian."

"Is Madame Pélardeau taking the cure as well?"

"Yes. . . . It seems they have no children. . . . They've joined up with some friends from Paris who are staying in the same hotel, and they share a table with them at meals. Occasionally they all go to the theater together."

"Have you got someone watching the hotel?"

"I've put a local man on it, until one of our people gets there, which should be about now. The local fellow, though he had every right to tell me to go to hell, was most co-operative."

Dicelle was obviously thrilled by the whole business.

"He must be the man we're looking for, don't you think?"

Maigret did not answer at once. He lit his pipe with great deliberation. They were less than a hundred yards from the house of the lady in lilac.

"I think he is," he said with a sigh.

The young detective stared at him in amazement. From the way the Chief Superintendent said it, one would really think he regretted it!

"I'm to meet my boss outside the hotel. He'll be there in twenty minutes at the outside."

"Did he say whether he wanted me there?"

"He said you'd be sure to come."

"I'll have to let my wife know first."

In the intermission, crowds of people poured out of the Grand Casino theater into the street. Most of the women were wearing sleeveless dresses, cut very low. They and their escorts looked up apprehensively into the sky, which was streaked with intermittent lightning flashes.

Low clouds swirled past, and, worse, to the west the stars were blotted out by a dense, threatening blanket of cloud, moving slowly toward the town.

Outside the Hôtel des Ambassadeurs Maigret and Dicelle waited in silence, watched by the hall porter who, behind his counter of polished wood, stood guard over his nest of pigeon-holes and panel of dangling keys.

Just as the first few heavy drops of cold rain were falling, Lecoeur arrived, and, at the same moment, a bell rang, signaling the end of the intermission. It took him some minutes of careful steering and maneuvering to park his car, and when he finally joined them he asked, with a worried frown:

"Is he in his room?"

Dicelle quickly reassured him:

"Number 105 on the first floor. His windows overlook the street. . . ."

"Is his wife with him?"

"Yes. They went up together."

A figure, a uniformed policeman whom Maigret did not recognize, loomed up out of the shadows.

"Am I to stay on watch?" he whispered.

"Yes."

Lecoeur, taking shelter in the doorway, lit a cigarette.

"I am not empowered to make an arrest during the hours between sunset and sunrise, unless a breach of the law is actually committed in my presence."

There was more than a hint of irony in his voice as he cited this section of the Code of Criminal Procedure, adding thoughtfully:

"What's more, there isn't enough evidence to justify a warrant for his arrest."

It sounded like an appeal to Maigret to help him out of his difficulty, but Maigret did not rise to the bait.

"I don't like leaving him to stew all night. . . . He must have guessed that he's a marked man—why else should he have changed his mind about telephoning?—and I'm puzzled by the presence of his wife, so close to the phone booth." Almost reproachfully, he added:

"What do you say, Chief?"

"I have nothing to say. . . ."

"What would you do, in my place?"

"I shouldn't be inclined to wait, either. . . . I daresay, by now, they're undressing for bed. . . . I should try and avoid going up to their suite. . . . The discreet thing would be to send up a little note."

"Saying what, for instance?"

"That there's someone downstairs who wishes to speak to him on a personal matter. . . ."

"Do you think he'll come?"

"I'm sure of it."

"You'd better wait out here, Dicelle. It wouldn't do for us all to be seen going in together."

Lecoeur went up to the inquiry desk, leaving Maigret standing in the middle of the vast entrance hall, looking about him vaguely. The hall, brilliantly lit by chandeliers, was almost empty, except for an elderly foursome, two men and two women, a long way off—in another world, almost—who were playing bridge. Distance and the deliberateness of their movements made them seem unreal, like characters in a film sequence played in slow motion.

The page-boy, with an envelope in his hand, went briskly up to the elevator.

He heard Lecoeur's voice, muffled:

"Well, we'll soon see . . ."

Then, as though struck by the solemnity of the occasion, he removed his hat. Maigret, too, was bareheaded, holding his straw hat in his hand. Outside, the storm had broken, and the rain was pelting down. They could see a little group of people huddled for shelter on the hotel steps.

In a very short time the page-boy was back.

"Monsieur Pélardeau will be down directly," he announced.

They were both watching the elevator. They could not help themselves. Lecoeur was smoothing his mustache with his forefinger, and Maigret could sense his excitement.

Somewhere up there, a bell was ringing. The elevator went up, stopped for a moment, and then reappeared.

Out of it stepped a man in a dark suit, with a florid complexion and graying hair. He looked inquiringly around the hall, and then, somewhat hesitantly, came up to the two men.

Lecoeur, who was holding his Superintendent's badge discreetly in the palm of his hand, allowed the man to catch a glimpse of it.

"I should be obliged if I could have a few words with you, Monsieur Pélardeau."

"Now?"

Yes, there was the hoarse voice, just as it had been described to them. The man did not lose his head. There was no doubt that he recognized Maigret, and seemed surprised to find him playing a passive role.

"Yes, now. My car is at the door, if you will be so good as to accompany me to my office."

The florid cheeks turned a shade pale. Pélardeau was a man of about sixty, but his carriage was remarkably upright, and there was great dignity in his bearing and expression.

"I don't suppose it would do any good to refuse."

"None. It would only make matters worse."

A glance at the hall porter, then another at the little far-off alcove, where the four bridge players were still to be seen. A quick look outside at the pouring rain.

"I don't suppose it would be possible for me to get my hat and raincoat from my suite?"

Maigret, meeting Lecoeur's inquiring glance, looked up at the ceiling. It would be cruel, as well as pointless, to leave the wife in suspense up there. It looked like being a long night, and there was little hope of the husband's returning to reassure her.

Lecoeur murmured:

"If you would care to write Madame a note . . . unless she already knows?"

"No. . . . What shall I say?"

"I don't know. . . . That you have been detained longer than you expected?"

The man went up to the desk.

"Can you let me have a sheet of writing paper, Marcel?"

He seemed saddened, rather than shocked or frightened. Using the ball-point pen chained to the desk, he scribbled a few words, declining the envelope that the hall porter held out to him.

"Send this up in five or ten minutes' time, will you?"

"Certainly, sir."

The hall porter looked as though he would have liked to say something more, but, unable to find the right words, merely bowed his head.

"This way."

As Dicelle, by this time sopping wet, opened the rear door, Lecoeur stood by, murmuring instructions in a low voice.

"Get in, please."

The industrialist bent down, and got into the car first.

"You too, Chief."

Maigret, aware that his colleague would not wish their prisoner to be left alone in the back of the car, obeyed. In no time, they were driving through streets crowded with people hurrying for shelter, and huddling together under the trees. There were even people sheltering on the bandstand, under the canopy.

The car turned into the forecourt of the Police Station in Avenue Victoria, and Lecoeur spoke a few words to the officer on duty. There were only one or two lights turned on in the entrance. It seemed a long time to Maigret before they reached Lecoeur's office.

"In here. It's a bit Spartan, but I didn't want to take you all the way to Clermont-Ferrand at this stage."

He removed his hat, but did not venture to take off his jacket, which, like Lecoeur's and Maigret's, was sopping wet about the shoulders. In contrast with the sudden drop in temperature outdoors, the room was very hot and stuffy.

"Take a seat."

Maigret had retreated into his usual corner, and was watching the industrialist, under cover of filling his pipe. The man's face was absolutely impassive, as he looked from one police officer to the other, wondering, no doubt, why Maigret was not playing a more active role.

Lecoeur, playing for time, pulled a memo pad and pencil toward him, and murmured, as though thinking aloud:

"Anything you say at this stage will be off the record. This is not an official interrogation."

The man nodded assent.

"Your name is Louis Pélardeau, and you are an industrialist. You live in Paris, in Boulevard Suchet."

"That's right."

"Married, I take it?"

"Yes."

"Any children?"

After an appreciable pause, he said with an odd note of bitterness:

"No."

"You are here for the cure?"

"Yes."

"Is this your first visit to Vichy?"

"I've passed through it in the car. . . ."

"You've never come here with the specific intention of meeting any particular person?"

"No."

Lecoeur inserted a cigarette into his holder, and lit it. There followed an oppressive silence, then Lecoeur said:

"You know, I presume, why I have brought you here?"

The man, his face still impassive, took time for thought. But Maigret could now see that his blank expression was a sign not of self-control but rather of profound emotional shock.

He was completely numbed, and it was hard to tell whether he realized even where he was, as Lecoeur's voice rang in his ears.

"I would rather not answer that. . . ."

"You came here of your own free will. . . ."

"Yes. . . ."

"You were not unprepared?"

The man turned to Maigret, as though appealing for help, and repeated wearily:

"I would rather not answer that. . . . "

Lecoeur, aware that this was getting him nowhere, doodled on his pad before returning to the attack.

"Soon after your arrival in Vichy, you had an unexpected encounter with someone you had not seen for fifteen years. . . ."

The man's eyes were watering a little, but not with tears. It was perhaps due to the harsh glare of the single naked bulb, which provided all the lighting there was in this bare, usually unoccupied room.

"Was it your intention, when you went out with your wife tonight, to make a telephone call from a public booth?"

After a moment's hesitation, the man nodded.

"In other words, your wife knows nothing?"

"About the telephone call?"

"If you like to put it that way."

"No."

"You mean that there are some matters regarding which she is not in your confidence?"

"You're absolutely right."

"Nevertheless, you did go into a public phone booth. . . ."

"She decided, at the last minute, to come with me. . . . I didn't want to put it off any longer. . . . I told her I'd left the key of our suite in the door, and that I thought I'd better let the hall porter know. . . ."

"Why was it that you didn't even finish dialing the number?"

"I had a feeling I was being watched. . . ."

"Did you see anyone?"

"I saw something move behind a tree. . . . Besides, by then I had realized that it was pointless. . . ."

"Why was that?"

He did not answer, but sat motionless, with his hands lying flat on his knees. They were plump, white, well-kept hands.

"Smoke, if you wish."

"I don't smoke."

"You don't mind if I do?"

"My wife smokes a lot . . . far too much. . . ."

"You suspected that the call might be taken by someone other than Francine Lange?"

Once again he did not answer, but neither did he deny it.

"You telephoned her last night, and told her that you would call again to fix an appointment. . . . It's my belief that, when you went into that phone booth this evening, you had already, in your own mind, fixed on a time and place."

"I'm sorry, but I can't help you there. . . ."

He was having difficulty with his breathing, and wheezing slightly as he spoke.

"I assure you, it's not that I want to be obstructive. . . ."

"You would prefer to consult your lawyer first?"

He made a sweeping gesture with his right hand, as though to brush this suggestion aside.

"All the same, you will need a lawyer."

"I'll do whatever the law requires of me."

"You must understand, Monsieur Pélardeau, that, as of now, you are no longer a free man."

Lecoeur showed some delicacy in avoiding the word "arrest," and Maigret was glad of it.

The man had made an impression on both of them. Here, in this tiny office with its dingy walls, sitting on a rough wooden chair, he seemed larger than life-size and this impression of stature was enhanced by his astonishingly calm and dignified manner.

Both men had, in their time, questioned many hundreds of suspects. It took a lot to impress them, but this man was truly impressive.

"We could postpone this conversation until tomorrow, but, as I'm sure you'll agree, it would serve no useful purpose."

This, the man seemed to be thinking, was the Superintendent's business, not his.

"What is your particular branch of industry?"

"Steel pressings."

This was a subject on which he could talk freely, and he volunteered one or two particulars, just to show that he was willing to co-operate where he could.

"I inherited a small wire-drawing business near Le Havre from my father. Then gradually I was able to expand and build a plant at Rouen, and another in Strasbourg."

"In other words, you run a very flourishing business?"

"Yes."

He seemed almost to be apologizing for it.

"Your offices are in Paris, I take it?"

"Head office, yes. We have more up-to-date office buildings in

Rouen and Strasbourg, but, for sentimental reasons, I've always kept the old head office in Boulevard Voltaire."

It was all past history to him. . . . This evening, in the space of time it took a liveried page-boy to deliver a written message, the greater part of his world had crumbled in ruins.

Probably because he was aware of this, he was willing to talk about it quite freely.

"Have you been married long?"

"Thirty years."

"A woman by the name of Hélène Lange was at one time in your employment, was she not?"

"I'd rather not answer that."

This was his unvarying response, whenever they stepped on dangerous ground.

"You do realize, don't you, Monsieur Pélardeau, that you're making things very difficult for me?"

"I'm sorry."

"If it is your intention to deny the facts which I shall lay before you, I would rather you said so now."

"How can I tell in advance what you are going to say?"

"Are you telling me that you are not guilty?"

"No. . . . In a sense, I am. . . ."

Lecoeur and Maigret exchanged glances. He had made this terrible admission so simply and unaffectedly, without the slightest change of expression.

Maigret was thinking of the park with its great, spreading trees, its expanses of grass which, under the lamp standards, seemed too green to be true, its bandstand and garishly uniformed musicians.

In particular, he was thinking of the long, narrow face of Hélène Lange as he had seen it when, to him and his wife, she was merely the nameless woman they had christened "the lady in lilac."

"Did you know Mademoiselle Lange?"

He sat motionless, gasping as though he were going to choke. It was, in fact, an attack of asthma. He grew purple in the face. He took a handkerchief from his pocket, held it over his open mouth, and was soon doubled up with a fit of uncontrollable coughing.

Maigret was thankful not to be in his colleague's seat. Let someone else do the dirty work for once.

"I told you . . ."

"Please take your time. . . ."

With eyes streaming, he fought to master the attack of coughing, but it persisted for several minutes.

When at last he straightened up, still red in the face, mopped his forehead and said: "I'm very sorry," the words were scarcely audible.

"I get these attacks several times a day. . . . Doctor Rian tells me that the cure will do me good. . . ."

He seemed suddenly struck with the irony of this remark.

"I should say, would have done me good. . . ."

They shared the same doctor, he and Maigret. Both had undressed in the same gleaming office, both had stretched out on the same couch, over which a white sheet was spread. . . .

"What was it you asked me?"

"Whether you knew Hélène Lange."

"There's no point in denying it."

"You hated her, didn't you?"

If it had been possible, Maigret would have signaled to his colleague that he was on the wrong track.

And indeed the man was staring at Lecoeur in genuine amazement. When, at last, he spoke, this sixty-year-old man sounded as artless as a child.

"Why?" he whispered. "Why should I have hated her?"

He turned to Maigret, as if appealing to him for support.

"Were you in love with her?"

His response was a puzzled frown, which surprised them both. Clearly the last two questions had thrown him off balance and, in some strange sense, changed everything.

"I don't quite see . . ." he stammered.

Then, once more, he looked from one to the other. At Maigret, he looked hard and long.

It was as though they were somehow at cross-purposes.

"You used to go and see her at her apartment in Rue Notre-Dame-de-Lorette."

"Yes," in a tone of voice that implied, "What of it?"

"I presume that it was you who paid her rent?"

He confirmed this with a slight nod.

"Was she your secretary?"

"She was a member of my staff."

"Did your affair with her last long, several years?"

It was obvious that they were still at cross-purposes.

"I used to go and see her once or twice a week. . . ."

"Did your wife know?"

"Obviously not."

"She never found out?"

"Never."

"Doesn't she know, even now?"

The poor man clearly felt that he was beating his head against a brick wall.

"Not even now. . . . All that has nothing to do with . . ."

Nothing to do with what? With the murder? With the telephone calls? They weren't speaking the same language, but neither realized it. No wonder they were baffled by their inability to get across to one another.

7

Lecoeur's glance fell on the telephone on his desk. He seemed about to pick up the receiver when he caught sight of a small white bell-push, and pressed that instead.

"Do you mind? . . . I don't know where this rings, or even if it's working. . . . We'll soon find out at any rate. . . . If anyone comes . . ."

He was playing for time. They waited in silence, avoiding one another's eyes. Of the three men, Pélardeau was probably the most self-possessed, on the surface at least. Admittedly, as far as he was concerned, he had staked his all, and had nothing more to lose.

They heard at last, a long way off, the ringing sound of footsteps on an iron staircase, then on the linoleum of a corridor, drawing nearer, followed by a discreet knock on the door.

"Come in!"

It was a very young, well-scrubbed policeman in uniform. In contrast to the three older men, he fairly radiated youthful vitality.

Lecoeur, who felt something of an interloper in this place, said:

"I wonder if you could spare a moment?"

"Of course, sir. We were just passing the time playing cards."

"We're going out for a moment. Be so good as to stay with Monsieur Pélardeau until we get back."

"It'll be a pleasure, sir."

The young officer, having not the least idea of what it was all about, kept darting puzzling glances at the well-groomed visitor. He could not but be impressed.

A minute or two later, Lecoeur and Maigret were standing in the doorway. The steps leading down to the forecourt were protected by a glass roof, but they could see a glittering curtain of rain in the darkness beyond.

"I was suffocating up there. . . . I thought you might be glad of a breath of fresh air too."

The heavy storm clouds, streaked from time to time with lightning flashes, were now overhead, and the wind had dropped.

The road was deserted, except for an occasional slow-moving car splashing through the puddles.

The head of the C.I.D. in Clermont-Ferrand, lighting a cigarette, watched the rain beating down on the paved drive, and dripping from the trees in the grounds.

"I know I was making a hash of it, Chief. I ought to have asked you to take over. . . ."

"He was at the end of his tether, numbed with shock. At first, there didn't seem any point in answering your questions. He was determined not to speak, whatever the cost. But, little by little, you won his confidence. What more could I have done?"

"I thought . . ."

"You succeeded, up to a point, in breaking down the barriers. . . . He was beginning to take an interest . . . to co-operate even. . . . Then something went wrong. . . . I don't understand it. It must have been something you said."

"What?"

"I don't know. . . . All I know is that it switched him off like a light. . . . I never took my eyes off his face, and at one point I caught a look of absolute astonishment and bewilderment. One would have to go back over every word that was said. . . . He had been so sure we knew more."

"More about what?"

Maigret sucked at his pipe in silence for a moment.

"Something that to him is patently obvious, but that we have missed. . . ."

"Maybe I should have had someone sitting in, taking a record of the interview. . . ."

"You wouldn't have got a word out of him. . . ."

"Are you sure you wouldn't prefer to take over from here, Chief?"

"Not only would it be irregular, a point which his lawyer might well exploit at a later stage, but I shouldn't handle it any better than you. Quite possibly not so well."

"I honestly don't know where I go from here. The worst of it is that, murderer though he is, I can't help feeling sorry for him. . . . I'm just not used to handling this sort of man. . . . He doesn't belong in the realm of crime. . . . When we came out of the hotel just now, I felt as though he had left a world in ruins behind him. . . ."

"So did he."

"Do you really think so?"

"He refused to play on our sympathy, like a beggar in the streets. . . . He was determined to keep some semblance of dignity, whatever the cost. . . ."

"Will he break down in the end, I wonder?"

"He'll talk."

"Tonight?"

"I shouldn't be surprised."

"Should we carry on here, or . . . ?"

Maigret opened his mouth as though about to speak, then, apparently thinking better of it, closed it again, and relit his pipe. At last he said evasively:

"Don't spring it on him all at once, but you might try leading up to the subject of Mesnil-le-Mont. You could, for instance, ask him if he'd ever been there."

Lecoeur couldn't make out whether he himself attached any great importance to this.

"Do you think the answer will be yes?"

"I couldn't say."

"Why should he have gone there, and what possible bearing could it have on what happened here in Vichy?"

"It was just a thought," replied Maigret apologetically. "When one is adrift, one clutches at straws. . . ."

There was another very young policeman on duty near the entrance, and, in his eyes, the two men standing talking on the stairs were persons of tremendous importance, who had reached the very pinnacle of eminence.

"I wouldn't say no to a glass of beer."

There was a bar on the corner, but there was no possibility of getting to it in this downpour. As for Maigret, the very word "beer" brought a wry smile to his lips. He had given his word to Rian, and he meant to keep it.

"We'd better go back."

They found the young policeman leaning against the wall. He sprang smartly to attention, and stood motionless, while the prisoner looked from one to the other of the older men.

"Thanks, young man. You can go now."

Lecoeur returned to his seat, and began fidgeting with the memo pad, the pencil, and the telephone.

"I wanted to give you a little time to think, Monsieur Pélardeau. I have no wish to harass you or tie you up in knots. For the present, I'm just feeling my way. . . . One tries to form a general picture, but sometimes one gets hold of the wrong end of the stick. . . ."

He was feeling his way, trying to strike the right note, like a musician tuning up before a concert. The man was watching him closely, but still betrayed no sign of emotion.

"You had been married some time, I take it, when you first met Hélène Lange?"

"I was over forty . . . no longer a young man. . . . I had been married fourteen years. . . ."

"Was it a love match?"

"Love is a word that has different meanings at different stages of a man's life. . . ."

"At any rate, it wasn't a cold-blooded marriage of convenience?"

"No. . . . It was my own free choice. . . . And, in that connection, I have nothing to regret, except the misery I have brought upon my wife. . . . We're very good friends, and always have been. . . . No one could have been more understanding. . . ."

"Even on the subject of Hélène Lange?"

"I never told her. . . ."

"Why not?"

He looked from one to the other.

"It was something I just couldn't talk about. . . . I've never had much to do with women. . . . I've worked hard all my life, and I think perhaps, even in middle age, I was a bit naïve. . . ."

"Was it infatuation?"

"I don't know if that's the right word for it. . . . Hélène was different from anyone I had ever known. . . . I was attracted by her, and yet somehow afraid of her. . . . She was so intense, I didn't know what I was doing. . . ."

"You became lovers?"

"Not at first . . . not for a very long time."

"You mean, she kept you dangling?"

"No, I was reluctant to . . . You see, she had never had a lover. . . . But all this seems very commonplace to you, I daresay. . . . I loved her, or rather, I thought I did. . . . She made no demands; she seemed content to occupy a very small place in my life, just the few hours once or twice a week that you mentioned. . . ."

"Was there ever any question of divorce?"

"Never! Besides, in a different way, I still loved my wife. . . . I would never have agreed to leave her. . . ."

Poor man! He should have stuck to his office, his factories, and his board meetings, where he knew his way about.

"Did she break it off?"

"Yes. . . ."

Lecoeur exchanged a brief look with Maigret.

"Tell me, Monsieur Pélardeau, did you go to Mesnil-le-Mont?"

His face took on an unhealthy, purple flush. With eyes lowered, he stammered:

"No."

"But you knew she was there?"

"Not at the time. . . ."

"Was this after you had parted?"

"She had told me she never wanted to see me again."

"Why was that?"

Once again, that look of utter bewilderment, as though he simply could not make out what was going on.

"She didn't want our child to . . ."

This time, it was Lecoeur whose eyes widened in amazement, while Maigret, apparently not in the least surprised, sat comfortably hunched up, like a contented cat.

"What are you talking about? What child?"

"Why, Hélène's . . . my son. . . ."

"In spite of himself, a touch of pride crept into his voice as he spoke of his son.

"Are you telling me that she had a child by you?"

"Yes, my son, Philippe. . . ."

Lecoeur was seething.

"And she hoodwinked you into believing that . . ."

But the man was shaking his head gently.

"There was no question of hoodwinking . . . I have proof."

"What proof?"

"A copy of the birth certificate."

"Signed by the Mayor of Mesnil-le-Mont?"

"Naturally."

"And the woman named as the mother was Hélène Lange?"

"Of course."

"And yet you never went to see this child, whom you believed to be your son?"

"Whom I believe to be my son . . . who is my son. . . . I didn't go because I didn't know where Hélène had hidden herself away to have the child."

"Why all the mystery?"

"Because she was determined that nothing should be done which might, at a later date—how can I put it?—place the child in an equivocal position."

"Wasn't that rather an old-fashioned view to take?"

"You might say so. . . . But Hélène was old-fashioned in some ways. . . . She had a strong sense of . . ."

"See here, Monsieur Pélardeau, I think I'm beginning to understand, but for the moment, if you don't mind, we'll leave sentiment out of it. . . . Forgive me for putting it so bluntly, but facts are facts, and there's nothing either of us can do about them. . . ."

"I don't see what you're getting at. . . ."

His outward self-assurance was beginning to give way to a vague uneasiness.

"Did you know Francine Lange?"

"No."

"You never met her in Paris?"

"No. Not in Paris or anywhere else."

"Didn't you know Hélène had a sister?"

"Yes. She used to talk of a younger sister. They were orphans. . . . Hélène left college so that her sister . . ."

Unable to contain himself any longer, Lecoeur got to his feet. He remained standing. If there had been room for it, he would have worked off his fury by pacing up and down.

"Go on. . . . Go on. . . ."

He wiped his forehead with the back of his hand.

"So that her sister should have the education she deserved. . . ."

"The education she deserved, indeed! Don't hold it against me, Monsieur Pélardeau, but I'm going to have to cause you a great deal of pain. . . . I ought perhaps to have set about things differently, to have prepared you for the truth. . . ."

"What truth?"

"At fifteen, her sister was a hairdresser's assistant in La Rochelle. She was also, at that time, living with a taxi driver, and he was only the first of heaven knows how many men. . . ."

"She showed me her letters. . . ."

"Whose letters?"

"Francine's. She was at a well-known boarding school in Switzerland."

"Did you actually go there and see for yourself?"

"No, of course not."

"Did you keep her letters?"

"No, I just glanced through them."

"And during the whole of that time, Francine was working as a manicurist in a hairdresser's in the Champs-Elysées! Don't you see, the whole thing, from beginning to end, was a sham?"

The man was still putting up a fight. . . . But his self-control, though still remarkable, was beginning to crumble, and suddenly his mouth twisted in an expression so pitiable that Maigret and Lecoeur could not bear to look at him.

"It's not possible," he stammered.

"Regrettably, it's the truth."

"But why?"

It was a last desperate bid to avert his fate. Let them say right out, here and now, that it wasn't true, that it was an ignoble police trick to undermine his resistance.

"I'm sorry, Monsieur Pélardeau. Until tonight, up to this very minute, I too never suspected the extent to which those two were in collusion."

He started to lower himself into his chair, but then sprang up again. He was still too overwrought to sit down.

"Did Hélène never raise the subject of marriage?"

"No. . . ."

This time, he sounded less confident.

"Even when she told you she was pregnant?"

"She didn't want to break up my home. . . ."

"In other words, you did discuss marriage. . . ."

"Not in the way you mean. . . . Only to explain why she was proposing to disappear. . . ."

"To commit suicide?"

"There was never any question of that. . . . But as the child would not be legitimate . . ."

Lecoeur sighed and, once more, exchanged glances with Maigret. Each knew what the other was thinking. Both, in imagination, were dwelling on the exchanges that must have taken place between Hélène Lange and her lover.

"You don't believe me. . . . I myself . . ."

"You must try and face up to the truth. . . . Self-deception won't help you now. . . ."

"Can anything help me now?"

With a sweeping gesture, he indicated the walls of the little office, as though, to him, they were the walls of a prison cell.

"Let me finish. . . . I know it will sound mawkish to you, but she wanted to devote the rest of her life to bringing up our child, in the same way as she had brought up her sister."

"And you were not to be allowed to see your child?"

"On what terms? How could she explain me to him?"

"You might have been an uncle . . . a friend. . . ."

"Hélène hated lying. . . ."

His voice had suddenly taken on a faintly ironic inflection. It was a hopeful sign.

"So she was determined that your son should never know that you were his father?"

"Later, when he came of age, she was going to tell him. . . ."

He added, in his strange, hoarse voice:

"He's fifteen now. . . ."

Lecoeur and Maigret listened in painful silence.

"When I saw her in Vichy, I decided . . ."

"Go on."

"That I must see him, or at least find out where he was. . . ."

"And did you?"

He shook his head, and this time there were real tears in his eyes.

"No."

"Did Hélène tell you where she was going to have the child?"

"In a village she knew. . . . She didn't tell me the name. . . . Then, two months later, she sent me a copy of the birth certificate. The letter was posted in Marseilles. . . ."

"How much money did you give her before she left?"

"Does it matter?"

"It matters a great deal, as you will see."

"Twenty thousand francs. . . . I sent thirty thousand more to her in Marseilles. . . . Naturally, it was my wish that, thereafter, she should have a regular allowance, to enable her to give our son the best of everything. . . ."

"Five thousand francs a month?"

"Yes. . . ."

"What reason did she give for wanting the money to be sent to a different town each time . . . ?"

"She was afraid I wouldn't have the will power . . ."

"Was that what she said?"

"Yes. . . . I had agreed, in the end, not to see the child until he came of age. . . ."

Lecoeur's look plainly asked Maigret:

"What's to be done?"

But Maigret only blinked rapidly two or three times, and bit hard on the stem of his pipe.

8

LECOEUR WAS SITTING down, having lowered himself very slowly into his seat. He turned to the man whose puckered face revealed all that he had just had to endure, and said, almost sorrowfully:

"I'm going to have to cause you still more pain, Monsieur Pélardeau."

The man responded with an embittered smile, as though to say:

"Is that possible, do you think?"

"I feel for you, and indeed respect you as a man. . . . I'm not fabricating all this to trick you into making admissions which, anyway, would be superfluous. . . . What I have to tell you now, like everything I have told you so far, is strictly true, and no one is more sorry than I am that the truth should be so harsh. . . ."

A pause, to give his hearer time to prepare himself.

"You never had a son by Hélène Lange."

He had expected a vehement denial, or at least a violent outburst of some sort, but he was met with a blank, expressionless stare, and silence. This was a broken man.

"Did you never have any suspicion?"

Pélardeau raised his head, shook it, and put his hand to his throat to indicate that, for the moment, he was unable to speak. He barely had time to get his handkerchief out of his pocket when he was racked by another attack of asthma, more violent than the first.

In the silence that followed, Maigret became aware that outside too it had grown silent. The thunder had ceased, and the rain was no longer thudding down.

"I'm sorry. . . ."

"You did have occasion to suspect the truth, didn't you?"

"Once. . . . Only once."

"When?"

"Here . . . that night. . . ."

"When did you first see her?"

"Two days before."

"Did you follow her?"

"Yes, keeping out of sight . . . to find out where she lived. I was waiting for her to come out with my son, or to see him come out alone. . . ."

"On Monday night, did you speak to her as she was going into the house?"

"No. . . . I saw the lodgers go out. . . . I knew she was in the park, listening to the music. . . . She always liked music. . . . I had no difficulty in opening the door. . . . The key of my hotel room fitted the lock. . . ."

"You searched through the drawers?"

"The first thing I noticed was that there was only a single bed. . . ."

"What about the photographs?"

"They were all of her. . . . Not one of anyone else. . . . I would have given anything to have found a photograph of a child. . . ."

"And letters?"

"Yes. . . . I couldn't understand it. . . . There was nothing. Even if Philippe was away at boarding school, he must have . . ."

"And she found you there when she got in?"

"Yes. I begged her to tell me where our son was. . . . I remember asking her if he was dead . . . if there had been an accident."

"And she wouldn't answer?"

"She took it all much more calmly than I did. She reminded me of our pact."

"That she would give you your son when he reached the age of twenty-one?"

"Yes. . . . On condition that I should never make any attempt to see him before then."

"Did she talk about him?"

"In great detail. . . . About when he cut his first teeth. . . . His childhood ailments. . . . The nurse she engaged to look after him when she herself was unwell. . . . Then school. . . . She gave me almost a day-by-day account of his life."

"But she never said where he was?"

"No. . . . She said that recently he had begun to take a great interest in medicine . . . that he wanted to become a doctor. . . ."

He looked straight at the Superintendent, without embarrassment.

"There was no such boy?"

"Yes, there was. . . . But he was not your son. . . ."

"You mean there was another man?"

Lecoeur shook his head.

"It was Francine Lange who gave birth to a son at Mesnil-le-Mont. . . . I confess that, until you told me so yourself, I had no idea that Hélène Lange had registered the child as her own. . . . The plan must have occurred to the two sisters when Francine Lange found she was pregnant. . . . If I know anything about Francine, her first thought must have been to get rid of it. . . . Her sister was more far-sighted. . . ."

"It came to me in a flash, as I told you. . . . That night, when I found that she was deaf to my entreaties, I used threats. . . . For fifteen years I had looked forward with longing to the time when I should see this son of mine. My wife and I have no children of our own. . . . When I knew that I was a father . . . But what's the use?"

"You took her by the throat?"

"To frighten her, to make her talk. . . . I shouted at her. . . . I demanded the truth. . . . I never thought of the sister . . . but I feared that the child was dead, or crippled. . . ."

His hands slipped out of his lap and hung down limply, as though all the strength of that great, burly frame had drained away.

"I squeezed too hard. . . . I didn't realize. . . . If only she had shown the faintest spark of feeling! But she didn't . . . not even of fear. . . ."

"When you read in the paper that her sister was in Vichy, it gave you fresh hope?"

"If the child was alive and Hélène was the only person who knew where he was, there was no one left to care for him. . . . I knew I must expect to be arrested at any time. . . . You must have found my fingerprints."

"Without knowing whose they were . . . though, in the end, we would have caught up with you. . . ."

"I had to know, to make provision. . . ."

"You worked your way, in alphabetical order, through the list of hotels. . . ."

"How did you know?"

It was childish, but Lecoeur badly felt the need of a boost to his self-esteem.

"Each time you used a different phone booth."

"So you had tracked me down already?"

"Almost."

"But what about Philippe?"

"Francine Lange's son was put out to foster parents soon after birth—a family called Berteaux, small tenant farmers at Saint-André-du-Lavion, in the Vosges. . . . The sisters used your money to buy a hairdressing salon in La Rochelle. . . . Neither of them took the slightest interest in the child. . . . He lived with his foster parents in the country until, at the age of two and a half, he was drowned in a pond."

"He's dead, then?"

"Yes. . . . But, as far as you were concerned, he had to be kept alive. All that about his childhood, his early schooling, his pranks, and his recent interest in medicine, was made up on the spur of the moment."

"How monstrous!"

"Yes."

"To think that any woman could . . ."

He shook his head.

"It's not that I don't believe you . . . but, somehow, my whole being revolts. . . ."

"It's not the first case of its kind in the history of crime. . . . I could tell you of others. . . ."

"No," he begged.

He sat hunched up, limp. There was nothing left for him to cling to.

"You were quite right, just now, when you said that you didn't need a lawyer. . . . You have only to tell your story to a jury. . . ."

He put his head in his hands and sat there, very still.

"Your wife must be getting anxious. . . . In my opinion, it would be kinder to tell her the truth—otherwise she'll be imagining much worse things. . . ."

He raised a flushed face to Lecoeur. He had probably forgotten her until then.

"What am I going to say to her?"

"Unfortunately, for the present, you won't have an opportunity to say anything to her. . . . I am not at liberty to release you, even for a very short time . . . You will have to accompany me to Clermont-Ferrand. But, unless the examining magistrate objects, which I'm certain he won't, your wife will be able to visit you there."

Pélardeau, deeply disturbed on his wife's account, turned, in desperation, to Maigret:

"Couldn't you see to it?"

Maigret looked inquiringly at Lecoeur, who shrugged as if to say that it was no concern of his.

"I'll do my best."

"You'll have to be careful, because my wife has suffered from a weak heart for some years. . . . We're neither of us young any more. . . ."

Nor was Maigret. Tonight, he felt old. He couldn't wait to get back to his wife, and resume the humdrum routine of their daily life, walking through the streets of Vichy, sitting on the little yellow chairs in the park.

They went downstairs together.

"Do you want a lift, Chief?"

"I'd rather walk."

The streets were glistening. The black car, taking Lecoeur and Pélardeau to Clermont-Ferrand, disappeared in the distance.

Maigret lit his pipe and, without thinking, put his hands in his pockets. It wasn't cold, but the temperature had dropped several degrees after the storm.

The shrubs on either side of the entrance to the Hôtel de la Bérézina were dripping.

"Here you are at last!" exclaimed Madame Maigret, getting out of bed to welcome him. "I dreamed you were at the Quai des Orfèvres questioning a suspect, and having beer sent up to you every five minutes. . . ."

But when she had had time to take a good look at him, her voice changed, and she murmured:

"It's over, then?"

"Yes."

"Who did it?"

"A very respectable man. He had charge of thousands of office and factory workers, but he never learned much about the ways of the world."

"I hope you'll be able to sleep late tomorrow morning."

"I'm afraid not. . . . I've got to go and explain to his wife. . . ."

"Doesn't she know?"

"No."

"Is she here in Vichy?"

"At the Hôtel des Ambassadeurs."

"What about him?"

"Within the next half-hour he'll be behind bars in the Clermont-Ferrand prison."

She watched him closely as he undressed, but could not quite interpret his rather odd expression.

"How many years do you think he'll . . ."

Maigret always liked to have two or three puffs at his pipe before going to bed. He was filling it now. Without looking up, he said:

"He'll be acquitted, I hope."

Epalinges, September 11, 1967